## THEY FOLLOWED A DREAM

**Quanming**—child of wealth and privilege, steely in his strength and rigid pride, torn between the Chinese wife that family duty demanded, and the American woman he passionately desired.

**Meiping**—a dangerously sensual and defiant beauty, rescued from sexual bondage and a life of unspeakable degradation by a love stronger than her shame.

**Fachai**—tormented by a faraway love, he could not forget the land he had left except in the arms of a woman who belonged to another.

**Loone**—the artist blessed and cursed by genius, he sought to turn life and love into things of beauty, yet found marriage to an exquisite enchantress the hardest challenge of all.

**They were the Children of the Pearl—bound by friendship and loyalty, divided by love and betrayal, heirs to hallowed ancestors and a shimmering past, builders of a shining future for themselves and their children.**

# CHILDREN OF THE PEARL

## CHING YUN BEZINE

A SIGNET BOOK

I dedicate this book to a man whose Chinese name is One Hundred Mountains, whose American name is Frank Bezine.

Being a Chinese, whatever feelings I have for my husband, I must hide.

Being also an American, I want to whisper: I love you, and I think this book is just as much yours as it is mine.

# ACKNOWLEDGMENTS

To my son, Everett, my love:
Believe me, please—the love between all the parents and children in this book, is inspired by the love between you and me.

To my agent, Ellen Lively Steele:
My parents' spirits watched me struggling in a foreign land as a frustrated, frightened, insecure writer. So they guided me, mysteriously to the most encouraging, kind, and positive person.

To my editor, Audrey LaFehr:
I came to you with a tremendous amount of apprehension, expecting to discuss the business of publication. Finding a friend to share my love for art, music, and literature, I left with endless gratification.

To the people in the Upper Peninsula of Michigan:
Thanks for making me feel like one of you, instead of a foreigner. Without a sense of belonging, it would be most difficult for me to write in a second language.

# PART I

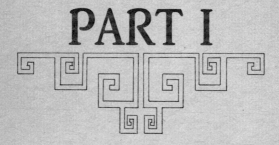

# 1

Gold shining brightly as the finch's wings,
Shall brighten the place where I must go.
But the thought of you,
Standing and weeping in front of the ancient gate,
Shall steal my sleep as I lie alone.
Watching the dying moon of dawn,
Tears shall be with me wherever I roam.
　　　　　　　　　—Li Po, Tang Dynasty
　　　　　　　　　Chinese Love Poem

THE PEARL RIVER flowed through South China, reached a village within the province of Kwangdung.

A hill bordered the north side of town, with huge marble blocks piled high on its top. These gleaming white stones could be seen from miles away, and because of their majestic presence the town was known as White Stone.

According to legend, a powerful warlord had come sailing down the Pearl centuries ago. He had had the marbles hauled over land and water, to build on the hilltop his future home. However, just before the construction began, he behaved carelessly and offended the emperor. The lord was beheaded, his dream of a mansion left unformed; the white stones remained on the hill. It was said that during stormy nights the headless lord could be seen wandering around, guarding his precious stones.

It was spring of 1911, the morning sun was shining

on a small red brick house at the foot of the hill. Beside its humble door, forsythias stood proudly in their golden robe. In the nearby woods, two whippoorwills were addressing each other in a riddled love call.

The door was opened, and a young man appeared. He squinted in the glaring light and stretched, welcoming another beautiful day.

He was tall like a northerner, with handsome, almost Eurasian features. The legs of his black pants were tied neatly around his ankles with white strips of cloth. Down the front of his black jacket was a row of white, knotted buttons. He had on his feet a pair of black shoes made from soft fabric. A bright red sash was tied tightly around his narrow waist. As he stood with his hands behind him and his feet apart, he carried himself straight and proud. On his eighteen-year-old face, the expression was that of a happy, worry-free child.

"Mama," he looked back at the door and called, "I'm going to the temple now."

A petite woman appeared at the door. She was no longer young, but age had little marred her delicate porcelain-white features that seemed even more fragile in contrast to her black hair that was pulled back tightly and pinned neatly into a bun.

"Quanming," she called out gently, wearing a frown of concern, "please be careful. That Master Lin of yours is too rough with his students. I'll never forgive him if he should hurt you."

Quanming smiled. "I'll be very careful, Mama," he promised. "Don't worry."

He started to walk away, and she stood leaning on the door frame, watching. Every few steps he turned to look back, returning her waves. The early sun was reflected on the mother's white robe, coloring it gold. Quanming noticed how small and venerable she appeared. No wonder Baba loved her so much! For her he had even given up the opportunity of going to America with his uncle.

The thought of his father brought an emptiness to his heart—his father had died a few years before.

Sung Quanming wished there could be no deaths or partings in life. Without them his life would still have been filled with perfect days—such as those when his father had been alive and teaching in the local school, and his older brother, Quanli, had been at home instead of at college in Kwangchow.

These reminiscences slowed his steps. By the time he neared the temple, the sun was already high over the horizon. In the courtyard under an arch, Master Lin had already started putting several students through a series of warm-up exercises. The moving figures varied in age: some were very young, the others had seen more than fifty springs. A few of the children were beginners, and they moved rather clumsily. Watching them from a distance, Quanming smiled and remembered how clumsy he had been ten years ago, when Quanli had taken him to the temple to be inspected by Master Lin, to see if he could become a qualified student. He had been greatly impressed that day, first by the Master's flowing movements and later the man's firm words: "Martial art is not to be used to harm people, you must remember."

Ten years had passed rather quickly. From a second-grader in the local elementary school, Quanming had grown to become a senior in the White Stone high school. He had been counting the days impatiently, eager to go to Kwangchow to join Quanli. *Only fifty-eight more days and I'll be graduated, and Quanli and I will be together again!*

He entered the temple. After bowing to Master Lin, he joined the class. As he moved through the various kicks, punches, and blocks, his chi began to flow, cleansing both mind and body. After the exercises, they started to meditate. The balance between yin and yang was soon reached, and Quanming was lifted to a higher spiritual plane. He felt himself rising from the ground, looking at things with a supremely keen awareness.

He saw a small figure coming into his vision from afar, gradually increasing in size. It was a young man who lived on the other side of White Stone.

"Sung Quanming! I have terrible news!" the young man yelled as he ran.

Quanming felt himself being pulled down abruptly to the troublesome earth. He opened his eyes wide and saw that everybody had stopped practicing to stare at the messenger.

With sweat streaming down his face, the boy looked apologetically at Quanming, then said breathlessly, "I hate to tell you this, Quanming, but my cousin has just arrived home from Kwangchow. He told us that . . . that a revolution has been started against the Ching Dynasty and the dowager queen. He said that many college students were arrested, and"—he bowed his head—"and your brother was one of them."

The sun was shining, but Quanming felt utter darkness come pouring over the world. He gazed at the news bearer incredulously, waiting for the man to take back that impossible statement.

"Quanming." Master Lin's voice forced him to face reality. "You had better go home immediately to tell your mother."

In a daze he raced home.

"Mama . . ." He tried to soften the news, but upon hearing it, Mrs. Sung collapsed in a heap at her son's feet.

Quanming picked her up and carried her to bed. "Mama, Quanli is all right . . . I'm sure he will be released," he said to her while washing her face with a wet cloth, but in his heart he knew that he was only making meaningless noise of empty assurance. Through the ages in China, when the commoners dared to fight against the authority, the blood that had been shed had always been the blood of the peasants.

The mother opened her eyes. She uttered only one word, "Come," then struggled to her feet, moving shakily toward the room once shared by her two sons to start packing for Quanming.

When the packing was done, she sat on the edge of the bed, her face livid, her voice a whisper. "You must go to Kwangchow immediately," she said. Her head was held high and there was a firm gleam in her eyes.

"Go to the prison and find out if they will let you see Quanli. Your father used to know a few people in the city, and you must go to each of them for help. After seeing Quanli, maybe you'll know what we can do for him."

In less than an hour Quanming was riding in a hired wagon. He looked at the misty mountains on one side of the dirt road, with their peaks floating in the fog of spring. In the vapor he saw Quanli's face, vigorous and full of mischief. He then turned his gaze to the other side and eyed the Pearl sparkling in the blazing sun. In the sound of the rippling water he heard the laughter of his family during the many trips they had made to Kwangchow together. As the wagon passed Jasmine Valley, the strong fragrance of flowers reached him. His eyes moistened as he remembered how his brother and he had planned to visit that village, but never actually taken the time to do it.

Arriving in Kwangchow at midday, Quanming went directly to the prison and asked to see Sung Quanli.

"Absolutely not!" the guard spat at him. "Why do you want to see him? Are you an accomplice of his?"

Quanming argued, creating a disturbance. An aged jailer was called, and the man shook his head with a look of warning. "Young man, if you don't leave right now, I'll have to throw you in jail along with your treasonous brother!"

Defeated, Quanming left the prison and started for the homes of those who had once been friends of his father's. Among over a dozen people, half refused to let him in their doors, the other half sent word by their servants that they couldn't afford to be seen talking to the brother of a traitor.

At midnight Quanming went to a hotel very close to the jail and rented a room. Lying on the bed with his arms folded behind his head, he stared at the ceiling, unable to sleep. His mind's eye kept casting glances at his childhood days. Though Quanli was two years older than he, the two had been inseparable. It was Quanli who had helped him to make the first lantern for the Lantern Festival, and Quanli who had convinced him that China was not really the center of the world. Quanli had told him about the mythological figure named Huang-ti who had separated earth from heaven, and made him proud of the fact that all Chinese were the descendants of this eternal king. *Quanli, are you really involved in the revolution against the queen? Why did you never tell me?*

Near dawn, he dozed off and dreamed. In his dream both he and Quanli were children again, playing on the hill behind their home. Quanli was trying to scare him by pretending to be the headless ghost of the lord. They ran around a tall forsythia bush; then they ran into the yellow flowers, and the golden petals started to fall over them like shining fragrant raindrops.

He was awakened by the shout of someone on the street right outside:

"Execution! Many heads will be chopped off! Bring your steamed buns and hurry!"

Quanming jumped out of bed, rubbed his eyes. Dawn was just breaking, and the crescent moon and morning star had not yet begun to pale.

"Execution!" This time the person was banging on a gong. "All the prisoners are young college students! All the heads will soon be chopped off! The queen has ordered the people of Kwangchow to watch them die. Watch and learn what'll happen to you if you dare to start a rebellion!"

Quanming was by now wide-awake. He dressed himself quickly and left the hotel. Standing on the sidewalk, he could see the prison wall; there was a group of soldiers gathered at the prison gate. The street was filled with people; everyone was following the sound of the gong, moving toward the outskirts of town. There were sleeping children carried by their mothers, and crippled old men walking on crutches. Peddlers were calling out their wares; the most popular item was the steamed buns. Everyone was caught up in festive excitement, as if celebrating a rare, happy occasion.

"Here they come!" someone yelled. Quanming

turned to see the crowd parting, making way for the ox-drawn wagons.

Standing in each of four good-sized wagons were more than twenty half-naked men guarded by armed soldiers. As the wagons came closer, Quanming saw that the prisoners were not men but youths, some still in their teens.

"No! Quanli can't be one of them!" He let out a cry and started to push his way through.

He was taller than almost everybody else on the street, and as the wagons rumbled nearer, none of the prisoners could escape his search. Studying each of them, he saw that from head to foot, they were all covered with dried blood. Their faces were bruised and swollen beyond recognition. Some of them had had teeth knocked out; some had had an arm or a leg broken. Their hands were tied behind them, and on their backs signs were tied with their names written. Unmindful of the bright sun and the roaring crowd, all the prisoners had a similar vacant look—as if they were being moved in a moonless night through an empty street; they could see or hear no one.

All of a sudden, bile rose in Quanming's throat. He stood frozen on the sidewalk.

"Quanli!" he yelled shrilly as he noticed that his brother was as battered as the others; if anything, he looked worse.

"Quanli!" he shouted again, feeling pain in his chest and tears in his eyes. He barged through the mob to the center of the street, then started to run after the wagons.

The procession soon left the city roads and began to head toward the Eastern Gate. Seemingly half the citizens of Kwangchow had dropped whatever they were doing to become entranced followers of the wagons. Once out of town, the wagons moved faster. The followers started to run; the children were being dragged, the cripples left behind, cursing. Quanming ran lightly on his feet, and with each step he shouted, "Quanli! Oh, Quanli, my brother!"

Once, and only for a brief moment, the two broth-

ers' eyes met. Quanming jumped up, waving frantically, and screamed out in agony: "Brother! What can
I do? How can I get you out of this? Please tell me!"

But the moment passed. The sign of recognition had
gone from Quanli's eyes; the tortured young man had
once again withdrawn from reality. Quanming kept on
calling his brother's name, but his voice fell only on
deaf ears.

The wagons stopped at the edge of an open field,
and the prisoners were pushed out. Those who fell
were kicked, pulled, and dragged to their feet. Then
one by one they were led to a rise in the center of the
lot, where an executioner stood waiting.

He was a middle-aged, dark, big man wearing a pair
of loose black pants tied at the ankles. He was naked
from the waist up; his fat stomach billowed out over a
red sash. His head was closely shaved, and beads of
sweat glistened on his scalp. He was holding a curved
broadsword; a piece of scarlet silk was tied to the handle, flapping in the wind.

The soldiers made the prisoners form a line. The
first was a bony young boy. Like a sleepwalker, he let
himself be led to the executioner and made to kneel.
The executioner approached him. With the slap of an
open palm on the back of the victim's head, the big
man sent the skinny figure toppling over with his neck
extended. The executioner raised his arms high, waved
the sword in a whistling arc. The arms came down
with tremendous force and speed. The blade of the
sword flashed like lightning, and the head was severed
from the body; the body stayed in its kneeling position
for a brief moment, then fell to one side.

Laying down his weapon, the executioner raised a
hand to wipe his brow, and then with a kick he sent
the head reeling. It rolled toward the waiting crowd,
and they started cheering.

In a frenzy, the mob flocked forward, and soon
broke through the cordon. Dividing into two groups,
they ran toward either the headless body or the bodi-
less head. With buns clenched in their hands, they
reached out to catch the blood spurting from the gap-

ing neck, fighting for the red elixir that promised a panacea of cures. While grinning, pushing, and yelling, they stuffed the soaked buns into their own mouths and the mouths of those who had come with them—the very old or very young or those sick enough to need this magic cure. The fresh blood of another human being filled their wide mouths, smeared their excited faces, running down their chins, dripping onto their civilized clothes. The first body and head were soon drained of blood, and the bloodsuckers waited impatiently for the next victim to fall.

Quanming tried to go to his brother. Four soldiers saw where he was heading, and, suspicious of this tall young man with the looks of a martial-arts expert, they surrounded him, pointing their bayonets at him, forced him to stand still. He stood in numbed silence, as if hypnotized. In front of his wide-open eyes, one more young man was led out of the line, the sword swung once more, one more head started to roll, accompanied by the thundering roar . . . it continued on and on.

And then he saw his brother being dragged and shoved to the center of the field. Then came the slapping hand and the flashing blade . . . he saw his brother's head rolling toward the wild forsythias in the field. Bumping into the bushes, it knocked the flowers off the stems—the yellow petals fell like golden raindrops over the head just as he had seen in his dream.

The sky turned black in front of his eyes; the ground was shaking under his feet. "Quanli!" he screamed, his voice broken, his legs weak. He fell on his knees, facing the direction where Quanli's body lay, dug his fingers into his hair, and started to pull frantically. The crowd charged past him; the soldiers saw that he was now a broken man and left him alone. He continued to kneel on the ground, shaking and sobbing at the same time.

"Quanli! Mama wants me to do something for you. Can you tell me: what can I do now?"

The families of those executed were expected to take

the bodies home. Quanming forced himself to stand up, to move on shaking legs and unsteady feet.

"You barbarians!" he spat, glaring at the people with fury burning in his eyes. "You bloodthirsty creatures! How dare you call yourselves the descendants of Huang-ti? What right do you have to look down at white people and call them uncivilized devils? No! There is no culture in China! Confucianism is but a joke!" He left a trail of fallen spectators as he worked his way forward.

"My brother!" Standing over Quanli's head, he regarded the empty, staring eyes. Those with the buns had already been there; there was no more blood pouring out of the evenly chopped neck, only broken veins, tissue, and small bones. "Quanli!" he called again, and then gingerly picked up the head by the queue. With the head in his hand, he fought every inch of his way to the body. The crowd had beaten him to this spot also; the blood had been drained from the opening on the body. He laid the head down and tossed the body over his shoulder, then once again grabbed the queue and made a path through the people. He kept walking until he was far from the execution field, where the crowd was thin. He stopped, lowered the body to the ground, and placed the head back where it belonged.

"Quanli! Quanli! Why were we born in this wretched country?" He sat next to his brother and started to cry.

# 2

On October 10, 1911, the Ching Dynasty was overthrown, and the Republic of China was born. After a severe winter a new year began.

Spring arrived in White Stone once more. At the foot of the hill, the forsythias were again blooming golden yellow, and the whippoorwills returned to make their love calls. Nothing much had changed in the village, for no one was particularly affected by the country's new government. The poor continued to farm and fish; the rich still lived in idle luxury. So did the small red brick house at the foot of the hill look the same from outside, but within its walls the occupants had been changed forever.

Mrs. Sung had been ill for almost a year. When she finally left her sickbed, her jet-black hair had turned iron gray, her once-bright eyes had lost their glow, and she had forgotten how to smile.

The carefree boy had deserted the body of Sung Quanming; in his place now existed a sad and angry young man. Quanming never did go to college in Kwangchow as planned; he had stayed home to take care of his mother. He seldom left his mother's side except to bring flowers to the graveyard for his father and brother, or to go to the temple to practice martial arts.

It was a lovely spring day, and long after the full moon had appeared with its following stars, the sky remained stubbornly light blue. Mrs. Sung had gone to bed soon after their early supper. Quanming was left sitting alone, not wanting to make any noise that might disturb his mother.

He walked outside absentmindedly, stood on the doorstep and breathed in deeply the twilight air. Suddenly the weight of his heart seemed to be lightened;

he felt less smothered than he had been in a long time. He listened carefully to make sure that his mother was soundly asleep, then started to walk slowly toward the temple.

That morning he had gone to the temple as usual. After class, Master Lin had reminded the students that they wouldn't be meeting for the next three days. "Lantern Festival is here again and, as usual, the temple will be filled with hundreds of lanterns and just as many people."

Once dusk had started to fall, it gained control over the earth quickly. By the time Quanming neared the temple, night had taken over.

With each step he could see more colorful dots twinkling in the dark, as if approaching a moonless field filled with fireflies. When he passed the pond, he saw lanterns floating on the water, in the shapes of ducks, fish, and other sea animals. *Quanli made me a fish lantern once, when I was ten.* Walking under the trees, he found them hung with lanterns made to imitate all kinds of birds. *I was twelve when the parakeet lantern Quanli made for me won the first prize in the lantern competition.* He was almost run over by children pulling lanterns shaped to resemble dogs and rabbits. *When we were much smaller, we used to pull the rabbit lanterns side by side, walking around the house at night.*

Once he reached the temple, he found himself walking into a sea of multicolored glistening dots, made by lanterns, candles, and sticks of incense. The poor villagers were dressed in their best, and the rich landlords had condescended to appear among the peasants. Peddlers were carrying their goods on their backs, and the hawking of their wares melted into a hundred other kinds of noise.

"I should've brought Mama here with me." Without knowing it, he spoke his thoughts aloud. "Seeing this festive scene, she might feel a little better—" He stopped suddenly.

Under the temple arch, not far from the gigantic statue of the Goddess of Mercy, a lantern shaped like a lotus was hanging from a tree. Its pink light softly illuminated the most beautiful image he had ever seen.

It was a girl standing with her back turned. She had on a white dress of a gossamer material, and the sleeves were impressively wide. When a gust of wind blew through the temple, the sleeves were uplifted and started to flutter like the transparent wings of a butterfly flapping delicately. Her hair was long and straight and shiny black in the candlelight, and was held together by a multicolored jeweled comb.

In the next moment she turned, and Quanming saw a pale heart-shaped face with two dark, slanted almond eyes. She looked around with the innocent expression of a child, and when she saw Quanming, instead of looking away, she returned his gaze steadily. As he continued to look at her, she slowly started to smile, and two dimples appeared dancing at the corners of her bow-shaped narrow mouth.

The idyllic picture was destroyed when from behind the girl a woman wearing a maid's uniform of black pants and white blouse stepped forward. "Sheo-jay!" she addressed the girl sternly, using the title "young lady," then took the girl by the arm and started to guide her away.

The girl's body turned reluctantly to leave, but her eyes remained on Quanming. And then the comb started to fall loose from her hair, dropping soundlessly to the ground. Unaware of it, she kept on walking.

"Your comb!" Quanming raised a hand and called, but she was already swallowed by the crowd.

He made his way through the lantern watchers to the arch, and saw at the feet of the Goddess of Mercy the ornate comb.

A glimpse of white appeared about twenty paces away. He dodged through the people until he saw the butterfly wings again. "Sheo-jay, your comb!" he yelled.

She turned. At the sight of him holding her comb, her face brightened. She shook her maid's hand off her arm and waited for him. When he caught up with her, she held out a hand. "Dor-jea," she thanked him in the Pearl dialect; her voice was like the sound of a silver flute. "I'd have been very sad if I had never seen my favorite comb again."

Before Quanming could place the comb in her hand, the maid quickly snatched it and gave him an accusing look. "Hm! Did you find it, or did you steal it from my Sheo-jay?"

Quanming looked at the woman angrily. Before he could say anything, though, the girl let out a soft laugh. "Don't pay attention to her. She's in a grouchy mood. Her big flat feet hurt, and my mother ordered her to accompany me here for the lanterns—"

The woman interrupted her loudly. "Sheo-jay! You're not supposed to talk to strangers!"

Ignoring the woman, the girl never took her eyes from Quanming's face. "I am Kao Yoto. Who are you?"

"I'm Sung Quanming, and I live beneath the hill with the lord's white stones—" Quanming was interrupted by a group of children rushing through, making a path between him and the girl.

The maid took the chance to pull the young lady away. Kao Yoto smiled at Quanming once more, then moved on. Quanming hadn't noticed until now that she was walking steadily without leaning on her maid. It was very unusual for a young girl from a rich family not to have bound feet. Quanming was not like the other men, who preferred crippled women. He had always considered it a cruel custom. He felt sad each time he looked at his mother's tiny, misshapen feet. The bones were broken and the toes folded under the heels. He had always wondered how much his mother must have suffered as a little girl. Now, watching Kao Yoto with admiration, he was convinced that her parents must love her excessively to have taken the chance of discouraging any rich man from wanting her for a wife.

Repeating her name, Quanming tried to follow, but over the flickering lights the temple was shrouded in smoke produced by the burning of incense and paper money for the dead. In only a few seconds Kao Yoto had vanished like a butterfly disappearing into the morning mist.

The next day, Quanming went to the town square and made some inquiries about Kao Yoto.

He learned that she was the only daughter of Mr. Kao, the richest man in White Stone. She had been tutored to read and write within the walls of her father's mansion, and musicians had been hired from near and far to give her lessons on a variety of stringed instruments. She was only sixteen, but already engaged to a boy named Ma Tsai-tu, son of the wealthy Ma family.

"She's engaged," Quanming mumbled on his way home, hitting his palm into his fist. When he reached home he immersed himself in work, trying hard to forget all about her. *A rich man's daughter. And engaged. The sooner I can get her out of my mind, the better.*

A few evenings later, just when he thought he had succeeded, he and his mother were eating their simple supper when they heard a knock on the door. He answered it, and his mouth dropped. Kao Yoto's unfriendly maid was standing there holding a letter.

Without a word of greeting, the woman said gruffly, "Sheo-jay sent me all over town to make inquiries about you, and now I'm supposed to give you this note." She then handed over a sealed envelope. "I was told to wait for your answer." She stood outside the door, refused to come in regardless of Quanming's offer.

Quanming opened the letter. Each character was written with a fine brush, in delicate strokes on a pink sheet of perfumed paper. It was a message inviting Sung Quanming to meet Kao Yoto later that night in the temple.

His heart pounding with joy, Quanming informed the maid with forced restraint, "Tell your Sheo-jay I'll be at the temple as soon as the moon reaches the midsky."

He was ready to close the door, but the woman was

not ready to leave yet. She looked at him, shook her head disapprovingly, and then her eyes saddened. She said in a pleading voice, "Please don't hurt my Sheo-jay. She is only a child . . . a spoiled child who doesn't know what she's doing."

"Why would I want to hurt her? You silly woman!" Quanming stared at her.

The woman shook her head again and muttered, "You may not want to, but you might anyway." She sighed, and experiences of life gleamed in her aged eyes. "Men forget easily; women don't. Many years from now, you will not remember Kao Yoto, but my Sheo-jay will still remember you. Your life can be happy without the memory of her, but for a girl like my Sheo-jay, her life might be shadowed forever by the memories of you."

"I don't know what you're talking about," Quanming laughed. "You sound like a stupid fortune-teller!" He slammed the door as the woman turned to go.

From behind him came his mother's soft voice: "My son, that woman is right. The Kao family are not our equals. Besides, the girl is engaged to the Ma boy; you must not lay your hands on something that belongs to another man—" Seeing the stubbornness in her son's face, the mother stopped in mid-sentence. Without another word she turned and went to her room.

That night, long before the moon reached the mid-sky, Quanming was already waiting in the temple.

The festival was over, the lanterns were gone. But inside the temple, hundreds of red and white candles were glowing in front of the many statues of Buddha, bathing the ancient building in a mystic golden hue. People came here to light red candles to pray for those who were alive, and white candles for the dead. While waiting in front of the Goddess of Mercy, Quanming dropped a few coins into a box and picked up two white candles. He lit the first one for his father. Peering into the dancing flame, he tried to communicate with his father in the world of the dead:

"Baba, maybe Buddha has wished for you to have Quanli, and for me to take care of Mama . . ."

Through the glow of the second candle, he tried to talk to his brother. "Quanli, I must tell you something wonderful: I'm in love. She is so beautiful. Please share my happiness."

Looking at the river of lights around him, Quanming counted twice more white ones than red. He thought of all the wars and famines that had touched White Stone in the past few years, and saw in each trembling flame the cruelty of life, the finality of death. *The life of a Chinese is like the flame of a candle in the wind. The winds of disaster can start to blow at any minute.*

"Sung Quanming, are you not happy to see me? You look like you're about to cry." Yoto's soft voice carried a pouting tone, accusing Quanming of not showing his appreciation of her arrival by jumping up and down at the sight of her.

Quanming turned to face her. All of a sudden he no longer saw the glow of the candles, but her alone. Yoto was wearing a pale green blouse and a long white skirt. A pair of jade earrings shaped like teardrops dangled from her ears. She was again wearing the ornate comb.

"Yoto!" Quanming took her hands in his and looked into her eyes. "Of course I'm happy to see you. It's just that I was lighting candles for my father and brother."

Unlike a truly old-fashioned girl, she didn't withdraw her hands. She smiled at him. But when he asked if they could go to the teahouse together, she shook her head. They couldn't go anywhere outside the temple: there were too many wagging tongues in White Stone, and her father must not be told. They started to walk around the temple grounds, holding hands naturally. They were soon involved in an animated conversation, as if they had always known each other. From above their heads the statues of Buddha looked down with saucer-sized eyes, glaring and unsmiling. From a distant corner, her maid kept an eye on them, disapproving and worrying.

"It's too bad that your father and brother are dead," she said lightly. "Mine are alive and well. My brother is five years older than I. He likes to play mah-jongg, smoke opium, and go to opera houses to look at the beautiful singers. My mother says it's all right, since he doesn't need to earn a living, but my father thinks that a young man should read, at least once in a while, a book or two. To my mother's disappointment, I don't like to embroider, but I love to read, especially poems. My favorite poet is Li Po—you know, the one who got drunk in a rowboat and in trying to catch the reflection of the moon, fell into the water and drowned.''

When they walked in the shadow of the red-faced Buddha who represented Truth and Loyalty, she was talking about her favorite musical instrument, the five-stringed Chin. When they were at the feet of the black-faced Buddha of Labor, she was describing her multiroomed living quarters. By the time they were hidden in the shade of the white-faced Buddha of Culture, she was telling him the details of her daily life:

''I get up around noon, then have breakfast in bed. I walk in the garden for a while, always with my maid holding a parasol to shield me from the sun. After lunch I'll read, and then practice my Chin. Sometimes I'll go to Kwangchow to shop with my mother. We always ride in a carriage with silk curtains on all sides to keep the dirty peasants from looking in . . .''

Beneath the outstretched arms of the Goddess of Fertility, Yoto started to recite the poem about a man who had to leave his beloved girl and his homeland: '' 'Gold shining brightly as the finch's wings . . .' ''

Quanming listened, but her voice was so beautiful that he couldn't concentrate on the words. When she finally stopped, he started to tell her about himself. She looked at him with her slanted almond eyes, and her bow-shaped mouth curled up into a smile, her dimples danced. Mesmerized by his handsome face, she hardly heard what he was saying. They continued to walk from one Buddha to another as he poured out his life story:

''. . . My father used to teach in our high school. He could have gone to America many years ago with his brother, but my mother didn't want to go, and he didn't want to leave her. After my father's death, my uncle wrote several letters asking my brother and me to join him, but my mother thought I was too young, and Quanli refused to go. My brother was very patriotic; he wanted to save China . . .'' His voice broke.

"You don't have to continue." Yoto softly touched his arm. "Everybody knows about everybody else's business in White Stone. I was told that he was beheaded and—'' She stopped. She didn't want to tell him that she had been warned not to go near the family of a criminal, even though the regime had already been overthrown and Sung Quanli was no longer considered a traitor.

Returning to the Goddess of Mercy, they stopped and looked up at the statue's serene face. "What are your plans for the future?'' Yoto asked casually.

"I would like to go to Kwangchow for college in the fall. But since my brother's death, my mother has become bitter toward our country. She said that life in China is worthless; men and women are killed like flies. She has been talking about sending me to America. She said that in the land of freedom, all people are protected by the same law—''

Yoto interrupted him with a low scream. "Oh, no! That barbarian land is meant for the white devils only. Don't you know? The white devils have transparent flesh, yellow hair, and blue eyes. They eat raw meat and walk around half-naked most of the time.'' She raised a delicate hand to hide the blush on her cheeks. "We Chinese are the descendants of Huang-ti. We must never put ourselves in the company of those who aren't truly civilized!''

Quanming laughed softly, and said in a sarcastic tone, "Descendants of Huang-ti? Well, if you had been in Kwangchow with me last year, I'm sure you would think differently . . . never mind. Who told you such nonsense about raw meat and being half-naked?''

"My brother, and his best friend, Ma Tsai-tu, the young lord from the Ma family.'' Yoto lifted her head, defending her statement with an unassailable source.

Frowning, Quanming said coldly, "I see. Ma Tsai-tu is your future husband, right?''

Yoto looked at him innocently. "Well, my parents and his parents want us to be married someday. But I don't think he likes me that much, nor I him. I never liked any man until the night of the Lantern Festival when I met you." She stopped talking, lowered her eyes, and hid her face behind an open silk fan.

She looked irresistibly beautiful at that moment. Quanming took her gently by the shoulders, turned her around to face him, then leaned down and kissed her quickly on the forehead.

Immediately a loud cough came from the shadows, and the maid advanced into the light. Quanming quickly stepped back, and Yoto looked up at him in astonishment. The candle shone on her, and Quanming saw a deep blush slowly rise from her throat into her cheeks. After a long silence she smiled and whispered softly, "No one has ever kissed me. Now you did, so I am yours . . . forever and ever."

# 3

THROUGH THE SUMMER, Quanming and Yoto met often in the temple. Hidden in the shadows of the Buddha, they exchanged vows. Like all young lovers, they started to plan for the rest of their lives together. That was when their arguments started.

Quanming told her what he had planned. "We'll run away to Kwangchow and get married there. When your father finds out, it will be too late."

Yoto disagreed quickly. "But then Baba'll be angry with us and won't give us any money . . . we'll be poor." She groaned. "Since you're not rich, we must have Baba's permission to marry so we can live on my dowry. If you truly love me, you'll go to my Baba and beg him. And if I keep on crying, we will soften his heart." She smiled slyly. "Baba can't stand my tears. I still remember when I was eight and the women in the house started to bind my feet. They tore cotton cloth into long strips, then soaked them in hot water. They wrapped the strips around my feet, with my toes bent under. When the cloth began to dry, the wrapping became tighter and the bones in my toes and arches began slowly to break. I cried and screamed. Other parents would have just ignored me, but my Baba couldn't stand it. He ordered the strips removed, in spite of the fact that I might never find a good husband with my big feet. . . . Quanming, please beg my father with me when I cry to him!"

"I've never begged any man for anything before, and I never will," Quanming answered proudly.

Yoto pouted. "What's wrong with begging my Baba? He's not a stranger. Nobody's asking you to get down on your knees and really beg. All you need to do is to go to him and talk nicely—well, maybe say 'please' a few times, and bow now and then. Can't you see that if he doesn't approve of our marriage, he won't give us anything, and we'll have to eke out a miserable life?''

Quanming retorted, raising his voice, "How can our lives be miserable? We won't starve. I'll be a teacher, like my father. We can live the same way my parents lived all their lives—without any servants, but with a roof over our heads and plenty of food to eat.''

"Without servants!'' Yoto's voice quavered at the incredible thought. "You want me to cook, wash clothes, and clean house? I'll have to do all those things and take care of your mother?''

"Yes, and you should be glad to do it if you really love me.'' Quanming looked at her, his eyes imploring.

Yoto didn't hesitate. "Well, to be honest, no matter how much I love you, I won't gladly do a maid's work. I don't know how to do it, and I have no intention of learning.'' She stamped her foot and began to cry. "I've never washed a handkerchief in my life. I'm not even allowed to set foot in the servants' quarters. I don't know what the kitchen looks like, and I don't wish to find out. To tell you the truth, I've poured tea for myself only once, because my maid was nowhere to be found and I was very thirsty. I burned my hand on the pot, and I cried for the rest of the day and had the maid fired.''

Quanming looked at her beautiful face incredulously and shook his head. "You are a spoiled brat who knows nothing about life. Your family are leeches that suck the blood from the poor villagers!''

"You . . .'' Yoto glared at him, her fragile body shaking with anger. "How dare you! My family are not leeches! I'm not spoiled! And you don't love me at all!''

She looked like a helpless flower trembling in a storm, and Quanming's heart began to melt. "I do love you. But''—he sighed, sensing the invisible walls rising between them—"unfortunately, we are worlds apart, and only Buddha knows how we can ever think of sharing a life together!''

* * *

In spite of their arguments, Quanming and Yoto continued to meet in the temple. After the cicadas had sung their last sad song, autumn came. Yoto's wedding to Ma Tsai-tu was supposed to take place soon, but still Yoto and Quanming had not agreed on how they would spend the rest of their lives together. Each insisted on his or her own way of thinking, and they argued more and more.

Two nights in a row passed while Quanming waited for Yoto in the temple, but she never showed up as promised. The third night she came late, and by the time she arrived, he was already furious.

"Are you too high and mighty to be on time?" he snapped at her, his voice hard and cold.

Tears quickly welled in her eyes. "It's not my fault I'm late. You have no idea how difficult it is for me to leave the house," she said, pouting like a child asking to be pampered. "You know the big day is near. Mother has hired several tailors to stay with us, making clothes for me day and night. They are constantly measuring me and asking for my opinion." Making a face, she started to imitate the voice of a lowly tailor: " 'Sheo-jay, where do you want us to sew the beads? Sheo-jay, what colors should the embroideries be?' " She let out a tired sigh. "And there are the furriers: 'Sheo-jay, do you want long strips of mink to be stitched together or short ones—?' "

Impatient, Quanming interrupted her with a roar. "Stop your stupid idle chatter! You sound shallow and vulgar. So you are a rich girl. So I'm a poor man. It still doesn't give you the right to keep me waiting!"

Yoto stopped talking. She stood looking up at him, her lips trembling, tears streaming down her face.

"I'm sorry," Quanming said, smashing his fist into his palm in desperation. "It's just that I have something to tell you, and I've waited for a long time." He laid his hands on her shoulders, and excitement appeared in his voice. "I have good news. I think our problem is solved. There is a letter from my uncle. He has sent me all the documents that will allow me to enter America legally.'' He looked into her eyes. ''If you and I were married immediately, then you could go with me as my wife.'' He went on with enthusiasm, ''We'll be sailing together on a large ship, going to the other end of the earth. We'll start a new life side by side, in a new world where all people are treated as equals. I'll work hard there to build you an empire, and you'll soon live the life of a queen.'' He smiled at her. ''Yoto, go home and pack a few things, and then we'll be on our way to Kwangchow. We'll be married there, and then go to Hong Kong to wait for the ship—''

With a jerk Yoto shook Quanming's hands off her shoulders. She stepped back, eyeing him as if he were a stranger. When she spoke, there was a hardness in her voice that Quanming had never heard before. ''You . . .'' She shook her head slowly from side to side. ''You don't know what you are talking about. Just go pack a few things and leave my home? Even if I were willing to go with you, I would need at least several wagons to carry my belongings, several maids to help me pack, and it would take me at least a month to get ready. But, Sung Quanming! I'm not going to pack anything, because I'm not going with you to that land of the white devils. Here, take a close look at me.'' She leaned toward him until her face was only a few inches from his.

She wore a crooked smile that looked harsh and ugly. ''I'm Kao Yoto, not a peasant girl. The Chinese in America are either working on the railroad digging tracks or cooking and washing for the white masters. What does your uncle do? Maybe he is a coolie in a gold mine, sweeping and dusting after his white boss? Oh, Sung Quanming, you are such a stupid fool!''

She turned to leave.

Quanming's anger reached a boiling point. He moved without thinking. He heard a loud crack, saw Yoto stumbling back, raising a hand to cover her cheek. He didn't realize until then that he had slapped her.

Yoto latched on to a post to balance herself and looked disbelievingly at Quanming. The numbness of her cheek gradually turned into searing pain. She didn't begin to cry until her maid appeared, running toward her from the other side of the temple. "You hit me! How dare you? You stupid brute! No wonder your brother's head was chopped off! They should do the same to you!"

She fell into the arms of her maid, burying her face against the woman's chest, sobbing uncontrollably.

From over Yoto's shoulder the maid looked at Quanming accusingly. "I asked you not to hurt my Sheo-jay," she said, hatred burning in her eyes. "Now I only hope she can forget you as completely as you must forget her."

Quanming started to say something, then changed his mind. He was devastated by what he had done. His whole body was shaking; his nerves prickled all over. He realized that if he said more to Yoto, things would become even worse. Words from him now would be like coals added to a roaring fire.

He turned and walked away, leaving Yoto sobbing.

He didn't want to go home. With one look at his face, his mother would know something was wrong. He walked out of town, feeling the night wind blowing on his burning face. Soon he had left the temple far behind and was approaching the graveyard.

By the light of a three-quarter moon he saw a small house at the edge of an empty field in the distance. It was the home of the grave-digger Bao and his family. His friendship with the Baos had been established during the past year. When he visited the graves of his father and brother, the grave-digger had been kind enough to invite him to his humble home, introduce him to his wife and shy daughter. Quanming had enjoyed their company and developed a fondness for all three.

As he walked toward the house, he heard someone screaming. He stopped, looked more closely and saw the usually closed door ajar; the screams were coming from within. Something was very wrong, and he felt the hair on the back of his neck turning stiff as he started to run.

The screams suddenly stopped. He ran as fast as he could. As he neared the house, he heard a woman sobbing. Rushing inside, he froze at what he saw.

The grave-digger and his wife were kneeling on the floor, trembling and crying. A few feet from them, their young daughter lay naked, her legs smeared with blood. Beside her lay a pile of torn clothes, and on the other side of the clothes a man was in a hurry to get dressed.

Quanming recognized the young man immediately—his name was Chow, a servant in the house of Yoto's future husband.

"Want to share the fun?" the man asked, grinning at Quanming. "Be my guest." He pointed at the unmoving girl. "I've already raped her. She's all yours now."

Before Quanming could answer, the grave-digger struggled to stand up, let out a wail and flung himself at Chow. "You ruined my little girl! I'm going to kill you!"

Chow quickly struck Bao and knocked him to the floor. At the same moment, Bao's wife haltingly crawled over to her daughter and covered the girl's body with her own. "My poor baby! Let Mama die with you!"

Quanming clenched his teeth. He had not forgotten the happy family the Baos had been. The girl had been extremely shy, and the parents had treasured her even though they were poor and she was only a girl. He stepped toward Chow, his eyes meeting the man's eyes, his hands slightly raised beside his thighs, his feet parted, and his legs bent.

"I see that you're ready to fight," Chow said, and with his last word he delivered a looping right hand.

Quanming parried the blow with his right forearm; his left palm, moving with incredible speed, caught his opponent under the chin. Chow's head snapped back; his eyes opened wide in astonishment as he stumbled backward and fell.

Quanming waited while Chow shook his head and slowly rose on one knee. As he straightened himself up, he reached inside his jacket and drew a knife out of his waistband. "You're going to die now, Sung Quanming!" he yelled.

At the sight of the knife, Quanming felt a chill go through him. For the first time in his life he was facing death. All the training he had received from Master Lin had been more or less a game; it had not prepared him for this situation.

His first instinct was to run. All of a sudden, though, the Master's voice echoed in his mind: "Forget yourself, let your chi guide you . . ."

He took a deep breath. His breathing became regular. He continued to move, no longer a participant but a cool observer.

Chow charged forward. The knife slashed in a curve, its razor edge trying to slice the target open. Quanming acted like a waiting tiger, his eyes riveted on the moving blade. At the last moment Quanming stepped back. The point of the weapon cut through his shirt and nipped his flesh.

As the blade went by him, Quanming grabbed hold of Chow's sleeve. Using the attacker's momentum, he pulled. Chow's body was forced to swing around. Quanming hooked his arm around the man's neck, and at the same time he stepped out with his foot swiveling his hip. The next second Chow was thrown to the ground.

Quanming stood watching, waiting for Chow to get up. Chow slowly rose, took a step forward, then stopped. Staring, he slowly sank to his knees. Only then did Quanming see the handle of the knife protruding from the man's heart.

The hatred in Chow's eyes began to fade; his hands grabbed the blade's handle, and he remained kneeling. He appeared to be praying, and then slowly fell forward and became still.

Quanming was too shocked to move. The gravedigger walked over slowly, turned the man over with the tip of his foot. Looking down carefully for a few moments, he then turned to Quanming. "The bastard's dead," he said.

Quanming stared at Bao. His wife had stopped sobbing, and the daughter was lying there without making a sound. The wind was blowing through the trees in a shrill whistle; somewhere in the distance a bird was singing a melodic night song. The world was at peace as always, and he would be waking up soon to find it was a nightmare.

"Sung Sisan," Bao called softly, using the term of respect, "you have destroyed what needed to be destroyed, and Buddha will understand. I'll take care of this piece of meat"—he kicked the corpse with contempt. "I have much experience with the dead."

"I must turn myself in," Quanming said. "It was self-defense, and you can be my witness."

Bao shook his head. "Sung Sisan, I'm a poor man, and you're the son of a schoolteacher's widow. We have just killed a servant of a very rich man. In court you'll have as much chance as a chicken in the hands of a starving beggar. Your head will roll, mark my words."

Quanming shivered. The picture of his brother's severed head rolling across the field flashed before his eyes. "What can I do?" he asked helplessly.

"Go home. Say good-bye to your mother and go away," Bao said. "Go as far as you can."

"But . . ." Quanming pointed at Chow's body. "What about him?"

The grave-digger shrugged. "He's already at the graveyard. While this night is still deep, I'll carry him over to where the weeds grow high and throw him in a hole."

"Won't someone come looking for him?"

Bao looked down at the body and shook his head. "He has no family in White Stone, and servants change masters all the time."

Quanming still hesitated. "I should help you bury him," he said. "And then I'll stay around, just in case he is discovered, so I can confess and you won't be accused."

Bao looked at Quanming silently, then sighed. "Sisan, let's suppose the bastard is discovered and I'm arrested. "If you're gone, then I can tell them your name without having to be tortured for long. If you're here, I'll bite my tongue and suffer. Please go.''

Before Quanming left the Baos' house, he looked at the daughter once more. The girl was being rocked in her mother's arms like a baby; she was no longer crying, but staring into space wearing a strange smile.

When Quanming reached home, his mother was still sleeping. He turned on her bedside lamp, sat on the edge of her bed, and shook her gently. She opened her eyes, looked at him, and her eyes widened. ''What happened?'' she asked, her voice already trembling.

Quanming told her the whole story.

''Killed a man . . .'' she murmured, all the blood draining from her face. Her ice-cold hands tightly gripped those of her son. ''You must go away. I can see the police coming for you. They'll put you in jail and torture you until you admit you're guilty. The law of China has always been like this: since we are neither rich nor powerful, you'll be found at fault, self-defense or no self-defense. They'll either shoot you or chop your head off, and that will kill me too. Son, if you don't want me to die, then you must leave for Kwangchow—tonight, right now. Go from there to Hong Kong, and then to your uncle.''

Quanming told her of his argument with Yoto. She listened without comment, then said calmly, ''I'll make sure that she gets a message, telling her not of the killing but of your whereabouts. I'll let her know that you're not coming back. If her love for you is strong, she'll join you either in Kwangchow or Hong Kong, and if not . . .'' She looked at Quanming intently. ''First love means more to a girl than a man. You'll forget her much more easily than she'll forget you.''

Quanming held the fragile woman in his arms. ''But, Mama, how can I leave you? You'll be all alone.''

''I'm stronger than you think.'' The mother forced herself to smile at her son. ''I can go live with my sister. Like all mothers, I would rather have you far away and alive than buried in a nearby grave.''

Over his mother's shoulder, Quanming looked out

the window at the clear night sky, brightened by a nearly full moon.

"Mama," he said, gazing at it, "I should stay with you at least a few more days, until after the Moon Festival."

"You silly boy! Do you want me to celebrate the festival by serving your head on a plate? Go! There'll be plenty more moon festivals to come. You can send for me from America. Or maybe someday, if China should fall into the hands of a good leader, it will become a livable place . . . then you can return, and we'll be together again. Go, my son, go quickly!"

Quanming left White Stone at dawn; the moon had not quite faded, but the eastern sky was already turning pink. His mother held back her tears as he walked away. He turned frequently to look at the hill with the white marble gleaming in the early light, and waved again and again at his mother. He also glanced toward the direction of the Kaos' mansion, but all he could see were the high walls. He looked at the temple, wishing he could have said good-bye to Master Lin. The bag he carried on his back was light, but he walked with a heavy burden.

He stayed in Kwangchow in the same hotel near the prison, and each time he wanted to change his mind about leaving China, he thought of Quanli's head rolling on the ground. He had to wait more than a week for the boat to take him to Hong Kong, and on the last day a messenger came from White Stone, bringing him a letter from his mother:

". . . Kao Yoto and Ma Tsai-tu were married on the day of the Moon Festival, so I didn't bother to give her the message from you."

# 4

The wind blew a leaf from the willow,
And it fell lightly upon the water,
Where the waves carried it out of my sight.

Time gradually erased the leaf from my memory,
As I watched a new leaf floating away.
Since I have forgotten you, whom I love,
I dreamed the days away in sorrow,
Living at a new water's edge.

But the leaf kept floating back to me,
And I knew that inside my heart,
The memory of you shall forever remain.
                          —Quan-tsi
                          Chinese Love Poem

ON A SPRING day in 1912, Willow Place, nestled on a
curve of the Pearl River, was already a beehive of activity by the time the stars began to fade in the eastern
sky.

Dots of yellow light from homemade oil lamps
started to brighten the windows in mud huts as women
began to cook over wood stoves. After eating their rice
gruel and salted fish, the villagers trudged toward the
rice paddies or toward fishing boats; farming and fishing were the two principal occupations of Willow
Place.

The sun continued its ascent over the edge of the
earth, painting the mountain slopes in a shower of

blazing hues. The rays soon became free of the mountaintops, beginning to bathe the farmers, who worked knee-deep in water bending to the task of planting rice, in a golden glow.

The sun also reflected on the river, creating an illusion of a million shimmering jewels. In the middle of the Pearl small boats struggled against the current; these were wooden ships with square sails still floating stubbornly after having passed through many generations of owners.

Aboard these vessels, the frail older men wore faded long pants and jackets. The young wore short pants and went without shirts, leaving their muscular limbs browned from the sun.

One of the boats carried six men: fisherman Li and his young son Fachai, along with four boys from the Wang family. Fachai was working the nets, and his shoulders and arms strained under the drag of the line. At seventeen, he was already a great deal taller than most of the village men. His handsome face was dark, his thick black hair braided into a queue. He loved the water and wanted nothing more than to be a fisherman.

"Another good day, Father," Fachai called out cheerfully, filling his lungs with the sweet clean air. "We should do well today. We'll fill the boat with fish and our pockets with money."

The father shook his gray head in annoyance. "Dreaming again," he mumbled under his breath. "Buddha won't let any of us get rich on this miserable river."

The youngest of the Wang boys yelled over to Fachai, "We'd be rich if we could net the Dragon King's treasure!"

The Dragon King lived in a shining castle hidden in the depths of the Pearl, accompanied by his beautiful daughters with seaweed hair. The king loved to gather the treasures from the sunken ships; the girls were eager to lure the sailors to their domain to become their eternal lovers.

"You better keep your mind on what you're doing,

before throwing yourself into the deadly arms of one of the king's daughters!'' Fachai shouted back as they pulled the net into the boat and released the catch on the deck.

The eldest Wang said, while throwing the fish into the boat's well, ''Talk about beautiful girls . . . someday I'll marry a girl with soft red lips and long black shining hair, who will wait on me without complaint.''

Hearing those words, old Li allowed himself a rare smile. He couldn't help wondering where such a woman could be found. On the rippling water he could see the face of his wife. She had been beautiful once, but it was impossible for a woman not to complain.

Sitting with his arms draped over the tiller, the old man looked up at the sky. He glanced over the sail, and noticed with disgust that it was in need of repair again. ''How, in the name of the Great Buddha, am I going to get the money?'' he moaned.

He then looked past the rigging and saw out in the distance dark heavy clouds rolling ominously toward the Pearl. He stared at the clouds intently; his whole body froze for a moment. ''Storm!'' he yelled.

Jumping, Fachai and the boys started immediately to haul in the nets.

As they pulled on the lines, Fachai kept glancing toward the approaching storm, hoping that they could secure everything in time.

The river was turning angry; a curtain of black clouds shrouded the sun, turning a lovely spring day into a frightening night.

As soon as the nets were secured, old Li, with the help of one of the Wang boys, turned the tiller toward shore. Suddenly a searing white streak clipped off the mast with a deafening explosion. The thick pole crashed to the deck, pinning the eldest Wang under its weight.

''Help!'' the boy screamed in pain.

As everybody rushed over, the boat tilted to one side. After a long struggle the boy was freed. The gunwale had taken most of the beating; except for a few bruises, the boy seemed to be all right.

The first drops of rain began to fall, and within a few minutes they turned into solid sheets of water. The crew could no longer see the shoreline, and without a sail they were at the mercy of the Pearl. A wave washed over the side, catching the boys off-guard. Two of them found a handhold; Fachai threw an arm around what was left of the mast and caught the youngest Wang with an iron grip—he was not about to give up any of the crew to one of the Dragon King's waiting daughters.

"Get to the oars!" Fachai bellowed above the roar, working his way to where they were lashed. The boys quickly followed, and after a desperate struggle they mounted the oars into the oarlocks. Only then did they gain some control of the vessel.

On their port side, one of the boats was caught by a powerful gust and reeled over, spilling out several men. The wreck was quickly caught in the roaring current and soon disappeared in front of their eyes.

Fachai and the eldest Wang rushed to the side, while the other Wang boys manned their oars. "More to the port!" Fachai shouted, reaching toward one of the men in the water. He got hold of the swimmer's queue, and pulled him by the hair until his partner could get a handhold; together they hauled the terrified boy aboard. They rushed back to the side of the boat again and managed to rescue another. After that, no matter how hard they looked, they could find no one else— the missing crew members were now in the hands of Buddha.

Of the two rescued boys, the elder one was bending over emptying his stomach. The younger one sat holding on to the broken mast, sobbing. The rest of them worked hard on the oars, trying desperately to keep the bow facing downstream.

Old man Li was yelling and pointing. "Over there! Head for the bend! Put your backs into it! There should be calm water beyond. Pull! Pull!"

Fachai and the others pulled with all their strength.

The muscles of their backs and shoulders knotted like rope. They moved diagonally across the current, slowly working the boat toward the land. Just when everyone felt he had no more strength left, the bow broke through the swift water and into the calm.

The rain beat down on them mercilessly as they lay draped over the oars, gulping air into their burning lungs. They were too exhausted to look up. Without casting their grateful eyes toward heaven, they mumbled their thanks to Buddha for helping them to escape once more from the Dragon King and his tempting daughters.

Farmer Liang had also been working since dawn, and by midmorning he was already feeling the strain. Standing with his feet buried in the muddy rice paddy, he decided to take a break. He rested his hands on his hips and arched his back. He stretched the aching muscles, let out a low moan.

Though he was only forty, his face was etched in deep furrows. The few teeth he possessed looked like ancient ivory that had yellowed with time. His thin queue, a braid of silver and gray, hung lifelessly from beneath a straw-basket hat.

Beside him, his only son, A-fu, stretched likewise, imitating his father. It was the boy's first day working in the rice field with true responsibility. Like any eleven-year-old, he was proud and eager to become a man.

A-fu was the son from Farmer Liang's second wife. The first had died giving birth to a daughter, Leahi. Old Liang had often wondered if the Great Buddha was a jealous god and had taken Leahi's lovely mother away because the two had shared too many happy years together and had failed to hide their happiness from the gods.

His second marriage had been one of convenience, and there had never been much happiness. He had needed a wife to run the house, and the woman, having passed her prime, had needed a husband to soothe her nagging family. He had felt little passion for this domineering female, but as the result of sharing a narrow bed night after night, they had produced a fine son. The woman fawned over A-fu like a brooding hen, while at the same time she hated the sight of her stepdaughter, the gentle, obedient Leahi.

A farmer couldn't afford too long a break. Once again the old man bent down and returned to his task, thinking that all his life he had worked side by side with the earth, each always on the edge of exhaustion, the overused soil and the overworked man.

A-fu quickly followed this example, determined to make his father proud. In one hand he carried the young plants; with the other he drove a single shoot deeply into the mud. Several times the seedling floated back to the surface and had to be planted again. His father noticed but kept working as if he had not seen. He knew the boy would learn on his own. And sure enough, after a while A-fu was able to keep the plants buried securely.

They soon finished working one mud-walled section, and A-fu followed his father out of the muddy water to head toward another patch. All of a sudden he started to jump up and down. "Baba!" he screamed. "Look at my legs! It's terrible! It hurts! Am I going to die?"

An army of leeches had fastened onto his legs. Here and there blood was dripping, and the sight was frightening. He used his fingers to pick at them, but as soon as he touched one he let go in abhorrence. Tears ran down his cheeks, and his screams caused workers in the other paddies to look up, some of them laughed at the boy's cowardice.

Their laughter hurt the father's pride. "Stop that crying and leave them alone before your legs are raw!" farmer Liang admonished his son severely. He took some salt from a pouch to rub it on the bloodsuckers, and continued more softly, "If you want to be a farmer, you must learn to endure hardships. Son, our life is not easy. If there is a drought, you pray for water. If a flood, you ask Buddha to return the sun. If there is no food, we eat grass, and if the leeches bury their heads inside your body, you simply wear them proudly like a fine garment.''

The boy stopped crying, picked up the young shoots, and once again entered the water. It pained the father to see his son growing up in a world that demanded so much and gave so little. It saddened him deeply that his son's life would be as poor as his—an endless struggle for every scrap of food through all his days.

Lifting his gaze to the top of the hill at the landlord's fine mansion, farmer Liang murmured, ''Why couldn't the Great Buddha, in all his wisdom, divide the wealth among us all instead of giving it to only a few?''

The gods in heaven answered him with a clap of thunder. The roar rolled from the mountaintop, echoing all the way down through the valley. Unlike the fishermen, the farmers needed rain. Liang smiled as he watched the heavy clouds moving in.

''It looks like a storm is on its way, my son. We are lucky, for the fields are getting thirsty.''

Large drops of rain started to fall, and the old man raised his grateful face to the sky, licking the precious water as it ran down his lined face.

In the downpour the father and son stood together, happily letting the wetness run over them. They looked at each other through half-closed eyes, and all they saw was a good harvest, some money, and an easier life.

A bolt of lightning cut through the sky, and the silver spear from heaven landed not far from them. Farmer Liang took his son's hand, and the two quickly ran for cover under a huge willow.

As the storm moved across the rice paddies, the raindrops created thousands of dancing circles. The ancient willow served as a giant umbrella; under it Liang and A-fu sat watching. On A-fu's face was youthful innocence, but the brief happiness on his father's had become tired resignation once more.

The storm soon abated, the sky cleared, and a beautiful rainbow appeared over the far mountain. The old and the young stood up, returned to work. Without letting his son know it, the old man looked at the boy with pride. After experiencing the leeches and the storm, A-fu was now a part of the land—a planter of dreams, a reaper of sorrow.

Toward midday their stomachs started to growl. They kept looking toward the village, and soon the boy saw a familiar figure. "Here comes Leahi with our lunch," he shouted. "I'm so hungry I could eat a whole water buffalo!"

When they stepped out of the water, they found more leeches on their bodies. The father took out more salt and rubbed it over the wiggling creatures. As he did so, a young girl appeared.

Less than five feet tall, she was small-breasted but with broad hips—a good sign for childbearing—something every future mother-in-law would be pleased to see. She had on a pair of faded baggy pants and a loose blouse. Her thick black hair was braided into a pigtail that reached her waist. She had a round-shaped face, dark almond eyes, and a full mouth. She came running to her father and stepbrother, then quickly set out lunch. She smiled as she worked, and her white teeth contrasted with her tanned skin.

Their dining table was the wet ground under the old willow. Farmer Liang leaned against the tree trunk, scratching his back on the rough bark and looking at his daughter. He could not get over how she had grown. It seemed but yesterday that he had bounced her on his knee. Now Leahi was a woman of fifteen, and according to custom it was time for her to marry.

"Have you eaten yet, daughter?" he asked with concern, knowing how tight his wife could be.

Leahi shook her head, and her father sighed. He then gave her part of his food, and the three ate in silent contentment.

While eating, Leahi looked toward the faraway river. The water looked peaceful and calm from a distance; it was hard to believe that a while ago the storm had hit while she was washing clothes along the bank. The water had suddenly turned into a roaring beast and the family's clothes were almost lost.

She was worried about Li Fachai. She knew that he

was out there somewhere, fighting another battle against the Dragon King and his vicious daughters. She prayed that he had won the battle and returned to the shore safely. *Does he ever think of me like I do him? I'm so ugly with my big feet and my dark skin. I'm nothing like the rich young ladies living in the landlord's mansion.*

As she stared dreamily at the Pearl, her thoughts flew back in time and landed on a very special day. She had been washing clothes at the riverbank. When the washing was done and she had gathered the wrung clothes into a basket, the voice of a man startled her: "My name is Li Fachai. I'm fisherman Li's son . . . and I want to know your name."

In the early-morning mist she saw him standing under the willows, tall, strong, and handsome. Her heart began pounding so hard that she thought it would burst. She blushed deeply, unable to find her tongue.

*Why didn't I say something? He must have thought me a fool.*

"Are you not hungry, daughter?" she heard her father ask.

"What?" She blushed again. "Oh! No, Baba, not very."

Immediately A-fu laid a hand on Leahi's rice bowl. "Can I have it, then? I'm still very, very hungry!"

Leahi handed the remaining rice to A-fu, then leaned against the willow next to her father, resting for a while before going back to her stepmother and the afternoon chores. Because she had never been to school and couldn't read or write, she knew no words to describe beauty, but she felt it all around her. She watched the clouds drifting across the blue sky, listened to the cicadas filling the fields with their unchanged refrain.

Liang laid a loving hand on his daughter's shoulder, watched his son eating with good appetite. He sighed. "Life is hard, but times like this make all the struggle worthwhile. If only Buddha can make our lives nothing but moments like right now . . ." As he spoke, his heart told him that he was asking for the impossible.

A-fu finished his rice and looked over at his sister with an impish smile. "Maybe you could marry into the landlord's family, and then we can all become rich and happy. But of course, we must first find a way to hide your big ugly feet." He giggled.

Sitting up straight, Leahi looked at her half-brother with an air of authority. "A-fu, don't you know anything? Bound feet are now out of fashion. They were forbidden by the law."

"That's impossible. Where did you hear such nonsense?" her father asked gruffly.

"Down by the river where the old men sit. I even heard one of them saying that there is also a new law that all men must cut off their queues."

The father shook his head in disbelief. "That's nothing but foolishness. Those old men didn't know what they were talking about. Our hair was given to us by our parents, and we have no right to cut it. Confucius said so thousands of years ago, and his words must be obeyed. I'll be damned if I ever cut my hair, and no other man should either . . . if he has any respect for his ancestors . . ." He continued to mumble his disapproval under his breath.

Leahi knew better than to argue with her father; she was not a disrespectful daughter. She started to gather the empty bowls, and then said good-bye to the men and left for home.

# 5

FACHAI AND THE crew secured the rented boat to its moorings. His father had made a mental note of the damages. The old man knew it would be useless to ask for help. The boat was his responsibility; the owner expected and demanded it. The rental agreements had always been made to benefit the owners, and the rule had already been in existence for centuries. The problem was, the Li family didn't have any money.

That evening, a family meeting was held around the kitchen table. Fachai, his parents, and the grandfather—all four tried to find a way out of the dilemma.

Old woman Li was scarcely taller than four feet and very thin. With tears in her eyes, she took from under the bedding a red silk wrapping. Her clawlike fingers trembled as she unwrapped the package and revealed a silver ring and a pair of matching earrings. They had been given to her on her wedding day by the Li family, and she wore them only on special occasions. They were her only treasures; she valued them as if they were the finest gold.

She placed the jewelry on the table; and without looking at anyone she announced firmly, "Let Fachai take either the ring or the earrings to Kwangchow to pawn . . . but please take only one, and leave the other for Fachai's future bride."

Fisherman Li watched his wife fighting back her tears, and his heart ached. In his blurred vision he could see her as his young bride, but as he blinked his eyes, her beauty faded. In front of him was a woman in her mid-thirties, aged in the merciless hands of life.

"Deu-na-ma! What a wretched life!" he cursed as he got to this feet. As the husband, he had to decide between the ring and the earrings for his wife. Point-

ing to the ring, he said curtly, "We'll pawn this!" and
with that he turned and walked out into the night.

In the cool night breeze, the old fisherman felt his
anger fading. Standing under the stars, he thought of
his mother, another woman who had struggled to feed
the family when times were bad, who had always kept
almost nothing for herself. His mother had died old
while still young, and now his wife was walking the
same path. He glared at the crystal-clear sky with the
moon hanging like a giant lantern, and whispered in
a pleading voice, "Maybe our next lives will be better.
Maybe both she and I will be born rich and powerful." He then turned and walked back to the hut.

The dirt road leading from Willow Place to Kwangchow was bordered by wildflowers. On one side, the
Pearl River could be seen flowing gently toward the
sea, and on the other side, one mountain peak after
another floated mysteriously over the low-lying clouds.

Walking to Kwangchow in the morning of an early-
summer day was a pleasant experience for Fachai. He
enjoyed taking off his cotton slippers, rolling up his
best pants, and wading knee-deep through one of the
small streams that fed the river. The water was cool
and clear. By cupping his hands he was able to drink
his fill. He passed several villages, among them White
Stone with its marble reflecting the sun and the fragrant Valley of Jasmine nestling between the mountains. The people appeared no different from those in
Willow Place; they all seemed to be wearing, like ox-
en's yokes, looks of despair.

It was noon when Fachai reached Kwangchow. His
clothes clung to his body from the heat, and he wondered how anyone could live in a place so crowded.
He couldn't even see enough space for a cool breeze
to blow through, and he was instantly homesick for
the farmland and the river.

People on the streets were rushing in every direction, shouting, cursing, spitting, laughing, elbowing
one another out of the way. Tired and thirsty, Fachai
spotted a free tea stand, and not knowing that it was

for beggars, he picked up the ladle and drank from it greedily. As people passed, they shook their heads at such a healthy young man taking tea from the needy. Fachai finished several dips before he heard one of the comments. Deeply embarrassed, he quickly put back the ladle and hurried on.

He had been told to look for a certain Fong's Pawn-shop on the main street. According to his father, Mr. Fong had always been known to be a very fair man.

Fachai had never learned to read or write, and so the street signs meant nothing to him. He discovered quickly how cold the city folk were, and those few who were willing to give him directions spoke in a dialect he barely understood. After hours of searching, he finally found himself at the entrance of a two-story building.

He walked in and saw a boy much younger than he, sitting behind a wire cage like a cooped-up chicken.

The caged boy looked up at Fachai, and his pale face broke into a fragile smile. "May I be of assistance to you?" he gently asked in the city dialect.

"I . . . I have something to pawn," Fachai stammered as he approached the cage and pushed his mother's silver ring through the small opening.

The boy leaned forward, picked up the ring, and studied it carefully. Fachai stared at the boy's soft white hands and long fingers; he had never seen such delicate hands in his life, not even on any of the girls at Willow Place.

The boy leaned closer toward Fachai and asked, "Is this beautiful ring yours?"

"It's my mother's." Fachai liked the boy instantly for saying the ring was beautiful, and volunteered to explain, "There was a storm, and our boat was damaged. We need the money to repair it, and I was told to come here to speak to Mr. Fong . . ."

A dark cloud suddenly came over the boy's bloodless face, and his thin, pale lips quivered. "You are too late. My father and my mother were killed during the last typhoon—"

Before the boy could finish, a man appeared and

pushed him aside. "What do you have?" he asked Fachai.

Fachai pointed at the ring. The man took it from the boy, looked at it briefly, then pushed it back to Fachai. "I'm terribly sorry, but I can't take it. In the storage room we have cases of silver jewelry already. My boy, you see, silver is something that the poor treasure, while the rich spit on it. In a time like this, when the poor are parting with their heirlooms, the rich are buying only emeralds, pearls, and solid gold."

Fachai's face dropped. He couldn't force his mother's precious ring on someone who didn't want it. He looked at the man and the boy behind the counter; they both looked at him apologetically. Bowing to them deeply, he pocketed the ring and left the shop.

The sun was setting by the time he had visited whatever other pawnshops he was able to find. He was exhausted, frustrated, and most of all, starved.

He was debating whether to look for more pawnshops or start for home when he accidentally bumped into a man dressed in a Western suit. "Please excuse me, Sisan, honorable sir. I beg your pardon one thousand times . . ." Fachai mumbled, and bowed again and again.

Frowning, the man checked to see if his light-colored suit had been dirtied by this country coolie. All of a sudden, though, he stopped frowning. His gaze swept over Fachai's broad shoulders and well-built body, and when he smiled, two gold teeth in his mouth flashed in the light of the setting sun.

"Little brother," he asked with a cunning grin, "what are you doing in this big city?"

Fachai bowed once more. "Sisan, honorable sir, I'm here trying to pawn my mother's ring." Standing on the sidewalk, wiping his sweating brow, he poured out the whole story.

The story was nothing new to the gold-toothed man, but he pretended to listen with interest. When Fachai stopped, he asked gently, "What's your name, my boy?"

"I'm Li Fachai, a fisherman from Willow Place," the boy answered with pride.

A food peddler passed them by, carrying steamed meat buns. As Fachai winced and swallowed, the man noticed right away. "Are you hungry?"

Fachai was embarrassed, but didn't know how to lie. He nodded. He was certain that the whole of Kwangchow could hear his stomach growling.

"Come, let me buy you something to eat," the man said, and pointed at a teahouse nearby.

Fachai had never been to a teahouse in his life. This one was dirty, hot, and noisy, but to him it was the finest place he had ever seen. The smell of food coming from the kitchen made his mouth water and his stomach rumble even louder. Young girls pushed around carts laden with an assortment of small bamboo steamers, and the man beckoned to one of them. As she came to their table, he said to Fachai, "Take whatever you like, little brother. Eat until there's no room left in your stomach."

There were spring rolls, chicken wings, duck feet, pork liver, steamed buns—Fachai had never seen such a variety of food, not even during the New Year or other festival days, when the poor splurged to eat a little better. He began to eat with youthful abandon. Meanwhile, the man lighted a cigarette and watched calmly behind a cloud of smoke. When finished, Fachai wiped his mouth on his sleeve. "Thank you, Sisan, the Great Buddha will reward you for feeding such an unworthy person."

The man smiled, then started to talk with a cigarette dangling from the corner of his mouth. "My name is Woo Ming, and I believe in rewarding myself more than counting on Buddha. By the way, you seem to be a decent young man. Would you like to be rewarded with an opportunity of becoming rich in a faraway land of gold? Have you ever heard of the Land of the Gold Mountains?"

"No." Fachai cocked his head to one side. "Is it in north China?"

Shaking his head, the man laughed. "The Land of

the Gold Mountains lies across the sea. Over there people can become rich by picking up gold from the streets . . .''

Spraying saliva all over the table, Woo Ming started to draw the picture of a heaven on earth. It took him a long time to finish, and by then Li Fachai was no longer the same young boy.

"There is actually such a place? How . . . how can I get there? I . . . I don't want to be as rich as an emperor, I only want enough gold to fix the boat." Fachai looked at the man with the same respect he would pay to the statue of Buddha in a temple.

Woo Ming's experienced eyes told him that Fachai had taken the bait; now it was time for him to pull the line. "I could lend you money for your passage on a ship, and give you a few silver dollars as an advance . . .''

Fachai could not believe what he was hearing. Here was a chance to go to a magic land with mountains made of gold, and to receive enough silver dollars to provide for his family's needs after fixing the boat.

"Please tell me more about the Land of the Gold Mountains," he said, his heart beating fast. "Will I be able to fish there? I love to fish, and I want to always be a fisherman."

Woo Ming moved closer, puffed smoke in the young boy's face. "I guarantee that the moment you step off the ship, someone will take you to the largest fishing boat you've ever set your eyes on." Then he asked abruptly, "Do you have a wife?"

"No." Shaking his head, Fachai blushed as he thought of Liang Leahi, in his eyes the most beautiful girl in Willow Place.

"Well, before leaving for the Gold Mountains, you had better find yourself a bride." Woo Ming was rushing toward the final settlement, anxious to close the deal. "When would you be able to leave?"

"I . . . well . . . I'll have to talk to my parents first."

Woo Ming frowned. He could already smell a sale, and he didn't want to lose it. "The ship sails in the middle of August by our lunar calendar, which will be sometime toward the end of October according to the Western calendar. This is only June; we have almost four months left. But I'll have to know your answer very soon to make the necessary arrangements. So your parents need to be quick in making a decision.'' He told Fachai how to find him again in Kwangchow, then reached into his pocket for a silver coin. ''Take this, and tell your parents there'll be a lot more when you sign up.''

Fachai's hand was shaking as he took the silver. He had touched only copper coins before. He placed the silver dollar carefully in his inner pocket, got off the chair, bowed deeply to the man. ''One million thanks, Sisan. I'm sure you'll be seeing me again very, very soon.''

Leahi awoke early, slid out of the covers, and stood looking at the crescent moon through her window. The night was far from fading, but she was wide-awake and couldn't sleep anymore.

Today she was to be married.

She started to prepare for her bath. A large wooden tub was soon filled with hot water, and in place of the usual coarse brown soap there was a fragrant bar—a secret gift from her father. She stepped into the water and slowly sat down. As she washed herself, she thought about what would soon happen and began to pray to the Great Buddha: ''Please, please help me to make Fachai happy . . . please.''

Suddenly she was frightened, worried, sad, excited—all at the same time.

Sitting in the water, she turned toward her bed. Her eyes fell on the silver earrings that her future mother-in-law had given her, and her heart was filled with gratitude. ''I'll treasure them forever. Why, such fine jewelry is good enough for a princess,'' she murmured.

Next to the earrings lay the beautiful quilt her father had bought as a wedding gift, over the protests of her stepmother. Looking at the quilt, Leahi almost started to cry. Knowing that tears on her wedding day would bring her bad luck for the rest of her married life, she quickly forced her thoughts back to Fachai.

A tingle went through her young body as the wash-cloth brushed gently across her small breasts. She looked down and saw her nipples standing erect. She was puzzled by the sensation traveling through her entire body as she continued to pass the cloth back and forth. The strange feeling settled between her legs, and Leahi quickly finished washing, stepped out of the tub.

She dried herself thoroughly, then began to get dressed in her wedding finery. According to tradition, the money to purchase her clothes had come from the groom's family. There was a red blouse trimmed in gold lace, a pair of red long pants and a skirt to wear over them. The lace cuffs would show from beneath the skirt as she walked.

While dressing, Leahi prayed once more that Fachai would always want her and that she would be able to bear him many fine sons.

She worked diligently to cover her dark face with a thick layer of white powder. Then she painted her lips and cheeks scarlet. The last thing she did was to put on the earrings. She then turned from side to side in front of the mirror. The girl who stared back was a beautiful stranger; she was pleased, no longer worried about Fachai not wanting her.

She checked her hair once more. While she made a few final adjustments, a loud knock shattered the silence. "What's taking you so long?" her stepmother's shrill voice came from the other side of the door. "You want to hide under our roof forever?"

"Coming," she answered. Nervously she looked around the room she had occupied her entire life. After today, she would become merely a visitor to this house. A wave of sadness overwhelmed her and she felt the tears coming; she scolded herself and walked out the door without looking back.

The narrow street was lined with villagers as the wedding procession slowly made its way. Leading the parade, farmer Liang nodded to his friends, looked down proudly at the embroidered quilt draped over his arm. It was his gift of love to his daughter, and he had prayed that it would keep Leahi warm through all the cold nights of her life. A-fu walked behind his father, dressed in a pair of new cotton pants and a new jacket, with a bright red sash tied around his waist. He enjoyed the journey for a while, but as they inched along the dusty road, he soon became bored. The sun was high in the sky, and its heat made him feel like a roasted duck for the wedding feast. He stepped closer to his father and whispered, "Can't we go a little faster, Baba? At this speed, we will never get there before the day is over."

The father ignored the boy. Going either too fast or too slow might mean a loss of face. Walking too fast, he would give the crowd the idea that he was anxious to get rid of his worthless daughter. Walking too slowly, he would be telling them he was too attached to a brat to let her go.

Leahi walked silently. Her steps remained deliberately slow to ensure that the old crones would have nothing to wag their tongues about. She could just hear them. "Look at her! See how impatient she is? Can't wait to get in the wedding bed!" She was also careful to keep her eyes lowered and her head modestly bowed. No one must know that inside her breast, her heart was pounding madly. A shiver went through her as she thought of her groom, and that slight tremble didn't escape the keen eyes of one of the old hags. The old woman shouted into the ear of her toothless friend, intended for the whole village to hear: "Did you see that? The bride is frightened! Must be a good girl! I remember how frightened I was, over fifty years ago."

Behind Leahi followed her stepmother, Mrs. Liang. The woman was miserable in the heat. She had combed a generous amount of oil into her hair to give it a youthful shine, and now the grease was running down her neck. Her new clothes were sticking to her skin, and her shoes, a size too small, were getting tighter with every step. She was ready to scream, but she

walked with her head held high, and occasionally even
managed a slight bow to a deserving friend. Her physical discomfort was compensated by the knowledge
that finally she was getting rid of Leahi, her husband's
little princess, the grain of sand in her eye.

When the procession turned the final corner, the Lis'
house came into view. On each door and window was
a sheet of red paper marked with gold characters, sym-
bols of good luck. A tall bamboo pole was hung with
strings of firecrackers, and as the group came nearer,
the fuses were lit; the sound of ten thousand explo-
sions echoed through the streets. Flying pieces of red
paper danced in the air, followed by white smoke carrying the acrid smell of burnt powder.

"The marriage is blessed! The evil spirits have been
driven away, making room for all the good luck to
enter!" the villagers cheered.

The cacophony continued as the bride reached the
front door. After a thick red veil was draped over her
head, she couldn't see anything. She heard her future
mother-in-law whispering beside her, "Come this way,
daughter." Leahi was then led to a makeshift table
covered with a red cotton cloth.

Fachai was standing to one side, nervously twisting
the red sash tied around the waist of his wedding robe.
After the bride took her place on the other side of the
table, the village elder, standing facing the two, began
to ramble. He talked about farming, fishing, and the
history of the village, sometimes getting lost within
his own rhetoric, much to the dismay of the already
perspiring and bored crowd. Finally he mentioned the
groom's and the bride's names:

"Li Fachai and Liang Leahi, you must not be influ-
enced by the changes that are trickling down from this
new government in Beijing. You should always be
faithful to the old traditions that have served us well
over the years. Li Fachai, you should always work hard
to provide for your elders, and when there is enough
left over, of course, you should also feed your wife. It
is the husband's duty to see to it that the wife always
obeys. If she does not, then as a good husband you

should beat her with a stick, but not so hard that she can't carry on her wifely duties. And you, Leahi, you should be a good daughter to the Li family and make life as easy as possible for them. You should remain in good spirits and good health, and above all, you must give the Li family many grandsons!''

Fachai and Leahi were made to get down on their knees to begin the ritual of kowtow. First they bowed to their ancestors, then to each living member of the two families. After that they were led to their bed-chamber, which had been Fachai's old room, now completely redecorated. The bed was covered with a bright red spread, and there were two pillows embroidered with mandarin ducks: the symbol of together-ness through eternity. Strips of red paper were strung from the four posts, and the quilt from the bride's father was placed neatly at the foot of the bed.

Mrs. Li had thought of everything. Two red candles were burning on the dresser, the left representing the life span of the groom, the right the bride. Giving fate a helping hand, the loving mother had lighted her son's candle a few minutes after the bride's.

The wedding couple were made to stand beside their bed, and then came the time for the groom to lift off the bridal veil. Fachai and Leahi were lucky to know what the other looked like; in most weddings, this was the first time bride and groom looked at the person with whom they were going to spend the rest of their lives.

After her veil was lifted, Leahi dared to raise her eyes only for an instant; what she saw filled her heart with pride. She couldn't believe this tall, handsome man was becoming her husband. He looked like a war-lord's son, standing so straight, with his shoulders fill-ing out his new robe. She knew she would obey his every wish willingly; though he had the right, he would never have to beat her.

Fachai gasped in turn, for the face he saw belonged to a stranger. He was so surprised that he just stood blinking. This white-faced impostor, this heavily painted clown, simply could not be his beautiful dimple-cheeked Leahi.

Next came the wedding feast, and everyone was moved out of the bedchamber. To several round tables borrowed from the neighbors food was brought, and the hungry guests started to eat. The sounds of laughing and toasting filled the air.

Fachai ate with his youthful appetite, but Leahi picked at her food, too nervous to swallow anything. Glancing over at her father and A-fu, she was glad to see both of them eating heartily, spitting the bones freely all over the place.

The sun had long since set and the moon rose high before the eating ended. The bride and groom were escorted to the bedchamber once more. Told to sit on the edge of the bed, the newlyweds folded their hands nervously in their laps. Their relatives and friends started to pour into the room to tease them, and the more the guests drank, the more suggestive the comments.

Fachai glanced over at his bride as she sat with her head bowed toward the floor. "I wonder how long this nonsense will go on," he whispered, his patience wearing thin as the drunks kept parading in.

Leahi didn't dare to answer. If she said something wrong now, she would be reminded of it for the rest of her life.

Finally, about three in the morning, all the guests had left. A-fu was the only one remaining. The poor boy was told to wait outside the bedchamber; he was not allowed to go home yet.

In the bedchamber, Mrs. Li walked toward the groom, pushed him aside, and took from under the bed a washbasin made of wood and painted bright red. In the bottom of the basin lay a piece of neatly folded pure white cloth. The mother handed them to her son and whispered, "Don't forget the instructions from your father." She then turned and left, closing the door quietly behind her.

Groom and bride continued to sit side by side, not knowing what to do next. Fachai finally gathered enough courage to reach over and take his bride's hand. "Leahi . . ." he murmured, saying her name for the very first time.

"Yes, my husband?" Leahi answered quickly, her heart pounding at the touch of his hand.

"You are really mine now . . . my wife. I've dreamed about this ever since I saw you that day under the willow beside the Pearl." As he talked, he cupped her chin in one hand, and using the other hand, he started to wipe away the white powder and rouge. When the real Leahi appeared beneath all the makeup, he took her awkwardly in his arms.

Leahi moved an inch closer to him, her heart pounding louder than ever. Slowly they worked their way toward each other on the bed, and it took them even longer to reach the stage of lying side by side. Fachai brushed Leahi's lips with his, and when she did not pull away, he let his mouth rest there. After a while her lips opened slightly. Like a hummingbird tasting the nectar of a new bud, his tongue began to draw in her sweetness. As his hands explored her young body, she quivered under his fingers, felt a thousand little needles under her skin. They were soon lost in the unfamiliar joy, wanting more but not sure how to achieve it.

Outside the room, A-fu sat in a chair, unable to keep his eyes open. He had been told to stay until Mrs. Li gave him permission to go—either alone when his sister proved herself pure, or with his sister if she failed to produce a bloodstained cloth.

The groom's mother was in the kitchen, trying to stay busy while waiting for the bedroom door to open. She had already washed and cleaned everything twice, and still the door remained closed. Exhausted from the long day, she finally sat down to rest.

When Fachai tiptoed into the room, he saw his mother slumped over, sleeping soundly.

"Mother," he whispered timidly from the door, holding in his hand a piece of bloodstained cloth. "Mother, wake up," he called louder, but she did not stir. "Mother!" he boomed.

Mrs. Li's head jerked up. She saw her son, then the cloth, and flashed a tired smile. "Took you long enough! I better cook a good pot of chicken soup tomorrow to rebuild your strength. But now I must go wake up the poor boy so he may return home with the news. The Liangs must be pacing the floor by now!"

# 6

SUMMER DAYS GAVE place to the autumn wind, and according to the Western calendar, it was October.

Fachai and his father had gone fishing in their fixed boat; at the house, the family was preparing for the Moon Festival. Grandfather Li was following Leahi around as she worked in the kitchen. He hobbled about on a cane made from a twisted root. His teeth were gone and his hands were knotted from hauling nets all his life, but his eyes still had a glimmer of mischief whenever he looked at Leahi. It was nice to have a pretty young thing around.

"Do you know, young girl, that ever since there were Chinese, the autumn moon has always been celebrated?"

"Yes, Grandfather," Leahi answered softly.

The old man dropped into a nearby chair and went on, "Togetherness is the most important element to celebrate this day. No matter how far people have traveled, today they must go home to be with their families. Next to being with the loved ones comes the food. Regardless of hard times, there must be something special on the table."

The Lis were eating unusually well this year. Leahi had already killed a hen, saving the blood for the soup, and the bird was now soaking in a rich wine sauce. There were also plenty of pigs' feet for everybody, and moon cakes baked with extra sugar; their sweet smell filled the kitchen. Tears welled in Leahi's eyes when she remembered that the reason they were eating well was that her husband was soon leaving for the Land of the Gold Mountains.

The thought brought a stabbing pain to her heart, and she quickly busied herself to keep her mind occupied by other things. The day passed slowly. The

almost white sky was eventually colored red and gold
by the setting sun. Then the glorious colors began to
fade, and a deep blue curtain was draped over the
heavenly stage. One by one the stars appeared, glowed
for a while, then turned pale as the moon in her orange
splendor began to rise gracefully, seating herself in her
heavenly domain like a true queen.

The fishermen came home late. It was Fachai's last
night of fishing on the Pearl River, and the Wang boys
were reluctant to let him go. When the men came
home, the women had already had the food on the table,
and the grandfather was complaining that the young
people these days no longer cared about the empty
stomach of an old man.

The family started to eat and drink, occasionally
going to the door together to look at the moon as it
slowly moved across the heaven. By the time everyone
had finished eating, the moon was almost straight
overhead, and it was time to cut and share the moon
cakes.

Many wishes were made, then the festivities continued. It was late when the women began to put things
away. Grandpa Li was the first to retire, and soon Fachai's father and mother followed.

Leahi was still busy in the kitchen when she felt a
hand on her shoulder. She turned with a start. "You
frightened me, Fachai. I thought you had already gone
to bed," she said, smiling at him gently.

"I can't sleep without you," he sighed. "Besides,
we have only a few hours left before I must leave. I
don't want to waste them sleeping."

Leahi turned away for fear of letting him see her
tears. She had to restrain herself from crying. If a
woman cried on a festival night, she would be blamed
for the rest of her life should any bad luck fall on the
family.

"Come," he said softly, taking her by the hand.
"Let's go to the river to watch the moon."

Pointing to his parents' room, Leahi hesitated.
"Won't they object?"

"They are too tired to notice." He smiled at her. "Besides, they were young themselves once."

The two walked in silence with the full moon's silver light guiding their way across the fields. The murmur of the Pearl grew louder as they neared its banks. They soon found themselves under the canopy of the ancient willows.

Fachai leaned back against one of the massive trunks, then pulled his wife gently toward him. His arms enveloped her tightly, his warm hands resting on her slightly swollen stomach: He was trying to hold both his wife and the child she was carrying.

With her head leaning against her husband's chest, Leahi looked up at the sky through the willow. Moonlight was sifting through the leaves, and as the breeze moved the branches, the light created black and white patterns on Leahi's blouse.

Fachai turned his wife around until they were face-to-face. Afraid to break the spell by saying something, he slowly began to remove the pins from her hair. Long black strands tumbled over her shoulders, ending at her waist. He buried his head in the scented softness. "I will miss you, my little Leahi," he whispered in her ear.

She held on to him tightly, biting her lip, wondering how she was going to live the rest of her days without him.

He raised his head and gazed at her for a long time. Then he gently raised a hand to lift her chin, and placed his lips on hers.

She quickly pushed him away. "We are outside our bedchamber! This is not proper . . . heaven has many eyes!"

She was still protesting when he pulled her to him once more, kissing her with such passion that she became dizzy. She wanted him to stop, but at the same time found herself responding to his desire.

His hand slipped under her blouse and cupped her small breast in his palm. She let out a gasp as he moved his fingers over her nipple. She could feel his hardness as they pushed against each other. The tradition that had been hammered into her head was now screaming: "This is wrong!"

But her body had become deaf to this cry. She found herself being lowered onto the grass, and he began pulling away her garments. His labored breathing became louder than the current of the Pearl, and she offered no more resistance. She welcomed him with a need she had never felt before. She wanted to scream and bite. She raised her legs to wrap them around him, her nails digging into his back. Her hips pounded upward, trying to take in all of him. They rocked faster and faster until she began to groan as if the world had come to an end.

They lay quietly for a long time. The only sound around them was the Pearl River making its way to the sea. Neither of them wanted to speak, knowing that soon he must begin his journey. As she listened to the wash of the Pearl, she wondered whether he would be like the rolling water: once gone, never to return again.

As if able to read her thoughts, he whispered to her, "Leahi, promise me one thing."

"One million things, my husband. Anything," she answered, choking back sobs.

He raised himself on his elbow and looked into her eyes. "On the next Moon Festival, if we are not together, please come to this very same spot, stand under this very same willow, and look at this very same moon. In the Land of the Gold Mountains, I too will do the same thing. On the face of the moon I will see your smiles, and while looking at the moon over the Pearl, you will hear my voice telling you that I love you and will soon come back."

"Yes, Fachai . . . I will do that. I will do that every year . . . under every full moon . . . until the day I die." The dam broke; she sobbed uncontrollably.

He kissed her wet lips, tasted the salt of her tears. Then he took her in his arms and held her tightly as she trembled.

The moon sailed to the west, the eastern sky turning white. He took her hand as they started back to the house. "I won't be gone too long," he said, forcing a lightness into his voice that he didn't feel. "Before our son can say Baba, we'll be together again."

She sobbed as she walked, "Fachai, please come back soon . . . there will be no life without you." She paused, then added timidly, "Fachai, please don't look at any of the female white devils—"

Without letting her finish, he gave her a hard slap on the rump. "How dare you say such a foolish thing? You stupid woman!" he yelled harshly. "Looking at a white cow? Never!" He continued more softly, "I'll be too busy earning money to look at anybody."

When they reached home, Fachai's parents and grandfather were already up and waiting. They had a quick breakfast, and as the dawn bathed Willow Place in a soft pink light, Fachai started for Kwangchow.

In front of the small hut stood the Li family. They watched quietly as Fachai slowly advanced down the narrow road. When he reached the lone willow at the end of town, he turned, set his bag down, and waved.

Leahi raised her arms, waving frantically, hardly able to make him out through her tears. He looked so small next to the tree. "Come back! Please come back to me!" Losing all the control she was expected to have, she screamed, "Don't go! Please don't go!"

The sun was rising quickly. She squinted in the blazing light to see him, but he had already faded into the distance. All that remained was the lone willow.

# 7

Flowers of the valley bloom,
Then they must fade and die.
While wild geese fly on the wind,
And the moon plays idly in the sky.
How far is the moon?
And how clear is the night!
I'll fly on the wings of birds,
In search of my heart's delight.
　　　—Chinese Nursery Song

THE BLAZING SUN had disappeared behind the high mountains, but Jasmine Valley still remained wrapped in a blanket of the steaming summer heat. For the people living alongside the Pearl River, day began at the paling of the stars and ended at the appearance of the moon. Most of the villagers had already eaten their last meal of the day, and in front of their grass-roofed houses they gathered under the graying sky, relaxing before going to sleep. Some of them were leaning against tall trees, while the others sat on the tree roots, waving their straw fans, chatting and breathing in the perfume of the night-blooming jasmine that grew throughout the valley.

Suddenly a man's angry voice boomed out of the back window of Yung's Teahouse. From the living quarter of its owner, the sound pierced the tranquillity like the crash of a cymbal.

"Sixteen years old, and no matchmaker dares to come to our house! You're going to be an old maid, and I'm stuck with you until I die! What did I do in my last life to deserve such punishment? Look at you! Those thick eyebrows, and that loud mouth of yours! Dear Buddha, why did you make my daughter so damn ugly and with a temper to match? Why have you inflicted such a curse upon my head?''

The villagers looked at one another, shaking their heads. Arguments between Yung Ko and his daughter, Meiping, occurred often. But no matter how many times they had already heard the same angry words, they still stretched their necks and listened carefully, not wanting to miss a single word—fights under another's roof had always been the best kind of entertainment.

Following the man's outburst came a girl's outraged scream: ''If Mama were still alive, she would have killed you for treating me like a slave! I cook, I wash, I mend your clothes . . . I never have any time for myself!''

''Time for yourself to do what? To go running all over the valley singing like a wild bird? That's all you do all day long! Your cooking is no better than ox dung! My clothes are dirtier after you wash them! Your needlework is the worst of all. If your mama were alive—oh, my great Buddha! Your mama would have never believed you were her child. She was the most gentle woman in the valley . . . so small, so pale, and so beautiful. Heaven knows what made you such a giant! Look at your long legs! They're like two trees reaching for the sky!''

''It's not my damn fault! You must have a northern barbarian hidden somewhere among your ancestors.''

''Deu-na-ma! Listen to yourself. Do you sound even remotely like a gentle daughter? If you were merely tall and dark and ugly . . . if you were not also known for your bad temper . . . some ignorant bastard with bad eyes might come along and I just might be lucky enough to dump you on him!''

''I know why you can't wait to be free of me! It's all because of that flirting widow of yours. She won't marry you with me in the house. How shameless! An old man like you wanting to get married! My mama will cry in her grave.''

The villagers heard a sound that rang out like the snapping of a branch. Their eyes lit up; things were getting more exciting. Like an audience waiting to see the next act of a play, they stared at the closed teahouse door.

Behind the door, the angered father, a short, heavyset man in his forties, had reached the end of his patience and slapped his daughter so hard he almost knocked her down.

The girl was about five-foot-six, more than a foot taller than the average village women. Her light brown skin was smooth, her long hair thick and black like a moonless night. Her eyes were large and forceful, her eyebrows two dark straight swords slanting upward. Her nose was high-ridged, her mouth wide, and her lips full. Her breasts were embarrassingly large when compared with the flat-chested village girls, and like her father had said, she did have very long, well-shaped legs.

She fell against the table, glaring at her father while rubbing her slapped cheek. The pain was bearable, but not her wounded feelings. She was determined not to cry. She blinked the welling tears away and eyed the table laden with the uneaten evening meal. She moved quickly. With one sweep of her arm she sent the dishes flying across the room.

Food sprayed all over the place, showering her father with vegetables and meat and salted fish.

''You wild bitch!'' the father roared, wiping his face and reaching for the bamboo stick leaning against the wall. ''I'll beat some gentleness into you!''

The daughter didn't wait. She moved quickly on her unbound feet.

The villagers watched the teahouse door fly open. Yung Meiping appeared, running barefoot with her father right behind her wearing most of the evening meal and waving a stick.

He intended to catch his fleeing daughter and give her a good lesson, until he saw his neighbors laughing and pointing. Meiping was too big to be whipped in public. And if he couldn't catch her, he'd lose face. He stopped. "You miserable bitch!" He raised a fist in her direction and bellowed at the top of his voice: "If you dare come back, I'll kill you!" He turned and slowly walked back to the house.

As Meiping kept on running, tears streamed down her burning cheeks. She looked neither to right nor left, but with her head held high and her loose hair flying behind. She pumped her long legs with the speed of a mountain goat, wanting to escape the watchful eyes as quickly as possible. She knew that her shame had been witnessed by the neighbors, and from the corner of her eye she saw them shaking their heads in disgust.

"How disgraceful! She doesn't even have shoes on! Look at her big feet!"

"She didn't even braid her hair! Her looks alone are enough to scare all the ghosts away!"

"No man in Jasmine Valley will ever want her as a wife, that's for sure! She is big enough to beat up a husband!"

"No mother in this village will want Yung Meiping for her son! Why, maybe she should go to some barbaric land in the West. I hear that the men over there are giants!"

She heard their stupid remarks as she sped by, but she didn't stop to fight. She'd give those miserable busybodies a piece of her mind some other time.

She finally passed all the houses and reached the jasmine-filled valley. The sharp foliage ripped her already torn pants and blouse, but she kept on going, heading for the hill. As she started to climb the mountain, the trees crisscrossed her body with scratches, but she forced herself to go on. Finally, exhausted, she reach the hilltop.

She collapsed on the green slope of her sanctuary. She sat on the grass and rested against a tree with her hands propped behind her head.

Around her the misty twilight began to fall, covering everything like a mother's gentle hand covering a

sleeping child with a soft blanket. She looked out toward the far horizon. Some fishermen must be getting
famished. It had long since passed their sailing hour,
but they were still on the water, trying to bring home
one more catch or two. She could see their sails like
the wings of birds resting upon the water. She shifted
her gaze and saw the box-shaped houses in the village.
She found Yung's Teahouse easily; its banner fluttered
slowly in the evening breeze, as if waving at her with
a recognizing hand.

Her breathing returned to normal, but her anger lin-
gered on. She stood up, cupped her hands around her
mouth, and screamed as loudly as she could, "I hate
you! I hate all of you!"

As her cry echoed from the hills, Yung Meiping sat
back down and began to weep. "Why am I so damn
ugly?"

She imagined herself shrinking, her long straight
legs becoming short and bow-shaped and her full
breasts turning flat. Her healthy, strong arms reduced
to puny sticks, and her fiery spirit disappeared completely. She saw herself transformed into a typical village girl, a frightened, obedient, lifeless little thing
that everyone considered a beauty.

"But, I don't want to be like that!" she shouted.

Then, amid the sound of cicadas and night birds,
she could hear her father's voice: "No one wants you.
You're going to be an old maid!"

Meiping sat with her knees drawn up to her chest.
She buried her face against her thighs, closed her eyes,
and let her thoughts drift to bygone days:

A petite, pale, gentle woman took the hand of a
little girl, and together they climbed the mountain.
They were looking for ginseng roots, supposed to have
the magic power of making the weak strong. After
filling their baskets with roots, they rested on the
mountaintop. The woman pointed first at the fishing
boats faraway and then the valley down below. "Isn't
Jasmine Valley beautiful?" the woman said, sighing
deeply. "The Pearl River will flow forever, and the
jasmine flowers will bloom every summer, and Mama

will always be here to love and take care of her Meiping. . . ."

And then the mother had taught the daughter a song, one that had never been written down but sung through the centuries by every mother to every beloved child.

The pant legs where Meiping had buried her face were all wet. She lifted her head. Drying her tears with the back of her hand, she walked to the edge of the knoll. She sat once more, now with her legs dangling over the edge. She lay back on the grass and looked up at the night sky. There were no floating clouds, the stars were bright, the moon watery and almost full. Suddenly, across the glimmering surface of the moon, a formation of wild geese appeared, flying slowly toward the mountain.

As her eyes followed the geese, her voice gathered into a song, and her words clearly carried across the valley, floating on the fragrance of jasmine: " 'Flowers of the Valley bloom. Then they must fade and die. . . ' "

Meiping's voice broke; she could not go on. In the distance a nightingale started to sing its haunting refrain, and a breeze traveled past the mountaintop, brushing her hair like the soft touch of a mother's hand.

She felt alone and frightened. *No one likes me in Jasmine Valley. As long as I remain here, I'll always be alone and unwanted. If only I could fly on the wings of the wild geese . . .*

Above the teahouse door a banner with characters long faded from the baking sun and the beating wind read "YUNG'S."

The place was small, and most of its seats never remained empty for long. Besides hot tea, Yung Ko provided simple meals with excellent homemade wine. His tea was always free, his wine and food surprisingly cheap. The villagers came to relax, tell jokes, and talk about fishing and farming. Yung Ko never made a great deal of money from the business, but he lived well and enjoyed the comradeship of his customers.

On this summer night the teahouse was filled with those who were not willing to go to sleep. Yung Ko had just returned from his unpleasant dinner break and resumed cooking and boiling tea. As he worked, he never stopped talking; he was the happiest when he knew he had everyone's attention. "Sometimes I think the Great Buddha has turned his back on me. I'm a peaceful man, and I work hard—well, hard enough. All I want out of life is to have a roof over my head, enough to eat, and a good woman by my side. The sweet wife I had, Buddha saw fit to take away. What Buddha left me with is a she-cat. You know what she did tonight? I'm sure you all heard her . . . ."

As he continued with his speech, a stranger walked in and took a table by the door. He was wearing a soiled light-colored Western suit, which made him immediately noticeable. The villagers turned to stare at him, and Yung Ko's monologue was forgotten.

Yung Ko shuffled over to the stranger. "Do you want tea or wine? Do you want noodles or rice? We don't have much to offer, I'm afraid, because I'm running this place all by myself tonight . . . my daughter and I just had a fight."

The man smiled, showing two gold teeth. He ordered wine and noodles, and then introduced himself to the teahouse owner. "My name is Woo Ming, and I've come from Kwangchow. The daughter of yours who dared to fight with her honorable father . . . I couldn't help overhearing about her a while ago," he said, shaking his head in sympathy. "A father's sorrow is a hard burden to bear. But I just might be able to offer a solution to your problem."

"You? Help me to solve my problem?" Yung Ko looked at the man distrustfully.

Woo Ming took out a pack of cigarettes, offered one to Yung Ko, then lit both of them. He blew a cloud of smoke into the air before speaking again. "First of all, let me ask a few questions about the girl. What's her name?"

"Meiping," Yung Ko answered hesitantly. "Her

mother named her. 'Mei' means 'beautiful,' and 'Ping' means 'peaceful' . . . what a joke!''

Woo Ming let out a low laugh. ''Well, is she really ugly?'' He eyed the father carefully. ''Is her face marked with pox? Is she crippled? Does she have all her teeth?''

Suddenly Yung Ko lifted his head high, and his tone of voice changed. ''My Meiping is only sixteen. Have you ever seen an ugly sixteen-year-old girl? That's like saying a blooming flower doesn't look pretty. Why, of course she has all her teeth. And her face is as smooth as a carefully peeled hard-boiled egg. Did you ask if she was crippled?'' Yung Ko threw his head back and laughed heartily. ''Not one man in Jasmine Valley can outrun my daughter! She has the strongest, longest legs you've ever seen!'' Looking around, the father met the eyes of the listening crowd and added, ''Besides all that, Meiping has such a beautiful voice that when she sings, she can make all the Buddhas smile in heaven.''

Woo Ming, also aware of the existence of the audience, took a long drag on his cigarette, then lowered his voice. ''I would like to have something to eat now. But later, after everyone is gone, I would like to talk with you some more.''

For the rest of the night Yung Ko was on pins and needles. His customers weren't easily sent away, for they all wanted to stay and hear what was going on. When they finally left, yawning, Yung Ko sat across the table from Woo Ming. In moments his attention was completely captured by the stranger's well-rehearsed sales pitch:

''I've been visiting several villages along the Pearl River, looking for young people who are interested in going to the Land of the Gold Mountains to become rich. I've found many young men, but nice young girls are as rare as precious gems. My employer will pay extremely high for such girls—provided, of course, they are healthy, not married, and willing to travel across the sea.'' He glanced at the father's suspicious face and added, ''They are needed as domestic helpers in decent homes. They'll be treated with respect.

They'll lead a life of decency. When they reach the marriageable age, they'll be married off by their employers properly, to the husbands good enough for them, with weddings fit for rich girls."

Taking a silver coin out of the pocket of his Western jacket, Woo Ming smiled broadly. "There are many more where this comes from, and they can all be yours." He threw the coin on the table, leaned back in his chair, and smiled.

On the yellow gleam of Woo Ming's gold teeth reflecting in the light of the oil lamp, Yung Ko saw a good future for his daughter, and an easier life for himself.

# 8

When the autumn moon is large and glowing,
Once again my lonely heart aches for home.
I can see the waters of the river flowing,
And a small room I call my own.
It has been written that few men go wandering,
Without the hand of fate and that alone.

                        —Unknown

KWANGCHOW WAS THE capital of Kwangdung province, and the largest city along the Pearl River. In the heart of this bustling metropolis, located at the most prominent spot on Main Street, was a two-story building with a sign that said "Fong's Pawnshop," seen from blocks away. The shop had been there for a long time. People of Kwangchow knew the Fongs well. Those interested in family histories could recall the Fongs' family records as accurately as they could their own.

On an early-autumn day in 1912, shoppers gathered in front of the store window. Looking into the display cases, they started to talk:

"This is more like it," said one man. "A pawnshop is supposed to get things cheaply from those in need of money, gain possession of the valuables, then sell them at high prices. But until its last owner died six months ago, this place never had anything for sale . . . they just bought and bought."

"That's because the last owner loved beautiful things," said a woman. "The Fongs loved them too much to part from them. Well, they were not very practical people . . . but it's all changed now.''

"Buddha is unfair," said another man. "The Fongs were still young . . . he was such a kind man, and she so beautiful. What a terrible death it was to be killed in a typhoon!''

"Their poor boy!'' exclaimed another woman. "How old is he? Fourteen? He's not as good-looking as his parents. Nor is he very sociable . . . I heard that he has never recovered from the shock of his parents' death. They said that in the past six months he has gone from bad to worse: at first he cried and wanted to die with his Baba and Mama . . . well, that's normal. But then he started to act kind of strange.''

The first man shook his head. "I heard that he's spoiled. His parents didn't bring him up as the son of a pawnshop owner but of a scholar. I was told that they had hired the best teachers to teach him all sorts of useless things, but never prepared him for facing real problems in life.''

The second man sighed. "Someone told me that Fong Loone is a smart boy . . . extraordinarily smart. He was able to read at four, and at six had already memorized many poems of the Tang Dynasty. He showed great talent both in writing and in drawing, and when he was eight, he had written and illustrated many works of his own . . . his parents used to show them to everybody.''

The first woman tried to peer through the window. "I wonder if the uncle and aunt are good to the boy. They moved in with their five sons, you know, six months ago.''

The second woman nodded. "Fong Mao and his wife are decent people. They are shrewd in business, but not cruel. It's rather nice of them to leave their own shoe store in the hands of the hired help and come here to help the brother's orphan.''

The first man said, "But I heard that Fong Loone doesn't want to be helped. He resents his uncle and aunt. I heard that the other day, when someone was ready to buy a Ming vase from the uncle, just when the deal was about to be made, Loone came from behind the counter and grabbed the vase from the buyer's hands. He was crying and shouting that he didn't want his father's favorite vase to be sold.''

The second man added, ''And I heard that it had happened many times: when the uncle was unwilling to buy something that had obviously no resale value, the boy suddenly appeared with a handful of bills he had taken from the drawer and threw them to the customers . . . he was weeping and saying that his father had never refused anybody, and he must keep up the tradition.''

The first woman said with concern, ''They said that the worst part about Loone is that he has not been eating or sleeping since the tragedy . . . he was a thin boy to start with, now even thinner.''

The second woman said with sympathy, ''I feel sorry for Fong Mao and his wife . . . stuck with a fourteen-year-old brat who makes it impossible for them to save the brother's business, and who's committing a slow suicide. No matter how decent and kind they are, I'm sure they wish to get rid of the boy somehow, if there's a way . . .''

The conversation went on. The people of the Pearl didn't believe in lowering their voices, and their words could be heard from afar.

A few feet away, leaning against a lamppost, stood a man in a light-colored Western suit, puffing on a cigarette. He had been listening intently. The tragic death of the couple didn't interest him, but when he heard about a fourteen-year-old boy being in his uncle's and aunt's way, he grinned, threw his cigarette down, then walked away with a firm nod of his head.

The voices of the people also reached the upstairs windows of the pawnshop, where the owners lived.

Behind the drawn curtains of one of these windows stood a young boy. He was bone thin, his skin parchment white. His narrow shoulders curved forward, while his concave chest appeared to sink into his backbone. The Western-styled shirt and pants hung loosely on him, for his legs and arms were crooked sticks. His long, thin neck looked far from strong enough to support his oversize head. In contrast to his thick black hair and eyebrows, his face looked frighteningly bloodless. What was by far his most striking feature, though, was his eyes: large, deep, and filled with wisdom. Since the sudden death of his parents two seasons ago, these eyes had changed a great deal. The innocence and happiness of a young boy had been wiped out, leaving only intense sorrow, fear, and anger toward the world.

His hands clenched the curtains tightly as he peeked at the street people. "You liars," he hissed at them, his voice thin and quavering. "My parents are not dead . . . they are merely away. They'll come back to me. My Baba and Mama love me too much to leave me all alone in this world!"

At that moment he turned from the window and looked at the securely locked door.

"Loone," a woman was calling, accompanied by a soft knock on the door, "your dinner tray is left untouched on the floor. The food is all cold now. Please open the door." She knocked again. "Come downstairs and I'll cook you something hot . . . anything you like."

Loone's body turned stiff. He glared at the door without answering.

"Loone, please, you must eat something," the woman continued. "I'm so worried about you, Loone, please . . ."

Loone remained silent. He had no intention of letting his aunt in.

After a long while the woman was forced to give up. "Loone"—her voice was soft and sad—"I'll leave you in peace, but if you want anything, please let me know."

Loone waited for her footsteps to disappear, then went to the door and cracked it open a little. With his body hidden in the shadows, he listened intently to the voices coming from downstairs.

"Poor Loone, he still won't eat anything," he heard his aunt saying, followed by a sigh.

"Will you forget that damn kid?" his uncle said, impatient and angry. "I've spent all morning going through this ledger; I have enough on my mind. Look at this! Can you tell me why my brother spent a fortune buying a string of pink pearls and then never tried to sell them?"

Loone's heart skipped a beat. *Oh, no! Not my mother's pearls! Not those too!*

An opium smoker who had lost his entire family fortune had come to the shop to pawn a string of perfectly matched pink pearls. Loone's mother's eyes had glowed at the sight of the clusters, and his father, after paying the man generously for the necklace, had said to her, "You should keep the pearls forever, because they are as perfectly beautiful as you.'

Loone blocked out everything else being said by his uncle and aunt. They must be busy searching for more valuables to sell!

He closed the door, locked it, then went over to one of the large antique trunks in the corner of his room. He opened the heavy lid, looked at all the art books and supplies, then took from it several jars of pastel watercolors and a roll of the finest rice paper. Bringing them to his desk, he carefully poured the paints into small porcelain saucers and mixed each color with white to make it even softer in hue. He glanced at the brush holder, carved out of a large piece of ivory, and selected among the many camel-hair brushes the finest one. He unrolled the paper with delicate fingers, and used two copper paperweights to hold it down flat on the desktop. He took a deep breath, dipped the tip of the brush into one of the saucers, and started to paint.

Stroke by stroke, a woman's head appeared on the paper. She had a beautiful oval face with a small mouth and thin lips. She was wearing a dark green dress with a high mandarin collar; around her neck a string of pearls glowed in a faint pink.

Loone stepped back, still holding the brush in his right hand, ready to add a touch here and there. He

looked down lovingly at the paper and smiled. Like
the light from a falling star that brightened a moonless
night, his face was brightened for a fleeting moment.
Then the smile died, his face darkened, and his lips
began to quiver.

"Mama," he whispered to the portrait, "you shall
always wear your pearls, for I won't let anybody take
them away . . ."

His voice trailed off. Abruptly he raised his arm and
forcefully threw the brush across the room. He turned
away from the painting, ran to his bed, and threw himself across it. As his feet touched the paneled wall, he
began to kick it.

"Mama! Baba! Why did you die? Why did you leave
me? What did I do? Did I drive you away? Why didn't
you take me with you?"

As he continued kicking, the wall shook and the
vibration reached downstairs. Within a minute his
aunt's voice could be heard again at the door. "Loone!
What happened? Are you all right?" she yelled.
"What's all the noise? Did you hurt yourself?"

Loone stopped kicking, lay with his eyes closed, his
entire body shaking. *This is still my house! I can kick
the wall if I want to. It's none of your business! Why
won't you leave me alone?*

Once more he waited until the woman was gone,
then got out of bed, cracked the door open, and listened to what was going on.

Fong Mao looked at his wife. "What's with that
idiot boy? Is he trying to tear the place down?"

His wife answered with a sigh, "I really don't know,
there seems to be no way to reach him." She shook
her head in frustration. "I just don't understand him.
He's nothing like our boys."

Fong Mao looked up from the vase he was trying to
price. "To tell you the truth, I'm running out of patience. If that kid is around when I find a buyer for
this vase and grabs it back from the customer, I just
don't know what I'll do." He sighed. "I'm tired of
fighting a losing battle. Maybe I should just sell this

place and let the family business change ownership, although my father and grandfather worked damn hard for this pawnshop and the shoe store.'' He shook his head. ''When my brother inherited the shop and I the store, the two places were of equal value. But in the past twenty years, our shoe store has been bringing in a large profit every year, while this shop is at the verge of bankruptcy. I'm trying so hard to save it, but the boy is fighting me all the way.''

His wife said wearily, ''I'm much more concerned with Loone's health than the Fong family business. Your brother and his wife have been dead for over six months now, but the boy is not showing any sign of recovery. I've never seen a son so devoted to the memory of his parents. Without them, he doesn't seem to have the will to live anymore.'' Tears welled in her eyes. ''Mao, what am I to do with him? I've tried everything. He doesn't eat enough to keep a bird alive, and he paces the floor night after night. He paints one portrait after another of his Mama and Baba, and then tears them all up. . . . If he doesn't snap out of it soon, he'll either die or become insane!''

At that moment someone coughed from the doorway. Startled, the Fongs turned and saw a man wearing a light-colored Western suit, smiling at them with two gold teeth showing.

''Who let you in?'' Fong Mao frowned at the familiar figure; everyone in Kwangchow knew Woo Ming, the labor trader. ''The shop is not open yet.''

Woo Ming invited himself in and took a chair. ''I'm not here to pawn things. I'm here to help you solve a problem.''

As the Fongs looked at each other, Woo Ming lit a cigarette, threw the match on the floor, and smiled. ''Don't you know that traveling is the best way for a boy to become a man?''

The Fongs looked at him in silence, and Woo Ming continued, ''Your nephew will never recover from the loss of his parents in Kwangchow. Every street and every person here will remind him of his Baba and Mama. He will ruin more than the family business if he doesn't leave this area; he will either become crazy or die young." He puffed deeply and looked at the couple. "You don't want that to happen, do you?"

"Of course not," Fong Mao answered quickly. Then he turned to his wife. "You know, traveling would do Loone some good. But where can he go? We don't have any relatives anywhere outside Kwangchow. The Fongs have always lived in this city."

Before Mrs. Fong could answer, Woo Ming raised a hand. "Wait," he said. "When I mentioned traveling, I didn't mean going from one town of China to another. All places are similar within the same country. Your nephew must travel far, very far . . . as far as the Land of the Gold Mountains."

Mrs. Fong gasped. "But that's the land of the white devils. No descendant of Huang-ti will go there, unless he is a starving peasant or wanted by the law."

Woo Ming smiled at her broadly. "No offense, Mrs. Fong, but you're wrong. America is the land of opportunity, as well as the land of excitement. It is a land for the young." He lowered his voice to a whisper, made his words as tempting as possible. "Americans are not bound by traditions; the young can do whatever they want. I understand that your nephew likes to paint . . . he'll find America a paradise for painters. Do you know that over there, no artist must follow the styles of the old masters? Creation—that's what they call it. The painters are allowed to create . . ." Woo Ming stopped. By now he had used up all the knowledge he had of Loone. "Trust me, this is the only way to save the pawnshop and your nephew's life."

Rising to his feet, Woo Ming reached into his pocket and came out with some silver coins. "It's customary for me to offer you something for the boy's traveling clothes and things. It'll also help to pay the pawnshop's debts."

"We can't take your money," Fong Mao grumbled. "That'll make it look like we're selling our nephew."

Woo Ming laid the silver on the table and started for

the door. "No one needs to know about it." Stopping at the doorstep, he turned to look at the Fongs. "You know, if you should decide to send your nephew to the golden land, when he grows up he'll be thankful to you for your wisdom."

Loone had been listening the whole time, sitting at the top of the landing.

*Mama and Baba, please don't let them listen to that slave trader. I don't want to leave Kwangchow. I'm scared of the white devils—they are mean and cruel. I won't interfere with the business anymore if they don't send me away. And I'll eat . . .*

His uncle and aunt left the pawnshop a while later to go to a teahouse. Loone waited nervously, wringing his hands, gritting his teeth, walking from one end of the room to another with his heart beating in his throat. He finally heard them coming in, and when they both climbed the stairs to knock on his door, his heart sank.

*I'm not going to beg them for mercy. I won't give them the satisfaction. I'll pretend to be brave . . . they must never know my true feelings.* He unlocked the door.

"Loone." Standing in the doorway, looking hesitantly at his nephew, Mr. Fong began, "You may not be aware of the debts that your parents have left behind and how difficult it is for me to save the shop. You may not know, either, just how your aunt and I have worried about you—"

Loone showed no expression as he interrupted his uncle with a voice sharp like a knife, "Save yourself the trouble, dear uncle," he said quickly, his words running together. "You're selling me to the barbaric land as a slave so you can take over my father's business, and I already know it.

The uncle was stunned; the aunt let out a low scream.

"You . . . you've been listening!" the uncle exclaimed in disbelief.

Hatred gleamed in Loone's eyes. "Of course I've been listening. My parents are dead, and the whole world is my enemy. I need to protect myself," he said, glaring at the two adults.

"If you really listened," Fong Mao muttered, shocked by the amount of fury on the young boy's face, "then you should know how much we care about you. We don't want to watch you deteriorating day by day."

"No, of course not!" Throwing back his head, Loone gave out a series of mock laughs, a sound that sent a chill through both of the grown-ups. "You only want to take over everything my parents left me, and send me to the land of the white devils as a yellow slave! No, you don't want to harm me!" He suddenly stopped laughing, and his face took on the look of a trapped animal's.

Fong Mao and his wife looked at each other, and after what seemed an eternity the uncle managed to speak. "Loone, let me explain . . ." He faltered, no longer sure of himself. "You need to grow up, to become mature and strong—"

Loone didn't let him finish. "Sure, you're selling me for my own good! Soon it'll be Moon Festival and the time to burn incense in front of the dead. Tell that to my parents and see if they'll believe you!"

"Loone . . ." Mrs. Fong took a step forward, wanting to take the boy's thin, trembling body in her arms to comfort him.

"Don't touch me!" Loone yelled in a broken voice, "I will go. I will leave Kwangchow and never come back again. I'm leaving because there is nothing and nobody left for me, and I'm leaving because I don't wish ever to see the two of you again!"

He raised a shaking hand and pointed at the door. "Get out of my room! You win, my dear uncle. You too, my dear aunt. What else do you want? Can't you leave me alone for the next few days? Or do you want to keep an eye on me, to make sure that I don't pack anything worth selling?"

His uncle and aunt exchanged a helpless look. Then both shook their heads and walked out the door.

For the next few days Loone never left the upstairs. His aunt brought all his meals to him; most of the time the food remained untouched. The uncle and aunt discussed many times whether they should forget about sending him away, but the final decision was always the same: it seemed to be the only way to save Loone.

Once in a while Loone opened his door cautiously, quickly pulled in the tray, then left the door ajar to listen to the voices coming from downstairs. When Mid-Autumn Festival arrived, he refused to go downstairs for dinner, but listened to the sound of his aunt and uncle having the festival meal with their five sons, talking and laughing. In this same dining room had he and his parents shared their daily meals and many holiday feasts, where they had once laughed and talked. He stood by the ajar door until his legs turned weak and his body numb; then he went to lie down on the bed, covered his face with a pillow, and started to cry.

*Mama and Baba! Please come to get me! I don't have the courage to kill myself, but I certainly no longer wish to live!*

The day before the sailing, the aunt brought Loone a tray laden with food and a small sandalwood box. Recognizing it immediately, Loone opened the lid with trembling fingers. His eyes filled with tears at the sight of his mother's pearls.

It was his last night to sleep in the only bed he had known all his life. With the door securely locked, he lay with the pearls tightly clenched in his hands. "Mama, Baba, I'm so scared," he whispered to each pearl, his thin body curled into a ball. "Help me, Mama. Hold me, Baba. Where are the two of you? Come to me, please . . . please don't let them send me away. I won't interfere anymore. I'll eat. Beg them for me, Baba and Mama, because I won't . . ."

From somewhere down the street, someone was singing a well-known old song:

When the autumn moon is large and glowing,
Once again my lonely heart aches for home.
I can see the waters of the river flowing,
And a small room I call my own.
It has been written that no man goes wandering,
Without the hand of fate and that alone.

# PART II

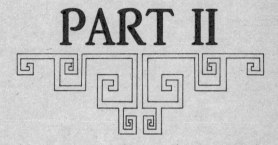

## 9

THE *LADY ANN*, coated with layers of paint like an old whore hiding her age, hugged a dock in Hong Kong harbor. Within her bowels, men drenched in sweat and coal dust cursed the heat as they stoked the hungry boilers. Their bloodshot eyes glared out from blackened faces, reflecting the fires of hell after a weekend's liberty. Most of them had a history of trouble: no other skipper but the captain of the *Lady Ann* would have them.

The captain was a Scottish Presbyterian and meaner than a shark during a feeding frenzy. He had no use for those who did not believe in God Almighty and Jesus Christ, and he had broken many a head spreading the Christian word. Every man was expected to attend his Sunday service, unless on duty. Before sailing for San Francisco he had given the crew specific orders: "As soon as we cast off, you scurvy bastards keep them yellow heathens alive but out of my sight!"

The first mate had been with the ship when she was in her prime, sailing between England and the new continent; it now pained him to see the *Lady Ann* reduced to a slave ship. Carrying out the captain's orders, he bellowed, "Watch that goddamn line, you dumb bastard! You! Yeah, you, you bloody imbecile! Get those yellow buggers aboard! I'm sick as hell at the bloody sight of them heathens!"

In an autumn wind the Chinese slowly made their way up the gangplank. Most of them wore patched loose pants, high-collared shirts, and cotton shoes. Some wore poorly fitted Western clothes, with foreign shoes that cramped their feet. Their belongings were wrapped in bundles tied with ropes, carried on their backs.

A Chinese interpreter in a felt hat, a sailor shirt

several sizes too large, and a pair of navy trousers which he kept pulling up was trying to relay the deck-hands' demands. No one was listening; the passengers were looking at the white devils in terror.

The ragged passengers were quickly herded below-decks, where each was assigned one of the bunks stacked five tiers high. There was no fresh air, and the heat of south China, even in the autumn, could be unbearable without the breeze. They would have to wait until the ship was under way for the large funnels on deck to suck in the cool sea air and send it below. Among the Chinese were farmers and fishermen accustomed to open air, and the confinement frightened them.

As the line snaked down the various passages, prayers to Buddha could be heard rumbling along the bulkheads, and the volume increased as they moved deeper into the belly of the ship.

Sung Quanming walked slowly up the gangplank. He had on a black cotton jacket secured down the front by a row of woven frog fasteners. His white pants were tied at the ankles, on his feet he wore comfortable black soft shoes, and slung over his shoulder was a canvas bag his mother had carefully packed for him. The only thing Western about him was his haircut; he had cut off his queue while waiting in Kwangchow. As he came aboard, one of the sailors reached out to give him a push. Quanming, unlike the frightened sheep before him, looked into the eyes of the foul-smelling deckhand and waved his finger. His expression conveyed a message: don't touch me. The sailor stared at him for a few seconds, then backed off.

In front of Quanming a tall girl suddenly dropped her bag. Quanming scooped it up and handed it back to her. She was very dark, wearing a bright red blouse and a pair of black pants. Her hair was combed into a thick long braid. Her big round eyes shone under two swordlike eyebrows. She had a full-lipped mouth and a high-ridged nose. She gave him an angry look, snapped the bag from his hand, and moved on without a word.

When everyone was on board and accounted for, the hatches were closed. The second mate worked his way down to the lower deck, followed by the interpreter. At each stop the mate spat, wiped his sleeve across his mouth, and called for attention; the interpreter repeated after him in Cantonese: "You'll get two squares a day and share the responsibility of carrying out the slop buckets. Once a day you'll be allowed to go on deck for fresh air, but your privilege will be taken away if you don't behave."

When the mate and the interpreter were gone, everyone started to talk at once. Each dialect attempted to overpower the others; the vocal racket gave the illusion of different kinds of animals being locked in the same cage—a human zoo. The few female passengers gathered in the far corner, trying to create a modicum of privacy by stretching sheets from bunk to bunk. The men were already settled and had started to get acquainted with one another.

"My name is Li Fachai. I'm a fisherman from Willow Place."

Quanming turned and saw a young peasant with broad shoulders. His forehead was shaved high and his remaining hair tied into a queue.

"Sung Quanming, from White Stone," Quanming answered with a slight bow.

Quanming had taken the bottom bunk; Fachai took the one above. As they looked up they saw a skinny boy trembling on the third bunk, huddled against the bulkhead. They noticed he was avoiding eye contact with them, and then saw that his bony fingers clenched a sandalwood box. A colorless face emerged from the rim of a funny-looking little cap, but as soon as he saw the two looking at him, he turned his back.

The noise was deafening. Anxious to get their minds off their fears, the passengers were saying things to strangers they would have never dreamed of repeating under normal conditions—most of them were talking about their lives along the Pearl. All the stories had a basic theme of sorrow, and every storyteller had a good reason for leaving home for the Land of the Gold Mountains.

Evening came, and the second mate asked for volunteers to bring down buckets of food. When it arrived, lines quickly formed; each person received a ladle of watered-down soup. Fachai was one of the men serving, and at the end of his line, the thin boy with the cap slowly approached. Fachai smiled at him as he filled the boy's bowl. Peeking at Fachai from the rim of his hat, the boy's sad face suddenly lit up. "I know you!" he shouted. "You were once in Fong's Pawnshop in Kwangchow!"

Fachai's face broke into a broad grin. "Now I remember. You were the boy behind the counter in the cage!"

The boy nodded, the smile gone. "My name is Fong Loone, and I was sold by my aunt and uncle." He took the soup and waited for Fachai to take a bowl for himself; together they walked back to their bunks.

Quanming offered his bunk as a table. As they ate, Quanming and Loone exchanged names, then gobbled down the strange food, not daring to question what was in it. When they had finished and washed out their bowls in the water bucket, they were allowed to go on deck for thirty minutes in assigned groups.

Once on deck they discovered they were confined to a roped-off area. While Fachai and Loone talked about Willow Place and Kwangchow, Quanming started to exercise. He flexed and relaxed his muscles, breathing in the sea air, using his chi to clean his inner self. When he was through exercising, he and his bunk-mates leaned against the railing and watched the rolling sea. Their eyes followed the flying fish breaking free of a wave and defying gravity, then gliding across the valley of water and disappearing into the next swell.

A piercing whistle was the signal for them to return below. Their momentary contact with open space and fresh air abruptly ended, they reluctantly started back down the passageway.

Through the first night of their voyage, most of them stayed awake. A few talked, while the others just lay in quiet contemplation. The light coming from the few portholes along the bulkheads was enough to reveal the glistening eyes on the passengers' faces, and muffled sobbing was heard throughout the hold. Fear and despair, like the leeches in a rice paddy, sucked away any prospect of joy in the future.

Fachai, accustomed to sailing with the wind blowing in his face, found it hard to breathe down in the belly of an iron ship driven by throbbing engines. "Loone," he whispered, "I don't understand how this metal ship can carry so many people and not sink. I know that iron is too heavy to float." He looked around, then in a low voice confided to his friend, "To be honest with you, I don't like being down here. I'm scared!"

"You have nothing to worry about," Loone whispered back. "I've read about these ships and—"

"You can read?" Fachai interrupted. "You must be awfully smart."

With a smile Fachai didn't see in the dark, Loone proceeded to relate what he had learned about a metal ship. His voice took on the pattern of a tutor instructing a small boy. Every so often Fachai would ask a question; he was amazed at the young boy's knowledge.

After Loone had finished, Fachai felt better. He sighed. "I miss the Pearl River, and I wish I were there: fishing in the morning sunlight, feeling the roll of the boat under my feet. I know I did the right thing by going on this journey, but I already miss my wife and family." He wrapped himself tighter in the quilt and rubbed his face against the soft fabric. "This quilt was my wife's dowry, and she made me bring it, Her name is Leahi, and before long I shall be a father."

Loone said with envy, "Someday you will go home and be with your family. But I'll never see my parents again—" His voice broke. Quickly he said good night, turning to face the wall.

Fachai soon fell asleep. Loone stayed awake holding the box that contained his mother's pearls. *Mama, I'm frightened. You know, until the last moment I still hoped my uncle and aunt would change their minds. What will happen to me? Will I die before this long journey is over? Will I really reach the Land of the Gold Mountains?* He pulled up his sheets and covered his face in an effort to hide his sobbing.

On the bottom bunk, Quanming lay with his head propped on his palms, his eyes wide open. Different images flashed through his mind: Quanli's head rolling across the wild field where the forsythias bloomed . . . the Bao girl lying on the ground with bloodstained legs . . . Chow's dying body falling forward . . . his mother standing and waving in front of the house . . . and then the image of Yoto appeared. She seemed to be floating above ten thousand lanterns and a million flickering candles.

*Quanming, I love you; why wouldn't you go and beg my father?* he heard her say, and his heart ached. Angrily he shook his head, trying to drive the thought away.

A rumor, one of many fanned by tongues with nothing better to do, was started on the third day out. Apparently there was not enough food to go around, and only the first ones in line would be fed.

Loone was waiting anxiously in line that day when all of a sudden a big man cut in front of him.

Outraged, Loone didn't notice the man's size but reached up and tapped him on the back; it felt as hard as the ship's deck.

The oaf turned and looked down at Loone. His eyes glared from beneath thick brows. His shaved head, resting on a bull neck, was a mosaic of scars. His bare arms looked like two large hams, and his ample stomach stuck out like that of a laughing Buddha. Yet not a trace of humor could be found on the face of this ape as he growled at Loone between clenched jaws, "What do you want?"

Loone stuttered, "I . . . I was here first."

"Deu-na-ma! Go suck your mother's milk!" the man roared.

After a brief pause Loone once again raised his pale

hand and tapped the giant on the back. "I said I was here first!" His voice was shaking but he stood his ground.

The man slowly turned, and with the back of his hand he sent Loone sprawling across the deck. "Anyone else object to Kim Shinma eating first?" He looked around, challenging anyone to open his mouth.

All eyes were lowered to examine the deck, except for Fachai, whose anger had overcome his better judgment. "Deu-na-ma! You son of a whore!" he yelled over his shoulder as he helped Loone to stand up. "Who the hell do you think you are?"

Without answering, Kim reached down with one hand. Pulling Fachai to his feet, he cocked back the other hand.

Just before Kim delivered the blow, two powerful hands gripped his wrist, twisting it with such force that Kim gave out a cry of pain. In another moment he found himself flat on his back.

Quanming stood over him, maintaining his hold. He began to turn Kim's wrist even more, exposing the man's right side. Kim Shinma looked up into Quanming's eyes and sensed the inner strength of this young man. For now, he knew he was in too vulnerable a position to fight back.

Quanming placed his right foot on Kim's side. "Make your choice, big man! Either get up and behave, or I'll kick in your ribs." Quanming never raised his voice, but in the stillness of the hold it rang out like thunder.

Kim Shinma had been around long enough to know this was no idle threat. Sweat popped out on his shaved skull, for the pain in his wrist was unbearable. "If you'll release me, I shall not cause any further trouble," he mumbled through his teeth. "I was only playing with the boys . . . I didn't mean them any harm." He looked at Quanming humbly, but beneath the facade his anger bubbled in a caldron of hate.

Quanming released Kim but watched him cautiously. Rubbing his wrist, Kim looked placidly at Quanming, wanting nothing better than to break his neck. "This voyage is not over, and I have a feeling that before we dock, I will find an opportunity to get to know you much better." With these words he turned and left.

As soon as Kim Shinma walked away, the boys rushed to thank Quanming. But he waved them away and went to sit on his bunk with his eyes closed and legs crossed. He remained motionless this way, until gradually the noise around him was blocked out and in its place came Master Lin's voice: "In a new environment, one should become part of the shadows. It's dangerous to be the tallest tree in a forest, for it is the one that gets chopped down before all others."

Quanming condemned himself for being a fool, wondering if he would ever learn. *Why must I act out of anger? The death of Chow should have taught me something. This must be the last time I lose control.*

The afternoon wore on, and still Quanming did not stop meditating.

Loone whispered, "He doesn't seem to be breathing. How long do you think he is going to stay like that?"

Before Fachai could answer, Quanming opened his eyes. He felt that a tremendous weight had been lifted from his shoulders. He stood up stiffly, stretched his legs, and began to massage the circulation back into them. While he rotated his upper body to work his back muscles, his eyes met those of Kim Shinma, who had been staring at him. Master Lin's voice echoed in his mind: "With one step, a person can make a mistake that cannot be corrected by the efforts of a lifetime."

Yung Meiping and three other girls had been sent for by Kim Shinma soon after they boarded the ship. When they stood before him, he announced:

"You're nothing more than merchandise to me, and each one of you is under my supervision." His eyes appraised them. "You must follow my orders during the entire trip, and never be out of my sight." He made clear that he was responsible for their well-being, including their maidenhood, until they were turned over to the proper hands in San Francisco.

It had soon become obvious that the three other girls preferred to stay together, while Meiping liked to be alone. She had watched Quanming fight Kim and enjoyed seeing him knock the smirking giant on his ass. From then on, she had started to follow Quanming with her eyes. He was the best-looking man she had ever seen—nothing like the stoop-shouldered boys back in Jasmine Valley. She also admired his prowess as a fighter: so strong, so brave, so unbeatable.

Meiping's admiration didn't go unnoticed by Kim Shinma. Born in Korea, he had been forced after several killings to escape to north China. While making his way toward the south, he committed more crimes, making it necessary for him to flee again for his life. He grabbed the first ship to San Francisco, and soon found himself employed by a powerful Lau Ban by the name of Wan Kon. One of Kim's many chores was to travel between California and Kwangdung to make sure that his boss's merchandise arrived undamaged.

Studying Meiping's long legs and the full curves of her body, Kim was certain that Wan Lau Ban, who loved petite girls, would not be too pleased by this big cow with tits to match. No customer would pay much for her first night, Kim considered. No, the Lau Ban would not mind if she was damaged a little. After tasting the bitterness of defeat from Quanming, like most bullies, Kim needed to reaffirm his manhood.

His groin ached with need as he walked toward Meiping, who had moved behind the sheet she used as a screen. He stepped around the hanging cloth and took her by surprise, wrapped his arms around her, taking her breasts in his massive hands. Meiping let out a scream and tried to wiggle free, but inflamed him even more as he felt her body moving against his swollen penis. All he could think of now was to drive himself into her.

At first her screams turned the others' heads. But when they saw what was happening, the female passengers closed their eyes and the men looked away—

nobody wanted trouble with Kim, and the fate of this tall dark girl was no concern of theirs.

With her adrenaline pumping, Meiping spun out of Kim's grip and began to claw his face; her nails raked deep furrows down his cheeks.

Kim grabbed Meiping by the wrist, and with his open palm he sent her sprawling across the metal deck. He quickly lumbered after her. He lifted her by her blouse with such force that the cotton fabric tore, exposing a white breast. The sight drove Kim into a frenzy. He ripped the blouse off and buried his head between her white mounds, gyrating his hips against her. As Meiping struggled to free herself, he bit down on her nipple, sending a searing pain through her body; her screams bounced off the walls.

Without realizing what she was doing, Meiping drove her right knee up, smashing it into Kim's groin with such power that he froze in shock.

From a distance, Quanming stood back in the shadows, determined that this time he would mind his own business. After all, he wasn't sure if the brute was the tall girl's husband and had every right to do as he pleased.

Meiping started to run as Kim, bent over, moaned in pain. Fleeing toward the darkness where she could hide, she ran directly into Quanming.

With a roar Kim came after her. From his waistband he drew a knife; its curved blade was ready to empty the blood out of the frightened girl.

Quanming caught Meiping as she stumbled into his arms, and over her shoulder he saw the Korean slowly approaching, swinging the blade from side to side. The next moment Quanming felt he had returned to the graveyard of White Stone, facing either his own death or that of the beast coming toward him.

"Deu-na-ma!" the Korean cursed in Chinese. "Let her go and give her to me, you son of a cur! If you dare interfere again, I'll kill you first and then that worthless whore."

Calmly Quanming motioned Meiping to one side, never taking his eyes off the advancing killer. "I do not wish to fight with you,'' he said in a low voice. ''But I can't let you hurt this girl.''

Fachai, also standing near Meiping, at last could no longer stand seeing her half-naked body being observed by all the men. He picked up the quilt from his bunk and threw it to the tall girl. Meiping gave him a grateful look and wrapped the quilt around herself. As she did so, Kim Shinma charged toward Quanming like an outraged water buffalo.

''I'll cut off your jewels and stuff them in your mouth!'' he thundered, the blade slicing through the air.

The crowd gasped loudly in horror at the near-miss. Had Quanming been without fast reflexes, he would have been opened up like a butchered ox.

The Korean attacked again. Quanming parried the knife with a downward movement of his left hand—the edge of his right clipped Kim's arm at the elbow. Kim grunted from the sharp pain, but still held on to his knife. With surprising agility for a man his size, the Korean spun on his left foot, brought his right foot around, and caught Quanming on the arm as he tried to block the kick. The force drove Quanming into the circle of cheering passengers that had now formed around them.

Quanming sprang to his feet again, a bit stunned. He had heard about the Korean style of kick-fighting, but this was the first time he had encountered it. How did one stop a man who used his feet? Kim slowly advanced, tossing the knife from one hand to the other. The two circled each other, while the crowd was going wild with excitement.

The commotion brought down several of the sailors, and when they saw what was going on, one of them turned to the other. ''I'm glad it's not me fighting that big bull, especially with that foot-long pigsticker. Don't seem fair to me. Let's see if I can even it up a mite.'' He took out a leather-wrapped piece of lead, then slipped the thong over his hand and started to work his way closer to his target.

Before Quanming had decided on a defense, Kim

attacked again. This time the blade pierced the sleeve of Quanming's jacket, cutting a gash in his arm. The Korean roared in triumph, strutting proudly around the circle, now certain of an easy victory.

In the meantime, the sailor had sidled next to Kim. "Aye, laddie. Just a mite closer, you hunk of lard! That's it, keep coming!" As soon as Kim was within reach, the sailor's hand whipped out, catching the knife with the lead sap. The blade flew across the deck with a clatter, stopping beyond the edge of the crowd.

Loone, standing out there alone, quickly snatched the knife, hid it inside his jacket, and squeezed his tiny body back into the crowd. He peeked from behind people, looked from one spectator to another. They were so engrossed in the fight that no one noticed him. Kim searched for the unseen assailant who had made him lose his knife. Those next to him stepped back, trembling under his glare. Loone met his searching eyes; the skinny boy looked at the big man innocently.

While Kim was screaming for the man who took his knife to show himself, Quanming came racing across the deck and leapt in the air with his feet tucked in tightly. Just before reaching Kim, his legs shot out, catching the Korean in the chest as he turned. Kim let out a cry that sounded like a spouting whale as the force of the blow drove the air from his lungs. He dropped to one knee, struggling to breathe.

Slowly Kim began to get to his feet, looking first at Meiping and then back at Quanming. Because the pain he was feeling was so acute, he knew his ribs were broken. He hissed at Quanming, "This is not over! Next time I'll see you dead!"

# 10

MEIPING WAS GRATEFUL for Quanming's defense, for Fachai's thoughtfulness in giving her the quilt, and for Loone's quick thinking in hiding Kim's knife. She felt a bond with all three young men and invited herself to join them wherever they went. At first the boys merely tolerated her presence, but as the days wore on they became great friends.

They talked freely about their homes and dreams for the future.

"I'll work hard as a maid for a while, then find myself a rich husband. When I go back to Jasmine Valley, my stupid neighbors will all die with envy!" Meiping smiled as she looked at the boys.

"I'll become a fisherman in the Land of the Gold Mountains, and save up enough money to go back to Willow Place to buy many boats," Fachai said. "Leahi will become a rich lady, and my son and I will spend the rest of our lives fishing together on the Pearl."

"I'll paint and paint and paint . . . and what else I want I just don't know!" Loone sighed.

"I'll do something useful for China, and make our beautiful land once more a good place for people to live . . ." Quanming left his statement unfinished because it sounded like too impossible a dream.

Friendship eased the pain of missing their homeland; companionship also lightened the worries about the unknown future.

The fury of the wind churned the still blue waters into an ocean of foam. Black clouds thundered in, covering the ship in darkness. All hands secured the hatches and lashed down anything that moved. The mountainous waves poured over the bow, washing away anything that was not tightly fastened. The

screws screamed in the air as the aft end came out of
the water. The ship's forward motion stopped; then the
vessel plummeted down. The screws bit into the sea,
and the ship lurched forward, toppling several deck-
hands.

Belowdecks, bedlam broke out. As the passengers
clung to their bunks, their belongings scattered about
the deck. They had been told when they came aboard
to lash everything down, but no one paid any attention. Some of the unlucky ones had already been injured by flying luggage. Many passengers were fighting
to get up the steep stairs; some, however, were too
sick to move. The area began to reek from vomit mixed
with the stink of slop buckets that had spilled.

Fachai was accustomed to storms, but not trapped
in the belly of an iron ship, and he panicked. He soon
joined the crowd climbing toward the upper deck, followed by Loone. The pitching of the ship almost
caused Fachai to lose his hold on the railing, and his
powerful arms were the only thing keeping him from
pitching downward.

"Help! Fachai! Help me!" Loone cried out, struggling to hold on. His arms were wrapped around the
metal framework, his feet dangling in midair.

Fachai turned to fight his way against the throng,
but before he went very far, Loone fell. He landed on
his feet and twisted his ankle. He didn't move.

Quanming and Meiping, who had seen what had
happened, reached Loone the same time as Fachai.
They struggled against the tossing of the ship and finally got Loone settled on Quanming's bunk. The ship
shuddered as it rammed into another wave, throwing
Quanming and Fachai on top of Loone.

"You clumsy fools! Are you trying to kill him?"
Meiping screamed in anger.

Quanming tried to remove Loone's shoe, but he
yelped in pain. Meiping shoved Quanming to one side
and took over; her gentleness surprised them all. The
hardness melted away; her features softened and for
the first time they had a glimpse of her beauty. She
smiled at Loone, and after examining his ankle she

reassured him, ''Nothing is broken, don't worry. I know, because in Jasmine Valley I learned to dress wounds and have fixed more than one broken bone.'' She went to get her ruined blouse, then quickly ripped it into strips to wrap Loone's ankle.

Loone looked up and smiled, enjoying the attention. ''Thanks for staying with me, my friends. It's nice to know that there are people who care.''

During the storm the plight of those below was forgotten by the crew, who were busy fighting to keep the ship afloat. As soon as the storm passed and the sea became calm, the hatches were opened and several sailors came down with buckets and mops, ordering people to clean up the mess.

No one paid attention, for they were all running around gathering their belongings. Their fear, like the passing squall, was forgotten, and arguments broke out as to what belonged to whom. The air was once again filled with the sound of many dialects shouting at one another. In other words, everything was back to normal.

Meiping left Loone with Fachai and Quanming and went to see if any other passengers needed her help. A woman was crying on a lower bunk, holding a small child of eight. When Meiping asked what was wrong, the woman answered helplessly, ''My son fell from the ladder and hit his head, and now he doesn't move or say anything.''

Meiping looked down at the child: his face was drained of color, and when she placed her hand on his head, it felt ice cold. Her heart went out to him. ''Don't worry,'' she whispered, ''I'll stay with you and do the best I can.''

For the next few days the boy drifted in and out of consciousness. When the interpreter came down, Meiping asked him to get the ship's doctor. He shrugged and left, not bothering to tell her that on this tub the doctor could care less for those belowdecks.

Neither Meiping nor the mother could get the child to hold down any food. The young boy's once-beautiful features became drawn, his skin almost transparent. The mother held him for hours, willing him to live. As she rocked him in her arms, she explained to Meiping that she was on her way to the Land of the Gold Mountains to meet her husband.

"He has a small business in the Tong-jen-gai section of San Francisco. In order to save enough money to send for us, he worked seven days a week, from early morning until late in the night. I have not seen him almost nine years now, and he has never seen our son."

Then the boy started getting better, and both the mother and Meiping were relieved. A few nights later, however, a piercing cry cut through the darkness, cutting into everyone's dream like a sharp blade. In the dim light they saw the mother holding the body of her lifeless son. She continued to wail, her shrieks tearing at the hearts of those around her. Meiping rushed to the mother and child, and when the woman saw her, she gave one final shriek and collapsed.

The death was reported, and a young sailor along with the first mate and the interpreter appeared. The sailor, seeing the dead boy, crossed himself, and the mate looked on dispassionately; death to him had become routine on these trips.

At the sight of the interpreter, Meiping leapt to her feet. "Deu-na-ma! You bastard! Did you ever tell the white devils that we needed a doctor?" She pounded the man with her fists until she was taken away by Quanming.

"Like all deaths that happened during the journey, your child will have to be buried at sea," the interpreter said to the mother, but the woman did not hear. She didn't turn to look at her son's body, which was now lying on the bunk, but continued to sit with her arms held as if she were still embracing her baby to her bosom. She was staring into her empty arms, smiling, rocking back and forth.

At daybreak the Chinese were herded up on deck. The boy, wrapped in white cloth, was placed on a flat board with one end resting on the railing. The first mate said a few words that no one understood, then crossed himself. He nodded, and the board was tilted and the body slid into the sea.

The mother looked on through sightless eyes, and when everyone was ordered to return belowdecks, she let Meiping guide her to her bunk where she sat motionless. She remained that way the rest of the day. Meiping tried to get her to talk, but her efforts were in vain.

Meiping stayed with her until it was time to go on deck. She left the woman sitting and joined the boys, needing to get some fresh air. When she returned, the woman was gone. Everyone searched for her, but she was never found.

During the journey, Loone never was without a drawing pad and pencil; he sketched constantly. He did sketches of the deckhands, much to their delight. They began sneaking extra rations to him, and Loone shared his bounty with his friends.

One sunny day, when the wind was strong, the four friends stood together, and Loone's pencil never stopped moving on the pad. When he was finished he showed it to his friends.

"How did you do this?" Meiping asked, her eyes wide with disbelief as she stared at a sketch of herself and the boys. "You've drawn not only how I look, but also how I feel. I know I have a loud voice and seem to be unafraid all the time. But you know me better, don't you, my little brother?"

Quanming took the sketch from Meiping and studied it for a long time. "Do I carry my feelings so openly? You made me look like the weight of the world was on my shoulders, and much more handsome than I really am." He smiled and passed the drawing to Fachai.

Fachai looked at it and was amazed by Loone's talent. "Loone, you surely are my best friend. You know exactly how I feel—are my eyes really that sad? I wish Leahi could see this drawing. Then she would know how much I miss her, and stop worrying about my looking at any other girl.''

Then they all pointed at the skinny little figure with a cap on his head, showing only half of his face. ''You're not very flattering to yourself. Do you not have enough talent to do a completed self-portrait? Why are you hiding under your cap?'' Quanming teased.

Loone quickly closed the sketchpad. ''I'm too ugly to serve as a model; I like to draw beautiful things. I can see beauty even on the faces of those deckhands, but not my own. My parents gave me everything except their good looks.''

Whenever the four friends were together, Kim Shinma was never far away. He never bothered them, but was always there like an ominous shadow, watching and listening. When Meiping started to talk about being a maid in some rich people's house, he thought how stupid the young girls from the Pearl River were— to believe that they were going to the Land of the Gold Mountains to earn a living with honest labor. He chuckled, imagining their expressions when the truth was discovered.

The sky was a clear deep blue over the Pacific, and the morning sun warmed the passengers as they huddled in groups. The gentle swells hugged the sides of the ship as she steamed her way to San Francisco.

Fachai whispered to Loone, ''I know you can read, and I need your help. But you must promise to keep this a secret.''

Loone nodded and Fachai continued. ''Before the labor trader got me on this ship, he gave me some papers to learn in order to pass an immigration test. He told me to find someone I could trust to help me read and remember these . . .'' He took from his inner garment several sheets of paper.

Loone looked at the papers and started to laugh. Then he told Fachai that he had also the same kind of documents to memorize.

In 1906 there had been an earthquake in San Francisco, and the city hall had burned to the ground, along with all its records. Every birth certificate had been destroyed, and as a consequence, many Chinese had grabbed the chance to claim that they were born in the United States, but were left with no papers as proof. Their claims could not be gainsaid, their wishes were granted, and they were called "paper citizens."

According to the immigration law at the time, there was only one way for Chinese to be admitted into America—one had to be the immediate family member of an American citizen who had a steady, well-paying job or a successful business. Suddenly all the paper citizens developed very large families. In some cases as many as ten children, twenty brothers and sisters, as many uncles and aunts, and numerous cousins, nephews, and nieces—all were called "paper sons," "paper daughters," and "paper relatives."

A new profession was born—the labor traders. Two traders worked as a team, one stationed in America, the other in China. The trader in America offered qualified Chinese-Americans money for adding another person to his family list; the trader in China searched for the poor who needed a living in the Land of the Gold Mountains. Both traders were paid well by employers in America, who needed cheap labor.

Sheets of detailed information were sent from America to China, and the newcomer had to memorize everything that a person needed to know about his adopted family. Upon landing, the Chinese would be questioned by the American immigration officers, and those who couldn't give satisfactory answers were detained or sent back at their own expense.

Li Fachai was supposed to be the son of an American-born Chinese couple who had visited their homeland eighteen years ago. The woman had become pregnant, and after her husband had gone back to America, she had stayed behind to give birth to the child. The baby had been a sickly infant, too weak to travel. The mother didn't want to take him on the long journey to the Golden Land; she had left him with a Li family in Willow Place. Now the boy had grown to

be a young man, and it was his birthright to be re-
united with his parents.

Except for a handful of people like Quanming,
whose real uncle in America had earned his right of
citizenship lawfully, most of the passengers had papers
to memorize. Fachai, Meiping, and Loone were only
three of them.

As the day of landing grew nearer, the sound of
mumbling filled every corner. Gone were the constant
screams and yellings in Cantonese; each passenger was
sitting on his own bunk reciting the lines he must use
to answer the waiting examiners.

# 11

BEFORE THE 1906 earthquake, the Pacific Street area had been the thriving business district of San Francisco, with the appearance of a neat, proud, and well-dressed gentleman. The quake turned the gentleman into a street bum with the sickening stench of a wino who was barely holding himself together.

On the body of this bum the Chinese immigrants found a gold mine of land inexpensive enough for them to own. Within a few years the whole district was given a new name: Tong-jen-gai, the Streets of the Chinese, or Chinatown.

By 1912, six years after the devastation, upper-class Americans had stopped coming to this area. Some said the gang fights had scared them away, some said it was the filth and noise that bothered them, while others claimed that the white devils were terrified of the yellow ghosts—the spirits of the Chinese that died in the fire of 1906. They were reported to wander in the dark of night, their burned and mutilated bodies floating in the air, wearing an aura of fog, searching for the soil of their homeland, where their tortured souls could once again find peace and go to rest.

There had been little reconstruction on Pacific Street. In the autumn of 1912 one could see only a funeral home, several warehouses, plus a building owned by an Italian family named Camerano. The Cameranos had a fleet of fishing boats, and every morning the catch was brought in to be cleaned and iced down. The boxes of fish were then loaded on horse-drawn wagons and delivered to markets and local restaurants.

The cleaning of fish was a miserable, backbreaking job. On one October morning, as the smelly, rough-looking workers stood knee-deep in fish heads and entrails, facing the tables piled high with the morning's catch, they bantered back and forth in a mixture of languages: Irish, Italian, German . . . and a smattering of English.

The conversation was centered on the new helper arriving today from China.

"Dino, you gonna get that Chink this morning, no?" asked a bull-necked man with a front tooth missing.

"That's if they can get that yellow heathen past those bastards at immigration!" answered Dino Camerano, the dark-haired owner.

"We've got enough of those sneaking little buggers taking jobs from us already. Christ! The slant-eyed bastards work for nothing! I don't like 'em, and I sure as hell don't want to have to work with one!" These words came from a blond man with a broken nose.

"Hey, Limey, don't you worry! He's gonna get all the fuckin' dirty work. Not bad—we'll have it easier in this shithole!" said a redhead with a scar across his face.


Not far from Pacific Street were Grant Avenue and Clay Street. On these streets were buildings that had partially survived the fire that followed the earthquake. These structures were now homes of the Chinese who had come to America a long time ago, some as early as 1850—almost all of them from the Pearl River basin.

In these rat-infested dwellings every available space was being used. At least five or six people shared one small room. Their toilets were metal buckets at the feet of their beds. For cooking they used galvanized pails resting on bricks, filled with charcoal. Because of these squalid living conditions, the Chinese tried to stay away from home as often as possible—when they had a few extra pennies, they ate in one of the many Chinatown restaurants.

All considered Yung Fa Restaurant their favorite eating place; it was just right for the poor. It served good food at a reasonable price, and the owners were very friendly. Having been poor themselves, the Chus were down-to-earth, understanding folks.

On this October day, near noon, smoke was pouring out of the grimy kitchen windows, carrying with it the smells of food being prepared in hot oil. Those sitting in the dining area could hear through the thin curtain concealing the door leading to the kitchen the sizzling sounds of frying and the banging of pots and pans.

The voices of Yung Fa's owners, Chu Ninpo and his wife, Chu Hasan, overpowered all other noises. From the Pearl River, the Chus were accustomed to shouting at each other.

"If Buddha sees fit, maybe by this time tomorrow the boy will be here and we'll be able to rest a little," said Ninpo, a man in his fifties. His clothes hung a size too large on his thin body, and wisps of white hair clung to his sweating brow. His few remaining teeth, rarely seen inside his sad mouth, were yellow and rotten with decay.

"Don't count on it, you old fool! The boy has yet to pass the interrogation of the white officers!" answered Hasan, a woman the same age as her husband. Unlike him, she was plump and neat in appearance. Her white hair was cut short like a man's, and over her blouse and pants she wore a spotless apron. On her fingers two jade rings sparkled; around her neck several solid gold chains gleamed.

Many years ago, Chu Ninpo's father had worked on the railroad, laying tracks between California and Chicago. Ninpo's mother had been a mail-order bride, and Ninpo was born in a small hut beside the railroad.

During the same year, Hasan's parents had been working in a mining camp. Her mother had cooked for the men; her father had washed their clothes. Hasan was born near the mine.

The railroad Chinese met the mining Chinese, and the four adults became friends. Both couples had saved some money, and they put their savings together, moved to San Francisco, and started the Yung Fa Restaurant as joint owners. The marriage between their daughter and son came naturally, and after the older generation died, Ninpo and Hasan became the restaurant's owners.

Affection was considered unnecessary between a Chinese couple, and often wife and husband hated each other. But the Chus loved each other. They were happy with their lives together, except for one thing—Hasan had never produced a child.

"You know," Chu Ninpo now said with a sigh, "it's been almost thirty years since we took over this place. Seven days a week, ten hours a day . . . I've been feeling the years in my old bones for quite some time now."

The old woman smiled, looking up from the food at her husband. "Well, it won't be long now. Fong Loone is fourteen. Like all children raised along the Pearl, he must know how to take care of his elders." She glanced at a statue of the Great Buddha on a high stand in the corner of the kitchen. "Let's pray that the immigration men let our boy land, and our troubles will be over."

On Grant Avenue, the open market was the source of all the noise and smells. Pigs, either half or whole, were hung from hooks with their blood dripping on the sawdust floor. Hanging alongside were plucked fat ducks, cooked chicken and pork, all dyed a bright red. On the butchers' counter pig heads stared out with cloudy eyes. Unwashed fresh vegetables and fruits were displayed in boxes along the sidewalk, partially covered with mud and fertilizer. All the Chinese frequented the market at least once a day; to them, food cleaned and refrigerated stopped being tasty.

There were also several herb shops, each displaying in its windows dried snakeskins, skeletons of small animals, and an assortment of hearts, spleens, and other body parts floating in small jars filled with liquid. The Chinese believed in the magic powers of these things; it was the knowledge of such power that separated them from the white devils.

The most prominent building on Grant was the House of Wan. This red brick structure was four sto-

ries high, and the massive black doors were trimmed
with highly polished brass knobs and hinges that reflected the activities along the street. Behind these
doors were over thirty young girls who had come from
China, some willingly, some ignorantly, to practice
the world's oldest profession under the protection of
Wan Kon, the Lau Ban.

The October sun poured brightly through a red-
curtained window into a large room on the fourth floor.
The brass frame of the large bed reflected the sunlight,
gleamed in the eyes of the two people lying there. They
were both completely naked. The man was Wan Kon,
the woman Limei.

"You lazy whore, get your fat ass out of bed! The
ship is arriving today and we need to go see what kind
of pretty things it has brought us." Wan flashed a rare
smile and gave Limei a resounding slap on her rump.

Only five feet tall, Wan Lau Ban was thin, almost
fragile in appearance. His beady eyes never stopped
darting around; his fingers, stained brown from chain
smoking, constantly toyed with his drooping mustache
whenever he spoke.

"Yes, my Lau Ban," the woman answered lazily,
annoyed and smarting from the smack. "Are you going to save one or two virgins for the customers? Those
tight young mounds might give you a sore rod. Remember, you're not so young anymore." As she
frowned, fine lines appeared between her eyebrows and
around her mouth.

Limei had been born in the House of Wan. Her
mother had been one of the working girls, and Limei
didn't know who her father was; she had never had a
last name. Limei was only twelve when Wan took her
as his woman, and when he became tired of her, he
had put her to work. She had proved to Wan that she
was more clever than the other girls in many ways.
She had earned her retirement at twenty and become
the madam. For the past fifteen years, she had been
solely Wan's woman.

"Deu-na-ma! You want me to shut your smart mouth
for you?" Wan Kon said angrily. It took very little to

change his mood, especially when his male prowess was involved.

Limei got out of bed without answering. She quickly dressed and started to prepare the Lau Ban's morning cup of tea.

Wan Kon stayed in bed, puffing on a cigarette, thanking the Great Buddha for that ridiculous law passed by the white devils in 1844. The law—that Chinese men were forbidden to bring in their wives from their homeland—had been very profitable to him. Because of that law, Chinatown had been known in the past fifty years as the Bachelors' Society. The law had brought forth an abundance of prostitution, and because of that, Wan Kon had become a rich man.

Back in China years ago, Wan Kon's grandfather had been engaged in piracy and smuggling. He had fled to America to save his neck from the chopping block, and in a short time he had established himself as the undisputed underworld power of Chinatown.

The first two generations of Wans faced competition from the Tongs, a well-organized establishment that dated back to the Ching Dynasty. Both the grandfather Wan and father Wan had been killed during one of those Tong fights, and Wan Kon had taken over the family business when he was only a man of twenty.

Wan Kon had gradually expanded his realm of power, and now the House of Wan was in control of gambling, liquor, opium, and prostitution. Chinese merchants were expected to pay a monthly protection fee to Wan, or their businesses would be visited by Wan's hired men.

Wan Kon was smiling again when Limei returned carrying a tray. "Bring me my finest silk robe," he said. "We're going to show the people on the dock who is Chinatown's most powerful Lau Ban."

Limei quickly obeyed. As Wan put on his robe, she applied heavy makeup on her face, piled her hair high on top of her head, and put on a silk gown of the brightest red.

The shining black carriage and its two handsome mares were Wan Kon's pride. The wheels were trimmed in gold, and on either side of the wagon were highly polished brass lanterns. The seats were of soft leather and the canopy overhead, edged with long red fringe, added an eye-catching touch.

As Wan Kon and Limei traveled through Chinatown on their way to the pier, people turned to look—some with envy, many with fear and hate. When they reached the dock, Wan Kon's beady eyes searched for a wagon that could match his. When he saw nothing was even remotely close, he smiled, nudged the driver with his foot. "Walk the team around the dock. Make sure that all the envious bastards can get a good look."

The driver, a huge Mongol who was also Wan's bodyguard, began to walk the horses slowly around the pier.

Near the edge of Chinatown, the skeletal remains of several burnt-out houses had been cleaned away in 1910, and after an entire year's work, a magnificent cream-colored building had been erected.

The Sung Wu Company was housed in this one-story complex that sprawled like a multiheaded dragon, taking up several lots. One of the dragon's heads faced Portsmouth Square, containing several offices that gave the residents of Chinatown free legal aid and other services. Another head of the dragon faced San Francisco Bay; it held classrooms where children were taught to read and write in Chinese and adults could get free lessons in English. On the south side was the warehouse, and to the east were offices for the import-export business, which was the backbone of the company.

The company was jointly owned by Wu Da-chung and Sung Tinwei. Wu lived outside Chinatown with his wife, three sons, and a daughter. Sung, a bachelor, had luxurious living quarters and an immaculately kept garden within the company structure.

The October sun shone on a lily pond. The pink, yellow, and white flowers floated in fragrant splendor, their large green leaves a haven for the carp that swam lazily through the clear water, their bodies sparkling like polished gold. Ornamental humpbacked bridges arched over the water, their reflection mirrored in the ripples. An array of flowering trees added a kaleidoscope of colors to this place, and large rocks were carefully placed to add just the right accent.

Sitting by the water on rattan chairs, two middle-aged men were drinking their morning tea. Sung Tinwei wore silk pants and jacket, Wu Da-chung a long robe.

"Are you nervous knowing that your nephew will be here this morning?" asked Wu Da-chung. He had a round face and a round body. His large innocent eyes belied his sharp and cunning mind; his kind smile hid the fact that he was a forceful businessman.

"I couldn't sleep at all last night," Sung Tinwei answered. "I'm worried." He was quite a bit taller than his partner, with a long, narrow face accented by high cheekbones and the eyes of a falcon on the hunt.

"Please put your mind at ease," Da-chung said reassuringly. "Everything shall go smoothly, since his papers are authentic."

"It is not his entry, but his ability to accept a new way of life that worries me. You and I waited a long time for a helping hand. My brother had refused, then my older nephew. What if Quanming doesn't like it here?"

Wu turned his face toward heaven. "Buddha will not be so cruel! One of my sons wants to be a lawyer, another a doctor, and my youngest an accountant—not one interested in the business. We are counting on Quanming. From what you've said, he will be a valuable asset. You and I have worked hard all our lives. Maybe now Buddha will turn a kind face in our direction."

"We've traveled a long journey together, my friend, and the road has been paved with thorns." Sung Tinwei sighed.

They had met on the ship that carried them from two different villages along the Pearl River, and after landing, they picked oranges in the same California orchard. When summer was over, they worked together in a sardine plant, and next they found themselves in Alaska, working in a salmon-canning factory. The next spring they returned to California to harvest asparagus, and then they put their savings together to start a small business—rolling cigars and selling them to stores in Chinatown.

One of their Chinese customers owned a bar on Grant Avenue. In return for a share of the profits, the man allowed them to set up a stand in his place. And when he decided to go back to China, Tinwei and Dachung bought the place. They turned it into a profitable business, with imported wine, fine foods, and a few tables for people to play mah-jongg. It developed into a small nightclub, which in time led to many larger ones. Because of their palacelike appearances, a few of them attracted the cream of San Francisco's white society, and the names Sung and Wu became known by the Americans.

While buying for the clubs, the two men started an import-export business. The business grew bigger by the day, and the Sung Wu Company was established exactly twenty years after the two had landed empty-handed in the Land of the Gold Mountains.

"It's still hard for me to believe that you and I, two starving kids from the Pearl, are now owners of the most powerful company in Chinatown. The police chief is our friend, and the mayor comes to our parties whenever we invite him." Wu Da-chung smiled as he remembered how they had been treated by the white people twenty years ago.

Sung Tinwei let out a soft laugh. "Don't be too proud, my friend. Don't forget that the Tongs would love to see us dead, and Wan Kon hates our guts."

"Well, all good things must be accompanied by things that're bad, that's life." Wu Da-chung took from the folds of his robe a gold watch, and informed his friend it was time to go to the pier. "Do we have to ride in that fire dragon again? I prefer the old wagon!"

Tinwei started to laugh. "I assure you, my old friend, that the car is absolutely safe."

They walked out of the garden, and when they reached the shuddering vehicle, Da-chung reluctantly hoisted himself into the backseat. Tinwei, with a young boy's excitement, sat by the driver.

The driver was from north China, named Liu Shih. He had to guide the vehicle by means of a curved bar, much like the rudder on a small sailing vessel. He handed his employers a pair of goggles to protect their eyes from dust and possible residue of the gas engine. He apprehensively increased the throttle, and suddenly the machine lurched forward in a series of neck-breaking jerks. Da-chung had produced a string of prayer beads, and was sitting with his eyes closed, mumbling over and over, "Ah Me Da Foo, Ah Me Da Foo . . ." a prayer said by the Buddhists when facing danger.

The vehicle began to pick up speed, and the engine quieted down, sending out an occasional backfire, followed by a cloud of smoke. As they chugged along, all heads turned; some ran in fear while others watched in astonishment. Da-chung began to relax, and when he noticed all the attention they were getting, he leaned against the leather seat, looking around with the air of a man accustomed to such a modern device. "You know, Tinwei, this is not bad!"

As the contraption belched its way to the wharf, a path was quickly cleared. Wan Kon jumped up. "What the hell is that racket?"

His driver yelled over the noise, "It's one of those horseless carriages—it belongs to the Sung Wu Company."

Wan saw the vehicle slowly bearing down on them. "Those old fools! What the hell are they up to now?"

Glancing over at her Lau Ban, Limei saw the expression on his face and said quickly, "What a nasty machine! How can anyone ride in such a thing? My hair and clothes would be a mess. Please, Lau Ban, let us never have one!" She exaggeratedly collapsed on the seat, holding a handkerchief over her nose as the smoke enveloped them.

Wan Kon was silent as he watched the faces in the crowd. A seed of envy, nourished by his mammoth ego, began to sprout. "If I ever get one, it will be much better than that!"

# 12

THE MORNING SUN burned away the fog, and soon the shore was visible to everyone on deck. The white passengers quickly disembarked, leaving the nonwhites lining up in front of a makeshift table occupied by four people. There were two immigration inspectors, one short, one very tall, a woman stenographer, and a young Chinese interpreter.

The interpreter had been born in San Francisco, but his parents had come from the Pearl River many years ago. They had struggled to send him to college, and he had a soft spot for all who came from his parents' region.

The line moved slowly. Each person had to go through the same procedure: first the documents, then the endless questions. Those who passed were allowed to leave; those who failed were moved to one side, waiting to be sent to Angel Island.

Kim Shinma led Meiping and three other girls to the immigration officers. He bowed and smiled as he placed their papers on the table and pointed to the sponsor's name, House of Wan. The officers knew that Wan Kon always paid well for certain favors. They glanced briefly at the documents and at the girls, then stamped their approval without asking any questions.

Meiping was excited. She couldn't wait to see the Land of the Gold Mountains. She was so glad that the clothes torn by Kim had not been her favorite red blouse and black pants. All the same, she had worn them several times during the journey, and they were dirty and smelled of sweat. She had combed her hair carefully this morning; her long braid was hanging to her waist. She wished that she had some white powder for her face, for she had stood on deck with the boys every day, and now she was even darker than she had been in Jasmine Valley. As Kim Shinma was leading her and the other girls away from the ship, she turned toward the three boys and caught their eye. She exchanged an unspoken good-bye, wondering if she would ever see them again.

Among the three boys, Fachai was the first to reach the table and present his documents.

He too was excited. He had not forgotten what Woo Ming, the labor trader, had promised: as soon as he stepped off the ship, someone would be waiting to take him to the largest fishing boat on earth. He had washed himself as best he could and combed his queue with care. But standing in front of the white officers, he suddenly felt small, filthy, and insecure.

"Li Fachai. You claim that your parents had left you in China all these years," the tall officer noted with a frown, after listening through translation to a story he had heard many times before. "How many letters have you received from them over the years?"

"How many? As a total? I . . . I've never counted." Fachai looked at the interpreter helplessly. According to the answers he had memorized, the question was not supposed to be worded like this.

"Would you say, five, ten, twenty letters each month?" asked the shorter one.

"Only one letter a month," Fachai answered quickly. He had rehearsed this question, and the white man had worded it correctly this time.

"How many pages in each letter?" The tall one leaned forward, looking at Fachai searchingly.

What kind of question was this? Fachai began to panic. The officers noticed it and were satisfied. They knew these yellow pigs well: once they panicked, they would not be able to lie well, and off to the island they would go.

Fachai looked at the interpreter again. The man was not looking at him, but Fachai noticed that he had folded his arms in front of his chest, and the fingers on his right hand kept on tapping first two, then three.

"Sometimes two pages, sometimes three," Fachai answered quickly with a faint smile on his face.

The officers were disappointed. The tall one turned to the short. "Since he's so calm, maybe he's telling the truth." He looked at his watch. It was getting late, and he was getting hungry.

More questions were asked, some trick questions. The interpreter gave Fachai a smile of encouragement with each question, and Fachai felt he had a friend. The notes he had studied became clear in his mind, and he answered the officers without hesitation. Finally they stamped his papers with the word "AP-PROVED."

"Let's take a break," the short officer said to the other, and then turned to the interpreter. "Tell the rest of them to wait for an hour."

When the interrogation started once again, Quanming was the first in line.

The short officer picked his teeth as he looked absentmindedly over the papers, and when he looked up he was surprised by the appearance of this tall Chinese. He studied Quanming's handsome young face, and became upset when Quanming met his eyes with a steady gaze instead of looking away in fear as a Chinese should, if he knew his place.

"Begin your story," the taller one said without looking at the papers. 'Let's hear what lies you have in store for us."

There was a different interpreter in the afternoon, and this one translated the question word by word. Quanming answered by referring to his uncle's letters. He spoke slowly, his voice calm and unwavering. All through his monologue he looked from one officer to the other as if they were his equals, and when he had finished, he just stood proudly and waited.

The short one wanted to smash that arrogant look off the Chink's face. Determined to reject this yellow bastard's request for daring to think he was as good as the whites, he started to throw questions at Quanming, hoping he could find an inconsistency. When one by one the questions were answered accurately, his anger overcame his judgment. He picked up the rejection stamp, ready to show Quanming his authority.

"Wait." His tall partner pulled him by the elbow, pointing at the Sung Wu Company's name. "Look."

The short one's hand stopped in midair. He asked Quanming, "This uncle you claimed to have . . . I never did get his name . . . is he working for the Sung Wu Company?"

"He owns it," Quanming said.

The officers were instantly transformed. The short one stammered, "I didn't realize . . . yes, we were informed of your arrival, but . . . I expected you to be much older." He quickly stamped the paper with his approval, handed it to Quanming, and extended his hand. "Please give your uncle our best regards."

Quanming ignored the outstretched hand and walked away.

The short man let his hand drop, feeling humiliated by the Chinese. "That yellow bastard!" he mumbled to his partner.

"Don't worry." The tall one gave him a sympathetic smile. "We'll get even." He pointed at the long waiting line. "There're plenty of them left yet."

Loone was the next in line.

His cap was pushed more forward than usual; he wished to hide not only his eyes but also his complete face if possible. Because he had packed plenty of clothes besides his art supplies, his white shirt was very clean, and there were creases on his pants. But as he handed over the papers to the two officers, his hands were shaking.

*They don't like me.* With one glance at the two white men he could read their minds. *I am going to fail!*

His thoughts showed on his trembling lips and paling face. The two officers took one look at the frightened boy and knew this one was theirs to kill. They didn't pay much attention to Loone's halting account, which at times was barely audible. They started to throw questions at him, watching his face drain of blood and his frail body shiver. The shorter one grabbed the stamp in his massive paw, slamming it down so hard that the table shook. The word "QUES-TIONABLE" appeared across the page.

A group of people was standing within a roped area, each looking like a prisoner waiting to be executed. Loone could hardly walk as he was told to join them.

# 13

KIM SHINMA SHOVED the four girls through the waiting crowd, knowing how eager his Lau Ban would be to see the merchandise. He rushed toward the black carriage, reached Wan Kon, and bowed deeply.

"It was a long, difficult journey, but I made it safe without failing in my duty—"

He was interrupted by Wan's angry voice: "What's that tall monster doing here? You brought her all the way back from China?"

Meiping, who stood a head taller than the other girls, glared at Wan Kon fearlessly. The little man with a big mustache looked very upset. She thought Wan Kon looked rather funny, and let out a small laugh.

Wan was infuriated, realizing that she was laughing at how small he was. "You call this fulfilling your duty?" he shouted at Kim. "What can we do with a girl so tall and ugly? Look at her thick eyebrows and big eyes! Her tits are as big as a white devil's! And those long legs! My Great Buddha!"

Kim bowed quickly and said, trying to redeem himself, "She was thrown in for practically nothing, Lau Ban."

"That is about what she is worth!" Wan Kon turned away from Meiping's steady gaze and surveyed the other girls, who by now were shaking in fear. They were all very short and none of them weighed more than perhaps eighty pounds. Eyeing them, Wan felt like a big man again. "Well, the rest of the goods are not too bad. No woman should be taller than four and a half feet, and you better remember it next time. Let's go home and get them cleaned up. They look awful right now, and smell even worse."

Kim climbed up on the wagon and sat with the driver, while the girls were instructed to sit with Wan

Kon and Limei, but on the floor. Wan turned his face away from the stench; Limei covered her nose with a perfumed handkerchief to dilute the smell.

Meiping completely forgot her humiliating position as she peeked over the edge of the carriage. With her big eyes wide open, she saw all the tall buildings and the hordes of white people. The streets were unbelievably spacious and clean, and all the people looked like they were in a hurry. She turned in all directions, taking in everything with deep interest, and her full lips parted slightly in childlike excitement. In utter contrast, the other girls sat low on the floor with their legs bent, their heads bowed, and their faces lifeless.

Ever since Meiping had gotten in the wagon, Limei had not stopped watching her. For reasons she could not explain, the woman felt that she was looking at herself many years ago, at a younger age.

Suddenly Meiping turned from her search to look at Limei. "Where are the gold mountains? I don't see them!"

Limei stared at the child for a moment, then started to laugh. "There is no gold mountain."

"No?" Meiping instantly began to pout. "Damn!" She cursed like a Pearl River peasant boy. "Why do people call it the Land of the Gold Mountains, then?"

"It's only a figure of speech." Limei wasn't aware of it, but she was looking at the filthy child with motherly tenderness. "People in China think it's easy to make money in this country, but believe me, the name is really quite unfit. All mountains in America are made of hard, solid, heavy rocks. When a person wants to get anything out of those rocks, he better be prepared for a lot of labor and many aching nights." Looking at the girl's uplifted chin, she couldn't resist the urge to reach out with her handkerchief and wipe the dirt off that stubborn-looking face. "Can you say 'America'? That's the name of this country. And can you pronounce 'San Francisco'? That's the name of this city."

"Ah . . . may . . . lee . . . ka!" Meiping repeated loudly. "San .. fa . . . lan . . . cis . . . ko!"

"Very good." Limei nodded with a smile. "Look," she said to Meiping, pointing ahead. "We're almost home. This is Tong-jen-gai, the Streets of the Chinese."

Meiping noticed that the view had changed drastically. The tall buildings had been replaced by shabby structures and narrow streets cluttered with debris. The people were no longer tall and well-dressed. They were thin and short, moving slowly, as if carrying a heavy burden. Their clothes looked as drab as their obvious mood. Even the air had changed: the smell of food reminded her of the markets in Jasmine Valley, and she suddenly realized how hungry she was.

The carriage stopped in front of the house, and Wan Kon quickly disappeared inside his kingdom. Limei, in charge of the girls, proceeded to take them to the third floor, using the red-carpeted stairs because the elevator was reserved for only the customers and Wan Kon. The first floor contained a bar, a gambling room, and a banquet hall. The second floor held many small rooms with mirrored walls; on some were peepholes concealed behind paintings of misty mountains in China. The girls worked in these rooms but lived on the third floor, where the popular young girls had larger rooms and the less popular and older ones shared closetlike spaces. The top floor belonged to Wan Kon and Limei, where they did their bookkeeping and held private meetings. Limei warned the new girls that they must never set foot up there without permission.

Meiping was overwhelmed by everything around her. As she walked through the lobby, the thick red carpet under her feet was softer than her bed at home. She couldn't resist the temptation to squat down and sit on it for a moment. And then she saw her reflection in one of the many mirrors that lined the walls. "My mirror at home is only big enough for me to see my face . . . this is so big and I look so funny!" she yelled, and started to make faces as she moved along.

As the curved stairway brought them through the second floor to the third, Meiping's hand glided over the wide banister, and her eyes brightened. "No, you don't!" Limei caught her just before she started to use the banister as a sliding board.

They walked through a long, narrow hall and stopped in front of a door. When Limei knocked, the door was opened quickly. A young girl appeared in a thin gown that hid very little of her body. The other three new arrivals blushed and lowered their eyes. "What a beautiful dress she has on!" Meiping exclaimed, her jaw dropping. She looked at Limei. "If I work real hard, will the Lau Ban buy me one?"

Limei didn't answer. She said to the girl in the transparent gown while pointing at one of the three new girls, "Clean her up, dress her in something of yours, and then bring her to the Lau Ban."

They went to two more rooms, and the other two new girls disappeared. "I'll take care of you myself," Limei said to Meiping. "I have other plans for you."

They climbed the steps and reached Limei's private suite on the fourth floor. Meiping stared at it in disbelief; never had she seen anything like this. The carpet was thick and green, like the spring grass in the meadows of Jasmine Valley. The walls were covered with pink paper, and the windows were covered by bright red curtains. A huge bed with a sparkling brass frame stood in the middle of the room, covered in red satin.

She was so absorbed by the splendor that when Limei spoke, she jumped. "My name is Limei. What is yours?"

"Yung Meiping, Limei Sheo-jay," she answered politely as she continued to look around.

"Just call me Limei," said the woman with a shrug. "Never mind the 'Sheo-jay.' There's no such thing as a lady in the House of Wan." Limei led her into the bathroom, and Meiping's jaw dropped once more.

Against one wall she saw a large white porcelain tub. "Oh, we have something just like this in Jasmine Valley . . . not quite so white and clean, of course," she said to Limei proudly. "We use it to store water for the whole village."

Limei shook her head again. "Meiping, get those rags off you while I run the water," the woman said as she turned the knobs.

Meiping watched the steaming water pouring into the tub like magic. "How . . . how can the water come out just like that? And how can you make it come out already hot?"

Limei smiled but didn't take the time to explain. "Now, get undressed."

"You mean, to take off my things in front of you?" Meiping raised her hands to her breasts, covering herself in advance. "I've never . . . Nobody's ever seen me naked!" She shook her head vigorously.

Limei, not known for her patience, put her hands on her waist and stamped her foot. "Get your damn clothes off, Yung Meiping, before I call in someone to do it for you!"

Pouting, Meiping reluctantly climbed out of her stiff, smelly clothes, then stepped unwillingly into the water. To her surprise, it was pleasant and warm. She gradually relaxed. She washed herself slowly, stopping now and then to smell the bar of fragrant soap. She then sank into the water to wash her hair. She had forgotten Limei was there, but the woman had never taken her experienced eyes from the girl, watching and thinking.

Limei could tell that this young girl had a bright future. She would be welcomed by American men.

There had been complaints from the white men. They were uncomfortable taking midget women to bed; they felt like they were molesting children. Limei looked at Meiping's full breasts and long legs and said to herself: This is not a midget, nor is she a child. Chinese men will feel small and insignificant in front of her, but the white devils will be happy to have something they're not afraid to break!

Limei left Meiping in the tub, went to her closet, and looked through her wardrobe. She picked out a set of Western clothes she had bought on impulse, something that was much too big for her and she would never wear.

An hour later, Meiping was dried, perfumed, and dressed in a black silk blouse with a very low neckline, along with a long green skirt that had a slit up one side. A wide black sash was tied tightly around her narrow waist, and her firm breasts were outlined against the thin fabric.

She was told to sit in front of the dresser. Limei began to pluck her eyebrows with some tweezers. Meiping cried out with each pull, looked at Limei accusingly, wondering why this nice woman now insisted on torturing her. Finally the task was finished: the swordlike eyebrows were gone, leaving two faint, thin willow leaves.

Next Limei began to work on Meiping's thick, stubborn hair. She brushed the strands until her arm was sore, but the hair soon hung gleaming all the way to the waist like a black waterfall. It took Limei another hour to make Meiping up, for the young girl didn't know how to stay still and never stopped asking questions. Then came the toughest part—Meiping had to put on silk stockings and a pair of high-heeled shoes.

"We're lucky that for a big girl, your feet are small. But you better trim those toenails of yours," Limei said, shaking her head. "They look like eagle claws."

Standing in high heels, Meiping's long legs looked even longer. "Now," Limei said, eyeing her creation with disbelief, "let's walk around the room." She took the girl by the elbow. "Being from the country, you should know how a willow moves in the breeze. Let's pretend that you're a willow tree: left, right, left, right . . . that's it. Swing your hips, but keep your upper body straight . . . you got it! I've never had anyone learn as quickly as you!" Limei said proudly.

Encouraged by the kind words, Meiping soon sashayed with confidence. With each long stride her slender legs showed through the slit of the skirt; her young body was a collection of sensuous curves.

She caught a glimpse of herself in the long mirror, gasped, and almost fell. "This can't be me!" She stared at the reflection of a tall, beautiful girl. "How come I'm not ugly anymore?" She turned to the woman with tears welling in her eyes. "Oh, Limei, you are a magician!" She ran to the woman and threw her long, strong arms around Limei, giving the woman a powerful hug.

Limei was surprised by such affection. She had been the unwanted child of a prostitute, and when she was six, her mother had died. She had lived in the house as a servant girl until Wan Kon took her into his bed-chamber. He had never been gentle to her even when she was young, and now that her beauty was fading, she was often lonely. The doctor had told her that she would never be able to bear children, and her maternal instincts were awakened by Meiping.

Clasping Limei in her arms, Meiping kept pouring out her happy thanks: "You're so good to me, Limei! You made me beautiful!" She kissed Limei on the cheek. "I wish the people of Jasmine Valley could see me now! I wish Quanming, Fachai, and Loone could be here!"

All of a sudden Limei felt uncomfortable. *How can this stupid young thing be grateful to me for turning her into a whore?*

From the pier, Fachai, along with several others, was picked up by a Chinese-American. The short greasy-faced man's job was to see that each of the newcomers was transported to his proper buyer. He hired a wagon, loaded the merchandise, and dropped everybody into the hands of his lawful owner.

Fachai had many questions to ask, but the man was not willing to answer. He felt much superior to these country punks, and he wasn't going to lower himself to speak to them.

Expecting to see the largest fishing boat on earth, Fachai was delivered to Dino Camerano's fish-processing plant.

"Am I going to work indoors? Am I not going fishing?" He looked from the white owner to the greasy-faced interpreter.

Through the interpreter Dino informed Fachai that a small room in the attic over the plant could be his if he agreed to pay for it out of his weekly salary. A percentage of his salary was also being taken away to pay back his passage, plus the money Woo Ming had given him in Kwangchow. Fachai must work seven days a week, ten hours a day.

Dino said to the bowlegged man, "Tell your fellow countryman that he can have all the fish heads he can eat. But he must buy his own rice—that is what you Chinks live on, right? Tell him there is a small Chinese grocery store a block from the warehouse. He can cook in his attic room, provided he doesn't set the place on fire."

The interpreter soon left, and Fachai was shown to the attic garret. He looked around, and his heart sank. It was a dark, low-ceilinged place filled with the smells of fish coming from downstairs. There were a few wooden boxes he could use for a table and chairs, and there was also a small charcoal burner. On his bed, some old burlap bags piled together, he sadly laid the quilt from Leahi.

He started work the next morning. His job was to take a fish from a pile, sever its head, slit it up in the middle, remove the entrails, scale it, then throw it into a barrel and start the whole procedure over again. As he worked, he wondered who would want to buy these headless fish. In China, a fish must be served as a whole. In fact the most famous dish was a fish already covered with tomato sauce and stuffed with ginger slices, but at the same time still able to open its mouth and move its tail.

Around midmorning the boss left. When the other workers grabbed the chance to step outside for a break, Fachai tried to follow.

The red-haired foreman took him by the arm and dragged him back to the bench. "You, Chinaman, stay! Stay!"

Fachai stared at him, not understanding a word.

"Stay, I said!" The man repeated it until Fachai got the message.

"Deu-ne-ma!" Fachai wanted so badly to fight, but instead cursed in Cantonese. "Deu-na-lao-bay!" He used all the foul words he could think of, keeping his voice pleasant and smiling as he bowed to the foreman.

He worked by himself for an hour. The last fish was cleaned, and he squatted down for a moment. The others had just returned from the break, and the big man with flaming red hair gave him a kick while passing. "Chinaman, get to work! Did you have permission to rest?"

The kick had not been hard; it had hurt Fachai's pride more than his flesh. He jumped to his feet, eyes flashing in anger as he advanced on the grinning man with the strange red hair. But before he could reach him, another big man with a missing tooth came up from behind, pinning Fachai's arms in an iron grip. Fachai struggled while all the white workers stood around laughing. Fachai suddenly remembered a move Quanming had taught him. He raised his arms straight over his head and quickly bent his knees, dropping his body down and out of the grip of the one holding him.

"What's the matter with you? You dumb Limey!" shouted the redhead. "The little Chink too much for you to handle?"

"He's as slippery as a bloody eel!" shouted the other man, looking puzzled.

Fachai backed into a corner, waiting for the next attack. His hate and anger swelled like a festered boil. "I'm a person! I'm a man!" he screamed, looking from one face to another. "Why do you treat me this way? Do you white devils have no heart?"

His words were meaningless to them, but his feelings were understood by everyone.

The fun was suddenly gone for the white men. One by one they looked away from Fachai, with shame on their rough but honest faces. They all remembered what it had been like to be new and all alone in this great land of opportunity. Without a word they turned and went back to work.

They had seen hard times themselves, and they knew what Fachai was going through. When they realized how much they had hurt him, and also understood that, like themselves, he too was a fighter, they grudgingly accepted the Chinese.

Later that afternoon, when it was time for another break, the same big redheaded man approached Fachai and motioned for him to join them. At first Fachai thought it was some kind of a trick, but the man continued to smile, and finally Fachai followed.

Sitting on the steps in the back of the warehouse, the other men tried to communicate with him. First they told him their names; he tried to say them and they all laughed at his attempts. He said his name, and none of them could pronounce it. While laughing, Fachai realized that he had become one of them, but this acceptance did little to relieve him of any of the dirty work.

Three weeks dragged by. On Saturday afternoon Fachai was told he could have the rest of the weekend off. He had just received his pay, less what he owed the company, leaving him with almost thirty dollars. He felt rich as a landlord. He had been living on fish heads, and except for buying rice, he had not spent a penny.

With his pocket filled with money, he walked down Pacific Street looking for Chinatown. He was ready to talk to both Chinese and the white devils outside the fish plant. During the three weeks, he had picked up an assortment of languages used by his fellow workers, and he now thought he was beginning to have an understanding of English.

At the entrance of Grant Avenue, he felt a touch of home: pig heads stared from butchers' counters, the bloody meat hanging from hooks. The dried lizards and snakes looked beautiful in the herb shops. He was tempted by the fresh vegetables and fruits with mud on them as a proof of their being fresh.

He looked around and breathed with relief. He felt comfortable walking once more among his own people. He noticed how different their clothes were from his. He liked their Western suits, but the ties around their necks made him think of the Willow Place dogs as they were being dragged to the market to be sold as someone's dinner. Then too, their hard leather shoes looked so uncomfortable compared to his soft slippers, but he envied the sound those shoes made with each step. He was shocked to see that almost all the men had cut off their queues, and their short hair was combed back, shining with oil.

He bought cooked chicken feet and carried them in newspapers shaped in a cone. He ate as he walked, throwing the scraps on the sidewalk. Seeing a barbershop, he made a decision. His young heart beat fast with excitement as he walked into the shop and said to the barber, "I want to cut off my queue!"

The old barber had been sitting against the wall, his face deeply lined, and his hair was completely white. His right leg was a wooden peg from below the knee, and his smile pulled his lips over toothless gums. "Newcomer?"

"Yes," Fachai answered, trying not to stare at the man's missing limb. "Three weeks to this day. I'm from Willow Place, along the Pearl River."

The old man's eyes brightened for a moment. "I too used to live near that beautiful river. I haven't seen the Pearl for forty years now . . ." The brightness disappeared as he asked, "How are things back home?"

As Fachai went on to describe his hometown, the man devoured every word with a hunger he had been carrying for many years. A dreamy look appeared on his thin face as his heart flew across the ocean and touched the land of his home. He had left that land as a young boy, and worked on the railroad until an accident took his leg. He had learned to cut hair, but the few coins he earned would never be enough to bring him back to the land of his birth.

As Fachai took the only chair, he looked in the mirror at the queue he had been wearing all his life. "I want a short Western haircut," he said firmly to the old man. "Please do it quickly before I change my mind!"

Thirty minutes later, Fachai turned his head from side to side, pleased with his appearance. The old man had been generous with the oil, and now Fachai's hair shone like black coal. The excess oil was dripping

down the side of his face and his neck, making him
feel rich, modern, and Westernized. The barber
handed his cut-off queue to him, knowing that someday, like all men, Fachai would want to be buried with
his hair in the same coffin.

Fachai paid the ten cents, thanked him, and walked
out of the barbershop, rubbing his bare neck. He felt
a sense of freedom and, for the first time, a part of
this new country. Coming upon a photography studio,
he stopped to look at the many portraits in the window.

As he stood looking, a well-dressed young man
stepped out of the door. "My name is Chen Bai, and
I am the best photographer in the whole Tong-jen-gai."
He smiled sweetly, resting his soft white hand on his
hip, tapping his neatly trimmed nails in rhythm. "You
look so handsome with your new haircut. It would be
a shame if you didn't have a picture taken."

Fachai thought of Leahi. She would be very proud
to see him with his haircut, but his parents and grandfather might be aghast to know he had cut off his
queue. He grinned self-consciously, wondering how
the man knew he had just had his hair cut.

Hesitantly he followed the photographer into the
shop, smelling the strong fragrance of perfume coming from the man. Chen Bai asked whether he wanted
to sit or stand for the picture, and Fachai considered
the question for a long while. "Stand, I guess," he
said uncertainly.

Chen Bai took Fachai gently by the arm and led him
up to a pedestal. "Yes, I think you've made the right
choice. You are such a tall man, and so strong and
powerful." He stepped back, tilting his head to study
his model carefully. "It gives me much pleasure to
take a picture of you, Sisan. You are such a handsome
fellow." He walked back to Fachai, took his arm, and
placed it carefully on the pedestal. He then gave Fachai's shoulder a soft squeeze. "Oh! What broad
shoulders you have!"

Fachai became very uncomfortable. Chen noticed
him frowning and quickly moved back to the camera.

"Hold still now, and don't be scared when you see the bright light. But what am I saying? Of course, a big strong man like you would never be frightened by a little light." He smiled. "Hold still now." He removed the lens cap and touched off the flash. It was followed by a cloud of white smoke, and the man said, "There, it's done! It didn't hurt a bit, did it?"

"When will the picture be ready?" Fachai asked, wanting to escape.

"Only a few days. I will rush it just for you," he said as he used the tips of his fingers to smooth his slightly mussed hair. "Early next week soon enough for you? Make it in the evening." He moved a little closer and flicked a few hairs from Fachai's jacket. "Come for your picture when you get off from work, and maybe you and I can have something to eat—my treat, of course. I wouldn't dream of making you pay. I live above the studio; it's a pleasant place to relax over a glass of wine or two . . . then maybe later, who knows . . . ?" He grinned, reaching out to touch Fachai.

"I'll come back for the picture," Fachai said as he fled the studio, and then yelled over his shoulder, "Never mind the wine!"

The fresh air was a welcome change after the cloying smell of the studio. Walking farther down the street, Fachai soon spotted a sign with a picture of a brush and an envelope. He was glad that all letter writers used the same logo, no matter where they were. He was soon sitting across the table from an old man with bushy white eyebrows, in a robe as ancient as he; it obviously had not seen soap and water for a long time. The man added water to his ink stone. With a hard charcoal stick he began to grind it into ink. When he was satisfied with its darkness, he picked up a brush. "Begin," he said gruffly. "I'm ready."

"My honorable Grandfather, Father, Mama, and Leahi," Fachai started in the correct order. "I've been in the Land of the Gold Mountains three weeks now, and life here is, I must say, much better than trying to scratch out an existence in Willow Place. My work in the fish market is not as dangerous as struggling on the Pearl, and I get ten dollars every week after they take out what I owe. I'm sending most of it home, so you can live well and buy a new boat. I don't need much money; with all the fish heads to eat, I feel like a landlord already. . . ."

Fachai gave a sigh of relief when the letter was finished, because he didn't know how to talk to his family without seeing them. He reached into his pocket and handed the old man the money he wanted to send home, then gave the address of the Li family in Willow Place.

## 14

WHEN THE SHUTTLE BOAT pulled up to the pier at
Angel Island, everyone was ordered to pick up his belongings and follow the guards toward a long wooden
building.

Before they entered, the Orientals were separated
from the few Caucasians. Loone had not been in
America long, but long enough that he realized that
no matter where the whites were being taken, they
would end up much better off than the Orientals. After
they entered the building, the men and women were
separated. Loone's group was made to strip and bathe;
then everyone was deloused. Every piece of clothing
was collected and taken away, replaced by ill-fitting
uniforms. Everyone dressed quickly, feeling embarrassed because none of them had ever appeared naked
in front of strangers.

In another room, the women, after much arguing
and prodding, were also made to strip, as the male
guards stood watching. The female detainees' sobbing
could be heard throughout the building. After they had
showered and were deloused, the guards gave the uniforms to the older women first and took their time
passing out clothing to the young and pretty ones,
boldly ogling them and laughing among themselves.
The women from the Pearl River had been raised in a
five-thousand-year-old tradition, and if there had been
a way, many of them would have chosen to end their
lives right then rather than be put through such shame.
The guards were ignorant of the tradition, but even if
they had known, they couldn't have cared less how
these heathens felt.

The bags of the detainees were taken away and
locked in a warehouse. Before that, an interpreter explained that each person should keep some money in

his uniform pocket, because even in the barracks, money was still used. Loone was in tears when forced to part from his mother's pearls, and although he was told that upon his release everything would be returned, he wondered how many, when finally set free, would dare to mention their missing valuables.

He was then taken to a room filled with a medicinal smell and made to strip again. Shivering in fear, he was thumped on the chest, made to turn his head and cough, while a cold hand pushed on the side of his genitals. Then he was forced to bend over and spread his cheeks. The young boy had never felt so humiliated. He was then tested for trachoma, hookworm, and filariasis. The examination was perfunctory, the staff bored and tired.

The group was led to a long dormitory. Along each wall there were narrow bunks stacked two high to make enough beds for a hundred people. The old-timers watched silently from their bunks as the newcomers were given a brief orientation by the interpreter.

Loone was assigned to one of the lower bunks, and as he sat on the thin mattress he looked around, studying each face: in some of the eyes he saw anger, in others he saw men long since resigned to their fate. Some of the people were quite content; still others stared into space as if they belonged to the world of the undead.

"Make yourself at home, because this just might be it for a long time." Loone jumped at the sound of the voice coming from over his head. "I've been here over two years now, and my name has never been called for interrogation."

Loone looked up and saw the pale face of a man with deep-sunken eyes and hollow cheeks, leaning over the edge of the upper bunk. "The first time I came to this terrible country I had just turned fifteen. I had forged papers then, but the white devils let me in  I worked in a laundry for seventeen years, saved my money, then went to the Pearl to visit my parents and find myself a young bride. When I returned to San

Francisco, the bastards said my papers were not in order. I've been waiting and waiting . . .'' The voice faded, and the pale face disappeared.

Loone shivered. Both the man's voice and his looks were like that of a ghost. ''Take it easy, you'll get used to that old man.'' Loone turned to the other side of his bunk and saw a chubby young man smiling a him.

He was glad to see someone his age. ''How long have you been here?'' he asked.

''Long enough to know my way around,'' the boy answered, moving closer to Loone. ''My uncle sent for me as his son, and I had hidden all my coaching notes in my hat. Aboard ship some of the guys took my hat and began to throw it back and forth. The notes fell out and a bully picked them up and wouldn't return them to me. When we landed, he gave them to the authorities, figuring that he could get on their good side . . . but the bastard also ended up here. He's in the next barracks, and someday I will get even with him!'' The boy laughed and slapped Loone on the back.

He also told Loone about an organization that had been established in the dormitory. Each member had to pay a fee. After that, should he be treated unfairly by the authorities or beaten by the guards, the organization would stand up for him. ''One thing you should never do is to report to the guards any theft or fights. Understand?'' When Loone nodded, the boy continued, ''The organization will kick you out, and you might as well be dead.''

''I'm tired,'' Loone said, cutting off the conversation. The boy left reluctantly, looking disappointed.

Lying on his back, Loone breathed in the musty odor from his blanket and sheets. The smell transported him back to Kwangchow, when he would sit in the pawnshop's storage room among all the antique books. His eyes filled with tears and he silently spoke to his parents: *Mama, Baba, are you watching me? Can you see where I am? I am no longer a worry-free boy surrounded by beautiful things. I am a prisoner.*

*The two of you have each other in heaven, while I'm
on earth all alone.*

Loone cried himself to sleep.

That night he dreamed he was a gull gliding effort-
lessly above turquoise water. The clear blue sky was
endless, interrupted only by an occasional wisp of a
floating cloud. He soared high and saw below him a
ship. Dipping downward to get a better look, he saw
on the deck his mother and father playing ball with a
small boy. The ball took a sudden high bounce, sailed
over the rail, and fell into a sea that had turned vio-
lent. As he watched helplessly, his parents jumped into
the water to retrieve the ball. The boy on deck
screamed in terror. A mountainous wave opened its
watery mouth and swallowed the couple. Loone discovered he was no longer the gull; he had become the
orphaned boy.

"Mama! Baba!" he screamed, and awoke on the
bunk, soaked in sweat.

Night had fallen while he slept, and the dormitory
was in darkness. He was disoriented at first, and then
the shock of reality jerked him fully awake. He jumped
up, bumping his head on the upper bunk, fell back on
the cot shaking, hearing only the sounds of his inmates. Some were snoring, others talking in their
sleep. He could make out the sound of crying and once
in a while someone calling out a dear one's name.

For the rest of the night Loone lay awake. He stared
out the window until dawn. With the first streamer of
sun, a guard came in and began blowing a whistle.
The men started to get up. Loone followed the others
to wait in a long line in front of the bathroom. When
it was his turn, he went into a tiny closet and found a
single commode and a sink in the corner. Flies filled
the room; everything was filthy. He took care of his
needs as quickly as possible and washed the best he
could. Long after he had left, the stench remained with
him.

They lined up to go to the mess hall, which was
located in a long building in the middle of the complex. The chamber was filled with several hundred

people, and at one end there was a huge kitchen, where the serving line started. There were many rows of wooden benches and tables on the cement floor and several large windows high on the concrete walls. To Loone's amazement, everything was very clean . . . cleaner than in China.

The rice gruel was sufficient to keep a person alive, but it had little flavor. Loone didn't see much meat or fish in it. He found a place to sit and picked at his food even though he was extremely hungry. When he couldn't force himself to eat any more, he pushed his plate to one side. It was quickly grabbed by the man next to him.

The whistle was blown and everyone again lined up. They washed their bowls in barrels of water that smelled of disinfectant. The wet plates were stacked and the chopsticks thrown into a large pail.

Once back in the barracks, everyone looked for something to do. Loone sat on his bunk watching. The majority were reading newspapers and playing mah-jongg. A few were acting out scenes from well-known Cantonese operas, while others were talking in small groups. Several buckets of water had been set up to wash clothes, and the wet things were hung between bunks to dry. A few men were just lying on their bunks staring into space.

Loone saw a man busy writing characters on a nearby wall with a brush. Curious, he walked over to take a look, and discovered that the man was compos-ing a poem. Loone then noticed many other poems. He read them slowly, and was surprised to see that many were very well written. Each poem was signed, but some were so faded with age that he could hardly make out the characters.

After lunch they filed out for fresh air. Loone stood in the shade of a palm tree watching a group of older men going through the routine of Tai Chi. He watched their slow, graceful movements, and wished he had had his drawing pad with him. He noticed that the detainees were divided into small groups and could hear a smattering of different dialects. The voices cre-

ated a cacophony matched by the screeching of sea
gulls. And as he listened, he realized that his country
could never be united as one.

The piercing sound of a whistle blared through the
air. Everyone started to walk back toward the barracks.

Loone didn't return to his bunk, but instead found
a small window, stood in front of it, and reached up
to hold on to the iron bars. He got up on his toes and
stretched his neck to look out.

Outside the window, the green grass was dotted with
gulls sleeping in the warm rays of the sun. He searched
toward the far end of the grass and saw beyond the
palm trees the waves washing against large rocks,
sending up a rainbow-colored mist. His heart sank at
the sight of the barbed-wire fence, which stood around
the perimeter of the island, reminding the several hundred men and women that they had committed the un-
forgivable crime of wanting to become a part of
America.

A bird flapped its wings and started to fly toward
the mainland. Watching the disappearing dot, Loone
envied the bird its freedom. *Baba and Mama, they say
that the dead know everything. Can you tell me, then:
how long must I be a prisoner? Will I ever be free
again?*

When it was suppertime, Loone talked to the guard.
Giving the man most of the money he had, he asked
for a trip to the warehouse to take from his luggage
his drawing pad and pencils. The guard nodded a silent yes, and the trip was made. As soon as Loone
returned to the barracks, he hid the pearls he had taken
without the guard knowing, then started sketching.
Soon he was lost in his work. His fear, self-pity, and
anger were all dissolving as his hand moved.

The first drawing showed two bony hands clinging
to iron bars, while beyond the window gulls soared
among the clouds.

The second picture displayed a large closed door;
an old man was kneeling in front of it, his hands raised
in fists, hitting the thick wooden panel. Through a

small opening a guard sneered down at the frustrated prisoner.

By this time several men had gathered, though Loone was unaware of their presence. As they watched the images take shape, the messages became apparent. Each prisoner understood what the boy was saying. Some of them turned away, their eyes glistening. Most of them stayed, mesmerized, not able to break away.

When Loone stopped to sharpen his pencils, he realized he had acquired an audience. He noticed one man in particular, whose eyes made him think of the eyes of a caged animal. He couldn't stop looking at his straight nose and thick lips, along with the square jaw and a chin with a deep cleft. The man's face was very dark, and his body was like a bear's.

Loone started to use this man as his next model, trying to capture the look he had seen in the man's eyes. As the finishing touches were being added to the sketch, the man thundered, "That's me!"

A hand the size of a bear's paw was laid on Loone's shoulder. *If he does not like his portrait, I am dead!* Loone looked up in fear.

The man smiled down at him, showing a mouthful of strong white teeth. "You made me look real good, little fellow," he said, and in the next moment he lifted Loone up above his head, like a child showing off his doll. He held Loone in midair for a long while, turning him in all directions. "I like this little fellow, he is my friend. He makes me look good!" the big man kept on saying.

Loone sighed with relief.

## 15

THE MORNING MIST rolled across the bay and glided silently into the sleepy streets. It swirled seductively around the legs of early risers rushing off to work. On its journey inland, the fog blanketed Chinatown as if ashamed of the litter in the streets and of the run-down, rat-infested shacks. The vapor stayed in the narrow alleyways, hugging the earth, where it waited, hoping to hide from the sun's rays that would soon find their way over the hills.

Quanming was looking out his bedroom window, breathing in the fresh air, gazing toward the invisible bay. His thoughts had been in White Stone. Everything he loved was so far away: his mother, Yoto, and his country.

He forced himself to leave the window, then changed into his workout clothes and walked into the garden. The misty courtyard made him feel as though he was walking into a dream. The base of the miniature mountain was gone; only the top could be seen floating above the haze. The pond was covered by a gray silk curtain, with a wisp of color from the water lilies filtering through the air. The brightly colored bridge looked like a pastel rainbow, and with each step Quanming felt he was moving along a mystic pathway to enter another world.

Standing on the wet grass facing east, Quanming clasped his right fist into his left palm and bowed. He remembered Master Lin's words: "Life is generated from the sun. One must bow to the east to honor this life-giving force, and ask his mind to be cleared in order to attain concentration."

As Quanming started to practice, the first rays of the sun began to burn away the fog, bathing the garden in a golden glow. He began to lose his concentration.

Four words appeared in his mind: Shin-yun-yi-ma; the heart is like a restless monkey, the mind a galloping horse. Lately he had been having trouble quieting the monkey and taming the horse. He kept thinking about a letter from his mother; he was extremely worried about her health. And he thought often of Yoto. The image of her in her husband's arms sent a wave of anger through his heart.

With a sigh Quanming sat on the top of a low stone table, crossed his legs, and closed his eyes. He sat like a statue, blending into the background. Gradually the self started to cease existing, and eventually he became in oneness with the universe. The restless monkey was tamed and the wild horse bridled.

Sung Tinwei entered the garden, and Quanming sensed the intrusion. Opening his eyes, he jumped off the table immediately. "Good morning, Uncle," he said, bending deeply at the waist.

The uncle bowed, then beckoned Quanming to join him. The two sat by the pond, watching the golden carp swimming lazily among the lily pads. Tinwei poured green tea and they sat sipping from small round cups, enjoying the fragrance of the tea leaves. The uncle soon began talking to his young nephew about the many complexities of Chinatown; it had become their morning ritual.

The garden was silent except for a rippling of water flowing over a miniature falls and the occasional splash of a jumping carp. Tinwei's voice was deep and low as he began to talk:

"In Chinatown, although we are all descendants of Huang-ti, there are many different people using dialects that are foreign to one another. Should we divide them by their origins, you would first find the Sze-yup people, who came from the four districts in the southwest regions of the Pearl, which includes the cities of Enping, Kaiping, Taishan, and Xinhui. Second, there are the San-yup people, whose original homes are in the three districts on the outskirts of Kwangchow, namely the cities of Nanhai, Panyu, and Shunde. People from Sze-yup don't get along with people from

San-yup, and within the same district, those from Nanhai will plot against the ones from Panyu. At first glance we seem like one big family. But look more deeply and it will become obvious that there is little loyalty among Chinese who are not from the same region. We are a very complex people.

"With, as you know, only one hundred last names for all Chinese, there has always been a bond between those carrying the same surname. They feel a strong kinship and wouldn't hesitate to join forces against those whose surnames are different. Grouping people by their last names, we come up with four important ones in Chinatown: Liu, Guam, Chang, and Chew. Each of the four families has established its own organization, known as a Tong.

"The Tongs are much feared because of their immense power. They lend money to newcomers to start a business, but when the businessman becomes successful, he'd better pay his debt with a sizable donation to the Tong. Those who fail to pay will soon wish they had never been born.

"Years ago, a few outlaws fled China and formed clandestine organizations in Chinatown that were interested only in stealing from innocent people. Merchants who owned stores and small businesses had gone to the Tongs for protection, and had been forced to pay the Tongs a protection fee. After a time some of the merchants had become tired of paying and formed societies to fight them." The uncle smiled at his nephew. "Do you follow me?"

Quanming answered, "Yes, I follow you." He thought for a moment. "But where do we stand, Uncle?"

The uncle lighted a cigarette and said proudly as he watched the smoke drifting across the garden, "We belong to the Sung-Wu Society, which is not only the most powerful but also the most respected. Our strongest opponent is the Tong of Wan."

"Who is the Tong of Wan?"

"A group of men led by Wan Kon. Before him, their leaders had been Wan's father and grandfather. Their

Tong has been prosperous, because in a bachelor society created by a crazy law, prostitutes are always needed—prostitution is Wan Kon's main business. Wan Kon and I have been on opposite sides for a long time. You see, until Da-chung and I came along, the Tong of Wan had always dominated Chinatown. You must be careful while dealing with Wan Kon. You should never turn your back on either him or any of his henchmen.''

Quanming asked again, "What makes the Sung-Wu Society so strong and respectable?''

The uncle clapped his hands, and a servant appeared with more tea. "Our strength lies in our dealings with the Americans. Your Uncle Da-chung and I discovered a long time ago that we cannot confine ourselves within the invisible walls of Chinatown if we wish to be truly successful. So, instead of calling the Americans white devils and hiding from them, we went to night schools to learn English and enable ourselves to interact with the white society. Now we are on good terms with Christian churches, law-enforcement agencies, and many prominent political figures. Our people respect us because when we deal with the Americans, we don't kowtow. We act like a Chinese embassy, functioning as mediators between the Chinese and the Americans, protecting our people and fighting for their rights.''

Tinwei put down his teacup and stood up; Quanming followed. "It's most important that you should learn English, Quanming, and I've already found you a tutor. His name is Paul Eddington. He was once a missionary to China.''

When Chu Ninpo and his wife learned that Fong Loone had been sent to Angel Island, Hasan broke down in tears and Ninpo became furious.

"Let's go visit Mr. Wong, the labor trader,'' Chu Ninpo suggested, and an hour later they walked into a shabby upstairs office in a run-down building on Grant Avenue.

A man in his late thirties greeted them from behind

a desk. He wore a white suit that looked as if he had slept in it, and a blue shirt with a collar much too large for his skinny neck. A bright red tie hung like a twisted rope with its ends tucked in his pants. "What can I do for you?" he asked, leaning back in his chair, tapping a pencil on the desk.

The Chus sat without waiting to be asked, and explained their predicament.

"Well," Wong said, "things like this cannot be helped. You must be patient and everything will be fine." He got up and walked to the door. "Thanks for coming, and keep me informed."

Neither Ninpo nor Hasan moved. The wife was first to speak, and there was a sharp edge in her voice: "How long will that poor boy be kept on the island?"

Wong shrugged. "I'm not a fortune-teller, how the hell should I know?" He stood holding the door, waiting for them to leave. "Good day!"

The husband stood up, stepped forward, and took a firm hold of Wong's thin arm. "Mr. Wong, we paid you quite a bit of money for this boy."

Wong tried to free himself but couldn't; the little old man had a grip of iron, "Well, what you paid me was barely enough to cover my expenses—"

"We paid you a thousand dollars, and now we want our boy." Chu Ninpo increased the pressure on the man's arm. "You'd better get your ass moving, or you'll find yourself warming a white devil's prison cell!" He released the arm.

Rubbing his arm, Wong moved toward the desk and sat on the edge, not believing his ears. He had counted on the fear that the Chinatown people had toward the law to make things easy for him, but now Buddha had to give him this crazy old bastard who seemed to have no fear at all. He forced a smile. "Let's not get excited. Of course you know that I wasn't going to ignore the problem. You see, I do have a cousin who works on Angel Island as a cook . . ."

He went on to explain that his cousin could pass some information to Loone and help the boy to prepare for his next interrogation. Loone would then be able to say things about the Chus concerning matters that he could not know unless he was truly a son. "My cousin can also bring word from the boy to tell you a birthmark or something he has that can only be described by his true parents.' Wong grinned. "The stupid white devils will have to let the boy go."

"You'd better be right!" Chu Ninpo said, gesturing his wife to leave. At the door the old man turned. "My wife has her heart set on having a son, and I can't live with a nagging woman much longer. If you don't get our boy out of that island, I might as well go to jail with you!"

In the past two months Loone's popularity as an artist had grown. Both inmates and guards had been coming to ask for their portraits to be done. They all agreed that there was something special about Loone's work. "When you draw us, the pictures not only look like us but also tell how we feel."

On this December day in the barracks, someone described his hometown, a village on the Pearl, to Loone and asked him to sketch it.

Loone started to draw a flowing river, a collection of low houses with ancient trees reaching toward the sky, and clumps of wildflowers along the path.

"That's it! That's my home!" The man pointed excitedly. "I've often walked on this road to go to work in my rice field . . . it was under this old tree that my family had gathered to watch the autumn moon!"

After that, another man came and asked shyly for a portrait of his wife. "We were married only a week when I left. Lying on the prison bed, I see her in every one of my dreams. But as soon as I open my eyes, she is gone. My days are so empty. Even if it's only a picture of her, I believe it'll give me something to hope for in the better days."

Loone agreed to do the portrait, and the man started to describe his wife: "She is beautiful. She has an oval-shaped face and very slanted eyes . . ."

Loone moved his pencil on the pad, and before long a beautiful village girl appeared. Her young body was clothed in a peasant blouse and pants, her hair braided into a long queue. She was staring at the river with a look of sadness, trust, and faith.

"My wife! That's my wife!" The man cried out a woman's name. "Be patient. I'll be released from here soon, and I'll work hard in this golden land. I'll send you a lot of money . . . you and the old ones will never be hungry again!" Then his voice broke. He grabbed the sheet of paper and ran.

With all the drawing, the days were not too bad. But Loone dreaded the nights. As soon as the lights went out, the storytellers would begin their tales. On this winter evening, there was no moon. As the hours passed, the wind began to blow. Lying on his bunk, he was forced once more to listen to ghost stories he didn't wish to hear.

The tales were spiced with imagination, although they were all based on true occurrences.

". . . a woman, after being kept on the island for over a year, was to be sent back to China. She sneaked a chopstick out of the lunchroom, and rubbed the end on the stone wall until it became very sharp. When no one was watching, she inserted the stick in her ear, tilted the point up, and drove it into her brain." The storyteller paused for effect, listening to gasps from those around him. "With blood pouring from her ears, she staggered around the room, reaching for help. She screamed in pain for a long time, but the guards never came to her aid. She finally sank to the floor and rolled into a ball, then slowly died."

The storyteller stopped once more, then whispered dramatically, "It's been said that many of us have seen this woman walking about the compound with a chopstick jutting out of her ear and blood dripping down her neck. When all is quiet in the night, she can be heard wailing until dawn's first light."

A second storyteller's voice came out of the darkness, starting another tale. "After several years of waiting, a man was going before the review board the following day. He became very frightened, and was certain that he would fail. He couldn't face the day, so he hanged himself at daybreak. And even now, people still see him walking about the barracks, his naked body blue and his staring eyes bulging, repeating, 'I might have passed, I might . . . I might . . .' "

After a period of silence the third began. "There were several young men who had been, before coming to this land, fishermen along the Pearl River. They came to believe that they could swim across the water surrounding this island, and on one starless night they tried. They were not aware of the difference between the ocean and a river, however, and they all drowned. During some nights their ghosts can be seen climbing out of the water, covered in seaweed, their flesh hanging from their bones. Their eyes are missing, eaten by fish. Their lips are long gone, and their white teeth gleam in the light of the moon, laughing at fate."

Loone pulled the blankets over his head, but couldn't keep the many more stories from making their way to his ears. Long after all the storytellers had gone to sleep, he still lay awake.

He could see the woman coming for him with a chopstick sticking out of her ear. He tried to hide his feet, for he could feel the icy fingers of the hanged man touching his toes. Even with his eyes covered by his trembling hands, he could still see the decayed bodies of the fishermen floating above his bunk, holding hands, forming a circle, laughing round and round.

After a sleepless night, Loone was tired and miserable the next day. He didn't feel like drawing for anybody. He walked over to one of the poem-covered walls and read each one slowly. He marveled at the sorrow and beauty contained in the simple compositions, and wondered what had happened to the authors.

Most of the poems were the writers' own creations, but some were quoted from the works of old masters. All of a sudden Loone's eyes were caught by the written lyrics of a well-known folklore of Kwangchow:

When the August moon is large and glowing,
Once again my lonely heart aches for home.

I can see the waters of the river flowing,
And a small room I call my own.
It has been written few men go wandering,
Without the hand of fate and that alone.

His vision was clouded by tears, blurring the words
on the wall. In his mind's eye he imagined once again
the comfortable room over the pawnshop, and his
beautiful childhood days. *So I'm not the only one who
knows this song. I'm not the only descendant of Huang-
ti forced to become a prisoner in a barbaric land.*

As December passed slowly, Christmas was near
and the island was bathed in a festive air. One day,
when Loone was standing in line waiting to be served,
the cook reached over and slipped him an envelope. As
soon as he returned to the barracks he opened it
and discovered several pages of thin paper. He had
been given detailed information about Chu Ninpo and
Chu Hasan.

That night, when no one was watching, Loone wrote
down many things about himself on a sheet of paper.
The next day in the lunchroom he sneaked it into the
hands of the cook.

A few days later, the inmates were served a special
Christmas dinner. There were turkey with bread dressing, sweet potatoes, vegetables, and pumpkin pies.
The Chinese cook on Angel Island had not devised the
menu; the authorization had fallen into the hands of a
higher official who was American and unfamiliar with
the Chinese taste. The detainees not only hated the
taste of turkey, but in China, both pumpkins and sweet
potatoes were considered food for either the starving
poor or pigs.

The inmates complained as they picked at their
Christmas dinner, wondering why there were no fine
delicacies such as chicken liver, duck feet, or pig in-
testines if Christmas was truly such a big day.

Soon after they had returned to their barracks, the
door opened and one of the officers entered. He wore
a rare smile as he called for attention. "Most of the
staff and the board members will start their three-week

vacation tomorrow, so a few of you will be questioned today. Listen carefully and step forward as I call your names . . .''

He started to read from a list of a dozen names. The twelfth was Fong Loone.

# 16

AFTER MEIPING HAD been dressed and made up, she was taken to Wan Kon. The Lau Ban's beady eyes widened at the sight of her.

"I can guarantee you, my Lau Ban, that Meiping can bring in more money than anyone else . . . if you will leave her completely to me," Limei said quickly before her Lau Ban's desire for Meiping was stirred too far.

Wan Kon looked Meiping over once more. "Well, she looks fine now, but I still don't think she'll ever become a gold mine. Most of our men are short, and their manhood will be threatened if the girl they're in bed with is taller than they."

Limei walked over and stood next to Wan Kon. "We have plenty of girls to work on the second floor. Meiping will be more useful at the bar. There are always plenty of white devils sitting there ordering drinks, and I've been the only one who can talk to them. With a little training I think Meiping can learn to handle them, and with her looks the white devils will be breaking the door down just to be around her. Once she learns to wait on tables, I can teach her how to mix drinks. She can save us a fortune when we fire that imbecile we have now as a bartender."

"Well, as long as she can bring in money, I don't care what she does," Wan Kon said. His interest in Meiping was waning the more he noticed how much she towered over him.

While Meiping was being trained to work in the bar, the three girls who had come from the Pearl with her were put to work. They argued vigorously, claiming that they had agreed only to be maids. Kim Shinma took them to the basement of the house and locked the door behind him. Soon their screams were heard throughout the place. They came out of the basement without any noticeable marks on their faces, but inside, their will to fight was gone. One by one, they were soon sold to the highest bidder. After losing their virginity, they were turned into profit-making commodities for daily customers; they smiled, talked, laughed, and made the customer happy. Only those close to them could tell that they were more like mechanical dolls than women. With one difference: they soon learned to hate men.

As for Meiping, she did rather poorly in the beginning. She dropped trays, spilled drinks, got all the bottles mixed up. But gradually she caught on, and eventually she was able to walk through a crowded bar carrying a large tray of drinks filled to the brim.

By November she still couldn't take orders from the white customers, however, and Limei talked to her: "Meiping, you must learn to speak English. It will ensure your position in the bar and make you more valuable. Study hard, and you'll get to keep your virginity until I find you a man who is kind and gentle. If you keep up the good work, I just might let you choose your own patrons."

Meiping immediately started to learn English, and she had no lack of teachers. They were every single white man who walked through the house's door. She was not afraid to start a conversation with a simple "Hi," although for a long time she had no idea what their answers were. She listened intently, trying to match the sounds of their words to their gestures and expressions; she gradually learned each word's meaning. She put her whole heart into the learning, knowing that her chance of delaying the unavoidable future depended on her mastery of this strange language.

Early in December a young American appeared at the bar in the evening. When he ordered a drink, Meiping was surprised to find herself understanding his complete sentence.

She stared at him for a moment, then shouted in his language, "I understand you! I know what you say! I learn English already! I no need go to bed with man yet!'' She was so excited that she gave the puzzled young man a big hug.

When he left, he left a large tip on the table. From then on Meiping was encouraged not only to speak English with the white customers but also to hug them.

By Christmastime Meiping was able to communicate fairly well in English, except when she ran into a person who talked fast or someone too drunk to speak clearly.

On Christmas Eve the bar was filled to capacity. A large Christmas tree loaded with decorations stood out in the Oriental surroundings. Limei wore a brocade gown in shimmering gold, accented with her finest jewelry. As she roved among the customers she looked like an aged ornament that had been plucked from the tree.

Wan Kon, sitting on a plush leather bar stool, was uncomfortable in the Western suit Limei had insisted he wear. *No wonder the white devils are always anxious to go upstairs and get undressed!* he thought. He took a long drag on his cigarette and began to choke. When he stopped he turned and spat on the red carpet. He looked up at the white customers in such holiday spirits, and wondered about the stories the church people had forced on him. Why should anybody want to celebrate the birthday of a carpenter who was later nailed to a cross and left to die? If the poor bastard couldn't even save himself, how could he be expected to save the world? And his father was supposed to be the biggest Lau Ban in heaven. And what's this talk about his dying for my sins? I wasn't even born when he died. How could he predict I was going to be a sinful man?

Wan Kon's philosophical thoughts were interrupted by a commotion. Seeing every head turning toward the stairway, he followed in turn.

Meiping was standing at the foot of the steps, wearing a peach-colored mandarin gown that hugged her body. A phoenix embroidered with seed pearls covered the front of the gown, matching the pearls on her satin shoes. A touch of red emphasized her full lips, and light rouge had been applied to bring out her high cheekbones. Through the slits in the gown were revealed her shapely legs, covered in sheer black stockings. Her hair flowed like a black waterfall ending at her waist. Like a proud child, she stood smiling, looking over the crowd, wholly unafraid.

Then she entered the room, moving like a willow in the breeze. She made her way between the tables, exaggerating the swing of her hips, playfully slapping the hands that reached out to grab her.

"Mah-lee Klees-mahs!" she shouted to everybody.

Wan Kon licked his lips, his eyes roaming up and down Meiping's body. He looked like a mouse seeing a delicious morsel. Glancing over from the other side of the bar, Limei realized Meiping was in danger. The woman went to the girl quickly. "You'd better go to the other end of the room and talk to that big white man who's sitting alone. I'll handle the customers at this end." She watched Meiping go, sighing with relief when the girl was out of the sight of her Lau Ban.

"Mah-lee Klees-mahs, Mr. David," Meiping said to a big middle-aged Caucasian sitting by himself at the counter having a whiskey.

David Cohen was a familiar customer. The son of an uneducated German Jew, he had become a wealthy jeweler, but he was not a happy man. Rebecca, his wife of twenty years, was a cold, hard woman who created standards no husband could ever measure up to. As a consequence, David was a lonely man, who came often to the House of Wan, sometimes only for food and drinks but sometimes a girl as well.

"Christmas is not really my holiday." He answered Meiping slowly, remembering her difficulty in understanding English. "You see, I'm not a Christian, I'm a Jew."

"You are not a Klees-chen? You are a Jew?" Meiping's eyes widened. "What are Klees-chens and Jews?"

"Well . . ." David looked at the young girl and knew it would be a waste of time trying to explain. "Never mind, just give me another whiskey."

As Meiping poured his drink, David remembered how clumsy and scared she had been the first time he had seen her. She had almost spilled a whole drink in his lap and then nearly cried. Now she looked so sure of herself, and her English was not really all that bad. "How did you learn the language so fast? Who taught you?" he asked.

"You." Meiping set his glass on the counter with a big smile. "You my teacha, like ev-lee-body." She waved her arm in a half-circle, pointing at all the customers in front of her. "Ev-lee-body talk, I listen, and I learn."

"Smart girl!" David lifted his glass to her. "To your future!"

"Future?" She tilted her head, looking at him with her large round eyes.

"A future is like many tomorrows," David said, lifting his glass once more. "May you have many happy tomorrows."

"Ah . . ." Meiping nodded. "Tomo-loo I work. I work many tomo-loos, and I rich girl. I go home to Jasmine Valley, I let my fa-der see my money. He so-lee then for selling me."

"Your father sold you?" David couldn't believe what he had heard. There was a great deal about Chinese culture that was beyond his comprehension.

"Yes." Meiping nodded again. "I too tall, I too ugly. I fight with fa-der, he no want me."

"Do you hate your father for doing that?" David said, eyeing the beautiful young woman sharply. He was six-foot-four and well-built, and in his eyes she was very small and very helpless.

"Hate?" Meiping shook her head. "I ang-lee with fa-der sometime, but no hate. Daughters no hate faders. No fa-der, daughter not born."

Such a simple philosophy! David stared at her and thought of his three sons. When they had been small and he was busy, their mother had shaped their personalities like a sculptor shaped wet clay. The youngest was now fifteen, and all three were like their mother in every way. They made it clear that they were glad to be rich, but not particularly proud of the fact that their father was merely an uneducated merchant. "I have three arrogant bastards for sale myself. Know anybody in China interested in white slavery? Oh, yes, and the mother of the bastards will be thrown in for free!" He took a large swallow of the liquor.

"What you say? I no understand."

He smiled at the wide-eyed girl with her innocent face and well-shaped body. As an experienced jeweler, he knew he was looking at a piece of uncut precious stone. If given a chance, could she be turned into a multifaceted gem? He peered at her closely. "Am I saying your name correctly, Meiping?"

Each of the American customers had his own way of pronouncing Meiping's name, and none of them had ever said it accurately. In order to save the white man's pink faces, Meiping had never corrected them. She was about to nod yes like she always did, but the sincerity on David's face made her change her mind. "Well . . ." She hesitated. "Meiping honest. Meiping tell the tooth . . . the tooth is, you say it funny like all white man say names in Chinese."

David started to laugh. It felt so good to laugh!

Meiping laughed with him, and from across the room Limei saw them. With her experience, she could read David's thoughts. She knew that sooner or later Meiping would have to be broken in by someone, and David Cohen just might be the right one.

# 17

PAUL EDDINGTON WAS twenty-five when he arrived in south China as a Baptist minister. His mission was in a small village not far from Kwangchow, and the villagers soon referred to him as Yung Mo Shih, the foreign minister. They grew to love him because he was eager to listen to their opinions and philosophy and beliefs, and never forced his religion on them, unlike so many other Christian missionaries.

A year after his arrival, there was another Boxer rebellion against the foreigners. One morning a small group of teenagers entered the village. The leader, no more than sixteen, came waving a long curved sword, marching down the middle of the street. He wore gray pants and a white jacket open to the waist; both were bloodstained. What's more, a red bandanna was tied around his head. He was caught up in the power of killing and was eager to find another victim.

An aged village man hobbled forward and bowed deeply to the young boy. "How may I help you, my honorable young sir?"

"Who the hell are you?" the boy jeered. "Get out of my way before I cut you in two!" He swung the blade in an arc and laughed at the old man.

"Sir, this unworthy person is the spokesman for the village. How may I help you?" Again the old man bowed deeply.

"Are there any white devils in your village?" the boy asked threateningly.

"There was a Yung Mo Shih, but we ran him off, and he should be far gone." The old man bowed his head.

The boy didn't trust the old man. He gave orders to search the village.

Hiding inside a well, Paul stood on a couple of slippery stones with his arms spread out, pushing against the curved wall. He could hear the commotion outside: the screams when houses were burned, the wails when animals were slain, the pleas of mothers as their girls were raped, the crying of children when their parents were tortured. He had to force himself to stay in the well, saying to himself repeatedly that by going out he would only get himself killed.

When the Boxers were ready to leave, they decided to have a drink of the well water. When one of them dropped a bucket into the well, Paul felt a sharp blow on his head. When the bucket hit the water he heard a splash, and as the bucket was being pulled back, he felt the rope rubbing against him, becoming wedged between his legs. Carefully he reached down and freed it. On its way up, the rim of the bucket caught him under the nose; the pain brought tears to his eyes. For a while he almost lost his hold. He could taste blood and had trouble breathing.

When the rebels were gone, the villagers hurried to the well. "Yung Mo Shih," they called. "Grab the rope! We're pulling you up now."

The rebellion was put down, and Paul's superiors wrote to ask how many heathens had been converted to Christianity. Paul replied, "Very few Christians, but many friends. And I'm learning a lot."

Shortly thereafter, he was replaced by another minister, who promised to use the fire of hell to convert the heathens. Paul returned to his home in San Francisco. He was assigned to work in a church not far from Chinatown, and his love for the Chinese took him to Clay Street, Grant Avenue, and Pacific Street often. Now that he had returned home, his constant companion was his niece Laurie, who shared his love for the Orient.

One day, when he was in a furniture store owned by the Sung Wu Company, admiring an imported teakwood desk, Sung Tinwei approached him. As they talked, the conversation led to the fact that the old gentleman was looking for an English tutor for his young nephew.

On a misty December morning several months later, Paul Eddington and Sung Quanming sat across a large desk in the well-furnished study. Quanming put his book down and looked out the window. "Paul, how do you say *wuh* in English?"

" 'Fog' or 'mist,' " Paul answered, then wrote the words in Quanming's notebook.

"Thanks. In China, when we are confused, we say, *'Yee-to-wah-shua,'* which means, "My head is buried in thick mist.' It's been two months now since you started to give me English lessons, and I feel as though I'm buried deeply. English must be the most difficult language in the whole world!"

"You are doing very well." Paul gave his student an encouraging smile. "Plus, your pronunciation is good. Unlike most Chinese, you don't have trouble separating R's from L's, or S's from TH's. Two months is a very short time; you need *nie-sheen,* patience."

"I'll try." Quanming picked up a steamed bun from the tray and took a large bite. "It's just that at times I feel so dumb," he mumbled with his mouth full.

"Wait!" Paul raised a hand. "I'm hired to teach you good manners as well. You've just made several mistakes. One, you must not talk with your mouth full. Two, instead of biting into the bun, you should use your fingers to break off a small piece, then put it into your mouth. Three, a gentleman should not chew with his mouth open."

"But why?" Quanming stopped eating and asked with a puzzled expression, "Food is to be enjoyed, right? If you have to worry about so many rules, how can you have any enjoyment?"

"I understand your point of view, but each society has a set of expectations that must be met by its people. In China, I used to take large bites, talk with my mouth full, and spit the seeds and bones on the floor. But if you don't want to be considered a barbarian in this country, you'll better learn your manners." Paul smiled and added, "Your first test is tomorrow night at the Christmas party. Some of San Francisco's most powerful people will be there."

"Are you coming?" Quanming asked. "I need your
. . . what do you call it?"

"Moral support," Paul said. "Yes, I'll be there,
and my niece Laurie will come as my partner."

"Partner? You are in business with your niece?"
Quanming asked. "What kind of company do you two
have?"

Paul began to laugh. Seeing the confused look on
Quanming's face, he explained, "The word 'partner'
has many meanings . . ." And the lesson continued.


Meiping was taking a nap when someone knocked
on the door. "Come in," she called.

Limei entered with a smile, came to the bed, and
handed Meiping a package. Sitting up in bed, Meiping
opened it. Her face lit up at the sight of a brand-new
robe. It was of a multicolored material that was light
and thin, like a butterfly's transparent wings.

And then Meiping's face dropped. She threw the
robe on the bedside chair without thanking Limei, and
after a long silence she said, "Do you give every girl
something like this on her first working night?"

Limei sat on the bed and answered calmly, "No. I
never give them anything, whether it's their first night
or not. I don't feel the same way toward the other girls
as I do toward you."

"Thanks for the special favor!" Meiping said sarcastically, turning away from Limei.

The older woman sighed and placed a hand on the
girl's head. "You may think I'm a mean bitch now,
because I'm pushing you into the meat market, but you
must understand, Meiping, that even if you were my
real daughter, you'd still have to do what you must do.
We are Wan Lau Ban's property: we have no choice."
The woman continued with a sad smile, "Well, your
fate is much better than mine. David Cohen is a kind
man and he likes you, and I know you like him too."

The sorrow in Limei's voice touched Meiping. She
turned back to face Limei without trying to hide the
tears on her cheeks, "I'm . . ." she whispered in a
trembling voice, ". . . I'm very scared."

Limei threw her arms around Meiping's shoulders and brought the girl to her bosom. "I know you are, child." She dabbed the tears away with a handkerchief. "But you don't have to be. You see, David is an experienced man. He'll be patient."

Limei soon left, and Meiping took a bath. When she stepped out of the tub, she looked at her body in the mirror, wondering if tomorrow she would look different. She picked up a bottle of perfume and sprayed herself with the scent of the night-blooming jasmine. She closed her eyes and imagined herself flying back to Jasmine Valley, looking at the village from the hilltop. *I wish I was back in China . . . I wish I didn't have to grow up. I don't want to become a woman . . . not yet.*

She opened her eyes, wiped away a tear, then put on the robe. She walked to the outer room and sat in front of the vanity table. She was starting to brush her hair when there was a knock. "Come in," she answered without looking around. She saw in the mirror, David.

Dressed in a light gray suit and a blue tie, he looked tall and handsome. Her heart started to beat faster, not because she was frightened but because she was stirred by him.

"Meiping," he called softly, walking toward her.

She had never been shy in front of him before, but she was now. She smiled at him in the mirror; in the mirror she saw herself blush.

He came to stand behind her and bent down to kiss her on the neck. "Meiping, my beautiful little Meiping," he whispered. He then took the hairbrush away from her, laid it on the vanity table, and lifted her up as if she weighed nothing. He held her in his arms for a while, and she buried her face against his chest, trembling. He kissed her on the top of her head, then carried her to the bed.

He laid her down gently, then sat beside her, looking at her with his hands resting on her shoulders. Beside her pillow, a lamp with a soft pink shade stood on the bedside table. The light bathed Meiping's flushed face in a soft glow. She looked up at him hesitantly, her lips parted, her breasts rising and falling quickly under her transparent robe. "You are so beautiful, Meiping," David said, and bent down to kiss her on the mouth.

Until this moment they had always met in the bar, in front of many people. There had been nothing remotely like a kiss. When his soft warm lips touched hers, she felt her apprehension and fear begin to dissolve. As he started running the tip of his tongue over her mouth, she felt something strange begin to happen. From somewhere inside, a ball of fire began to rise and spin, sending powerful heat waves to every part of her body. She closed her eyes tightly, circled her arms around his neck, pulling him close, kissing him back. She tried to call his name, but her mouth was covered by his. She could not find her voice. All that came out was a soft moan.

While he kissed her, his hands gently stroked her hair, her face, her neck and shoulders, then moved down to remove her robe. His lips left her mouth and followed the path paved by his hands. She soon lay naked, feeling him touching and kissing her body. She started to tingle with sensations she had never experienced before, as if that fire ball had now multiplied in number, burning inside of her, setting her aglow.

"Don't be afraid, my little Meiping. I will not hurt you," he said softly. Then he began to take off his clothes.

She opened her eyes just a little to see his naked body sliding next to hers, and then quickly closed them again. She felt his hand touching her between her legs, and unknowingly let out a soft cry. As he probed and teased patiently, his fingers were like a thousand magic fans kindling a spark, which soon turned into a roaring flame. She twisted her hips on the bed, lifting herself on her heels, feeling that at any moment she was going to leap out of her skin. She wanted him to stop, while knowing that if he actually did, she would die.

"David, David!" She called, turning her head on the pillow from side to side. She felt him climbing over her and opened her eyes once more. She saw him lowering himself toward her. She smiled at him faintly and closed her eyes.

She felt him entering her, first just a little, and he moved slowly; she felt no pain. Then he gradually began to go in deeper and faster, and finally with a savage thrust he penetrated her body. Feeling the pain, she screamed.

"Meiping, my darling little Meiping," she heard his voice soothing and comforting beside her ear, and the pain changed into pleasure. In movements independent of her thoughts, her body reached up to meet his. "Oh, David!" she called again.

She had no idea what was happening, only that she was living through the most wonderful moment in her life, a moment of combined agony and pleasure. She wouldn't mind if it lasted forever. He pumped faster and faster, and eventually he shouted her name and filled her with his orgasm.

At that instant Meiping saw herself jumping off the cliff in Jasmine Valley. But instead of falling, she flew higher and higher, like the wild geese she had envied all her life.

She didn't drift back to earth until much later, and when she did, she realized that David was lying beside her. She moved her face very close to his, looked into his eyes, and whispered in his ear, "David, I liked it . . . it feels so good. Please tell me, is it always like this?"

The Sung Wu Company Christmas party was held in the Chinese Pagoda, one of the company's many holdings and the finest restaurant in Chinatown. The decor was a pleasant blend of East and West; the waiters wore Chinese uniforms, while the maître d' was in a black suit and tie. Moreover, Tinwei and Da-chung had donned Chinese silk robes, whereas Quanming looked tall and handsome in a Western suit.

The Americans arrived early, the gentlemen dressed in tuxedos, their ladies in floor-length brightly colored gowns. The Chinese, in satin and silk robes and laden with gold and jade, made sure they were at least an hour late. Arriving on time would mean they were anxious to enjoy a free meal, and they would lose their honorable face.

The three hosts stood at the entrance of the banquet room greeting their guests. Tinwei and Da-chung welcomed people with "Lay-ho" and a bow. Quanming, wide-eyed and eager to practice his English, met every new arrival with a firm handshake and a loud and clear "How do you do?"

Quanming needed all of his willpower to keep his eyes off the American ladies' strapless gowns that exposed an ample amount of their white breasts. He looked at all the low-cut necklines with curiosity: *I don't think gowns like these would work with Chinese girls. They have nothing to hold them up!*

Just then his eye was caught by a young girl in a long yellow dress. Her hair was red as flame. As she advanced toward him in the long greeting line, there was something special in the way she carried herself. *Her yellow gown looks like the home of the golden sun. Her red hair is the source of all the fire on earth. I wonder what her face looks like.* He couldn't see her face because she was talking to a man behind her in line. And then she turned, and he saw the man behind her was Paul Eddington.

"Paul!" Excited to see his teacher, Quanming called, waved, and when it was Paul's turn to be greeted, Quanming took the teacher's hand, held on to it, and wouldn't let go. "Your face is the first familiar one!" he said, pumping Paul's hand up and down.

"Quanming, I would like for you to meet my niece Laurie," Paul said, trying to free himself. He turned to the girl in the yellow gown. "Laurie, this is the bright young man I've been telling you about, Sung Quanming."

"How do you do?" Quanming mumbled as he bowed.

The girl extended her hand and greeted him with a warm smile. For Quanming, that smile instantly brightened up the entire banquet hall. He stared at her, feeling as though he were standing in the warmth of the sun on a beautiful spring day. He looked into her green eyes. He remembered seeing such green color only once before, when he had been in a museum, admiring a fine art object made of translucent jade.

". . . and we'll see you later, Quanming." Paul's voice seemed to have come from far, far away. Quanming blinked, found himself holding Laurie's hand, keeping all the guests waiting in line.

He dropped her hand, feeling the rising warmth on his face. "Yes, Paul . . . and it was a pleasure meeting you, Miss Eddington," he murmured.

"Please call me Laurie." She smiled at him once more, then walked away.

Quanming gazed after her while shaking hands with the other guests. The guests were many, and among them was Wu Da-chung's family.

Mrs. Wu was short and fat, dressed in silk and wearing a great deal of jewelry. She was followed by three shy, pale-faced boys in tailored suits, and hiding behind them was a slight girl in a jade-green robe. Like her brothers, she refused to lift her eyes to look at Quanming directly. Why do my people like to avoid eye contact? Quanming thought. It's so irritating the way they study you when you are not watching! Then he almost laughed out loud at the sight of a huge red bow perching precariously on top of the girl's head.

Smiling at Quanming, Mrs. Wu pulled her daughter forward with a jerk. "A-lin is a very good cook. You must come to our house and taste her food." As soon as the mother loosened her grip, the girl quickly escaped, the red bow bobbing above her like an injured bird trying to take flight.

"My daughter is modest," Mrs. Wu explained, "but will make someone a fine wife—" The woman obviously had much more to say, but behind her the guests started to cough impatiently. Mrs. Wu reluctantly moved on.

There were over two hundred people, each table accommodating ten. The most influential guests had the place of honor facing the door—a centuries-old Chinese tradition based on the principle that should an assassination take place, those facing the door would be the first to spot danger. Quanming, Tinwei, and Da-chung each sat as host on one of the three head tables, and Quanming found himself sandwiched between two middle-aged American couples. He kept looking across the room at Paul and Laurie sitting with some of the workers of the company; he wished he could join them. Paul met his eyes and lifted his glass in a silent toast. Laurie also looked his way and smiled. As Quanming smiled back, he felt a hot blush rise from his throat and stain his cheeks.

When he looked away from Laurie, he was still smiling. Then the smile froze on his face. He saw his uncle looking at him from another table, and on his uncle's face was such a troubled, angered expression.

Uncle Tinwei is upset because I'm not acting as a good host! Quanming thought. Quickly he turned to the guests at his table.

There were no other Chinese at his table, so he started to explain to the Americans each of the many exotic dishes being served. He had a good deal of trouble finding the English words he needed, and as he watched them picking at their food, he wanted desperately to tell them that it was not poison.

"How long have you been in our country?" the man sitting on his left asked slowly and loudly, hoping his young host could understand.

"I have been in your country a little over two months," Quanming answered, emphasizing the word "your."

The man's wife leaned past her husband. "You speak pretty good English, young fellow, and you're a lot better-looking than most of the runts around Chinatown. Are you all Chinese?"

"As far as I know, madam," Quanming answered politely.

The woman on his right picked up the conversation. "You look very different from the ones the good reverend and I have to deal with. You seem so clean."

Her husband explained, "I am a minister, and we

have been involved in charity at times. We sure have had our share of handling your poor, unfortunate countrymen.''

Quanming wished he had never learned to understand English. He tried to bite his tongue, but still the words escaped: ''It must have made you sick, sir. That was exactly how I felt on the ship when I saw my first white man. The smell coming from the white sailors' dirty bodies was just awful.''

The American guests looked at their young host, exchanged looks, and the atmosphere became chilly. The man on Quanming's left finally broke the silence by lifting his glass to Quanming. ''How do you say 'Bottoms up' in Chinese?''

''Gum-bay,'' Quanming answered, picking up his drink.

''Gum-bay! Gum-bay!'' the man said, and the others followed. No one talked for a while, occupied in eating and drinking.

After many more Gum-bays, the man excused himself and headed for the rest room. His wife moved over and sat next to Quanming. ''Sure am enjoying everything, young fellow,'' she said, leaning over so that a good part of her breasts protruded over the top of her gown. ''To be honest, I was not too happy to come here. I was afraid I'd end up eating dogs or monkeys!'' She roared with laughter, her breasts bouncing up and down. She gave Quanming a wink.

When the husband returned, the woman did not return to her chair. She had decided to remain next to this handsome young Chinese.

Quanming almost dropped his glass when he felt her leg rubbing against his and then her hand resting on his thigh. He gave out a gasp when the hand started to move slowly up and down his leg. From the corner of his eye he saw the woman calmly eating and drinking. He couldn't move. He didn't know what to do but to blame his teacher. Why hadn't Paul included this in their lessons?

The hand found what it was looking for, and Quanming let out a moan. Fortunately, someone was shouting "Gum-bay" at the time, and the moan went unheard.

Quanming was disgusted with himself when he realized that his sexual hunger had given him an erection in spite of this old woman's cowlike appearance. He felt himself throbbing in her hand, and saw from the corner of his eye again that this was much to her delight. There was no way for him to get up now; the bulge in his trousers would certainly be obvious to everyone. He sat looking around the table with a caricature grin on his face, knowing that any minute he would be in serious trouble.

Finally he jerked his body toward the guest on his right, at the same time reaching down and removing the lady's hand. He crossed his legs and waited for his penis to return to normal. He then jumped up, mumbled an excuse, and walked away. *I must ask Paul in the next class: what's the American way of handling a situation like this?*

He found an empty seat at the table where the three Wu boys sat, and stayed there for the rest of the party. He talked to the three young men, but trying to get them to talk was like trying to get milk out of an old dried-up cow. But at least, with them, he was safe.

The meal, after many succulent dishes, came to an end. Soon thereafter, the guests started leaving, and Quanming and his uncles went to bid them good-bye.

When Paul and Laurie appeared in front of Quanming, Laurie gave him her hand. Behind her was a door leading to the terrace, and the city of San Francisco lay beneath with a million lights shining like a glittering net. The lights made Quanming dizzy. He took Laurie's warm hand with both of his hands and kept it there. He looked into her eyes, and she looked back with a steady gaze. Their eyes searched each other deeply in a silent embrace.

"Quanming!" He jumped at his uncle's sharp voice. "Are you deaf? Miss Wu has said good-bye to you three times, and you haven't even answered her once!"

"I'm sorry." Dropping Laurie's hand, Quanming looked down and saw Wu A-lin with her big red bow.

He caught a glimpse of her mouselike face: she was trying to smile. "Thanks for coming to the party, Miss Wu," he said to her, and when he looked up from the red bow, Laurie was gone.

An hour later, Quanming was back in his room, in his pajamas, lying in bed with his head propped on his hands. He was wide-awake. He could hear from afar the fog horns in the bay, sending out mournful warnings to the ships at sea.

"Laurie, Laurie . . ." he whispered. Then he heard a soft rap on his door.

Sung Tinwei didn't pay attention to the surprised look on his nephew's face. He walked softly across the room on his cotton slippers and sank into a chair. "I'm very tired, Quanming, but I need to talk to you."

Quanming saw the deep concern in the old man's eyes and wondered what had put it there. "Shall I pour you a cup of tea, Uncle?"

"No, thank you." Tinwei pointed to the chair next to his and told Quanming to sit. "I've heard good things tonight that made me proud of you, but I also saw some things at the party that disturbed me greatly."

"Disturbed? Did I do something wrong, Uncle?" Quanming asked, puzzled. "I tried my best to be a good host—"

Sung Tinwei interrupted the young man, "That girl, Paul's niece." His voice turned cold. "I couldn't help noticing how you looked at her, and how shamelessly she looked back at you, instead of looking away like a good girl should. I didn't like what I saw."

But . . . why?" Quanming started to blush. "Is it very wrong to look at a beautiful girl?" He tried to smile at his uncle. "Didn't you look at them when you were my age?"

"That's beside the point!" his uncle cried. "Let me tell you, if you should let looking lead to liking and even deeper feelings for that red-haired white cow, you'll get hurt!"

"Hurt? Who's going to hurt me, Uncle?"

Tinwei let out a long sigh. "You are a naive boy

from the Pearl, and Laurie is an American girl raised in the city of San Francisco. Her experience in life is ten times greater than yours, and you are no match for her—''

Quanming couldn't help interrupting. "Match? Laurie and I are not having a duel.''

"Be quiet!" Sung Tinwei looked at Quanming angrily. "Listen to yourself! You've been in America only two months, and already you are arguing with your elder. What I'm telling you is for your own good. I don't want you to have anything to do with Laurie Eddington or any other American girl! Do I make myself clear?''

Quanming couldn't believe what he saw. Tinwei's kind face was now a picture of fury. "Yes . . ." he answered. "But may I ask . . . why?''

His uncle's answer came quickly: "Because you are my brother's son, and I love you too much to see your heart get broken.''

"You mean . . . you think Laurie Eddington will hurt me? You know something about her? Is she a bad girl?''

"I know nothing about this Laurie." Sung Tinwei left the chair and started for the door. "But I do know American girls. They are all the same. They like to play games. You are not heartless enough to play with them.'' At the door, the man turned and gave the boy an encouraging smile. "If you are ready for girls, why not go pay Wu A-lin a visit? With a good old-fashioned Chinese girl, you'll be safe.''

# 18

STARTING EARLY IN December, the workers at Camerano's started getting caught up in a holiday mood. Every morning some were unable to work due to a monstrous hangover, and Fachai ended up putting in long hours doing their chores. By Christmas Eve he was exhausted. His spirits were boosted a little, though, when he received his pay and found, to his surprise, a few extra dollars as a Christmas bonus.

He slowly climbed the ladder to his attic room at the day's end and collapsed on the makeshift bed. Lying there, he looked at the improvements he had made during the past two months. The dark walls had been painted white, and a red paper lantern was hanging from the ceiling. Pasted here and there were gold Chinese characters written on red papers, works of an old man in Chinatown.

He was too tired to cook another fish head. He had a sudden urge to go to Tong-jen-gai for a meal in one of the restaurants. Wearily he got out of bed, washed up, and put on his newly acquired Western-style clothes; each piece was his pride and delight. He dressed himself in a blue shirt, a brown pair of pants, a bright yellow vest, and a scarlet-red tie. He pulled on a pair of thick white socks and then stepped into his black leather shoes. He didn't forget to put on his gray felt hat. He started down the stairs, idly wishing Leahi could see how great he looked, and the thought of her dampened his spirits. *If you were here, Leahi, we'd make such a handsome pair!*

From Pacific Street he walked through Portsmouth Square. He did pass the Sung Wu Company, but didn't know that was its name because he couldn't read the sign. He marveled at its splendor, and wondered if Quanming was living in a place half as nice as this.

He walked to the water's edge, then stood in the wind to watch the whitecaps.

The night air was cold. He stuck his hands into his pockets and rounded his shoulders against the chill. Dim lights were shining far away, reminding him of the lanterns gleaming from the fishing boats along the Pearl. In his mind's eye he saw the ancient willows along the bank. He quickly turned away from the bay to continue his journey.

On Grant Avenue, as he passed the red brick building of the House of Wan, he saw two young men standing in front of the black doors. He couldn't help overhearing one telling the other:

"It costs a week's pay to screw one of those whores! Can you believe it? I wish I had the money . . ."

Fachai now knew what kind of place the tall building was. Embarrassed, he hurried on. He was very hungry, and could think of nothing but pig feet and chicken necks at this moment. He reached Clay Street.

Without being able to read the sign, he knew the name of the place: Yung Fa Restaurant. He had been here before, had liked both the food and the prices. He decided to treat himself to a top-notch meal.

Yung Fa's small dining room was packed with customers. The place reverberated with the joys of eating, and the aroma of food floated on layers of thick cigarette smoke that filled the air.

Chu Ninpo was moving quickly on his short legs, taking orders, serving food, and bussing tables. Behind a greasy curtain in the kitchen, Chu Hasan was cooking over several woks and multilayered bamboo steamers.

"Hey, Ninpo," one of the customers shouted. "For an adopted son, that boy is not doing much. Tell me, does he ever get out of that chair?"

"Well . . ." Chu Ninpo turned to look at the corner table and whispered to the customer, "The poor child was confined on that Angel Island for almost two months, and just got here three days ago. He needs to rest."

Another old man said to Chu, "He's not resting. He's bending over a notebook. What is he writing all the time?"

"You old fool! He's not writing," Ninpo answered, "he's drawing. That boy can draw anything."

"Drawing? You're going to serve pictures in your restaurant? Does he do anything useful?" asked the third customer.

"Look, he comes from a good family," Chu said. "His old man owned a pawnshop, and the boy is not used to hard work."

"You mean, you paid a thousand bucks for a pair of helping hands, and end up having an artist with a good appetite? I saw your old woman bringing to his table one dish after another. And I also saw that when the dishes were emptied, it was you who had to clear them away!"

Chu shrugged and started for the kitchen. On his way there he was caught by another customer. "What did the child say about this country? I like to hear the newcomers praising the Land of the Gold Mountains. It always makes us old-timers feel lucky to be here."

Chu shook his head and leaned closer to the man. He had been defending his adopted son, but now a trace of unhappiness showed in his voice. "We picked him up from the boat that took him from the island. We hired a wagon because my old woman wanted him to look at the city. She kept on pointing out things for him to see, but he closed his eyes as soon as he got into the wagon, and opened them only briefly now and then rather unwillingly. He said that he has seen better views before, that nothing is worth seeing, from what he saw, that he thinks Tong-jen-gai looks like a poor man's district compared with the city of Kwangchow!"

The customer's jaw dropped. Chu shook his head. He now sounded hurt. "I guess I'm too old to understand the young. When we reached home, the kid walked away from the wagon empty-handed, and I had to carry his luggage all the way upstairs to his room." He raised his voice, now unable to conceal his anger. "If it weren't for my silly old woman wanting this kid so much, I'd send him back to his precious Kwang-chow on the next boat!"

"Give the boy time, Ninpo," one of the men said, trying to comfort the old man. "He'll learn to adjust. Someday he'll learn the business, and you'll be able to retire."

Chu Ninpo shook his head pessimistically. "I'm too old to have silly dreams. The boy thinks Yung Fa is a dump, and his room upstairs is not good enough for him. He doesn't talk much to us, as if we were not up to his level. Besides sleeping and eating, he has done only two things: look at a string of pearls and draw pictures of people he sees." Shaking his head, Chu picked up a stack of dirty dishes and walked away.

Entering Yung Fa, Fachai stood in the doorway and searched for an empty table. In the far corner he saw a familiar fragile little figure sitting by himself.

"Loone! Fong Loone! My little brother!"

## 19

In China, Dr. Sun Yat-sen, father of the new republic, decided to withdraw from the political world, leaving Yuan Shih-kai to carry on the new government. Yuan, once the favorite of the dowager queen, soon became discontent with his position as president; he decided to become an emperor with absolute power. Those who had helped to establish the new China rebelled at his proposal, and a bloodbath followed.

In the meantime, the Pearl River continued its endless journey toward the sea. People in the villages knew little of what was taking place, since, as usual, they were busy struggling to stay alive.

Early in the spring of 1913, a drought descended on southern China. Like a giant sickle it swept mercilessly through the population, leaving in its path starvation, death, and sorrow. By midsummer none of the villages along the Pearl had escaped its strokes.

Sitting in a small hut, in Willow Place, old scholar Hsu gazed out his open door at the thirsty earth. He was small, with a thin frame. His gray hair was tied back into a braid, but his eyes, in contrast to his ancient features, gleamed bright and alive from below his bushy eyebrows.

Many years ago he had wanted to serve in the Imperial Palace, but though his knowledge was vast, his prose magnificent, each time he approached the emperor's examiners for his tests, his terror transformed him into a stuttering fool. After a few unsuccessful attempts he decided to give up his ambition and retreated to this peaceful village, devoting his days to teaching the illiterate villagers. Occasionally he was paid in food, but most of the time his services were free.

His view was interrupted by the form of a young

girl standing in the doorway. Her belly protruded in a mound; she was obviously in the last stage of pregnancy.

"Mrs. Li," the scholar greeted her warmly. "Another letter from your husband?" He offered her a chair.

The young woman nodded, then wearily took the chair. She handed him several sheets of paper but held tightly to the envelope. The scholar looked at her and wondered how a young girl could lose her glow so completely within only a few months. It had been at the end of the previous year when he had first seen Li Leahi. She had come with her in-laws to listen to the letter from Li Fachai. She was quite beautiful then, with her round face and childlike smile. Now the sparkle had vanished from her cheeks, and looking at her was like watching a flower losing its radiance. With a sigh the scholar squinted at the characters and slowly began to read:

My Dear Family,

I am now a restaurant worker. The work will be less tiring than that in the fish market, and the pay more. I am a very lucky man.

Fong Loone is one of the young friends I made aboard the iron ship. Since then he has been adopted by an old couple named Chu, and now his name is Chu Fong Loone. Mr. Chu owns a restaurant, and is kind of old. The old man talked to me yesterday and told me how tired he and his wife are, and I offered to help him without pay. He was touched by my offer and gave me a job as his full-time helper. He'll set things straight for me with the labor contractor and my previous employer.

You'll find five dollars in this envelope, and next time I will send more. I'll not have to pay rent anymore, because Loone said that I could share his room over the restaurant. I'll put some money in the bank here, saving it to buy a fishing boat. I don't want to work too long as a cook and waiter; I am a fisherman.

Many people are waiting in line to write letters home, so I must go. Burn an extra stick of incense in front of the Great Buddha, as thanks for granting me good luck.

Scholar Hsu laid down the letter. "Do you wish to answer him now?"

"Yes," Leahi said, taking the letter back and holding it to her heart. "Tell him that we are happy for him . . . tell him that things at home are fine . . . tell him that we are all in good health."

The old scholar looked at the young woman. "Are you not going to let him know the truth?"

Shaking her head, Leahi tried to blink away her tears. The drought had killed her father and little A-fu. Grandfather Li had been another victim. Both her father-in-law and mother-in-law were very sick right now, and there was little chance that they would recover. What's more, during the drought the mail delivery had been delayed, and when Fachai's money didn't arrive in time, her silver earrings and Mrs. Li's ring had been sold to a servant in the landlord's house for medicine. "You may tell Fachai that I pass the Pearl River each day . . ." she said hoarsely. "Tell him that the Pearl's water is running shallowly, and the willows have wilted. But every night, when there is a moon, I always stand under the leafless branches and look up at the sky . . ." Her voice broke. She sobbed quietly for a while, then with an effort pulled herself together. "Tell him that I remember our promises . . . tell him that I miss him so very, very much."

She got up slowly. Taking a coin out of her pocket, she placed it on the table, turned, and left.

"No! You don't have to pay me!" scholar Hsu yelled, but the young woman was already gone.

Leahi walked quickly down the path. The summer wind dried her tears, for she was too exhausted to even raise a hand to her eyes. Breathing hard, she stopped at the side of the road and gently patted her huge belly. The baby was kicking, and the little pokes brought a smile to her weary face. "Your Baba has sent us money," she whispered lovingly. "Mama will be able to buy something to eat now."

She continued her journey home, and just as she saw the house, a piercing pain shot through her lower back, causing her to drop to her knees.

When the pain subsided, she struggled to her feet, started to walk again. But after only a few steps the pain struck once more, followed by a burst of water that ran down her legs.

Someone passing heard her scream and helped her back to the Lis' house. Her in-laws were too weak to help, but the neighborhood women quickly came and began to prepare her for the arrival of her child.

For hours she lay naked from the waist down, covered by an old sheet. Time seemed to stand still. She bit her lip to hold back the screams, but then she had to give in to the intense pain. Each time she cried out, the old women clicked their tongues and shook their heads in disapproval.

"There's no need for all this noise!" an old hag hissed. "We've all been through this with far less noise."

"The younger generation can't do anything without complaining," another old one sighed. "When I had my first, it was out in the field. I popped it out, cleaned it up, strapped it to my back, and went right back to work."

Though Leahi tried her best to be brave, the contractions came with such power, she couldn't hold back more screams. Finally a woman peeked under the sheet and yelled, "Here comes the little thing! Push! That's it! Don't just lie there!"

Leahi tried—she felt like she was being ripped open. She sank her teeth into her lip and tasted blood.

"A boy!" a woman yelled.

Leahi heard a slap, followed by a child's cry.

"Fachai," Leahi called with her eyes closed and tears streaming down her cheeks, "please come home to see our son!"

In White Stone, the Mas' household was in turmoil.

"Go find me enough sweet rice for the festival, or you'll be sold!" Ma Yoto shouted while sitting in bed,

propped up on three embroidered pillows and covered
by a silk quilt. A pink shawl was wrapped around her
shoulders, and her hair was tied back with a purple
scarf. Contrasting with her white skin, it gave her face
the look of a porcelain doll.

A wooden tray with carved legs rested on her lap,
filled with delicacies. The cook, an old man, stood at
the foot of the bed with his head bowed, his eyes intent
on the patterns on the rug. "Tai-tai," he addressed his
mistress in a low voice, "there's this drought, and no
sweet rice is to be found—"

A teacup filled with hot tea was thrown at the man,
accompanied by Yoto's piercing voice: "I'm not interested in the stupid drought! I want my sweet rice! Now,
get out before I lose my temper!"

Bowing deeply, the old man backed out the door,
not daring to wipe off the tea leaves or check to see if
he was burned until he was out of her sight.

A young girl, hired only recently after the death of
Yoto's old maid, remained beside the bed and quickly
poured her mistress another cup of tea. The girl's
hands were shaking in fear that her lady's anger would
now shift to her.

To the maid's relief, the young master, Mr. Ma Tsai-
tu, appeared.

He was wearing a dark blue satin robe and a pair of
black leather shoes. Like all the rich, who had no need
to work in the sun, he was very pale. Since he had
rarely lifted anything much heavier than a pair of
chopsticks, his body was soft and delicate. He looked
at the maid's curvy young figure with interest, then
turned to his wife. "Did someone dare to upset my
lovely Yoto?"

Yoto tried to smile, but didn't quite succeed. "This
is my first festival as a married lady, and I must have
sweet rice for the cakes. I don't want to lose face in
front of all the relatives and have all our friends laugh
at me." While talking, she picked up a large shrimp
from the tray. Chewing it slowly, she continued, "Tsai-
tu, my husband, I really don't know what to do." As
she ate, tears filled her eyes.

Ma Tsai-tu hated to see women cry. They were so much prettier when they smiled or laughed. All the young maids cried after he had deflowered them—what a hateful sight! Only the singsong girls and prostitutes knew how to behave properly. He glanced at his gold watch, searching for an excuse to leave and go join his friends. They were all like him: rich, educated, with nothing to do. They would carry their caged birds to secluded gardens and talk about inconsequential matters—things such as a game of chess or a verse of a poem.

Restless, Ma Tsai-tu looked at his watch again. "I'll go ask around. Maybe some of my friends can help with the sweet rice—"

There was a soft knock on the door, and the cook entered. The young master hurried out as soon as the servant started to report that some sweet rice had been found.

As the old man talked, Yoto looked dreamily at a yellow finch out the window beside her bed. She had stayed within the courtyards of the mansion since her marriage, and it had been quite a while since she had seen a tree or a bush that was not neatly trimmed by her gardener. Something was stirred inside her by the sight of this free little bird; she suddenly wanted to fly beyond the garden walls and take a look at the outside world.

". . . and I'm on my way to the mill to have it ground into flour, Tai-tai," the cook was saying.

"Wait!" she yelled. "Tell them to get the wagon ready. I'm going to the mill myself."

The maid started to dress Yoto in her new summer clothes: a soft pink blouse and a long white skirt, both covered with embroidered yellow butterflies.

In the bright sunlight, as the wagon proceeded slowly toward the countryside, Yoto sat under a parasol held by her maid. She had not known what had happened to White Stone in the past few months until this moment.

She saw the parched earth, the dead trees, the lifeless fields. The chimneys on the farm houses betrayed no smoke coming from cooking fires. The villagers were in rags that barely covered their emaciated bodies. Most of the children were naked, and at the sight of her wagon they came running with their hands outstretched. "Please, rich Tai-tai, give us something to eat!"

Yoto shrank toward the center of the wagon, where the children's dirty hands could not reach. "This is disgusting," she said to her maid. "Tell the stupid driver to crack his whip and make the horses go faster!" She then covered her face with a perfumed handkerchief. "Are these fools too lazy to bathe?"

The maid, who had come from a poor home, didn't answer.

The wagon sped up, leaving the disappointed children behind. The driver did not slow the animals' pace until they were far removed from the shouting crowd. Yoto breathed with relief when she was no longer bouncing on the soft cushion. As the maid started to fix her hair and adjust her wardrobe, Yoto said with a sigh, "I must look a mess!"

Soon they reached the temple. Yoto could see the large iron urn supported by three fierce dragons. Smoke drifted from hundreds of incense sticks, and the gray cloud almost hid all the statues of Buddha. As they drew closer, she saw the faceless shadows of people gathered under the arch like floating ghosts, some praying on their knees, others walking aimlessly, everyone holding on to a thread of hope and wearing the mist like a shroud.

As Yoto stared at the scene, she saw once again a tall, handsome young man running after her, holding her lost comb.

*Sung Quanming, where are you? Do you still remember me? Before she died, my maid told me to forget you, because she said you had forgotten me already. I will never attain happiness if I still think of you, she said, but . . . Quanming, how can I forget?*

On her wedding night, when her husband had held her in his arms, she had closed her eyes and visualized Quanming as her groom. Through the long winter she had wished for the fire in the warm stove to burn away the image of her first love. Her buried feelings, a fertile seed lying dormant in the darkness of her memory, now became alive, riding on the fragrance of the incense from the temple.

She tried to drive the memory away with a steady stream of chatter. "I'm going to take up the game of mah-jongg. It would be a diversion from reading or writing poetry. I'm a married woman now and should give up all sentimental foolishness. I can wear all my fine jewels to the game table and be the envy of the other women. I can play the time away when my husband is busy . . ."

The wagon passed under the glare of marble, White Stone's namesake. The hill was devoid of any signs of vegetation. At its foot was the empty home of Mrs. Sung. The red brick house was boarded up and looked abandoned. Shocked, Yoto asked her maid, "Is nobody living there now?"

"My cousin knows the lady who owns that house," the maid answered. "The son went to the Land of the Gold Mountains, and his mother has gone to live with her sister."

Once more the past tried to pry its way int Yoto's consciousness. Her vision blurred, and the maid quickly held up a handkerchief. "Tai-tai, let me remove the dust from your eyes."

The little house was left behind, and Yoto leaned back to watch the thin line of the Pearl. *The Pearl goes to the sea, and across the sea lives Quanming* . . . Yoto was silent until the wagon reached the miller's home.

As the driver carried the bag of sweet rice into the stone mill, Yoto followed with the help of her serving girl.

The miller, a big, rough-looking man, poured some of the rice on the flat stone and started to push against the wooden bar that rolled the heavy wheel. He walked around and around, and soon the rice was turned into flour.

Yoto stood watching, and when her eyes became adjusted to the gloom, she noticed in the dark corner a young girl. She wore a pair of black pants white with dust. A tear on her tattered brown blouse gave a glimpse of a round, firm breast. She was barefoot, and was smiling into space.

The maid addressed Yoto over the noise of the wheel. "My Tai-tai is looking at the miller's wife. Her father is the grave-digger. Her maiden name is Bao A-teem. At one time she was rather pretty. The morning after their wedding night the miller dragged her back to the Baos, complaining that they had given him a piece of damaged goods. Her parents talked the angry husband into keeping her, but what can you expect from a man in a situation like this? He's been beating her often, and she becomes crazier every day."

The girl looked at Yoto and the maid. Knowing she was being talked about, she smiled at the attention and started to sing:

All trees have died but one.
All souls are buried in coffins except one.
One carries on his chest a tree in bloom,
One was buried under the mid-autumn moon . . .

Yoto shivered. "That is a terrible song! It sounds like a riddle, and I certainly don't want to know the answer." She strode outside and stood trembling, chiding herself for overreacting to a crazy peasant woman's melody of horror.

In front of her the Pearl River slowly moved on. The water was low, and the ripples sparkled in the bright sun. *Quanming, will I ever see you again?*

To the rich of Kwangchow, the drought was an inconvenience but not a tragedy. To the north, the Yangtze River had become the city's life line, ferrying food down to it each day.

Summer had arrived, but there were no flower peddlers lining the main street. In their place were hundreds of peasants selling their children.

The fathers kept up a constant chant: "You can take

my son and daughter for only a handful of coins, as long as you promise to feed them.'' The mothers held on to their children, reassuring them that the rich ladies and lords would be kind, that parting was much better than starving to death. Even as they spoke, however, the mothers recalled the tales of noblemen's cruelty, and they trembled for their babies.

The children had flesh as thin as rice paper, and their eyes were sunken dark holes. A few lay already dead in their mothers' arms, while the fathers, totally unaware, were still pleading for buyers.

Once in a while a rich man stopped to examine a boy, the way he would a pig or an ox. Arguing over price, he would pinch the frightened child. ''With some good whipping, the brat might be of some use. But by the time he is strong enough to do any heavy work, a fortune will have been spent on food!''

Now and then a lady in silk paused to look at a girl as if she were an orange or a melon. Pulling her hair hard, she would force the bashful child to lift her head. ''With constant beating, she might become an obedient servant. When she's old enough, she can be added to my husband's bedroom collection!''

Buffeted by a summer wind, Fong Mao and his wife left their shoe store and headed down the main street toward the pawnshop. Being parents of five sons, the sight of the children for sale bothered them deeply, especially Mrs. Fong.

She stopped in front of a boy no older than five, who had just been sold. The buyer was dragging him away, and he was screaming for his mother. The bony young woman had in turn collapsed to the pavement. She raised her arms, straining toward the direction of a wagon as her baby was thrown into it and driven away.

''What a cruel world! What a cruel life! How can Buddha not have a care?'' Mrs. Fong's voice was quavering, her eyes filled with tears. ''And look over there. That boy, doesn't he look just like Loone?''

Fong Mao had known this was coming. Glancing

quickly at the child, he said, "No. That kid is at least four years younger than Loone."

"But Loone is small for his age, so that makes them look alike—look again! The expression! So sad, so angry, so frightened. That's exactly Loone's expression when he boarded the ship. I see his face in all my dreams, and I'll never forget that look as long as I live."

"But these children are for sale. We didn't sell Loone!" Fong Mao said patiently in a very tired voice. "We only sent him away for a little while, for his own good. I'm sure he is doing fine in the Gold Mountains, maybe eating well and getting fat. He will return home someday, and find the pawnshop being turned into a profitable business. What's more, it will remain in his name."

Mrs. Fong didn't seem to have heard her husband. She kept looking at the children around her. "These people have an excuse for selling their children. We didn't—not really!"

Fong Mao tried to get his wife to move on, but she remained standing still. Ever since Loone had gone, she had lived under a burden of guilt. She cried every time she saw a stray dog or a bird that had fallen from its nest. For Fong Mao's part, he had rationalized to her what they had done, but found his own guilt surfacing every time.

They had not heard one word from Loone, and had no idea whether he was alive or dead.

Fong Mao raised his eyes toward the summer sky, started to pray to heaven. "Loone, wherever you are, please be well. For our sake, please be careful!"

His wife joined him with all her heart: "Loone, please be healthy and happy. And please forgive us for what we have done!"

In Jasmine Valley, Yung Ko had served tea without charge throughout the drought.

"Come, come! As long as the Pearl doesn't run completely dry, we can always enjoy a hot drink!" he had repeatedly urged the depressed villagers, moving his short, stumpy body from table to table.

The villagers had accepted his tea, and in return for his generosity listened to Yung's monologue about Meiping, even though their minds were preoccupied with their mounting troubles.

On this summer day, Yung's Teahouse was filled with customers. Yung Ko stood behind the counter, and across the room, behind the stove, was his bride, a quiet, understanding woman. She listened more than she talked, and when she learned a secret, she never let it be known.

While busy preparing food, she listened to her husband's voice coming from the other side of the room:

"Meiping is working in the house of a rich Chinese couple named Wan. They like her so much that Meiping is constantly showered with new clothes from her mistress." Yung Ko took from an envelope a photo, not forgetting to flash the green American bills that had come with the letter. "Look, this is her most recent picture."

The proud father passed the picture around, and the villagers took their time studying it.

"Ahya!" They saw Meiping wearing a tight, shining gown, with dangling earrings and a string of beads hung from her neck.

"Ooooo!" They noticed that her hair was piled high, decorated with a jeweled comb.

"How beautiful she looks! Not the Meiping we used to know!" said one villager.

"As a maid, she can afford to dress herself this way. Can you imagine what her Sisan and Tai-tai must look like?" said another.

"The Land of Gold Mountains must really be the heaven on earth!" said the third. "I'd like to send my son and daughter there!"

Yung Ko's wife watched her husband's face drop as the last comment was being made.

Over the past months, numerous villagers had asked Yung Ko to ask Meiping through the letter writer to help them to send their children to the Golden Land.

Yung Ko had given their messages to his daughter, but Meiping had never mentioned her willingness to help in her letters.

Mrs. Yung heard the voice of an angry villager: "Is your daughter too high and mighty to help us? She knows life is hard on the Pearl. Doesn't she care?"

Mrs. Yung saw the embarrassed look on her husband's face. She knew he was now sorry that he had ever brought up the subject of his daughter.

Mrs. Yung left the cooking stove and stepped forward. "You people hold your tongues!" She walked to her husband and stood beside him. "Have you forgotten how you used to treat our Meiping?" She glanced around the tearoom, and most of the customers turned away from her gaze. "She has every right to ignore your plea for help! Each of you called her names and made fun of her. You laughed at her for the way she looked, and you teased her for the way she behaved. Now you have the nerve to ask her for help, and when she ignores you, you dare to upbraid my poor kind husband!" Mrs. Yung stopped, caught her breath, and added, "If you don't show your appreciation for the free tea, maybe from now on we will charge every one of you."

The villagers bowed their heads, and Mrs. Yung knew they would not bring up the subject again. She waited until happiness and pride reappeared on her husband's face, then returned to her cooking stove.

While cooking, she remembered what she had heard the night before and many other nights, her husband murmuring in bed when he had thought her soundly asleep:

"Meiping, how come you're dressed like this? How can you afford to send me so much money? Are you doing more than the honest work of a maid? If you are, may the Great Buddha forgive me for what I've done! Meiping, can you ever forgive me for sending you away?"

# PART III

# 20

CHINA NEWS, A Chinese-language newspaper, came out once a week. Within its six pages were articles on China and the Chinatowns of San Francisco, New York, and Chicago, though most of its space was given to advertisements. It was now 1917 and the world was at war; Germany had just announced the beginning of unrestricted submarine warfare. This horrendous news was hidden next to a large picture of ginseng roots. The article about the establishment of a new Russian government by Prince Lvov was overshadowed by the announcement of a big sale on water pipes and the best brands of tobacco.

Every Wednesday in San Francisco the Chinese could be seen reading on the worn stoops of their tenements. In every restaurant the customers read as they ate. Even in the parks the benches were occupied by people engrossed in the paper. Since many residents were illiterate, those who could read, read to others. Small groups formed, and a babble of dialects filled the air as the latest news was announced, punctuated with exclamations and comments.

On a late-autumn day a bundle of papers had just been dropped at the Yung Fa Restaurant. Li Fachai brought them in, the customers grabbed them, and within a few minutes they were all gone.

Fachai was in a hurry, but was stopped by an old man on his way to the kitchen. "Boy, you must take a look at this girl. Even my old blood is boiling at the sight of her."

Glancing over the old man's shoulder, Fachai saw on the front page several pictures of a beautiful girl in different costumes. "Well, she looks fine . . ." he said, starting for the kitchen again. "But my wife in Willow Place is much prettier."

The old man started to laugh. "Come on, don't compare your woman with Yi Moi, the leading opera singer in Hong Kong!" He went on to say that the Sung Wu Company had engaged the actress to come to the Land of Gold Mountains for a tour. "She'll be here soon, and will stay in San Francisco for a whole week. I'm taking all my savings out from under the mattress to watch her every night."

Illiterate customers from other tables began to bring their chairs to the old man's table to look at the pictures and listen to the great news. Even the Chus, sitting at one of the tables making wontons and spring rolls, pricked up their ears at the man's words.

Shaking his head, Fachai murmured, "Well, my Leahi really is much prettier." He then went into the kitchen and started to wash the dirty dishes.

Through the curtain over the doorway he could still hear the old man saying proudly, "Listen closely, now, all of you. I'm going to read you the true-life story of Yi Moi." He then waited until the room was silent. "Yi Moi was born in a small village along the Pearl River. Her parents were poor farmers. One year, when things were going badly for them, they took her to Kwangchow and sold her to an opera school. She was only four." The man paused, probably drinking tea, Fachai thought. "For many years Yi Moi was strictly trained. She learned to sing, dance, do acrobatics, fight with swords, and act."

Out of the corner of his eye, Fachai caught some movement, and he jumped, almost dropping the bowl he was washing. "Loone! Why do you always tiptoe around? You don't make a sound coming down those stairs!"

In the past five years, all the good eating in Yung Fa had put weight on Fachai. But Loone had stayed rail thin. Giving Fachai one of his rare smiles, he picked up a steamed chicken wing and started sucking on it. "Sorry if I scared you." He yawned. "I'm so tired. I painted half the night, you know, and then all the racket downstairs woke me up." He grabbed a plate and stacked some more wings on it. "I'm going to my table to eat and see what's going on."

"Wait! On your way out, will you bring a pot of tea for the people at that large table? I'm all tied up with the dishes."

"No! I'm not a waiter!" Loone grumbled, and was gone.

Fachai sighed. *Life is unfair! For five years now I've cooked, cleaned, waited on people, and am still far from having enough money saved up to buy a boat. But Loone just sits at his table in the corner of the dining room, watches people and draws them, then turns the drawings into paintings through the night.*

When he had the whole kitchen cleaned, he carried a tray of pots of hot tea into the dining room. To his surprise, he saw that instead of sitting in his corner, Loone was standing behind the old man reading the paper. Fachai placed a pot of tea on the table and whispered into Loone's ear, "Lowering yourself to the company of us common peasants, my honorable artist?"

Smiling, he waited for Loone to hit him or yell at him. But Loone didn't even look at him. "Are you sick, my little brother?" Fachai peered at Loone closely and saw an expression on his face that he had never seen before.

Loone was staring intently at the picture of Yi Moi. There was a certain tenderness in his eyes, one that had appeared only when he looked at his mother's pink pearls.

Time had changed Paul Eddington and Sung Quanming to a considerable degree. Paul had seriously taken up the art of eating; his girth had expanded to a point that he was far more comfortable in a loose Chinese robe than in tight Western shirt and pants. Quanming had lost much of his color, and his body no longer carried the hardness that had once given him the appearance of a kung-fu fighter.

As the last wind of autumn blew through the garden, the two had worked hard all morning in the study. It had been Paul's idea to use the *China News* as a textbook. Quanming was told to translate the writings from Chinese into English.

"Paul, I can't believe this!" Quanming shook his head at the paper. "With all that's going on in Europe, every page is filled with news about this little actress."

Paul glanced at Yi Moi's pictures. "She certainly is a beauty."

Then they began to work together on the article, Quanming translating as Paul looked on to make necessary corrections. Sometimes it took both of them to come up with the correct words. A Chinese character is usually multifaceted in meaning, and to conjure up a word from the restricted idiom of English was at times impossible. In the past five years Quanming had become as proficient in English as most Americans. Although he still spoke with a heavy accent, he could now read most English publications fluently.

Looking up from the paper, Quanming said, "I used to go to the opera in White Stone. My mother loved those high-pitched songs . . ." He paused, becoming sad. "She's been dead two years now, but it's still hard to believe that she's not waiting for me to come home anymore." He sighed. "She, my father, Quanli—all my loved ones are gone . . . all, except—" He swallowed the name he was about to mention as the door opened and his uncle walked in.

Time had been kind to Sung Tinwei. He still carried himself erect and moved with a grace that belied his age. At fifty-five, his face was almost free of wrinkles and his eyes still gleamed with an inner intensity.

Both Paul and Quanming quickly rose to their feet and greeted Mr. Sung with a respectful bow.

"Would you like a cup of tea, my uncle?" Quanming asked.

The uncle lowered himself into a chair, sipped the tea, then asked, "Have you read the paper?"

Paul and Quanming nodded as Sung Tinwei continued, "It is our responsibility to pick up Miss Yi at the pier with a welcoming committee." He looked at

Quanming. "Da-chung and I have decided that you should head this little project. You should arrange a welcoming party, and then, before she leaves for Chicago, a small, intimate farewell is in order. I'm most confident that you are more than able to handle everything."

Unwilling to disturb Quanming's study further, Sung Tinwei got up to leave. At the door he turned. "Remember to invite the best people for both parties. We cannot afford to slight anyone. Mrs. Wu and her daughter are stopping by later. You should come to talk to A-lin and ask her to act as your hostess at those parties." He closed the door quietly behind him, without giving Quanming a chance to reply.

Quanming turned to Paul with a disgusted look. "Wu A-lin! That mouse! For five years now my uncle and her father have been pushing us together every chance they get!"

"Poor girl." Paul shook his head. "She's not a bad-looking girl. It's her personality. Her mother trained her to be that way, I guess."

Quanming sighed. "I would love to have Laurie as my hostess. Before Uncle Tinwei came in, I was just about to tell you that I have only Laurie to love now."

Paul looked at his student with concern. "Laurie had told me that she feels the same way about you. But it's the two of you against the world, you know."

"I'm afraid we do." Suddenly Quanming thumped a fist on the desk and made the pencils and books shake. "This damn law of yours that forbids interracial marriages. I'm considered colored, and she white. People don't like to see us in restaurants and theaters together. We can only meet on beaches or in parks when no one else is around. We can't even meet here in my home, because if my uncle should find out about us, the sky will fall!" He looked at his teacher pleadingly. "Please, Paul, can you think of a way for Laurie and me to get married? We love each other, and our feelings will never change. When I was a young boy in China, I had once thought that I was in love. But that was only an infatuation—the girl was pretty, but we had nothing in common. Laurie and I are the best friends. We talk about everything, and we enjoy each other's company.''

Paul reached over to place his hand on Quanming's forearm. "I would love to see the two of you married, but I can't think of a way to change the law and the people. Maybe with time—'' He was interrupted by a knock on the door.

A large man in his early thirties entered.

"I'm sorry to interrupt, Sisan,'' Liu Shih said, bowing. "But Miss Wu and her mother have arrived, and Sung Lau Ban wants you to accompany the young lady on her shopping trip to buy the new clothes she'll need as your hostess in the coming parties.''

Grumbling, Quanming got up to follow his uncle's longtime servant and bodyguard.

Thirty minutes later, the wheels of the company automobile were rolling over the autumn leaves on the streets, bringing Quanming and A-lin to the stores. As Wu A-lin chattered on, Quanming stared at the back of the driver and thought about what his uncle had told him about this man.

Through the arrangement of a trader, Liu Shih had left China to come to San Francisco to work for the House of Wan. On the ship he had met and fallen in love with a young girl who had also been sold to the Wans. When they arrived in San Francisco, Liu pleaded with Wan Kon to let him marry the girl, but Wan only laughed in his face. "Idiot, I'm a whorehouse owner, not a matchmaker.''

Liu and the girl tried to escape before she was put to work, but they were caught and taken to the basement, where there was an old filthy bed. Two men tied Liu to a post in the middle of the room, while a third held the girl.

Kim Shinma walked in, looked around, and smiled. He gave orders to tie the girl spread-eagle to the bed, and had one of the men hold a knife to Liu's throat, forcing him to watch.

"Keep your eyes open wide!'' Kim grinned at Liu, then turned to the girl. He grabbed the top of her dress, and with one powerful tug he tore it from her shaking body. "My sweet little thing, I'll give you what you need!" He took her like a savage animal, her screams driving him into a frenzy.

Liu struggled and cursed, and then felt a sharp pain in his side. The last thing he saw before passing out was Kim Shinma with his head thrown back, laughing as he brutalized the girl.

When Liu awoke in the hospital, he learned that the girl was dead. He himself had been left to die in an alley. One of the workers from the Sung Wu Company had found him and informed Sung Lau Ban, who had taken him to the hospital and volunteered to pay all the bills. After Liu was nursed back to life, he became Sung Tinwei's most loyal man.

When Kim Shinma entered the fourth-floor room with the *China News*, Wan Kon and Limei were having lunch.

Wan tossed a chicken bone to the floor, spat out a piece of gristle, then wiped his hands on the corner of the tablecloth. He grabbed the paper from the Korean and dismissed him with a nod. As Wan glanced from page to page, he reached for a pastry and popped it into his mouth. In the middle of chewing, he abruptly stopped. Looking up from the paper, he started to shout, spraying food across the table, "Now I know what a true beauty looks like!"

From across the table, Limei looked at Wan, trying to suppress her anger as he went on to fill her with the news about the arrival of the opera star.

Limei was still a striking woman even with the added weight she now carried and the few more lines on her face. As the Lau Ban rattled on, she gradually calmed down. She realized that now her Lau Ban was interested in this Yi Moi as a spoiled child is eager to have another new toy. She sighed resignedly. In her way she cared for Wan Kon, but had learned long ago that she had no right to be jealous.

Wan Kon finally laid down the paper. "Limei, go fetch Meiping. I want the two of you to go shopping

for the most eye-catching clothes you can find. We
must show Yi Moi that the women in Wan Kon's house
are dressed like queens. She will become envious, and
she'll want to become one of your girls. Can you
imagine? With her presence in the house, our business
will increase ten times!'' He took another sweet cake
and sat smiling to himself.

Leaving him to his happy dreams, Limei went
downstairs to see Meiping.

The girl now lived in the largest suite on the third
floor. She had not been up long. As she stood by a
window in a yellow silk robe, her hair cascaded over
her shoulders. She was toying with a ruby ring given
to her recently by David Cohen. Her complexion was
much whiter than five years ago, and she had acquired
the look of a city girl. But, an untamed lioness still
lurked inside, ready to leap out when she was angered.

As Meiping watched the people beneath the window
on Grant Avenue, her face darkened. She remembered
another autumn day like this four years before, when
she had encountered Quanming, Fachai, and Loone.

It had been the day of the Autumn Lion Dance, and
Grant Avenue was filled with people shouting, singing, and eating the many treats offered by street vendors.

A long lion carried by twenty-four young men
wound its way through the crowd. Strings of firecrackers hung from poles and buildings were set off, sending showers of red paper floating down on everything.
The sounds of screaming adults and crying children
accompanied the lion as it slowly made its way, with
its magnificent head rearing up each time the puppeteer extended his arms.

Suddenly the puppeteer's eye was caught by something alongside the road; his arms stopped in midair.
The lion's head stopped moving, and all the men down
the line quickly froze. The lion had stopped at the
sight of Meiping, who was standing in a carriage
watching the parade. She was wearing a long green
velvet gown embroidered in silver and gold; around

her neck she wore a gold choker with matching earrings and several bracelets.

The puppeteer started to flirt through the lion. The beast tilted his head from side to side, the eyes open and the mouth agape.

Limei, who was standing next to Meiping, started to laugh. "Little sister, you've taken the lion's roar and changed it to a whimper."

Meiping brought her head up, smiled, then reached over and kissed the lion on its forehead. The eyes of the lion shyly closed and the head dropped. The crowd roared their amusement.

Meiping was having the time of her life. She was looking around proudly when she spotted a group of men walking on the opposite side of the street. Her heart skipped a beat when she recognized them.

She met Quanming's eyes looking at her with a puzzled expression. She saw Loone jumping up and down, shouting her name. She watched Fachai waving and was about to wave back and call them each by name—then her hand dropped.

From the looks of her three friends, she knew they must be doing well. She looked at herself and realized that no velvet gown or expensive jewelry could change the fact she had become a whore.

She quickly turned away, ashamed. She had lost interest in the lion and the parade.

She had avoided her friends not only that day but also from then on. She had chosen to remain within the walls of the House of Wan, going out only when necessary. She worried about running into one of the three boys, for if they should ask her what she was doing, she wouldn't know how to answer.

Returning from her reverie, Meiping murmured, "It has nothing to do with you, David. I don't mind being your whore. It's nice of you to pay Wan enough to keep the other men from getting into my bed, but the whore to one man is still a whore!"

Moa Lau's tailor shop carried only the finest silks directly from China, and was well known not only in the Chinese community but also to the American buyers interested in things Chinese.

The owner, Moa Lau, a man in his thirties, was always dressed in the finest traditional Oriental clothes. He made a point of welcoming all his customers with a low bow, and treated each one with the greatest respect. While humbling himself to their every demand, he enjoyed watching the fools pay for goods that were worth only a fraction of the price.

The carriage from the House of Wan stopped in front of the store, and Moa Lau saw Limei and Meiping stepping from the rig. He quickly opened the door and shepherded them into the shop, knowing that these two whores always meant a good sale.

Bowing deeply, Moa asked in flawless Cantonese, "And how may this humble person help you two Sheo-jay today?"

"Sheo-jay? Hell, Moa Lau, I'm no more a lady than you! What are you going to charge us for a couple of gowns that will knock people's eyeballs out?" Limei asked.

"Ah, don't worry, my lovely Sheo-jay, you know I always give you the fairest price and the finest material." Moa bowed again.

"I can fry spring rolls with the oil that pours out of your mouth! We're not a couple of white devils who'll fall over themselves when you start oozing out that charm," Limei said acidly. "Shut up and show us the overpriced rags that you're so proud of."

For the next two hours Limei and Meiping looked over the various cloths, argued over prices, then picked out the patterns. Moa Lau measured Meiping with delight, and then measured Limei. "You've put on a little weight since the last time." He smiled as he read the tape.

"My weight is none of your damn business!" Limei replied.

"I'm sorry, Sheo-jay. I didn't mean any disrespect. What I meant was that it's most becoming—"

The door opened and Sung Quanming walked in with Wu A-lin. Meiping found herself face-to-face with her old friend. As their eyes met, she had to brace herself against the counter to keep from falling.

After searching her face, Quanming recognized her. "Meiping! I can't believe this! Where did all the dirt go? And where are the old rags?" With a warm smile he walked toward her with an outstretched hand. "How good to see you! You look wonderful!"

"Quanming," Meiping stammered, taking his hand. "It's been a long time. You look great . . ." She blushed, and tears were forming in her eyes. She wished she could hide, but it was impossible now. She also wanted to tell him everything, but didn't know where to begin.

"Quanming!" the mouse-faced girl cried shrilly. "How can you acknowledge this trash?" A-lin looked at the interlocked hands of Quanming and Meiping; on her face there was shock.

Meiping looked down at the short, skinny girl. A-lin lifted her head and glared back with obvious revulsion. Meiping had the urge to strike her, but then A-lin opened her mouth and uttered the word Meiping dreaded above all others: "Whore!"

All the blood drained from Meiping's face. She bit her lip, her hands clenched into fists. Without looking at Quanming or saying good-bye, she turned and fled from the shop, leaving Limei standing there. *Now Quanming knows! Now all my old friends know!*

Limei rushed to the carriage behind Meiping, and after they had ridden silently for a long while, she asked the girl, "How long have you known the nephew of Sung Tinwei?"

Meiping did not answer right away. When she did, she could hardly control her voice. "I knew him a long time ago . . . I was still a poor good girl from Jasmine Valley."

"Are you in love with him?" Limei asked curiously.

"No," Meiping answered, "but he is a friend. I hate to have my friends see me the way I am today. Besides, they make me remember myself the way I used to be, and will never be again."

Limei didn't say anything else. All girls in the house had trouble facing people they had once known.

When they arrived at the House of Wan, Meiping ran to her room without a word to anyone. She locked the door. When Limei came to call her to go to work in the bar, she refused to answer.

They were shorthanded in the bar. Soon everybody in the house knew Meiping was throwing another one of her fits. Kim Shinma was all for kicking the door down and straightening the bitch out. Wan was debating whether to let Kim do that or to be concerned with the cost of the repair on both the girl and the door.

Limei tried to calm Wan down. "Don't worry, David will be here soon, and she'll open the door for him.

Wan Kon hissed, "That David Cohen is a stupid fool. What he sees in the Giant I'll never know! But as long as he pays, who the hell cares?"

Limei spotted David Cohen the moment he walked in. His tall frame was hard to miss. He was well tanned and moved with youthful grace. He was a man who exercised regularly; he met time head-on and refused to let it turn him into an old man.

On this day there was a dark cloud over his face. He was emotionally exhausted from another row with Rebecca. The argument had been caused by many reasons, among them the fact that he had become a stranger in his own house. Neither his wife nor his sons showed any affection toward him, and he was either ignored or found himself on a battlefield each time he stepped in the door.

David was counting on finding relaxation in the bar, and later comfort from Meiping.

As soon as he approached the bar, Limei started telling him about Meiping. ". . . Will you go up and see if there's something you can do?"

"Damn, all I need tonight is Meiping in one of her moods!" David could not hide his anger as he asked for a drink.

He tossed the liquor down, ordered another, and drained it. Then he sat for a long while twirling the glass in his big hands. For the past five years he had given in to Meiping's every wish. God, how he loved her. She had become everything to him.

No other man had ever touched her; his money had seen to that. Wan Kon had no argument with the arrangement as long as he was well paid. David had thought about getting Meiping out of this environment, but he still felt a certain loyalty to his family that would not allow him to do such a thing.

*I can't get her out of here, so I feel guilty toward her. Because of my guilt, I've spoiled her rotten!*

David's thoughts were interrupted by Limei. "Mr. Cohen, do you mind a little advice?"

He looked up and handed her his glass. "Does it matter if I do?"

Limei filled his glass and set it on the bar. "In a way, you're responsible for Meiping's high-handedness. You've been paying a good price for her, and she is your woman. I think it's about time that you let her know who's the boss."

"What do you suggest?" David groaned.

"Make her realize she is yours. Reassure her that you will keep her as yours forever—the Chinese way. Make her see that you will not put up with any nonsense, because you want to keep the relationship between you a lasting one. Let her know that you don't mind to trim the tree now and then, because you intend to see the tree grow."

"Trim the tree?" David asked, bewildered.

"Yes." Limei smiled. "You know, like a gardener. It may hurt the tree a little, but the feeling of security and a certain pride should follow." She winked at David and moved away.

David sat thinking about what Limei had said. She was obviously suggesting he teach Meiping a lesson. Limei didn't know Meiping like he did. He shook his head and stood up, heading for the upstairs.

Reaching Meiping's suite, he knocked on the door and called her name. There was no answer. A couple of the girls stuck their heads out of their doors to see

what was going on. When they saw David and the sad
look on his face, they smiled.

"Meiping!" he called again. "Open the door for
me, please!"

One girl whispered to another in Chinese: "Did you
hear that? I think he is begging her to open the door!
The barbarians are strange! Doesn't he know that a
man should never beg a woman? I bet his ancestors
are crying in their graves right now! He should just
break the door down, charge in, and give her a good
whipping! Meiping would become a better girl then,
and learn to respect her man as she should."

The other girl shook her head in doubt. "It would
work with you and me, but Yung Meiping is different." She shook her head once more, then closed the
door. Her friend followed her example.

David stood in the empty hall for a long time, not
knowing what to do.

"Meiping, please let me in!" he called again, and
was ready to leave. He would come back the next day,
and perhaps Meiping would be in a better mood.

The door opened.

Meiping stood there wearing a pair of loose, faded
black pants and a red blouse made of coarse material.
She had braided her long hair into a single queue and
washed off all her makeup. She had black cloth shoes
on her feet, and a small bundle in her hand. She looked
at David with her eyes wide, tears streaming down her
cheeks.

"What's this?" David glanced over her clothes, then
stared at her face. "You look like a peasant now . . .
the most beautiful peasant, of course . . ." He tried
to smile, but his heart was sinking. "Why are you
carrying that silly-looking bundle? Haven't I given you
enough purses? Are you going somewhere—?"

"Will you help me?" Meiping interrupted. Her tears
continued to fall.

"Help you?" David murmured. The determination
in Meiping's eyes frightened him, and his heart continued to sink.

"David . . ." Meiping said softly. She swallowed

hard. Tears poured out of her eyes like a string of pearls with the thread broken. She forced herself to continue: "Help me to leave. Hide me somewhere until there is a ship to China. I want to go back to my Jasmine Valley . . ." She waved an arm around the room. "I won't take anything you gave me. The clothes, the jewelry . . . they are expensive, I know. You give them to some other girl, and buy me a ticket on the ship. You may have to pay Wan Kon something too, for my freedom. I cannot repay you in this life. In this life, I'm a poor girl. But I'll pay you in my next life, I promise. I haven't done too many bad things so far, so I will ask Buddha to make me a rich person in my next life . . ." Her voice broke. She couldn't go on.

David felt cold. He saw the dark days ahead. Meiping gone. What would be the use of his success in business? How could money buy the happiness he had found with Meiping? He stepped toward her, put his hands on her shoulders. "Meiping, don't you know that I love you?"

Meiping raised a hand to wipe her tears. She shook her head. "Love is only a word for white people. You say it often, but you don't mean it. Because if you did, you would not leave me in a whorehouse. You would not let my friends laugh at me, and let some mousy girl look down on me in a dress shop . . ."

David took her by the arm and guided her to a chair. He sat, pulling her onto his lap. She went reluctantly, still holding her small bundle. "In Jasmine Valley, people told me I was ugly. My Baba beat me sometimes, but he always protected me from bad things. He thinks I am here working as a servant. He will die if he knows I am a whore. I want to go home to Baba . . ."

"Meiping, your father is remarried. You'll be in their way. Besides, he sold you once, and just might sell you again," David said, kissing Meiping softly on the forehead. "What if he sold you to someone worse than Wan Kon? And Limei won't be there to help you." He kissed her on her tearstained cheek. "And

I won't be there . . . you will miss me, won't you?
Just a little?''

Meiping leaned back to look at David. She tilted her
head to one side, bit her lower lip, thought deeply.
She looked into David's eyes. ''I couldn't bear to be
without you.'' She studied his face for a long while,
then blushed. ''We Chinese are not supposed to say 'I
love you,' David . . . but I do!'' She closed her eyes
and began to cry once more, then suddenly became
angry. ''It's all your fault!'' She started to hit his chest
with her fists. She dropped her bundle and didn't
bother to pick it up.

A smile appeared on David's face. He knew that the
worst of the storm was over. Now he must wait for the
sky to clear up, and the sun would shine again soon.
''Meiping,'' he said tenderly, ''you are a clever girl.
Clever girls know how to block out the bad parts of
life and see the good parts alone.'' He kissed her
mouth, tasted the salt of her tears. He stood up with
her in his arms, and she continued to look into his
eyes. ''I promise you, Meiping, I will get you out of
here as soon as I can. It will not be tomorrow or next
month. It may not even be next year. But someday we
will have a home of our own.''

The promise was like a check that couldn't be
cashed. But Meiping didn't argue. She let out a little
sigh, then buried her face against his chest as he
walked toward the bed. He laid her down carefully and
unbuttoned her blouse, then fumbled with the string
on her pants. He pulled both the blouse and the pants
off her and threw them to the floor. He undressed himself and they soon lay naked beside each other. She
got up on her knees and straddled him.

Slowly she lowered herself, feeling him slide inside
her, hot and throbbing. She looked down at him with
a shy smile and began to gyrate. He lifted himself to
hold her, and soon they were lost in each other.

Meiping closed her eyes. She imagined herself back
in Jasmine Valley, on top of the hill. She saw one of
the wild geese soaring through the sky. All her trou-

bles were forgotten. She was floating over the clouds, rising, sinking, and rising again.

They rolled over. Just when David was ready to climax, Meiping dug her nails into the flesh on his back and let out a scream. David could hold back no longer. As he threw his head back and let out a moan, Meiping screamed his name. She had soared once again on the wings of pleasure, and fell back to earth completely spent.

She opened her eyes then. David had collapsed on top of her. She couldn't see his face, and knew that he could not see hers either. She felt tears filling her eyes once more. She let them fall soundlessly onto the pillow. Suddenly she felt much older than her age. She mumbled in Chinese: "Fate is unfair. The Great Buddha wants to make me a whore, who am I to argue?"

"What did you say?" David asked without moving.

"Nothing." Meiping tried to sound cheerful. "Nothing except that I will block out the bad parts of life from now on."

## 21

WHILE WU A-LIN was showing her mother the items she had purchased, she mentioned the tall girl in Moa Lau's shop. "She was nothing but a common whore, Mother. You should have seen her. It was disgusting. I was so humiliated." Her timid demeanor was nowhere in evidence. She did not have to pretend in front of her mother as she did in the presence of Quanming.

"Why should you care?" Mrs. Wu asked, admiring some new jade earrings. She walked over to the mirror and held them up to her ears. "Like all men, Quanming must go to the whores now and then. It's part of their nature to release their animal lust."

"But, Mama," A-lin protested to her mother's reflection. "When he is my husband, he must stop going to places like that." As the two stood side by side, it was obvious that A-lin was her mother's child; the wrinkles and double chin on Mrs. Wu's face did little to hide the resemblance.

Mrs. Wu laughed. "My foolish daughter, no man belongs to one woman completely. A marriage means the husband provides a house and many servants. In return, the wife gives him children. It's a fair trade: money is hard to earn, and the pain of childbirth is hard to bear."

"Mama, it'll be impossible for me to share Quanming with other women. I . . . I love him." A-lin blushed, and at that moment she looked tender.

Mrs. Wu raised her voice. "My daughter, you had better grow up and get such a foolish notion out of your head. Quanming doesn't know it yet, but it has been arranged that he should become your husband, so the Sungs and the Wus can be brought together. It has nothing to do with love."

"To marry Quanming but not to love him?" A-lin murmured incredulously, staring at the mother.

"Remember, my daughter, to be a wife is to grab all the money, for that alone will give her the controlling power. And then she must teach the servants to fear her, and the children to listen to her instead of their father. The very last thing she should be interested in is her husband's love. What's the use of something you can't see, taste, or wear?"

A-lin listened, absorbing every word. After all, she could not remember her mother ever being wrong. She smiled. "Thank you, Mother, for arranging the marriage. I will try my best to be the wife you want me to be . . ." She hesitated. "But I still love Quanming . . . very much, and I don't think I'll ever be able to allow him to love or touch another woman."

The opera star Yi Moi had lived in a China that was divided into regions ruled by warlords, and she had seen her girlfriends become victims of these cruel men. The luckier ones were raped and set free; the unfortunate ones were imprisoned forever in the warlords' mansions. Those who dared to fight back were killed, their naked bodies dumped outside the city walls.

During a recent performance in Kwangchow, she had noticed such a man in the center of the front row. His shaved head glistened with beads of perspiration, and his eyes never stopped undressing her. A cold chill coursed down Yi Moi's spine, causing her to stumble over the next lines.

Backstage, she learned from the manager that the man was known as King of Hearts. "He is Lord Chiang, the warlord of Kuelin. He loves to kill people and eat their hearts."

The following morning a heavy package was delivered to Yi Moi's dressing room. She opened it and saw two solid gold bars on top of a short note: "Lord Chiang has to go on an important journey, but will be back in ten days. You are expected to have dinner with him. Be ready for the lord's personal aide, who shall come and fetch you upon the lord's return.''

It was then that Yi Moi started to search for a letter she had cast aside a month ago, an invitation from the Sung Wu Company in San Francisco for her company to tour the Land of the Gold Mountains.

As her ship pulled slowly out of Hong Kong harbor, Yi Moi and those company members willing to follow her stood on the deck watching their native land fading into the horizon. Some of them were excited, but most of them worried. They all knew that anyone flouting a warlord's wish had better forget about ever returning to China.

Being the Lau Ban of the opera company, along with her fame and money, Yi Moi was allowed to stay in a first-class cabin. The members of the troupe were herded into the crowded quarters belowdecks. She saw them only during the brief moments when they were allowed to come up for a breath of fresh air. They filled her with stories of the conditions below; the scenes were painted with a theatrical flair for the sole purpose of terrifying their Lau Ban.

When the ship docked in San Francisco, Yi Moi and her people had little trouble with the immigration officers.

''What a beauty!'' said one official to another. ''I didn't know the Chinks could look like her. I sure would like to have her cook me a dish of chop suey and serve it between her legs. And while I nibble on her bean sprouts, she can taste my hot dog!'' The two men began to laugh as they eyed the girl. Yi Moi just smiled politely, having no idea what they were talking about.

In preparation for landing, she had donned a white satin pantsuit with red coral buttons, and tied a red sash around her slim waist. Her hair was held up with two ivory chopsticks. Her only makeup was a touch of color on her lips.

She passed customs and started down the gangplank. She looked toward the waiting people and saw a tremendous crowd. Her eye was caught by a huge banner with red letters: "WELCOME MISS YI MOI AND COMPANY." She surveyed the crowd below with the practiced eye of a performer, discovering that most of the people didn't look any better than poor villagers along the Pearl River.

She turned to a musician in back of her. "I thought this was the land of plenty. I'll be damned if they don't look worse than some of the beggars in Kwangchow."

As she neared the dock she noticed a very tall, handsome young man with broad shoulders. Next to him were a pale skinny boy and an old couple. She gazed over their heads and saw a black carriage; a man with the face of a weasel was sitting with a woman wearing an exquisite dress, and with them was a strikingly beautiful girl, overdressed and covered in jewels. The driver was a big man with a shaved head.

Yi Moi shivered. Something in the weasel's face reminded her very much of Lord Chiang, the King of Hearts. She decided to stay clear of that group if at all possible.

She had seen only pictures of automobiles, and her eyes widened as a distinguished vehicle stopped in front of the pier. A young man wearing a gray Western suit stepped out of the car, and when Yi Moi set foot on the dock, the young man came toward her.

She turned to her supporting actress and whispered, nodding her head in the young man's direction, "By the Great Buddha! Look what's coming this way! He has to be the best-looking man I've ever seen!"

Her supporting lady began to giggle. "Look what's trying to keep up with him—that little mouse wearing red. She looks like she belongs in a comic opera. Do you think she could be his wife? If she is, the handsome man has terrible taste in women!"

Yi Moi found herself blushing as the handsome young man came up to her with a friendly smile, followed by a deep bow. "I am Sung Quanming, representing the Sung Wu Company. On behalf of my uncle and his partner, I welcome you to San Francisco."

Quanming introduced Wu A-lin as the daughter of one of the two Lau Bans, then escorted Yi Moi to the waiting automobile. Cameramen began taking her picture, and people pressed forward, shouting for her autograph. Only with great difficulty did she pass through.

Yi Moi and her troupe stayed in the Sun Wu Company's hotel, and that evening a welcoming party was held in the banquet room on the main floor.

The actress walked into the room wearing a long pink skirt and a white blouse, escorted by Quanming in a cream-colored suit. He guided her to the head table and introduced her to many of the guests with charm and dignity. It didn't take her long, however, to sense that Quanming was preoccupied, and only going through the motions of a perfect host. She was disappointed by his lack of interest, because she had intended to avoid going back to China by way of marriage, preferably to someone handsome and rich.

Throughout the party, Yi Moi used her beauty and charm as a bait, searching for a good catch among the men. The few who showed interest in her had been in the Golden Land for a long time, and by the look of them the years had not been too kind. They were uneducated and still carrying the tradition of male dominance in their manners. They had lived the lives of bachelors for so long that their ways could no longer be changed. What bothered Yi Moi most, though, was that they cared so little for their appearance; their yellowed teeth and greasy hair turned her stomach.

When she met her sponsor, Sung Tinwei, she was impressed by the elderly gentleman. Like nephew, like uncle. She didn't think of his age as an obstacle. However, his interest in her was strictly fatherly, and she was disappointed once more.

Quanming then led her to meet the Wu family. She had met Wu Da-chung earlier and liked the fat, happy man. Mrs. Wu and the three boys left a more unfavorable impression, and she remembered A-lin as the funny-looking girl who had accompanied Quanming on the pier. Here in the ballroom A-lin looked like a clown in a flower-patterned gown with a huge yellow ribbon on top of her head and outlandish jewelry dangling from her ears. Yi Moi tried to hold back her laughter, but couldn't keep her lips from curling up.

A-lin took the actress's smile for a friendly gesture, and immediately began to inform her that she knew all the best stores in San Francisco and would be glad to take her shopping soon.

"Miss Yi," Quanming interrupted A-lin, "please come with me and meet my two closest friends."

He guided her to a table and introduced her to Chu Fong Loone, who was standing with a nervous smile on his face, looking at her as if she were a goddess. His pale face turned red and he stammered, "Miss Yi, I would like . . . if you don't mind . . . to paint your portrait."

Moi smiled briefly at the boy and quickly turned to Li Fachai, appraising him with keen interest as she was being introduced. She remembered him immediately: the man with broad shoulders who had first attracted her attention at the pier. He didn't have the aristocratic air possessed by Sung Quanming, but neither was she, Yi Moi, born as a true princess. She felt her cheeks turning warm under Fachai's steady gaze. She couldn't understand why, after all these years of theatrical training, she should feel like a silly village girl in front of this man.

"How . . . how about . . . the portrait?" Loone asked once again, stammering. "My room above the Yung Fa Restaurant is a studio, and I . . . I would love to paint you there. If . . . if you don't want to be alone with me, my friend Fachai also lives there, and he can always keep us company."

With her eyes still on Fachai, Moi answered absentmindedly, "Why, of course. I would be flattered to have my portrait painted by you."

Quanming was waiting for her to meet the other guests, and as she was walking away with him, she realized that although Li Fachai had never stopped looking at her, he had not said a single word to her.

After she had met everyone else, Quanming escorted her to the far corner of the ballroom. "Now

I'm very proud to introduce you to my English teacher, Paul, and his niece Laurie.''

Moi was very surprised when Paul spoke to her in Chinese. Then, with one look at how Quanming and Laurie greeted each other, Yi Moi realized why he was not interested in her. *So, no wonder he doesn't look at me! He is so obviously involved with this white girl with her red hair . . . and she with him; I can see it in her eyes. I feel better now that I know I'm not defeated by a little mouse.*

The party was a great success. Pictures were taken for the local newspapers, and the guests pushed each other aside while putting on their best smiles for the cameras.

When the party was over, Quanming took Yi Moi to her hotel room and quickly left.

After soaking in a hot tub for a long time, Moi went to sleep, exhausted. Soon she was having a twisted nightmare: Lord Chiang was running after her, his bald head gleaming. In his outstretched hand he was holding a knife covered with blood. ''You thought you got away from me, but you won't find a husband in the white devils' land. Now you're back in my domain and your heart is mine!''

Moi woke up screaming, and for the rest of the night she lay in bed thinking. *I can't go back to China! I must stay here . . . I'll marry somebody, anybody!*

## 22

EVERY SEAT IN the theater was filled. In fact, folding chairs were packed into every available space for extra seating. People arrived hours before the performance. They were eating food brought from home, throwing the wrappers and empty containers on the floor.

The musicians began to practice behind the closed curtains, and the beating of drums, along with brass cymbals and stringed instruments, overpowered the sound of the audience.

"Make way for Master Wan!" Kim Shinma shouted, pushing aside everyone in his way. Wan Kon strutted slowly toward the front, making sure the crowd noticed Meiping and Limei. Their silk gowns and jewels had cost him a fortune, and he wanted everyone to know that working for the House of Wan was like being an emperor's courtesan.

"Whores!" someone shouted, and several others joined in. Wan Kon's face turned red, and Kim Shinma turned in search of the sources. All eyes evaded the Korean's angry look; all faces appeared innocent.

Meiping, in a gold gown with red rubies on her ears, whispered to Limei, "That word doesn't bother me anymore. What does it matter if the world calls me a whore as long as I know that I am really David's devoted woman?"

The soft lavender-colored gown helped mask Limei's age, and she looked very proud when she smiled at Meiping. "I'm so glad you feel this way now. He sure has a gentle way of changing your opinion, doesn't he?"

Meiping started to blush.

The curtains were pulled aside, and the audience started yelling, "Hao, hao!"—Good, good!. The cheers were deafening. But as soon as Yi Moi stepped into the lights, a hush came over the theater. The story of the White Snake began, with Moi standing in a white flowing gown, her face powdered white and her eyes heavily made up. After the proper pause, Yi Moi began to sing the first song.

The story was about a white snake that had acquired the human form of a beautiful woman and fallen in love with a scholar by the name of Sen. They married and soon had a baby boy. A monk came to their house and advised Sen that it wasn't very healthy to be the husband of a snake. At last Sen was persuaded to poison his wife. Mrs. Sen was transformed back into a white snake and imprisoned forever in a pagoda. The final scene ended with a heartbreaking melody.

When Yi Moi's beautiful voice sang the sorrow of a devoted wife and loving mother bidding her son and husband an eternal farewell, all the women in the audience sobbed.

After many encores, Yi Moi was glad to get back to the dressing room. She had been settled for only a short time, however, when the door swung open. Filling the opening was Kim Shinma, his bald head shining in the overhead light.

He bowed. "My master, Wan Kon, would like to have you as his guest for dinner this evening."

Moi walked to the door and started to close it. "I'm very tired. Please tell your boss that I'm not having dinner with anybody."

The Korean placed his big foot in the path of the door. "I don't think you understand. My master is an important Lau Ban, and it's not wise for you to turn down his invitation."

Moi felt once again back in China, being threatened by a warlord's aide. Before she could say anything, Kim Shinma was shoved to one side and the weasel-faced man appeared. "I am Wan Kon, and I've come here to offer you my invitation personally. Did I hear it right, that you don't wish to be in my company?"

Wan Kon entered the room uninvited. He smiled at Yi Moi, then made a slight bow. "Miss Yi, your performance was magnificent. I have great admiration for you, and your presence in my house would be a great honor.''

As Wan Kon's eyes swept over her, Yi Moi felt a hissing adder trying to undress her with an invisible hand. She brought up her arms to hide her body, and could smell the lust of this loathsome man. She wondered what had become of Liu Shih, who was supposed to be her bodyguard at all times.

Wan Kon looked around the room, one of his hands pulling on his mustache, his beady eyes darting everywhere. ''Maybe you have already made plans to have dinner with someone else?'' he asked suspiciously. ''Is that the reason?''

Moi backed against the dresser; the room seemed to be closing in on her.

Suddenly Quanming appeared at the door, and behind him was Liu Shih.

''Is everything all right?'' Quanming asked Yi Moi. ''I'm very sorry that I couldn't come earlier.''

Liu Shih and Kim Shinma glared at each other; Quanming and Wan Kon likewise exchanged stares. The tension in the small space was as thick as the morning fog, and the hatred was almost visible in the air.

Yi Moi felt as though she was trapped in a cage of wild animals that at any moment might start tearing one another apart. Then she saw Quanming smiling at Wan Kon. ''Welcome to the theater of the Sung Wu Company.'' He bowed. ''At long last we meet. It's my honor to have this chance to know such an important member of our community.''

Outside the dressing room, several men of the Sung Wu Company had gathered by the open door. They stood silently in a semicircle, their arms folded across their chests.

Seeing these men, Wan Kon narrowed his eyes, then returned Quanming's bow after a brief hesitation. ''It's indeed my honor to meet the young master of the Sung Wu Company.'' He turned to Moi. ''You and I shall meet again.'' He bowed and left.

* * *

The Sung Wu Company's limousine pulled up in front of the Yung Fa Restaurant. Liu Shih opened the door and Yi Moi appeared. Dressed in a gray silk pantsuit, she was wearing little makeup and her hair was braided in a queue. Loone, Fachai, and the old couple Chu, all dressed in their best, greeted her at the door.

Chu Ninpo bowed, his face lighting up with excitement. "Welcome to our humble establishment. Please excuse the place. I'm sure you'd be much more comfortable in more elegant surroundings."

Moi smiled at the old man. "I like very much what I've seen so far. You have a lovely little place, and the smells coming from the kitchen are making my mouth water."

"Ah," Chu Hasan exclaimed with pride, "that's the smell of fried fish that our cook Li Fachai has prepared especially for you."

Moi's eyes brightened. "Fish is my favorite. I have not had any well-prepared fish since I left China. The food on the boat would kill an ox."

They were soon seated and Fachai served the food. She looked at him and smiled. He bowed, then quickly withdrew from the dining room. Her eyes followed him and color appeared on her pale face.

Loone, who could not take his eyes off her, saw her blushing, but never noticed it was caused by Fachai. All he could think of was that soon she would be posing for him and he would be able to transfer all that beauty onto his canvas. The first chance he had, he moved close to her side and whispered into her ear, "I'm so happy to see you here. I couldn't believe it when Quanming told me you were coming today."

The actress smiled without answering.

Fachai had the table set for only four; the old couple, Loone, and Moi. While they sat and ate, he took care of the other customers. Each time he looked to see if their table needed anything, Moi looked back with a smile and wouldn't look away.

Without any help from the *China News,* word had traveled with the speed of lightning. More people poured into Yung Fa and soon all the tables were filled. The customers placed their orders but ate absentmindedly; all eyes were watching Moi.

Being the focus of attention was nothing new to the actress, and she continued to eat undisturbed. She wasn't trying to please when she said she liked fish. She picked up the fish head, plucked out the eyes, popped them in her mouth with a sigh of delight. She then licked the juice from her fingers and sat back contented, "Ah, tonight I will dedicate my performance to the chef."

Those watching her smiled. Her hearty way of eating pleased them: the famous singer was as down-to-earth as they. They now liked her as a human being instead of as a goddess.

After the meal, Loone took Yi Moi to his room without anybody following. He had worked hard to show the room at its best. There were new sheets on the bed, and the sofa was piled with colorful satin pillows he had purchased the day before. He had also groomed himself carefully: his white shirt was spotless, his gray pants sharply creased; he had even parted his hair a different way. Nevertheless, he looked drawn, for he had not slept much the night before. Every time he closed his eyes, he had pictured Moi's face.

Moi went to the sofa, kicked off her shoes, sat comfortably like a little kitten. The light coming through the window fell softly on her delicate features; her braid was draped over her shoulder, resting in a curve around her breast.

"Please be patient," Loone said, his voice shaking and his fingers trembling. "I'll have to do several sketches first, then choose the best as a study for the painting."

Moi nodded. "Who taught you to paint?" she asked casually, watching Loone's eyes peering over the edge of a huge pad.

"Myself," Loone answered as he started to sketch in the pillows behind Moi. "My parents were art lovers, and as a child in Kwangchow I took up water-

colors. Fate took the good days away, and I was sold
to the Chus. When they realized there was no hope in
my becoming a cook, they allowed me the freedom to
paint. I've visited all the bookstores of San Francisco
and bought many books on Western art. I discovered
that Western artists are not like Chinese painters, who
believe only in copying the masters. I was greatly excited by this discovery, because I had always wanted
to create my own unique style. It was a difficult tran-
sition from working on rice paper to painting on canvas, and more difficult to change from watercolors to
oil . . .'' Loone kept on talking as he drew. He didn't
know he was talking so much—much more than he had
ever said to anybody else.

Moi looked at Loone, and her eyes widened at the
change. Somehow he was not the same person anymore. His trembling hand became steady the moment
he picked up his drawing pencil, his quaking voice
firm as soon as he started to discuss art. He was no
longer an insecure, scared child. With a confident glow
in his eyes, he was now an artist, a man.

Loone laid down the pencil and picked up a stick of
charcoal. His hand moved with firm strokes as he continued to talk. ''. . . It was through oil painting that I
began to see a new world, an unlimited field to journey
through. I started to travel along the path of a world
of art, stopping along the way only to explore further
the wonderful new mixture of colors or the effect of
the juxtaposition of two hues on the viewer's eye.''

Moi understood only half of the words used by
Loone, but she listened carefully in puzzlement as he
went on. ''A little over a year ago I was blessed with
the most encouraging event of my life. A small gallery
owner came to visit Chinatown with his Chinese interpreter, and happened to come to Yung Fa to eat.
He saw me sitting there sketching customers and
walked over to watch me. After a while I was persuaded to show him my paintings, and he offered to
buy them. I sold him a few, thinking that would be it.
But soon he came back and wanted to buy more—and
this time he raised the price. He told me that people

like my work . . . not the Chinese, of course, they scorn my barbaric style. It's the Americans who consider my technique good and my subject unique. Anyway, the man told me I would be very famous someday. Well, I don't really care about either fame or money. I paint because I have so much to say, and my brush speaks better than my mouth.''

Loone paused to pick up a rag and wipe off a line he didn't like. ''The Chus think differently about me now. I've been giving most of the money I've earned from the gallery to them—I have no need for money except to buy books and supplies. They buy clothes for me, and Mrs. Chu is forever after me for not eating enough. They are very kind people and I guess I should be grateful to them. Without them I wouldn't have been here painting the way I do. But there is another person I must thank, and that's my best friend, Fachai. You know, he doesn't really like to do the work he is doing. In his heart he is still a fisherman—that's what he was in Willow Place, his home. But he never complains as he buries himself in the kitchen or waits on those stupid people. He does the dirty work for the Chus so I can do what I like. He is truly a good friend.''

For the first time Yi Moi responded. ''Tell me more about Fachai,'' she said, interest creeping into her voice. ''Did you know each other in China? In this Willow Place you've just mentioned?''

''No . . . I thought you knew I was from Kwangchow. We came over on the same ship, the *Lady Ann*. There were four of us—what a sad bunch! Fachai, Quanming, Meiping, and I. Fachai missed his wife terribly; he talked about nothing but her through the whole trip. They had not been married long when he left her . . .''

When Loone glanced up, he noticed that Moi looked grief-stricken. He stopped drawing. ''Are you all right?'' he asked with deep concern. ''Have I kept you sitting in one position too long? You want to get up and move around a little?''

Moi forced a smile. ''I'm fine. You go on with the sketch.''

Loone continued sketching that day, and every day afterward. Soon the whole of Chinatown had learned about Yi Moi's being in Yung Fa every morning after rehearsal. They talked about her staying there for lunch and not leaving until it was time for her evening performance. The little restaurant quickly became the most popular eating place around. Long before her arrival the tables filled. The Chus had to hire temporary help, which was no problem, for many people would have been glad to pay the owners for a chance to wait on the famous actress.

Wan Kon was furious. "Going to that rat hole every day but turning down my offer for even one meal? She must be crazy! I was willing to pay her for her company, you know."

He and Limei sat at the dining table, and in his distress Wan was stuffing himself. The floor was covered with chicken bones.

Limei mumbled, "Maybe she is not crazy. Maybe she just happens to be one of the many things that don't have price tags."

Wan threw a piece of chicken at her. "Are you getting smart with me? You want to find your ass out on the street?"

Limei dodged the flying missile and answered with mock sweetness, "I'm sorry, Lau Ban. It's just that you always talk about buying people—"

She was interrupted by a bang on the door. Kim Shinma barged in.

"Well, what did you find out?" Wan shrieked.

The Korean wiped his brow. Because he knew how impatient the Lau Ban was, his words flowed out in one breath. "Yi Moi still goes to Yung Fa every day to have a portrait made by that adopted son of the Chus. The guard dog Liu Shih takes her there from the hotel and waits to take her back. I was told that at times Sung Quanming also goes upstairs to the little room where the painting takes place. Sometimes laughter can be heard by the customers downstairs."

"Deu-na-ma! I knew it! It's Sung Quanming! That

young smart-ass who thinks he owns Chinatown!''
Wan's face turned scarlet as he remembered how young
and handsome the upstart was, and concluded instantly that he had found the true reason for Yi Moi's
spending so much time in that miserable little place.
''I knew all along something was fishy. No one would
be stupid enough to waste time on a portrait with all
those photographers around.''

Wan's weasellike face was twisted with pain. Yi
Moi's rejection had become more unbearable since he
now believed he had been beaten by a member of the
Sung family. ''They're openly insulting me. Everyone
must be having a good laugh! I've been made to look
like a fool!'' Anger twisted his face and deformed it
as he raged on. ''They'll soon be laughing out of the
other sides of their mouths when I'm through with
them! Every last one of the fornicating bastards!''

He moved Kim away from Limei and spoke to the
Korean in hushed tones: ''Find out when is the busiest
time at the little dump, and pass the word to our friends
that it may not be a healthy place to have meals. You
understand? Go!''

Looking at Wan Kon from a distance, Limei felt a
chill coursing through her body.

Yi Moi's last appearance in San Francisco was performed, and she now had to depart for Chicago. A
farewell party was given by the Sung Wu Company,
and once more she was given a chance to mingle with
the elite of Chinatown. As for the welcoming party,
she dressed herself carefully and tried to use her youth,
beauty, and charm to hook a husband. But again she
was met with defeat and disappointment. Her fans were
many, her suitors few. Men regarded her as if she were
an art object in the Palace Museum; most of them
admired her without the intention to possess, and those
with the intention to possess her, she wouldn't want
near.

The morning after the party, Quanming picked her
up and drove her to Yung Fa for a small farewell gathering planned by the Chus.

They had closed the place to the public so that Fachai would be freed from the customers to join them.
In the middle of the room a table had been carefully
set with red buns for good luck, green vegetables for
sound health, and many golden cookies for a prosperous future.

Moi looked at Fachai with a sad smile and said
softly, "You arranged all this, I know. I envy your
wife, she must be the luckiest woman on earth. She
must be very proud of you for what you can do. Everything you cooked looks not only delicious but also
beautiful."

Without meeting her eyes, Fachai let out a small
laugh. "Leahi proud of my cooking? She would die!
She is a woman who doesn't believe a man should pour
himself a cup of tea if he has a wife . . ." He stopped
with a sigh.

Chu Ninpo agreed with Fachai. "You're from the
Pearl, Miss Yi. You know it's true that in China a man
would never think of cooking or washing clothes. Actually, none of us Chinese came to this country to be
cooks and laundrymen. We started by working on the
railroad and in the mines. Then, since there were no
women to cook or wash for us, we did the chores. The
white men liked the smells of our food and were surprised by the taste after they came up with the courage
to try. They also noticed our laundry was cleaner than
theirs and offered to pay us for doing it. And pretty
soon, before we knew it, all the Chinese had become
laundrymen and cooks."

Fachai seldom talked in front of Yi Moi. But all of
a sudden he began to speak, his voice hoarse and low,
his eyes trained on an empty dish. "I've become a
cook because I'm a coward. I'm afraid to fight for what
I truly want—the white man's world frightens me. Life
as a cook in Yung Fa is safer than going out of Chinatown to try to find a place for myself in the world
of the white fishermen. I'm very ashamed." He
paused. Moi opened her mouth but couldn't think of
any comforting words. Fachai continued, "I've promised my family to stay here only for a short time.

They've counted on my returning home with enough money to buy our own boat, but my parents and grandfather have died without seeing me return—my wife didn't even let me know about their deaths until almost a year later. I miss the Pearl so much. In all my dreams I see it flow. Even last night I dreamed I was fishing there again, and felt the swell of the waves under my keel. I was fishing with a boy, a boy who looked like me, but it wasn't until he called me Baba that I knew he was my son—''

Fachai suddenly stopped. He raised his eyes, looked across the table at Moi. He wasn't sure if it was his imagination or if there were actually tears in her beautiful eyes. He quickly stood up and left the table. "I . . . I have to check on something in the kitchen," he stammered.

Ever since Loone had turned to oil painting, the smells of turpentine had forced Fachai to move his bed into the downstairs storage room. He ran into the room and sat on the edge of the bed with his elbows resting on his legs and his head propped on his hands, looking in dismay at a faded quilt.

He could never forget how his young bride had given it to him before he left, and each time he looked at it his heart ached. It reminded him of the Autumn Festival night, and he saw again the image of Leahi and himself under the ancient willows, making love in the beams of the full moon. The memory of the fragrance of her body and the feel of her softness came back to haunt him and make his homesickness unbearable.

Covering his face with his palms, Fachai started to sob. "I want my Leahi . . . I want my son! I'm so lonely . . . I want to go home—''

Someone called, "Fachai! Come! We're going upstairs to see the portrait!"

Unable to stop sobbing, Fachai looked at the many bottles of cooking wine on the shelf. He quickly reached for one, uncorked it, and started to drink. After several large gulps he dried his mouth with the back of his hand, then yelled to the people waiting for him, "Coming!"

* * *

Everyone stood silently in front of the painting, their mouths open, their eyes wide.

The background was a stormy sky painted with a blending of colors that produced a misty living gray. Across the canvas were the pillows, their pigments and arrangement giving the appearance of a rainbow. A woman with a heart-shaped face was reclining in a white gown that sometimes blended into the clouds or melted into the rainbow. Her long slanting eyes gazed out of the portrait, reflecting an inner fire. Her perfectly shaped red lips were slightly parted, and around her slender long neck was a string of pearls, their pink luster so real that it seemed they could be lifted from her neck.

Yi Moi's intake of breath broke the silence. Tears streamed down her cheeks as she stood staring in awe. "Oh, Loone, you've created a goddess. Is this how you see me? And, Loone, the pearls! You've told me how much they mean to you, and now you've painted them on me." She walked over to him and, to the amazement of everyone, embraced him.

Loone turned so red that he was about to ignite. His arms remained stiffly at his sides; he looked over Moi's shoulders and searched for help, but everyone just stood and smiled. It was considered unladylike for a woman to hug a man in public, but everyone understood Moi's emotion. Seeing the painting was, for everyone, an overwhelming experience.

The old woman suddenly frowned. "Yi Moi looks so sad in this portrait." She walked closer to the painting. "I see her as the white snake in the final act. She looks like a woman who is about to sing a farewell song to her husband and child."

The old man's face was darkened by his wife's words. As he looked at the portrait carefully, he felt the hair on the back of his neck turning stiff. Moi, sitting among the clouds, looked inhuman. A goddess, yes. A very sad goddess, who represented tears and sorrow, pain and suffering . . . perhaps even death. Quickly he asked, "You are taking the portrait with you to Chicago, I'm sure?'' He suddenly couldn't wait to get rid of this bad omen.

"Oh, no,'' Loone said quickly. "She can't. It's not dry enough to be moved. She'll have to come back for it when she's through with her tour.''

The railroad station was crowded, and the Occidentals wondered where all the Chinese had come from. Yi Moi stood on the steps leading to the car, smiling at all the people who had come to see her off. The whistle blew and the train began to inch forward. Moi was entering the car, but stopped when she heard Loone yelling her name.

She turned to see him running alongside the train, and as the wheels began to gather speed, he threw a small box to her, with the expression that he had thrown her his life. "Catch it! I want you to have it! I . . .'' The rest of his words were lost in the blast of the whistle.

Yi Moi settled in her seat and opened the package. Nestled in a fold of red silk was the pink pearl necklace.

# 23

QUANMING DROVE TO the outskirts of San Francisco and stopped at a deserted spot by a quiet hill. A gentle waterfall whispered down the protruding rocks, then changed into a clear stream shaded by several tall trees. Not far from the falls, white flat stones formed a giant throne. Sitting on one of the stones, Laurie was waiting for him.

The trees were dressed in their autumn colors; wild-flowers were still in bloom. Laurie stood up with a bouquet she had just gathered and ran into Quanming's outstretched arms. Their lips met, two bodies pressed together trying to melt into one. When they finally broke away from each other, they whispered soft words of love.

"I missed you so much," Quanming said, out of breath from running up the hill. "I'm glad Yi Moi is gone. It has been so difficult seeing you at the parties but not being able to hold you."

"And I missed you terribly," Laurie answered as they walked arm in arm toward the top of the hill. "I was beginning to worry. That actress is so beautiful, and you were with her a great deal."

"There was never any need for worry. You are the only one I love. There can never be anyone else."

"Nor can there be anyone but you for me. Oh, Quanming, I wish the world would leave us alone!"

Both of them were thinking about the difficulties that lay between them, but as they walked together, neither wished to talk about it.

The pressure from Sung Tinwei for Quanming to marry A-lin had become harder to bear. Quanming knew he would have to tell his uncle soon that he wanted to marry Laurie, but dreaded the confrontation. Laurie's parents had been told about their daughter's Chinese young man, and were heartbroken. It hurt Laurie to see them on their knees praying to God to bring their daughter to the good senses of a true Christian and forget this yellow heathen.

"I've packed a picnic basket, with all your favorites," Laurie said, trying to sound cheerful.

There were chicken-salad and ham-and-cheese sandwiches. They were not really to Quanming's liking, but he wasn't going to hurt Laurie's feelings. There were also a bottle of wine and two crystal glasses. Laurie had even brought a red-and-white tablecloth, with polished silver utensils and a little vase for the bouquet of wildflowers.

"I like the way you Americans eat," he said. "We Chinese pay attention only to the food, but you create an enjoyable atmosphere."

He was sitting with his legs crossed, and Laurie noticed how his once-flat stomach now protruded over his pants. She playfully poked him. "My man is getting fat."

Chewing on a chicken-salad sandwich, Quanming shrugged. "I haven't been exercising like I should. My uncle has given me a lot of responsibility, and I've become more of a businessman than a fighter."

"You shouldn't stop exercising, Quanming," Laurie said with scorn. "You know very well that if you wanted to keep up with your workout, you could have made time. You're so young. You shouldn't let yourself go. You've been eating too much at all those parties, and you've been lazy in a way—"

Quanming raised a hand. "That's enough. If you want to be a good wife to a Chinese you'd better learn not to interfere with your lord and master. And if you dare to tell me what to do in front of our guests . . ." He shook a threatening fist at her, then poured himself another glass of wine, trying to keep a stern look.

"What would happen if I did, my lord and master?" Laurie asked with exaggerated innocence, her head tilted and eyes wide.

"In order to save face, I'd have to give you a good beating in front of all the guests."

"What about my loss of face?"

"Your face wouldn't be lost, because you would be honored by the fact that your husband loved you enough to put you in your place."

Laurie's green eyes flashed. "I wouldn't classify beating as love! Sung Quanming, that would be wife abuse!"

Quanming began to laugh, and Laurie realized he had only been teasing. She started to hit him with her fists, and he grabbed her in his arms, kissing her anger away. At first she tried to avoid his lips, but soon was all too happy to give in.

Unknown to the lovers, Liu Shih was hiding at the foot of the hill, watching and listening. He had followed Quanming on orders from Sung Tinwei. It had been a painful chore for him, because the laughter of the lovers reminded him of the laughter that had once existed between himself and the only girl he had loved, who was killed by Kim Shinma.

He waited patiently for Quanming and Laurie to leave the hill. He watched as his young master walked the red-haired girl to her car. When Quanming drove away, Liu Shih raced toward the car the company had given him and followed Quanming to Yung Fa Restaurant.

Quanming walked into the restaurant at its busiest hour. Fachai was in the kitchen, and the Chus were running in circles. Loone was sitting in his corner, reading a book. Joining him, Quanming was surprised to see Loone reading about the marketing of art.

"Hello, Loone. What has turned you into a businessman?"

"I have something to tell you. I . . ." He stood up, and continued excitedly, "I've gathered my best sketches, and am ready to bring them to the gallery. I'll ask the owner about my turning each drawing into a painting and having a show. I want to become a successful artist—with fame, fortune, and everything. I've decided that I'll need them after all . . . not for myself, but for someone else, someone wonderful."

He smiled at Quanming. "Wait here, I'll go get the sketches."

While Loone was gone Quanming poured himself a cup of tea. As he lifted the cup, he sensed a sudden silence in the restaurant. Because Loone's favorite table was at the end of the room facing the kitchen, Quanming had his back to the front door.

He turned to look. His hand froze in midair, holding the teacup. Standing there were Kim Shinma and two strangers. One was wearing a red bandanna, the other a gold earring.

The Korean looked at Quanming and smiled, then nodded to his friends. The two men sprang into action. The one with the bandanna flipped the lock on the front door; the other ran to the rear, barring the exit.

Most of the customers remained glued to their chairs in fear; the few who had gotten up quickly sat back down when Kim looked their way. The crowd was a herd of sheep facing the sharp teeth of a wolf.

Chu Ninpo, who was standing with a pile of dirty dishes in his hands, asked in a quavering voice, "Please . . . what do you want?"

In answer to the old man's question, the earring man drew a short metal pipe from beneath his tunic, and with a flip of his wrist he hit one of the seated customers on the side of the head. The victim fell soundlessly to the floor.

Ninpo dropped the dishes. The diners panicked. They jumped to their feet, knocking over tables and chairs to race for the door. Kim Shinma knocked several of them down as he plowed through the screaming crowd, making his way toward Quanming.

Chu Hasan ran toward her husband just as the bandanna-man pulled out a knife. Holding it by the handle, he made an overhand toss that sent the razor-honed blade toward Quanming. The terrified old woman entered the path of the flying knife; the handle smashed into her skull. She collapsed at her husband's feet with blood seeping from the wound. The old man dropped to his knees, holding his wife, wailing in anguish.

Still in the kitchen, Fachai cautiously peeked through the curtains to see the source of all the commotion. Shocked at what he saw, he started to join the fight. Then he remembered how all the fights on the ship had ended between Kim and Quanming, and was confident that his friend could take care of the situation. He raced toward the kitchen door and was on the back streets a few seconds later. The thought of calling the police never crossed his mind; Chinatown had always handled its own problems. He ran without stopping until he reached the Sung Wu Company.

Liu Shih, who had followed Quanming, had seen Kim and the two strangers entering Yung Fa Restaurant. He hesitated but a moment before he rushed over, but not in time; the entrance was already locked. He moved back several paces and barreled into the door, hitting it with such force that it was torn from its hinges.

Seeing the door down, the crowd rushed toward it. Their panic had turned them into a stampeding herd, mowing down anything that stood in the way. Liu Shih, being directly in their path, was knocked backward. He lost his footing and fell, and when he got up his head was swimming. He had barely stumbled into the entrance when suddenly he felt a sharp pain in his side, doubling him over. He reached around and felt the handle of a knife. When he looked around, he saw one of thugs moving toward him.

Liu Shih was transported back to the room where he and his girl had been tortured; the features of the gold-earring thug changed into the face of Kim Shinma. With a scream his hands shot out and grabbed his attacker by the throat. His thumbs madly pressed against the man's windpipe.

The thug struggled, hitting and kicking for his life. His hand found the hilt of the knife, and with a tug he pulled it out and drove it into Liu once more. At the same moment his windpipe collapsed and Liu released him. The man fell to the floor, his eyes bulging, his hands holding his throat as the body jerked in its struggle for air. Then he was still.

Kim turned to help, but realized it was too late. He

shifted his anger to Chu Ninpo, who was still rocking his wounded wife. "Shut your damn mouth!" he bellowed, chopping down with the side of his hand, breaking the old man's collarbone, knocking him unconscious. The Korean stepped over the old couple, his eyes burning with hate as he saw Quanming coming toward him.

The bandanna-man was closer to Quanming and reached him before Kim. The man shot his hand out, his fingers rigid. Quanming sidestepped, bringing his left arm up in a sweeping block. With the palm of his right hand he smashed upward into the attacker's nose. Blood flew as the nose was parted from the face. A piece of the cartilage had broken off, driven by the force of the blow into the brain. The man was dead before his body hit the floor.

Quanming felt the ominous presence of Kim before he saw him. The Korean smiled at his old enemy. "Well, it's you and me again. I've waited a long time for this. Today you will die!"

Quanming knew he was no longer a match for the menace that loomed before him. As Kim talked, Quanming searched frantically for a weapon. He spotted a table leg that had been broken off and quickly grabbed it.

Quanming swung the club with all his strength, but Kim's hand caught the wooden stick on the edge of the palm. The wood splintered, leaving Quanming holding a short stump.

Quanming started to retreat, and Kim advanced slowly toward him, tossing the overturned tables and chairs out of his way, the smile never leaving his face.

"Time to die, you pretty boy!" He came at Quanming with a bellow that echoed through the room, and his fist shot out. The fight would have ended right then if Quanming had not been fast enough to deflect the blow. Still, the force sent him sprawling backward. He lost his balance as his foot struck a chair, and he toppled over, landing on his back.

Shinma stopped and looked down. His smile broadened as he beckoned with his hand, the fear in Quanming's eyes feeding his ego. "Take your time, pretty boy. I'm in no hurry." He stood with his fists resting on his hips, watching Quanming trying to untangle himself from the chair.

Quanming got to his feet, sucking in deep breaths of air through his open mouth; he felt like his lungs were being roasted over hot coals. Before he could move out of the way, Kim hit him again, sending him into one of the tables. The table skidded across the floor into the wall. Quanming could taste the blood in his mouth, and his vision blurred. Another blow to his side caved in a rib, but he still did not go down.

"Pretty boy, enjoying this?" Shinma hissed, moving in.

Quanming kept shaking his head, trying to clear it. He managed to sidestep the next attack, and with his two hands clenched together, he hit Kim in the kidneys with a force that made the big man roar in pain. Kim leaned on one of the upright tables, snarling.

They stood facing each other. Through sheer willpower Quanming began to calm himself. His vision cleared, and his breathing became more normal. All the years of discipline began to mold him back into a fighting machine. His skills compensated for his physical weakness; he took his stance as he had done many times in the temple at White Stone and waited.

Kim Shinma charged in a maddened rage. "You're dead, you son-of-a-cur!"

Quanming brought from his diaphragm a sound that began softly but built into an ear-piercing yell. As Kim came in, Quanming moved like a cat: he shifted his head and his body with perfect timing so that the Korean's blows met nothing but air. Kim was breathing with difficulty as he stood now in bewilderment. Quanming instantly raced toward the Korean, jumping high into the air, his legs drawn in against his chest. Then, with flawless timing, he shot them out. One foot hit Shinma in the face, breaking his nose and throwing his head back; the other caught him in the throat. Kim went crashing into a table, breaking it under his weight.

Quanming landed gracefully on his feet and came at the Korean again, but stopped in his tracks when he found himself staring into the muzzle of a gun. He dived for cover. Kim fired. Quanming had not moved fast enough, and felt a searing pain in his left shoulder. He rolled behind a table as a second shot took a chip out of the floor. Again the gun went off, the bullet tearing through the top of the table, sending needlelike splinters into Quanming's face. The young fighter kept dashing about, with his left arm hanging uselessly at his side.

Kim fired again and a slug tore through Quanming's leg. He continued dodging, trying to drive away the pain. Another shot rang out, then another before Quanming spotted a knife just within reach. He scooped it up and hurled the blade just as Kim raised the revolver once more. The Korean squeezed the trigger, but the hammer fell on an empty cylinder. Quanming's knife completed one revolution before the blade embedded itself into the advancing Kim. The big man staggered back, bewildered by this disastrous about-face, and began to weave his way toward the exit.

Loone was getting his sketches when all hell broke loose. He ran to the stairway to look down and then froze. The sight of the bald-headed man recalled a chilling childhood memory, when the warlords' soldiers had swept into Kwangchow and killed at random on the main street.

"Hide, my baby, you must hide. And don't make a sound until they are gone," his mother had said then, and right now the same words reached his ears again. Quickly he obeyed.

In a trance he retreated to his room and crawled under his bed. He lay on the floor, flat and stiff. He heard the screams and shouting coming from below, and at times he thought the whole building was about to be torn apart. His body turned ice cold; he lay still, staring up at the bottom of the mattress that was a bare inch from his face.

Only long after everything had quieted down did he

begin to regain his senses. He worked his way from under the bed and cautiously stepped into the hall. He noticed he was covered with sweat. He placed one foot on the first step and waited. Now the silence frightened him, and he shakily forced himself slowly down the steps. He stopped and held his breath when his weight caused one of the boards to creak. He remained rigid, listening, then once again proceeded. When he finally reached a little way below the level of the dining room's ceiling, he squatted to take a look through the rungs of the banister.

In the dim light he could make out tables and chairs, their legs tangled like the antlers of fighting stags, most of them shattered beyond repair. Broken dishes covered the floor, along with the food they had once held.

He stepped down carefully, but still slipped and almost fell before he reached the light switch. He threw the switch, and to his horror he realized that he was standing in a pool of blood. He felt sick. He leaned against the wall with both hands, emptying his stomach.

He took several deep breaths, then continued to look about. Blood was everywhere. He noticed a broken window and the front door off its hinges. He wondered: Who had created so much havoc, and where was everyone?

He walked slowly through the debris and spied a faded plastic flower. He picked it up, imagining Chu Hasan placing it in a small vase. He looked over to where his corner table had been, and saw it now stood on three legs. He kept staring at the corner, and thought he heard Mrs. Chu's gentle voice: "Loone, my son, would you like me to bring you something nice to eat? You're so thin. Maybe after you have eaten, you would like to help a little? That'll make the old man so happy."

Loone held his hands up to his ears and began to scream.

## 24

THE EMERGENCY ROOM was a bedlam of activity. There were five dead: Liu Shih, the bandanna-man, the one with the earring, a diner with a caved-in skull, and another with a broken neck. Chu Ninpo was on an operating table, a tube in his arm replacing the blood he had lost. His lung had been punctured by a broken bone, and his condition was not stable enough for an operation. The doctors could do little for him except to make him comfortable. Chu Hasan, with a critical head wound, lay next to him in a state of shock.

Kim Shinma's wound had been cleaned, his shoulder bandaged. The knife had severed the nerves that fed his arm, and there was nothing further the doctors could do. He lay there wondering why he was not able to move his hand or arm.

They had removed two bullets from Quanming, but because of the amount of blood he had lost, the doctors were not sure whether he would survive. He was taken to the new intensive-care unit, and outside, Sung Tinwei and Wa Da-chung waited.

The others in the waiting room were all Americans, and some were disturbed by the presence of two Chinese. But when they went to check with the head nurse, they were told, "It's because of the donation made by these two Chinese gentlemen that it was possible to add this beautiful new wing. They are the owners of the Sung Wu Company."

Tinwei and Da-chung overheard the conversation. "Even in the hospital we are not spared the arrows of prejudice," Da-chung said to his old friend. "What have we done to deserve such hatred?"

Sung Tinwei, however, was concerned about only one thing at this moment. "Do you think the doctors are doing everything they can to save Quanming? Will they do less for him because he's Chinese?"

Da-chung thought it over carefully before he answered. "Dr. Weinstein is a good man. I have known him for many years and I have no reason to believe that he is biased against us Chinese." The old man's eyes were filling with tears. "I love Quanming as if he were my nephew instead of yours. I want him to marry my A-lin, and see them have many sons."

Just then Fachai walked in with Paul Eddington and Laurie.

After the police and ambulance had been called by Sung Tinwei, Fachai had quickly returned to Yung Fa with several employees of the company. When he arrived, he had seen Quanming being carried on a stretcher. Quanming had beckoned to Fachai, then had gathered enough strength to whisper only one word: "Laurie."

As soon as Laurie entered, she ran to Sung Tinwei. "Where is my Quanming? How is he?" she sobbed in a state of panic.

Tinwei frowned. Laurie's eyes were red, her hair a mess. She had not gone through the customary greetings of respect, which were expected no matter what the circumstances were. "Young woman, are you talking to me, or are you addressing the wall?" he asked, his voice cold as ice.

Laurie was taken aback by the old man's remarks. She bit her lip, not wanting to tell him off. Instead she bowed to Tinwei and said stiffly, "Good evening, my honorable sir. Please excuse my manners, but my fear for Quanming has blinded me to *your* standards of conduct!" Try as she might, she could not keep the bitterness from creeping in. "My concern is for your nephew, not the precious protocol that you seem to cherish more than life. Now, are you going to tell me how my Quanming is, or do I have to prostrate myself on the ground and kowtow to you?"

Paul Eddington knew immediately how big a mistake his niece had just made. She had ridiculed not only Sung Tinwei but also five thousand years of Chinese tradition. Her wrongdoing could be neither tolerated nor erased.

Tinwei stared at Laurie. "Since when has my nephew become your property? You shameless Fangui-nui!" After calling Laurie a foreign-devil-girl, the old man turned his back on her, ending any further conversation.

Tears rolled down Laurie's cheeks as she walked around to face Tinwei. "Mr. Sung, I don't know why you hate me so, but I love Quanming, and he loves me. Please tell me how he is."

Sung Tinwei answered her with slow deliberation: "Keep away from me, young woman. There are other rooms where you can wait. If you must know Quanming's condition, I suggest you check with the nurses down the hall. Now, will you please remove yourself from my sight?"

Before Laurie could create a scene, Paul took her by the arm and led her out of the room. As Laurie stood in the hallway shaking in anger, Paul returned and apologized to Tinwei for disturbing him during his hour of trouble. Tinwei didn't answer. Paul left, knowing he had lost a good friend.

Wu Da-chung placed a hand on Tinwei's shoulder. "I have not seen you so angry for a long time, old friend. You were very hard on that young lady—"

"Young lady!" Tinwei roared. " 'Young devil' is more like it! She acted as if she were already betrothed to our Quanming!" He paced the floor, each heavy step a step of anger.

After studying Tinwei for a time, Da-chung said, "My friend . . ." His voice was low and understanding as he walked in step with Tinwei. "It's not this girl who is bothering you. It's the same old ghost, the American girl who broke your young heart all those years ago. You are taking it out on this Laurie for fear that she will hurt our Quanming as the other one hurt you."

Sung Tinwei stopped pacing and stood looking at his friend. Then he sighed. "I don't want to talk about the past. Let us pray that Quanming is out of danger soon. He and A-lin must marry as soon as he gets out of this hospital.''

Wan Kon walked into the bar excitedly, telling Limei and Meiping what had happened.

''The young Sung is going to die, and the Sung Wu Company will soon collapse. I, Wan Kon, will be the biggest Lau Ban of Tong-jen-gai again!'' He poured himself a drink to celebrate, not the least disturbed by the death of the five people. His only concern was that Kim Shinma might have talked too much and involved the House of Wan.

In the middle of his toast, though, he reconsidered the matter. His beady eyes swept from Limei to Meiping, and he finally said, ''I wish the two of you could be of some use. Can either one of you go to the hospital to visit Kim and find out if the fool has told the police anything? I really must know.''

Limei looked at Wan Kon angrily. She had given her whole life to this man, and he had not even the slightest concern for her safety. ''Sure,'' she said to Meiping sarcastically. ''The Lau Ban won't change a light bulb himself because he is afraid of being electrocuted; he makes us women do the changing. Now, if Kim has told the police that everything was carried out by orders of the House of Wan, then there will be policemen waiting beside Kim, ready to take us to jail. What does it matter to our Lau Ban as long as he is safe?''

'Deu-na-ma!'' Wan Kon cursed. ''For so many years I let you stay under my roof, and you won't even show me the smallest bit of gratitude! You ungrateful bitch!''

He walked toward Limei with an open hand. In turn the woman flinched, ready to take the blow. Meiping quickly stepped between them. ''I'll go!''

''But, Meiping!'' Limei protested. ''What if they arrest you?''

Meiping did not answer, not trusting herself to speak. Instead she glared at Wan Kon, wanting to spit on him.

Wan Kon dropped his hand, and Limei was spared.

He mistook Meiping's offer for loyalty, and allowed her to be driven to the hospital in his new car.

On the way, Meiping looked through the car window and saw a crescent moon wearing a necklace of stars. She was reminded of the evenings aboard ship with her Pearl River friends—how young and naive they had all been. She regretted not having contacted them all these years. "Don't die, Quanming,' she started to pray to the moon. "If you stay alive, the four of us might become friends again."

Kim opened his eyes to see Meiping standing at the foot of the bed. "It's about time!" he bellowed. "What took you so long? Where are the others? Why am I here in this room with all these poor bastards? I never told the police one word about the Lau Ban, and he must take good care of me! So, when will he have me transferred to a private room?"

Meiping didn't answer immediately. She stood staring down, hating the sight of this animal. With a grin she leaned forward and whispered, "There are two reasons you are not dead: hell rejected you, for one, and the other is that Quanming is still alive. If he had died, I would have killed you myself."

Kim sat up, wincing from the pain. "Listen, you whore, I followed the Lau Ban's orders and now we will see whom he appreciates. Sung Quanming will die. I shot him several times point-blank. Just the thought of seeing him go down gives me a great deal of pleasure."

"He's not going to die," Meiping said calmly. "I talked with his doctor before I came to you. It's you, Kin Shinma, who might as well be dead. Your days of killing and raping are over. You're about as useless to the Lau Ban as tits on a male dog now that you have only one arm." Seeing the disbelief on Kim's face, she drew even nearer and grinned. "I've also talked to your doctor, who told me that you will never be able to use your arm again. Eventually it will shrivel up and hang at your side like a limp dick."

"What are you talking about?" Kim yelled, and

tried to move his arm to prove she was wrong. The arm refused to obey. He poked it with his fingers; it felt like touching a piece of cold meat. "Wan Lau Ban will get me the best doctors in San Francisco. He'll do anything for me after all I have done for him!" he screamed, on the point of hysteria.

Meiping stood smiling at the tormented man and whispered. "Do you really believe that Wan Kon wants the police to think he had anything to do with what happened? You know him well enough to realize that his only loyalty is to Wan Kon. Look, you're in a city ward. The white doctors will do little to save the arm of a Korean bastard. They'll throw you out in a day or two, just to have the bed for someone else. When you get out of here, the police will be waiting. The Sung Wu Company is pressing charges, and there are more than enough witnesses to nail you for the deaths of five people"

"No!" Kim shouted. "Wan Lau Ban will get me a powerful lawyer. He'll not do this to me . . . you lying whore!"

Meiping tilted her head back and laughed. "You are denser than I thought. Wan Kon never lifts a finger for anyone if it's not to his benefit. What you are to him now is nothing but a useless cripple with five murders on your head. If he finds a lawyer, it would be for himself, to deny anything you say. His lawyers are paid highly to be good, and you are as helpless against them as your wasted arm." Meiping turned and left, not giving a damn if Kim and Wan both rotted in prison.

Out in the corridor, she could still hear Kim screaming. She smiled at the policeman guarding the door and proceeded toward the floor that held Quanming.

Loone stood at the door, looking in at the Chu couple. The old man had not regained consciousness and was lying there hooked to many tubes. Chu Hasan was sitting next to him on a chair, her head wrapped in a bandage.

"How are you feeling, Mama Chu?" Loone asked,

using a title he had been determined never to use. He knew how much pleasure it would give the woman, but at the same time it made him feel disloyal to his own mother.

Chu Hasan never took her eyes from her husband. There was a string of Buddhist prayer beads in her hands, and she was counting them, mumbling over and over the four simple syllables. "Au Me Tau Foo . . ."

"How is Papa Chu?" Loone asked as he stepped closer.

The old woman continued to mumble as if he were not there. "Au Me Tau Foo . . ." Her fingers journeyed from bead to bead.

Loone made several vain attempts to comfort Chu Hasan, but finally left crying. "This is not fair!" he sobbed as he walked down the hall. "Why must I lose everyone who cares for me? I should have treated them better! I will let them know how much they mean to me as soon as they are well."

After Loone left, the old woman leaned toward her husband, resting her head on the guardrail. Her fingers moved slowly over the beads; her lips quivered silently, her eyes closed.

In her mind, she was once again young, wearing a bridal gown. Her groom was standing next to her, so handsome. She shyly glanced at him now and then, proud to become his wife. They were standing in front of a Buddhist monk whose face was covered by a hood. "Au Me Tau Foo . . ." the man chanted, blessing the married couple.

All of a sudden the monk stopped. He removed the hood, revealing a grinning white skull. His skeletal hands clutched Chu Ninpo by the shoulder, and as he threw back his head, she saw its empty sockets as black and deep as a moonless night.

"Mrs. Chu, please wake up." Chu Hasan opened her eyes to see a doctor standing over her, shaking her by the arm and trying to stop her from screaming.

She looked up and asked, but already knew. "How is my husband?"

The doctor took her hand. "I'm so sorry, Mrs. Chu. Your husband expired a few minutes ago."

As the old woman stared at the doctor, the flesh on his face seemed to dissolve, leaving a grinning white skull. She screamed. Leaping out of the chair, she ran from the smiling abhorrence. A searing pain gripped her chest; she could not breathe. Leaning against the wall, she slowly slid down, landing in a heap on the sterile floor.

Not able to live without her husband, she had joined him.

Loone was in the waiting room when the doctor told him that they had both died. He turned and left without a word. He walked the streets throughout the night, and by morning he had reached a decision: if death insisted on taking those he loved, from now on he would love only his art. That was something that even the grinning bastard death could not destroy.

Standing in front of Yung Fa at dawn, Loone began to visualize how to rebuild the place. It would become the showplace of Chinatown, he decided, in memory of the Chus and the blood and sweat they had put into it. "I'll not let you down, Papa Chu and Mama Chu. You loved me, and I also loved you!" He went in, ran up the stairs, and with his jaw set firmly, he began to paint.

Quanming saw himself returning once more to White Stone. Beyond the white marble on top of the hill, the setting sun had dyed the clouds a pastel pink. At the foot of the hill he saw his home, and through the windows the lamplight glowed a warm yellow.

He saw his mother walking slowly toward the house; she was again young, with shining black hair. He called out to her, but she didn't seem to be able to hear him. She entered the house and left the door open. His father and brother were both waiting to welcome her. "Let me join you! I want to come home!" he shouted to his family, but was ignored by them. The picture began to fade into a white mist.

A bright ray of light burned a hole through the fog,

its heat quickly drying away the vapor. A young girl appeared in a beautiful robe, and in her long hair she wore a colorful comb. "Yoto!" Quanming called out. The girl looked not at him, but at a man who was offering her a jade plate heaped with gold. The two walked hand in hand; the light faded and the mist returned.

Quanming was suddenly flying high, looking down at a patch of green grass. He swooped down to take a closer look, then landed on a flat rock near a waterfall. A young woman appeared sitting on a giant boulder, the sun shining on her bright red hair. She was crying, and through the sobs he could hear her calling his name: "Quanming. Please don't leave me. I love you. Please don't die."

He called out to her. She smiled and threw him a bouquet of wildflowers she was holding. "Catch them, Quanming. They are the magic you need!"

He reached for them but missed, and the flower petals began to fly away. He raced after them; the girl was screaming for him to run faster. In desperation he leapt through the air, his hand outstretched. The minute he caught the bouquet, he could feel their magical power. "Laurie! I'll not leave you! I'm coming back! I love you!" His eyes opened.

All that day he drifted in and out of a coma, but by the following day he was able to sit up. Two days later he was able to take solid food and have visitors.

Meiping, wearing a pink silk suit and a pair of gray alligator shoes, reached into her matching purse to get a mirror, and as she checked her hair, she said loudly, "I'm glad Buddha has brought us together again! But couldn't he have found an easier way? I'll have to give him a good talking-to!"

From his bed, Quanming smiled. "I pity poor Buddha. He had better hide!"

Sitting on a chair next to the bed, Fachai added, "You're right, Buddha is in big trouble. There's no place to hide when Yung Meiping gets fired up."

She walked over and gave Fachai a punch. "What are you trying to say?"

"Nothing . . . not a thing!" Fachai put up his hands to defend himself.

Leaning on the wall opposite the bed, Loone held a piece of charcoal and a sketchpad, working silently. He looked up at his friends horsing around like children and smiled.

Meiping moved away from Fachai, went to look at the drawing. "Oh, my!" she said, and snatched the pad away from Loone. "I want you all to look at this! We sure have changed since we were on that miserable ship."

"Wait, it's not finished!" Loone cried, reaching to get his pad back, but Meiping easily pushed him aside.

The pad was brought to Quanming, and Loone waited for comments. Meiping and Fachai went to either side of the patient, and together they studied the sketch.

Quanming pointed at the drawing of Meiping. "Once a scarecrow, now a beauty. Loone has captured your look, a look that's more impressive than your jewelry or clothes."

Looking at the drawing, Fachai added, "I hate to mention this, but there is a softness in her eyes. I've noticed the same expression in David Cohen's whenever he looks at Meiping."

Meiping blushed with joy. She looked at the pad again, then looked at Fachai. Not one for being delicate, she added abruptly, "Fachai, how come you look so old and so bad? You're only in your twenties; we all are. Why such a haggard look?"

Quanming looked over at Meiping, shaking his head. "You are too blunt for your own good. Of course Fachai looks tired. He has to take care of so many things at the restaurant now the Chus are gone."

"No, Quanming, Meiping is right. Blunt and rude she may be, but she is honest." Fachai's voice was low and weak. "Among the four of us, I am the only one who has accomplished nothing. In a few days it'll be the Mid-Autumn Festival again. I promised Leah to watch the moon with her, and each year as I stand at the water's edge looking out over the bay, I never fail to make wishes.'' He sighed, bowed his head. ''All the wishes have been but the same empty words: Let my wife and son join me. Let me become once more a fisherman . . .'' Fachai's voice faded to a whisper.

''You know, Fachai, I can lend you the money for a boat—''

Fachai interrupted Quanming. ''I'll need much more than a boat. The fishermen's association will not take in a Chinese as a member, and Sung Wu Company doesn't own the fishing industry. I can't make much money by fishing on my own, and there is always the need for money to be sent to Leahi and the boy. I'm stuck in the Yung Fa Restaurant for reasons far beyond what you can understand.''

Loone was studying Fachai closely. ''Fachai, I must do a portrait of you, and title it *The Dreamer.* You will be wearing a cook's hat and an apron, standing by the water, looking at a faraway fishing boat. Since so many Chinatown people are from the Pearl River, I'm sure there will be many who will understand exactly how you feel.''

''Is there anything else for you but art?'' Meiping asked Loone. ''I know your first show is coming soon. I'm sure it'll be a big success. David and I will be there for the opening.''

Quanming was looking at himself in the drawing, and suddenly he pushed the pad aside. ''Thanks, Loone, for letting me see myself so clearly. I've changed into a lazy, overweight, and out-of-shape bum! I'm going to change that right now.''

He worked his way out of bed, ignoring his friends' protests. He stood holding on to the bed, his legs shaking. Then he started walking toward the other end of the room. ''I'm going to work out every day, and I'll cut down on my eating, and never touch another drop of liquor. You have no idea the feeling of helplessness I had, lying on the ground waiting to be killed by a madman. I'll never let that happen again!''

His friends watched and waited, knowing he

wouldn't want their help. When he had toured around
the room and made it back to the bed, Meiping and
Fachai each put an arm around his waist to support
him; Loone came to join them.

"Look out the window. What a beautiful sight,"
Quanming whispered.

Above San Francisco Bay, a full moon was rising.
As the four of them looked at the silver beams dancing
on the water, they were for a time transported back to
their homeland and became the children of the Pearl
again.

## 25

DR. HU SHIH was a Chinese college graduate who had been to America to further his studies. He had received his Ph.D. from Columbia University, and upon returning to China decided to change the thinking of the nation. He and his followers started to preach individualism, denouncing the old traditional family system. They worked for women's rights, democracy, and modern technology. The youth of China quickly accepted this modern doctrine, and it soon became a strong force.

During this time China was still, so succinctly stated by Dr. Sun Yat-sen, "a sheet of loose sand." The warlords dominated the people within their jealously guarded provinces; the central government's authority continued to disintegrate; its military force in Beijing could not enforce its edicts.

In reality, China was like a large quilt that contained small independent areas patched together by very thin thread. Each piece of the fabric was held in the iron fist of its own ruler, without the slightest intention of being a whole.

In 1919, World War I was over, and the Versailles Peace Conference took place. When the meeting ended, it was announced that the former German rights in the Shantung peninsula of China had been given to Japan. No one bothered to ask China to participate in this decision. The intellectuals of China, led by Dr. Hu Shih, protested angrily. The fire carried in the hearts of the youth exploded into an inferno when the announcement was made. On May 4, over three thousand youths in Beijing protested against the interference of foreign powers. The government, in its zeal to put down the rebellion, arrested hundreds of students. This only spread the flames of dissension fur-

ther, and soon the cry for a China free of outside
intervention was carried throughout the land.

Japanese goods were boycotted; merchants closed
their shops. Except for the warlords and the aristo-
crats, all of China was behind the movement.

The movement first spread to the major cities, then
began to touch the small towns, until finally its pre-
cepts reached everywhere. Even the most peaceful villages along the Pearl River were affected, and the
villagers' lives were never the same again.

In 1919, Kwangchow was the leading metropolis of
the south, much like Beijing was in the north. The
students' movement had made its way here in early
June, and on the main street, both Fong's Pawnshop
and Fong's Shoe Store were closed in protest. Fong
Mao and his wife, together with their five sons, were
infuriated by the Versailles decision.

"This is the least we can do to show how we feel,"
Fong Mao said, burning with anger. "Those stupid
white pigs! What right have they to cut us up like a
cooked duck, then throw the pieces to the highest bidder?"

"If they treat the whole of China like dirt, I wonder
how our poor Loone is being treated, living as a Chinese among all the white devils?" Mrs. Fong sighed,
near tears.

Mr. Fong and the boys blamed the Japanese not only
for taking their Shantung peninsula but also for making Mrs. Fong cry.

The students' movement wasn't heard in Jasmine
Valley until the following winter. At Yung's Teahouse,
Yung Ko in a fit of rage smashed a Japanese tea set,
stamped on the pieces, and hissed, "May the Great
Buddha break the heads of the Japanese the same
way!"

One of his customers yelled out, "How about all
the white devils who helped pass the decision? Are
you going to curse them also? Do you think your
daughter is still on our side?"

Yung Ko looked at the man and growled, "I'm sure the white devils who helped give away China's land deserve to be cursed. But I don't think they have anything to do with my Meiping."

Yung Ko stopped jumping on the tea set, reached into his pocket for a photograph he had just received from his daughter. "Did I show you Meiping's latest picture? Look at her. She may wear fine Western clothes but she is still a Chinese. That will never change.

Most of the people in Jasmine Valley were Yung Ko's loyal customers, and according to them, even if all the white devils of the world had participated in giving Japan Chinese land, those in the Land of the Gold Mountains who were friends of Yung Meiping had to be innocent.

In the spring of 1920, some of the participants of the students' movement escaped the government's arrest and traveled on foot to White Stone. They lived in the homes of the peasants and helped in the fields. After work they would gather the townspeople into small groups to fill them in on news of the outside world. Within a short time the poor had become aware, and the rich began to worry.

It was a hot summer day in White Stone, but in the Mas' living room the rays of sun had melted into the bamboo curtain, leaving only a warm glow that enveloped the interior.

There were three people sitting on separate teakwood chairs: Ma Tsai-tu, his wife, Yoto, and Yoto's brother, Mr. Kao. All three were young, but all had already turned round and soft, with pale skin, double chins, and girths of great proportions. The quick movements of their youth had now slowed down, like an unwound phonograph.

Ma Tsai-tu, the head of the household since his father's death, was agitated by the rumors of a student revolt. "I don't know what this country is coming to. This is what happens when a peasant like Hu Shih is allowed to attend college. Education must always be

the sole right of the upper class. It's we who understand how to deal with such knowledge.''

He lifted his jade cup and smelled the sweet fragrance before sipping it. Holding up the cup, he
continued, ''Take this spring tea, for instance. Give
it to a peasant, and he would slurp it down, making
enough noise to wake the dead, having absolutely no
idea of the delicacy of this magnificent, outrageously
expensive brew.''

Mr. Kao looked at his brother-in-law and nodded in
agreement. ''Hu Shih wants us to copy Western ways,
but he is absolutely wrong. Would you rather learn
from an infant or a wise old sage? Our culture is over
five thousand years old, and the white devils are still
prancing around in their swaddling clothes.''

Yoto, the lady of the house, listened as she lazily
waved her sandalwood fan, nodding now and then in
agreement.

Her brother took a deep pull on his cigarette, then
blew it toward the ceiling, watching the smoke curl in
the soft light. ''This group of intellectual peasants will
disappear as soon as the first winds of force blow their
way.'' He waved his hand in the floating smoke and
smiled. ''That's exactly what happened ten years ago
when that group of rebels tried to change things. All
they got for their trouble was the chopping block!''

Yoto's heart missed a beat, and she stopped waving
her fan as her husband picked up the conversation.
''I'm not sure it'll blow away so easily this time. I was
in the town square the other day, and watched a young
fellow from Kwangchow speaking to a rather large
crowd. They seemed to be hanging on his every word;
he had a way about him that was positively infectious.
The crowd responded to his questions with energy,
even anger. What he was saying seemed to appeal to
their very souls. I didn't like it. To be honest with you,
I was uneasy.''

Yoto was lost in her own thoughts. The conversation
between the two had triggered a memory of Sung
Quanming. It had been nearly eight years since he had
left White Stone, but already her days of youth seemed

like a lifetime away. She was now the mother of three sons and two daughters. Although she was only in her mid-twenties, little was left of her beauty. Her husband had begun to ignore her some time ago, making no secret of the fact that he was interested in chasing girls much prettier and younger than she.

She looked at her jeweled fat fingers and wondered how Quanming looked these days. Was he still as handsome as he was in her memory? She glanced over at the porcelain plate filled with sweet cakes, picked up a nut-filled bun, and took a bite. The bun was very sweet, but in her heart she tasted only life's bitterness. As a true Chinese lady, she acted in front of people as if her husband's attitude didn't bother her. But she couldn't help wondering at times: If I had married a different man, would I still have been ignored this way? What if I had gone with Quanming to the Land of the Gold Mountains? Would he treasure me no matter how I've changed in looks?

She cursed herself for having such crazy thoughts. In the white devils' land, with no servants, living on barbaric food, doing all that hard work, she'd be either dead or looking like an old dried-up hag. Quanming would be too busy working as a slave for his white bosses to notice her anyway. She took another bite of the sweet bun, the bitterness now gone as she chewed the tasty morsel.

"We don't have to worry. The students' movement will never touch us. The rich of China shall always be rich," her husband was saying, but she was only half listening. She had resumed fanning, bathing in the luxury that she knew she could not give up.

Some of the fleeing students found their way to Willow Place and decided to stay on. In time their pale skin darkened from working in the sun, and by 1921, even if the soldiers had come to search for them, they would have had difficulty telling them apart from the local farmers and fishermen.

On one day in June, when Willow Place was being baked by the sun, Leahi was at home sewing. The house was steaming, and she stopped occasionally to pick up a torn fan and wave it in front of her son, Kwanjin, and herself. Neither felt any cooler, but at least the flies were driven away.

Kwanjin was seated at the only table in the room. In front of him were several books borrowed from scholar Hsu. Looking lovingly at the boy, Leahi thought how fast the years had rolled by. It had been nearly nine years since her husband had left, and by Chinese calculation all babies were born a year old, so Kwanjin was now ten.

When Kwanjin had been a baby, Leahi had carried him on her back to the house of scholar Hsu. While Fachai's letters were being read, the boy was on the floor eating the sweets given to him by the scholar. The lonely man had taken a special liking to the child and repeatedly told Leahi, "Your son is going to live up to his name and be a great success!

When Kwanjin was three, he sat on the man's lap and learned to read simple characters. A year later he learned to write. He had an insatiable appetite to learn, and with the help of scholar Hsu he had soon become proficient at reading and writing.

For years Leahi had thought of nothing but Fachai and his return, until one day it had dawned on her that Kwanjin was right here with her while Fachai was but a memory. Ever since that day, all Leahi's love had been lavished on her son.

One night she had gone to the Pearl River and looked at the moon hanging over the willows. "Fachai, forgive me, but now I love Kwanjin more than I do you," she had murmured. "You can't hear me, you're too far away. Our son is real, and his sweet voice answers me each time I call. He is all I have now."

"Mama, did you know that our country has no strong leader, just like you and I have no Baba?" the boy said, looking up from his book.

Leahi stared at her son. "What? I don't understand you. Your Baba still sends us money. He has not forgotten us, and someday he will be back." But she did not believe it even as she said it.

"Mama, you should go out more. Your world is too small," the young boy said to his astonished mother. "Scholar Hsu took me to the town square the other day, and we heard a very clever man talking there. He said that all the foreigners are mistreating us, and it's very unfair. Mama, you wouldn't want all the neighbors to come to our house and divide our things among them, would you? Well, the clever man said that's exactly what's happening to China."

Leahi looked at her son in puzzlement, wondering what he was talking about. She didn't have the heart to forbid Kwanjin to visit Hsu, but every time when the boy came back from the man, she discovered that she had lost more ability to understand her son.

Kwanjin turned away from his mother and returned to his books. "Mama, do you know what a communist party is? Well, when I grow up, I'm going to become a member. According to that clever man, the communists are the only ones who can make China strong."

Leahi picked up the fan and shooed away the flies. She was so proud of Kwanjin, but couldn't understand the boy, no matter how hard she tried. She thought of the old saying "A woman's place is to obey the three men in her life: as a young girl, her father; as a wife, her husband; as a widow, her son."

"Well if you feel this way, my son," she said, returning to her sewing, "I'm sure you are right."

# 26

WORLD WAR I had lasted only eighteen months for the United States, but to the people it seemed an eternity.

President Wilson had returned from the Versailles Peace Conference pleased by what had been accomplished. The decision to turn over the German-held territory in China to Japan seemed perfectly rational to all the participants of the conference, including Wilson.

After losing so many lives in Europe, the Americans wanted to return to their former inward-looking ways. Senator Warren Harding of Ohio became the next president, running on a platform of old-fashioned isolation.

Within its closed doors America grew rapidly. Electricity reached almost every home; every house had a radio. More people were buying cars; new roads were being built. The nation was soon enjoying economic prosperity and the highest standard of living it had ever known.

In 1921, Royal Palm Heights was a new residential area in the outskirts of San Francisco. Accessible roads and affordable cars had made it easy to sell these beautiful homes, and on one beautiful summer day a real-estate agent was busy selling a luxury home to a client. "Mr. Cohen, I'm sure you'll like this place. It has four bedrooms, two baths, and a spacious living room. The dining area is custom-made for large parties, and the view . . . well, just take a look!"

As they walked through the house, the salesman pointed out every feature. They returned to the living room and David stood in front of the large window looking out over the bay. "I'll take it," he said.

On his way back to the city, David smiled. Since he

couldn't offer Meiping marriage, at least he should give her a home of her own, safe from the pressure she was about to face.

Above Grant Avenue, Meiping was staring out her third-floor window, wondering if David would ever come to her again. They had been careful throughout the years, but now this had to happen!

About a month ago she had started to feel sick in the mornings, and had eventually gone to see a doctor. She was told that she was pregnant. It had taken her a few days to muster the courage to tell David, and that had been two weeks ago. She had not seen or heard a word from him since then.

Limei had tried to put her at ease, as had the other girls of the house, but it had done little to lift her spirits. No matter what they said, she was afraid she would never see her David again.

She looked down at the street, where the people of Chinatown were shuffling along the sidewalk with their heads bent and backs hunched as if the burdens of the world were on their shoulders. *I must get out of here. I can't let my child become one of them!*

Suddenly she became furious. All the sweet words of love meant nothing! He had said that he loved her and that she had become his reason for living. Through the past years he had given her jewels, clothes, and had continued to pay Wan generously to keep her from being touched by any other man. But he had never divorced his precious Rebecca, and now he was gone.

She turned from the window, walked to the closet, and started to pack. She had always had the freedom to come and go on her own, and no one stopped her when she left the house carrying a suitcase.

The outside of this large house looked no different from any other in its neighborhood, except for the Oriental garden, which could be viewed from the street.

Once inside, however, one was surrounded in Chinese luxury. There were Chinese scrolls of both paintings and calligraphy hanging on the walls. Ivory, jade, and porcelain works of art were displayed throughout the rooms. All the furniture was of teakwood, and on every chair was an embroidered pillow.

In the living room, Quanming was reading the paper and A-lin was drinking her tea. The clock could be heard ticking, for not a single word had been exchanged between the two.

In the past four years, Quanming had lost all the extra weight and now once again looked fit. His wife, A-lin, now the mother of a boy and a girl, had also changed over the years. Although she still looked like a frightened mouse, her disposition was nothing of the sort. Being the wife of a prominent man, she was no longer intimidated by people. She had stopped feeling it necessary to be congenial to others, especially those beneath her station.

A male servant appeared at the door. "Master Sung, there's a lady to see you, by the name of Yung Mei-ping."

"Show her in," Quanming stood up immediately.

A-lin slammed her teacup down, spilling hot tea all over the teakwood table. "A whore in my home!"

Quanming's face turned red with rage as he looked at his wife, wishing she would drop dead. "You may leave at any time if you don't want to be in the company of my friend."

A-lin, deciding she didn't want to miss anything, remained sitting and watching.

Meiping appeared in a gray suit accented with a pearl necklace and matching earrings. Her black high heels made her as tall as Quanming. As she walked toward him, she held her head high and her back straight.

"Meiping, what a surprise!" Quanming welcomed her with a broad smile and outstretched hands. "Please sit down and have some tea." Looking at her, he noticed her face was pale and she seemed worried.

Meiping remained standing; she turned and addressed A-lin, but the lady of the house didn't bother to return her greeting. Meiping shrugged and turned back to Quanming. "I've come for your help," she blurted. "I'm pregnant."

A-lin made a noise that sounded like something between a cough and a laugh. Quanming turned to her with his hands clenched into fists. "I want you to leave! Now!"

A-lin didn't push her luck; if her husband hit her in front of this whore, she would lose too much face. She walked toward the door, and as she passed Meiping she brought her handkerchief to her nose. She was lucky that Meiping was too concerned with her own problems to notice.

Quanming asked what he could do to help.

"I need to find a place to live, a lawyer to fight with Wan Kon for my release, and a doctor to deliver my baby. I also need a job, so I can support myself and my child."

"What about David?" Quanming inquired with concern.

"He doesn't want me anymore. He's only a mean white devil after all—"

The doorbell rang. There was a commotion in the hall, followed by loud running footsteps and the protesting words of a servant. The door opened and in strode David. "Have you seen Meiping? I've already been to the Yung Fa Restaurant. They haven't seen her, and I hope she didn't do anything foolish, I—"

At the sight of Meiping, the anxious look on his face melted into a wide grin, and he opened his arms.

"David!" Meiping ran to him. "You still want me! You didn't leave me because I'm going to become fat and ugly!" She kissed him, sobbing, laughing, and talking all at once.

David stepped back to look at her carefully. "First, tell me that you didn't do anything to the baby."

Meiping was puzzled by his question. "Of course not! How can you think of such a silly thing? It's your baby, and even if you didn't want me anymore, I'd still want my little David."

"Thank God." He pulled her to him, holding her tightly. "I went to the house and found you gone.

Some stupid girl there told me that you had gone to a doctor to solve the problem the only sensible way . . .'' He suddenly held her at arm's length, angry. ''Why did you scare me so? I ought to put you over my knee right now for almost giving me a heart attack.''

Meiping laughed and kissed him, unafraid. ''No, you won't. Not in front of Quanming, and not in my delicate condition. Anyway, it's your fault for not showing up these past two weeks.''

David's voice softened. ''I'm sorry about that. It was thoughtless of me. But I had to make a decision. It's not every day that a married man finds himself in such a position. I debated asking Rebecca for a divorce, but then knew it would be a waste of time. I thought of other things we could do, even considered running away . . . I haven't slept much in the past two weeks. When I finally decided what to do, I immediately went to check with my attorney, a close friend, about how to deal with Wan Kon. And then I went to a real-estate man . . .'' He smiled, and held her face in his two huge hands. ''Meiping, I have bought us a lovely home overlooking the bay!''

Quanming stood looking at them, his heart filled with envy.

Laurie's flaming hair was tied back with a yellow ribbon to match the yellow flowers on her beige dress. As she welcomed Quanming at her apartment door, love glowed in her green eyes. He closed the door behind them and they flew into each other's arms. In her embrace Quanming felt his tension fade, like a man who had just found a warm fire in a cold winter night.

They walked toward the bedroom with their arms around each other, kissing all the while. Their lovemaking was a maddening whirl of need and desire. Afterward they held each other quietly for a short time, then started all over again. Only this time they did it slowly, bringing each other to the brink, then backing off, until they could no longer wait. Later they fell back exhausted. Quanming lay on his back, his stomach muscles rippling as he sucked in air, his body glistening with sweat.

"I love you," Laurie whispered, breathing hard. "I'll always love you, no matter how long you stay married to her." She turned away.

"Laurie . . ." Quanming said helplessly. They had gone through this so many times already. His marriage to A-lin had been an invisible wall between them, and it continued to stand erect no matter how hard they had tried to tear it down.

With her back turned toward him, Laurie said, "Don't say anything, Quanming. Let's try to enjoy the time together. Soon you'll have to go . . . to your work . . . to the home and children you share with her." She tried to hold back her tears, but he heard the pain in her voice.

"Laurie . . ." He tried to say something again. She suddenly turned to face him, put her arms around him, and started to cover his mouth with kisses.

"Please don't talk," she said in between kisses. "I know what you'll say. I've already heard them many times before. Those words can't help things. They can only bring back unpleasant memories."

The memories of the unfortunate incident in the hospital between her and his uncle, for instance. Soon after Quanming had left the hospital, the old man had used obligation and tradition as a weapon, and forced his nephew to marry the girl of his choice.

Laurie didn't know how she had managed to live through Quanming's wedding day. She had locked herself in her room and imagined the things happening between the bride and groom. Through the night she had cried. Early the next morning she had heard someone at the door.

"The obligation is done, and now I'm all yours." She had found Quanming standing there, his face colorless, his eyes filled with suffering. She had tried to close the door on him, but he had pushed his way in and taken her in his arms, kissed away her tears. From that day on they had been lovers.

"Laurie, my darling," Quanming said, "there'll be a way. Please be patient."

"Patient?" Laurie let out a small laugh. "I've been your mistress for almost four years now; I'm still waiting to be promoted. You can't accuse me of being impatient, I'm sure."

"I know it's difficult." He kissed her and looked at his watch. "You've cut yourself off from your parents and friends. The only person you see now is Paul. Well, Laurie, I love you." He looked at his watch again.

After Quanming had left, Laurie tried to find things to do, to rid herself of the depression and anger she always felt after they had been together. *A man doesn't have to look at his watch when he is with his wife. Whether he loves her or not, he can give her all his time. Quanming loves me, but I'm his mistress. He can only fit me in in between home and office. What's the difference between me and the shoeshine boys on the street? He stops to see us both!*

There was a knock on the door, and she ran, thinking that Quanming had returned. She could not hide her disappointment when she saw Paul. "Oh, it's you."

"Thanks for the warm welcome."

"I'm sorry, Uncle Paul. It's just that I thought you were Quanming."

Paul didn't say anything until they were seated in her small kitchen over two cups of coffee. "I have something to tell you," he said, unable to conceal the excitement in his voice. "I've been chosen by the mission to go to the Hawaiian Islands, the island of Maui, as a minister in a place called Lahana. It's a whaling village . . ." He went on to tell her more about the island and his assigned job.

"That's wonderful, Paul, I'm so happy for you!"

"Wait, Laurie," Paul said, taking her hand. "I'm authorized to bring an assistant with me, and I've given them your name."

Laurie stared at him. "But I'm not trained . . . I don't know how to be a missionary's helper. Besides,

Hawaii is so far from . . . Oh, Paul, I can't go!''

"But you must, Laurie." Paul reached across the table and took her hand in his. "You can't spend the rest of your life in San Francisco as Quanming's mistress. I love Quanming, but I can't let him destroy you. You are so young and beautiful and you deserve more." Paul stopped, looked at her for a long time. "Please, Laurie, think about it." Then he added with a smile, "By the way, Hawaii is not bound by American law. If Quanming should ever become a free man, he can always come to the islands to find you, and the two of you can get married."

Once Paul had left, Laurie sat at the table for a long time, thinking.


David and Meiping had moved into the house in Royal Palm Heights. One morning, when they were having breakfast, Meiping suddenly laid down her utensil and looked at David with a stern expression.

"What now?" he asked, continuing to eat.

"I want us to have a wedding," she said. "Not a public one, because of the stupid law and all that. But a good old-fashioned private ceremony, done in the traditional Chinese way." She poured him more coffee. "It'll give me much face."

Drinking his coffee, David said, "Anything that'll make you happy. What is a Chinese wedding like? Do you need a bridesmaid?"

"Yes." Meiping looked at David thoughtfully. "In China, when a man takes a second wife, the first wife comes to the wedding to give blessings and receive kowtows. Shall we ask Rebecca to come?"

"Good Lord!" he bellowed, laying down his cup with a thump. "Are you out of your mind? Do you want the wedding to be a bloodbath? How dumb can you be?"

Meiping was instantly angered. "Who's dumb? You're dumb! You white devils know nothing about tradition! You're all dumb barbarians!"

"Meiping," David said with a frown, trying his best to be patient, "Chinese tradition doesn't hold in this

country. Over here, people think it barbaric for a man
to have more than one wife." He had to make sure
that she understood. He couldn't afford to have her
inviting Rebecca on her own. "A man must not invite
his wife to his wedding. Because in America the first
wife will not give her husband's second wife any blessing. Rebecca will probably come with a loaded gun."
He shook his head. "Some of your traditions are considered barbaric by American wives."

Meiping slammed the coffeepot she was holding on
the table. "Do you agree with your Rebecca? What do
you mean, my traditions are barbaric? Are you calling
me a barbarian, you mumzer?"

David started to laugh. He grabbed her hand, pulled
her off the chair, and dragged her to his side. "Where
did you learn to curse in Yiddish?"

Meiping struggled to free herself. "From you,
mumzer!"

"If you were not pregnant, I'd spank you so hard
you wouldn't be able to sit for a week," he chided her
in mock anger.

"Promises, promises," she laughed. "All right, you
win. No Rebecca. I didn't really want to kowtow to
her anyway." She sat on David's lap, circled her arms
around his neck, and became serious. "I don't really
want a wedding. It's just stupid talk. You and I are
husband and wife already." She rested her head on his
chest. "We've been married for a long time . . . ever
since that night many years ago when you took me and
made me your woman."

David held her close. Over her shoulder he saw a
hand-carved wooden statue of Buddha, a housewarm-
ing present from Quanming. A lantern was hung
above, casting a soft glow over the Buddha's serene
face. On either side of the statue red candles were
burning. Meiping had searched a long time for incense
with the fragrance of night-blooming jasmine, and now
the sweet smells rose from a brass urn, filling the
room.

"Come with me, Meiping," David said, gently lifting her off his lap. He took her hand and they started

to walk toward the statue.

In front of the Buddha, David knelt and pulled Meiping beside him. She was surprised to see how serious he was. He turned to face her and then took her hand. She was touched by the tears in his eyes. "Until you came into my life, I was a married man, but without a wife. You, Yung Meiping, are my first wife, and the only one. I will treasure you forever."

Then, lifting his eyes to Buddha, David started to pray: "Should you have the power, Buddha, please grant us as many happy years together as possible."

Meiping felt herself swell with pride. She knew without a doubt that she and David were truly married now. She looked from David to the statue, and when she spoke, her voice was trembling with emotion. "Thank you, my Great Buddha, for giving me to Mr. David Cohen. Please never let him be tired of me, so he'll keep me forever. I'll be a very good wife to him, and I want him to be my husband not only in this life, but also in all the lives hereafter."

When she had finished, David picked her up, feeling like a groom carrying his bride to their wedding bed-chamber.

# 27

IN THE PAST four years, Chu Fong Loone's name had appeared repeatedly in San Francisco newspapers.

In 1918, after his first one-man show, an article had been written by a well-known American art critic:

> A young man has come from the Pearl River of China with a magic brush, landed in San Francisco, and touched American hearts with his unique art style.
>
> The viewers were deeply impressed by *The Burden of Tradition*. Within the frame we were shown a village nestled along a flowing river. As our eyes traveled along a curved dusty road that led to several small houses in the background, we could see, near the center of the canvas, an old man in a torn jacket and patched pants. He was struggling under the weight of a large burlap sack. Etched on his weathered face were the lines of sorrow from dreams long gone; hidden in his sad eyes were the signs of hope that had vanished . . .

Soon after that, there had been a banner headline on the front page of *China News:*

> The leading actress of the Pearl River delta, Yi Moi, recently returned to San Francisco from a nationwide tour and immediately married the young artist Mr. Chu Fong Loone. The wedding took place in a Chinatown Buddhist temple, and Mr. Sung Tinwei of the Sung Wu Company gave the bride away. One of the best men was Sung Quanming, the young Lau Ban who recently recovered from an assassin. The other was Li Fachai, manager of the Yung Fa Restaurant, owned by the groom.

In detail, it had described the clothes of the bride and her maid of honor, Yung Meiping. The paper succinctly reported that the reception that followed was "a royal feast that went on forever."

A year later, when Chu Fong Loone had his second show, another influential critic wrote:

> In one of Mr. Chu's paintings, *The Faint Memory of a Few Happy Days,* the artist has once again captured the sorrow and anguish of his people. He has shown us a toothless old woman sitting on a flight of worn steps, leaning against a weathered door in the glow of the late-evening sun. She is wearing a patched robe, her eyes half-closed, and there is a faint smile on her weary face. The viewer feels immediately that she is remembering a happier time and a better place. . . .

The next year, when Loone gave his third show, the prices of his paintings had increased tenfold. *The Ship Is Waiting* was a work fought over by many collectors, and eventually was auctioned off at a record price. It was painted on a huge canvas, showing a misty horizon and a ghostlike ship waiting at the pier. A crowd of people in shabby clothes carrying their meager luggage waited onshore and walked up the gangplank, each with a sad, frightened look.

During the past four years, the rich of San Francisco, with or without a true appreciation for art, had flocked to Loone's shows. It had become fashionable to own a Loon original. Chu Fong Loone had become a well-known name in the art world, although few could claim that they knew the secluded artist personally.

On an early-summer morning in 1921, in a spacious house set on several acres, the reclusive artist was working in a studio he had designed himself, busy getting ready for his fourth major show.

His pale fingers worked the brush into the colors on his palette, his thin body bent close to a canvas several times his size. Once in a while he would glance away from his work toward one of the three large windows and gaze at the garden below. In the early-morning mist the garden had a fairyland quality, and he could see his fairy princess, a petite figure in a white robe, walking slowly.

*It's so nice to know that she is right there,* he thought. He quickened his strokes, hoping to accomplish what he had planned to do early enough to join his wife for brunch. *I don't think I've seen her in the past twenty-four hours . . . or has it been longer than that? I wonder if she slept well last night.*

They had started to sleep in separate rooms soon after they were married. Loone had suggested it, since his hours were so irregular and he hated to disturb Moi's routine of having breakfast by herself and then taking a walk in the garden alone.

She liked to get up early every morning, a habit she had acquired in her opera-school days. On this morning, on her way out of the house, as she passed the studio and saw the light beneath the door, she had wondered whether Loone had not yet gone to bed or was up and painting already. She had wanted to knock on the door and ask him to join her for the walk, but then changed her mind. No, she must not disturb him.

The mist covered every inch of the garden, and Moi walked slowly. She glanced up, trying to locate the windows of the studio, but the fog was too heavy. She knew that her husband, as usual, was somewhere behind one of those windows, painting. He would probably paint through the entire day, and with the show coming, might even work long after she had gone to bed. *When was the last time we had a meal together?* she wondered. *When will we go out again and have some fun? I am safe from the warlords of China and I am living well, but I don't have a man at all.*

Staring in the direction of the unseen windows, she sighed. There was a thick layer of mist in their marriage as well. She had tried hard to find the true Loone behind his shielding fog but had failed. Even when the two of them were at their most intimate moments, Loone still managed to put himself behind an invisible screen. She had made numerous attempts to reach him, but her efforts had only made him withdraw further.

*My Great Buddha, I feel so lonely at times! Why must he
hide from me? Why can't he share his life with me?*

As she bent to touch a red flower's new petal, she
remembered her wedding day. Loone had known nothing about lovemaking, and she, for all her sophistica-
tion, had been still a virgin. Sensing Loone's anxiety,
she tried to forget her own and did everything she could
to put him at ease. He had finally entered her and had
climaxed after only a few moments.

As they lay in each other's arms, Loone suddenly
pulled away, having seen the blood on the sheet. "I
did this to you!" he gasped, pointing at the stains.
"I've hurt you! I . . . I'm so sorry!"

Moi was shocked by his expression. He seemed to
hate himself for what he had done. During the next
few months their lovemaking had become less and less
frequent, until finally it came to an end.

By the time the sun began to burn away the mist, Moi
had wandered through most of the garden and returned
to the fish pond. Standing on the little bridge, she once
again looked up at the studio and whispered into the
fog, "I wish to have you, my husband, to walk through
the garden with me and hold me in your arms . . ."

At the time the Mexican maid served Moi her lunch,
Loone was still painting. After eating, she decided to
get dressed and take the car Loone had bought her and
go into town to visit a few friends.

Quanming and A-lin? No, she decided. They are
probably having another one of their fights. Meiping
and David? No, I'll be an intruder in their love nest.
She finally decided to go to Yung Fa Restaurant and
bring something back for Loone's evening meal.

The remodeling of Yung Fa had been completed
three years before and now the restaurant was a proud
focus in the middle of Clay Street.

In the morning fog, a man walked out of Yung Fa's
back door, heading toward San Francisco Bay. He was
only in his late-twenties, but his rugged features had
already turned soft and pale; the broad shoulders were
stooped and the back bent. Looking at him, it would

be difficult for people to recognize him as the well-built fisherman of Willow Place.

He walked past the drunks lying on the street, the overflowing garbage cans, and the refuse scattered everywhere. He was soon facing the ocean and breathing in the salty air. As he looked across the water he felt once again close to home, and a sad smile appeared on his thin face when he began to picture the fishing fleet and the men pulling in the nets. He was soon visualizing the ancient willows with Leahi standing beneath them, and he started to frown when he imagined his son, a boy without a face. He tried to put his own face and the face of Leahi into one, but he was not good in conceptualizing.

He stayed by the bay until it was time to return to Yung Fa to open the restaurant.

As soon as he reached there he started to cut vegetables. The knife beat a staccato on the cutting board, and with each chop he cursed the people who had made up the immigration law. In 1922 the law still forbade Chinese laborers to bring over their families. Even with the Sung Wu Company's attempts to help, Leahi and the boy were still not able to come to the Land of the Gold Mountains.

"Deu-na-ma!" Fachai mumbled, and started to clean the first case of iced fish that had been delivered to him this morning.

The fish looked at him with dead white eyes, and Fachai felt that they looked as hopeless as his future. No wife, no son, no possibility of ever becoming a fisherman again. In the past ten years such a realization had made him die a little with every passing day.

"Deu-na-ma!" he cursed again, and started to tell Buddha exactly what he thought of life. His three friends from the Pearl were now each successful in their own ways; he was the only one left behind, drifting further and further from his dream.

When it was time, he shuffled over to open the front door for the waiting customers and tried to smile at the crowd. The majority of them were tired and lonely men: vegetable vendors, noodle makers, shoe-factory workers, laundry owners. They hated being alone, so they came to Yung Fa every day to share their misery with each other. On their faces Fachai could see himself. We are all a part of Chinatown, he reflected. Like the bricks that pave the sidewalks, we too are stepped on by the feet of fate day after day, getting worn down by the weight of time, never able to escape.

He seated the people, then moved from table to table serving hot tea. Following the rules established by the Chus, tea was always free. "I'm glad to see you alive and kicking, brother," a customer said to Fachai with a smile. "I was worried about you yesterday, when I saw you standing by the bay, looking miserable and lonely. You know, many people do kill themselves by drowning when the misery and loneliness becomes too much."

"Me?" Fachai quickly denied. "Miserable and lonely? You must be mistaken!"

Another man, a noodle maker, slapped Fachai on the back. "You're a happy man, I'm sure. Didn't I just run into you last week in the dark hallway of Madame Wong's House?"

Many of them smiled understandingly, and Fachai forced himself to smile with them. He had started to frequent prostitutes about three years ago, and had often seen his customers there. They were all members of this bachelors' society, all victims of an absurd law.

An old-timer stopped Fachai as he tried to pass. "Have you heard about Mr. Wu of the herb store?"

Fachai stopped. He knew the man: a longtime resident of Chinatown who had always been easygoing and full of jokes.

"Hanged himself last night in the storage room behind his shop," the old man said. "Came to Chinatown when he was nineteen. Worked hard and earned himself the store with sweat and blood. Twenty-six years without seeing his family—a wife and two boys—given up hope of bringing them over." The old man shook his head and continued, "He received a letter informing him that his wife and two boys had died in the plague."

Fachai had heard stories like this before, but this one hit him especially hard. He stood in a daze until someone shouted for him to take an order, and he snapped back to reality. He continued waiting on tables until the part-time helper he had recently hired arrived, then went to the kitchen and started to cook.

As he was frying vegetables he thought of the recent suicide again. The man had been a scholar in China, and had never really been happy selling herbs. *Just like me. A fisherman now confined in a restaurant as a cook and waiter.*

Peering through the curtain at the miserable crowd, Fachai felt that he was looking at a roomful of prisoners within the wall of Chinatown. Outside that wall lay a much better world, a world controlled by the white people. The wall was made not only by the color of their skin but also by their inability to speak the English language.

With determination and hard work, people of Chinatown can jump over the wall, he thought. It's been done. The white devils are not all that bad. Once you have proved your worth, they forget your skin color . . . but I just don't have that determination. I'm too weak inside.

When the lunch rush was finally over, the hired help cleaned the tables, shut the doors, and left. Fachai soon sneaked out the back door and headed once more toward the shore. He stayed there staring at the water until the wind started to blow and large drops of rain began to fall. He rushed back to the restaurant, but was still soaking wet by the time he got there.

He ran up the stairs, unbuttoning his wet things and pulling them off, dropping them to the floor. Naked from the waist up, he was unbuckling his belt when he saw Moi in a white silk dress, lying comfortably on his bed.

"You were not here, so I let myself in. I've been waiting for a long time. I was tired, so I lay down for a nap. I hope you don't mind," she said, slowly stretching her beautiful body. "Fachai, you're all wet!"

Staring at her, Fachai thought of the first time they had met. How his eyes had looked into hers, and how he had felt a thrill surging through him like a lightning bolt. While awake he could never forget the fact that she was his best friend's wife, but when dreaming of making love to Leahi, in his dreams Leahi had frequently turned into Moi.

Lying in bed and dressed all in white, Moi looked now very much like she had onstage as that ill-fated white snake. Fachai could not take his eyes off her. Feeling his blood boiling inside, he stood unmoving, afraid to break the spell and make her vanish.

"Fachai, are you afraid of me?" Moi let out a small laugh. "I didn't plan this. I've come here to bring some of your marvelous food home. But . . ." She started to purr in a voice soft as a kitten. "You are a lonely man, and I am a lonely woman. Your wife is far away, and my husband sees only his art. Come, we won't hurt anyone."

Fachai swallowed hard. *She is right. We are both lonely. We want each other. We've been wanting each other since the first time we met.*

"Come to me, Fachai, please come . . ." Her voice was warm and inviting as she began to take off her dress.

Fachai closed the door and walked toward the bed.

A tired-looking old man walked into Moa Lau's store and took from his pocket a multilayered package. He unwrapped it with shaking hands, then placed a white jade pendant in the shape of a phoenix on the counter.

"This comes from the Pearl River, a good piece of antique jade. It used to be my grandmother's. She worked all her life for a rich family, and the mistress gave this to her when she quit to get married; it was all she had to show for those years of hard labor. When I left China, she gave it to me and told me to give it to my future wife. I've been here fifty years now, but have never found a wife."

Moa Lau stared at the pendant. Since he had taken

over the shop after his father's death nearly twenty years before, he had never seen anything so beautiful.

The man was saying, ". . . through even the difficult times I refused to part from this, because it represents my home and my grandmother. I was going to have myself buried with it under my tongue to preserve my body, but now I've changed my mind . . ."

The man went on to say that he wanted to sell the pendant and enjoy the money when he was still alive. "How much will you give me?"

Trying to hide his excitement, Moa Lau named a price high enough to tempt the man but far below the jade's actual value. The old man was delighted by Moa's offer and quickly took the money.

The following day, as soon as Sung A-lin walked into the store, Moa Lau greeted her with a big smile. "Mrs. Sung, please come and see what I've kept just for you!"

He produced the pendant. She took it with a condescending air, but after one look at the almost transparent gem and its intricate design, her expression changed. She had been trained by her mother from an early age to recognize true antique jade.

Moa Lau whispered into her ear, as if telling her a top secret, "I'm sure you've heard the ancient story: white jade was for royalty. Those who were anything less might be allowed to wear rubies or diamonds and green or yellow jade, but never a piece of white jade. This particular pendant once belonged to a queen when she was her king's favorite. I've saved it for you, because I think only a true lady like you is fit to wear it."

A-lin hung the pendant around her neck and gazed at the mirror. "What a perfect picture!" Moa Lau said, his voice sugar-coated. "You and the jade are born to belong to each other."

The price Moa Lau asked was far more than the amount of money A-lin had with her, and she had never been an impulsive buyer. "Keep it for me. I would like very much for my mother to see it," she said, reluctantly returning the pendant.

A-lin went to her mother's house to find Mrs. Wu with a cold. By the time she was able to go shopping with her daughter, it was a week later.

As soon as they entered the shop, A-lin said to Moa Lau without a word of greeting, "Bring out the white jade pendant. My mother would like to take a look at it."

Moa Lau looked at her, puzzled. "The pendant? Don't you already have it?"

"Fool! You know very well I'm talking about the white jade phoenix!" A-lin shouted at him. "Of course I don't have it yet!"

Moa Lau looked at her strangely. "Mrs Sung"—he swallowed—"your husband was here two days ago. He bought the jade phoenix, and I never doubted it was for you."

"My husband? He bought the pendant?" A-lin's face turned white. "Did he say whom it was for?"

"No. You mean he didn't . . . ." Moa's hand flew up to his mouth. "Oh, my goodness! Let me see . . . he only told me that he was looking for a present for someone's birthday. I almost asked him to give you my birthday greetings. I showed him the phoenix, knowing it would make you happy . . . He didn't mind the price at all." Moa Lau was amused by the change of expression on A-lin's face. "He told me to find a nice box for it and to gift-wrap it with a red ribbon."

"My birthday is five months away, you damn fool!" A-lin screamed, shaking with fury.

"Oh, I'm so sorry! I guess, like most men, Mr. Sung forgot the date."

"You simpleminded idiot! He knows my birthday as well as his own! He forgets nothing, except where his loyalty lies!" A-lin shouted.

"Let's go home to discuss it," her mother said, trying to calm her down. "You must not behave this way in public."

A-lin wasn't willing to leave, and Moa Lau quickly offered the two ladies his most comfortable chairs and a pot of tea. Being too upset to move on, they accepted his offer.

* * *

"You'll have to find someone else to go to Hawaii
with you," Laurie said to her uncle. "I can't leave
Quanming." Paul started to interrupt her, but she
shook her head. "Please, Uncle Paul. My head knows
all the reasons, but my heart refuses to listen. It is no
use for you to try to persuade me."

Paul looked at her for a few moments, then nodded
without saying anything. Laurie was thankful that he
understood.

As she got ready to leave, she looked at his tattered
old robe and decided to buy him a new one as a farewell present. Knowing how much Paul liked things
made in China, Laurie went directly to Chinatown to
look for one made of silk with an embroidered dragon.

She walked into Moa Lau's tailor shop, which also
carried antiques and expensive jewels. When she saw
A-lin and Mrs. Wu drinking tea, she knew that they
had already seen her; it was too late for her to retreat.

Moa Lau's thin face brightened at the sight of the
white-devil-girl. His shop was one of the gossip cen-
ters of Chinatown, and he new very well who Laurie
was. Flashing his best business smile, he walked toward her. His eyes swept quickly from the red hair to
the long legs, enjoying her hourglass figure. "May I
be of service to you?" he asked with a deep bow.
Then his eyes widened in surprise.

Laurie was wearing a black pullover sweater, and
the white phoenix was hanging from her neck, resting
in the deep valley between her breasts, standing out in
contrast to the dark background.

"I'm here for a robe," Laurie said, turning her back
to the two other women. "A man's robe."

"Yes?" Moa said, again bowing deeply. "Oh, yes.
This way, please." He led Laurie directly to A-lin and
Mrs. Wu, making sure they would not miss the splen-
did piece of jewelry.

Laurie hesitated, then followed Moa without showing any sign of recognition to the Chinese ladies.

"Please take your time," Moa said, pointing to a

rack. "I'll be with you in a moment . . . a bit of unfinished business."

He walked over to A-lin and whispered, "I believe we've found our lucky birthday girl."

A-lin had immediately recognized not only Laurie but also the white phoenix. "Mama!" she screamed, pointing at Laurie's chest. "This is the pendant I wanted you to see! Look who's wearing it!"

Mrs. Wu took a deep breath. As a mother, she was very angry for her daughter. As an experienced wife, she wanted to avoid a direct confrontation between A-lin and this white-devil-girl. "Let's go home," she said softly, getting out of the chair. "We'll have a talk with Quanming."

A-lin was now hysterical. "What can he say? That he spent a fortune on his white whore? I'm his wife. I'm the one who deserves to have such an expensive piece of jewelry! Did he ever buy anything half as nice for me? No! Never!"

She bolted from her chair and stormed over to Laurie. Her hand shot out, tearing the phoenix from Laurie's neck. "Whore! You have no right to wear this!" she screamed, her voice shaking beyond control.

Laurie was taken completely by surprise. She stood rubbing her neck where the chain had cut into her, leaving her skin raw. She watched the jade swinging to and fro in A-lin's hand, as if she were mesmerized.

"So you're buying a man's robe!" A-lin continued to scream, while dangling the white phoenix from the chain. "Is the robe for my husband or the husband of another woman? You had better buy one to fit all of them!"

A series of events began to play at a high speed through A-lin's mind: Quanming's remote attitude and cruel comments, his ignoring her, his lack of passion . . . A-lin drew back her hand and slapped Laurie across the face with all the strength she could gather. "Leave my husband alone, you miserable whore!"

Laurie's head was knocked to one side; she stumbled and almost fell. Her ear was ringing and she could taste blood in her mouth. As her hand touched her cheek, the stinging pain brought tears to her eyes. She could barely make out the blurred image of A-lin standing there with her head thrown back, laughing and swinging the white jade.

Laurie turned and ran out of the store, knowing that she had to get as far away from her present life as possible.

Quanming turned the key and walked into Laurie's apartment. He had come to take her out to dinner. "Laurie, I missed you so much yesterday," he called, hanging up his hat. "I brought the meeting in Los Angeles to an end as quickly as possible and rushed back to you."

When there was no answer, he called out again. It was then that he noticed the place seemed different. The embroidered pillows were missing, and as he turned to look at the dining table, he saw it empty—no candles or fresh flowers. Then he saw that all the books had been stripped from the shelves, all the paintings taken from the walls.

"Laurie!" he yelled, running to the bedroom.

There were no sheets on the bed, only bare pillows. The perfume bottles and makeup jars no longer lined the dresser. The closet doors were open, revealing an empty row of hangers.

"No! Laurie, no!" he shouted, and then saw the letter on the bedside table.

Dear Quanming,

Uncle Paul and I are sorry for not saying good-bye. But if we wait for you to come back from Los Angeles, I just might not be able to do what I must do.

Like a thief caught with stolen goods, I was caught as a woman who had stolen another woman's man. I was humiliated in public. I knew I was wrong, and like a thief, I ran.

You know where Paul and I will be, and we'll be writing you many letters. If someday you should become a free man, and you still love me as much as I love you, Quanming, I'll be glad to be yours completely and legally.

In the meantime, I'll miss you terribly, but I'll never be a thief again.

Yours,
Laurie

Quanming left the apartment and rushed to the pier like a madman. The ship for Hawaii had already sailed. As he stood staring at the tiny black dot moving toward the far horizon, he suddenly realized that the woman he had loved for ten long years was being carried farther and farther away with each passing second.

He started to scream, "Laurie, I can't live without you!"

People on the pier turned to look, but he didn't care. "I'm coming to you, Laurie!" he shouted at the disappearing ship, and decided to buy a ticket on the next ship for the islands. But first he must go home and settle his affairs.

He waited until the ship was completely out of sight and the ocean had become vast and empty. He got into his car and drove, feeling a void in his heart that could only be filled by Laurie.

He parked in front of his house, then trudged wearily across the lawn. Entering the front door, he saw A-lin sitting in the living room, drinking tea. She turned in his direction with a self-satisfied smile, and he quickly turned away. Just the sight of her was enough to make him sick.

"Baba, Baba, you're home early! I'm so happy! I missed you the whole day! Please come and play with me!" A plump boy in a sailor suit dashed down the stairs and jumped from the last few steps without doubting that his father's strong arms would be there to catch him in time.

Quanming held his three-year-old son close to his chest, feeling the boy's soft arms encircling his neck. As he kissed Hwa-hwa's soft cheek, the special sweet smell of a young child filled his nostrils, and his heart ached.

*If I go to Laurie, then I'll never see my son again!*
He felt like a rope being pulled by two forces: his love for Laurie and his love for his boy. In the struggle between the two, his heart was to be torn asunder.

# 28

MEIPING HAD A baby girl, seven and a half pounds in weight, twenty-three inches long. The baby had thick black hair and a high-ridged little nose. Her eyes were dark brown, almost black. Her high cheekbones and full lips were her mother's.

Meiping's shoulders were covered by a pink shawl. Her hair, wet from sweat, looked like a waterfall. She was propped up in bed with pillows, holding the baby in her arms and repeating for the hundredth time, "She's the most beautiful baby in the whole world!"

Standing next to the bed was David, along with Loone, Mòi, Quanming, Fachai, and Limei. None of the hospital staff complained about having too many visitors, not at the price David was paying for the room. The conversation was being carried out in two languages. Fachai couldn't speak English; he had discovered a long time ago that what he had learned at Camerano's was not really presentable. Loone had learned to speak through dealing with the art-gallery owners but was reluctant to talk in a foreign tongue. Mòi had learned only a mixture of Spanish and English through her Mexican maid. Quanming, Limei, and Meiping were the interpreters for David.

"You're not being very humble," Loone said with a smile to the new mother. "Bragging about a worthless female child! But of course, ever since I've known you, modesty was never in your character."

"Let me show you what you should do, Meiping." Mòi, the actress, bowed to the new father with exaggeration. "I'm so sorry, honorable husband, for giving birth to a useless girl. A terrible shame has been put upon our house, and I beg my husband's forgiveness. Please don't sell me or send me away. I'll try to do better next time. I'll pray every day for Buddha to grant us a son to carry on your honorable name—''

Before David could say anything, Fachai answered in his place, acting the father. ''I'm not sure if I should forgive you, stupid woman! My hard-earned money will now go to feed a worthless girl, who will eventually grow up to become a useless woman who can't even carry my name or take care of me in my old age. And if she should be able to find a husband, I'll be forced to give her a dowry!''

While everybody was laughing, Limei added, ''I think I'd just sell the child to a madam right now and let her become their headache!''

Meiping turned to Quanming. ''You have not said a word since you walked into this room. Aren't you going to pick on my poor baby like everyone else?''

Quanming stared at the little pink, wrinkled face. ''What a beautiful result of mixing two different races!'' he sighed. *It's strange that nobody in the hospital seemed to mind the pairing of David, a white man, and Meiping, a Chinese girl. It's the other way around that they don't like to see.*

A young nurse walked in, said to the mother cheerfully, ''It's time for little Rachel to go back to the nursery.''

David wouldn't let them take his daughter until he had held her in his arms once more. The baby looked tiny in his large hands, and he was so careful not to break his fragile little jewel. ''My little Rachel, my treasure,'' he whispered softly.

Watching the way David held and spoke to the baby, Meiping felt a lump in her throat. She glowed with pride, and tears of joy began to roll down her cheeks.

As soon as the nurse left with the baby, Meiping patted the bed for David to sit by her. She reached for his hand and brought it to her face. Rubbing against his palm, she asked, ''Do you really not mind that she is a girl?''

He didn't answer for a moment. She looked up and saw tears in his eyes as he smiled at her. ''Mind?'' He shook his head and sighed. ''This is the first time I feel like a real father.'' He turned to Meiping's friends and explained, ''When each of my three sons was born, my wife and her father, a rabbi, merely told me the name they had already chosen. Why bother to consult me? I was only an outsider. And then when the children were bigger, no one ever asked my opinion about their education or future. As soon as each boy was old enough to be brainwashed, he was told that I was only an ignorant merchant whose words carry no weight in the house.'' He sighed again. ''But now, my friends, I feel very much like a proud papa.''

''Rachel, Rachel,'' Meiping repeated softly. ''David has picked such a perfect name. 'Ra' in Chinese means 'all things that are great,' and 'Cheal' means 'autumn.' Our daughter's Chinese name is Splendid Autumn, and she is born in my favorite season of the year.''

David bent toward Meiping and kissed her. She circled her arms around his neck and returned his kiss, ignoring what her Chinese friends might think.

The onlookers turned away from the couple, embarrassed. Limei jabbed Quanming, pointing to the diamond bracelet Meiping was wearing. ''For giving him a daughter, he gave her that. She is some lucky woman!''

All of a sudden, fear appeared in Meiping's eyes. She pushed David away. ''Oh, no! We've all been so careless!'' She looked around, asking all her friends, ''Do you think the jealous spirits have heard us?''

Immediately Limei raised her voice. ''Poor Meiping, she's so unlucky! Her man never gives her anything, but beats her every day! He's going to beat her harder now because she has given him an ugly baby girl. The spirits in heaven and earth have no need to be jealous, no, they don't need to at all!''

Following Limei, everybody in the room, except David, started to say how ugly the baby was and how unfortunate the new parents were. And gradually a smile of relief came back to Meiping's face. David was confused; it was a feeling he had experienced often since starting to live with Meiping—especially when they were with her Chinese friends.

The thing that interested Loone the least was bookkeeping. Once in a while Fachai needed to go over the details of Yung Fa's business with him, and he was very glad to let Moi take his place. It soon became a routine that Moi and Fachai must meet at least twice a month, and only occasionally was Loone present.

On one summer day, Loone accompanied Moi to Yung Fa. As usual, Fachai had some business to discuss with Moi. Loone knew it would take them at least a couple of hours to be through, so he left them for a walk. He wandered over to the town square and stopped at the fountain. Seeing people feeding the birds, he took out his sketchpad. When he finally thought to look, two hours had passed, and when he rushed back to the restaurant, he was relieved to see that his wife seemed content and happy.

For the next two months, as summer faded into autumn, Loone worked on a painting titled *The Pigeon Feeders*. On the canvas slowly appeared buildings with pointed roofs and signs written in Chinese. Spouts of water arched out from several nozzles of a moss-covered fountain, and around it rusted iron benches formed a circle. There were pigeons everywhere: on the ground, in the air. Chinese of all ages were feeding them with hands outstretched, and expressions on their faces showed the pleasure it gave them in their otherwise miserable existence.

On a breezy autumn day, as Loone was adding a few final touches to this completed painting, he looked at it with satisfaction and thought it might become the central theme for his next show. He laid down his brush and realized that he was exhausted and hungry. He often neglected to eat and hadn't had dinner the night before or breakfast that morning.

He walked to the window and looked down at the garden. It was near noon, and the mist had cleared. The sun had painted Moi's favorite white dress gold, and she looked like a golden goddess sitting by the lily pond.

He remembered their wedding night, and a feeling of shame appeared like a dark cloud, casting a shadow over his happiness.

*I wish I were a big strong man who knew how to please my bride. I wish I didn't feel so guilty after-*

*ward and act so foolishly. But most of all, I wish I could make love to her right now. It's just that to me she's a combination of a goddess, the sister I've never had, and the mother I've lost. How can I make love to a goddess, a sister, or a mother? I'm lucky that she is of a spiritual nature and can feel my love without having a great deal of physical contact.*

Still looking at Moi, he sighed softly. "I love you so much . . ."

Turning pale, he raised a hand to cover his mouth, and fear appeared in his eyes. "I take it back!" he shouted, looking first up to heaven, then over his shoulder at the invisible evil spirits. "I didn't mean it!"

He had been careful never to tell Moi that he loved her. Neither before nor after their wedding had he mentioned the word to her. He was angry with himself now for being so careless. *If I should allow myself to display my love for her openly, then the jealous spirits of the evil world will come and take her away, the way they took my parents and the Chus.*

He looked down at the garden, worried. The lily pond was immense, and Moi was merely a slight dot next to it. Her favorite color was white, and in it she looked like a tiny snowflake that could easily melt away. Loone shivered. *If I should lose her too, I'll die.*

Down beside the lily pond, Moi was staring at the floating flowers and thinking about Meiping's beautiful baby. The pink little face was far more delicate than the petals of a lily, and the wet, tiny mouth was always waiting for her mother's kisses. Moi wanted so much to become a mother. *Then I'll not be so lonely, and I'll be able to stop going to Fachai. Our meetings are becoming more and more painful; the feelings of guilt have become unbearable for both of us.*

She looked up and saw her husband standing by the window. She started to run toward the house, with an urge to tell Loone what she and Fachai had done. *Maybe he'll be very angry with me for a while, but then he'll forgive me and pay more attention to me. He'll realize that I'm not a goddess but a woman; I'm made of flesh and blood and I have passion. He'll understand that I need a man . . . and later maybe we'll even have a baby.*

Loone had seen Moi running and came to the stairway to meet her. "Come, let's go to Yung Fa and have some of Fachai's delicious cooking. I've painted all night and I'm famished."

Moi gazed at him, trying to hold on to her resolve to tell him everything. "Would . . . would you like to spend a day with me alone? It's so seldom that you put down your brush. I can cook for you and we can enjoy an intimate meal . . . just the two of us."

"But Fachai is my best friend!" Loone answered, hurt. "He and you are the two most important people in my life. Must I be with only you and not him? I thought you liked him. Did he do something to make you upset?"

Moi hesitated for a few moments, then forced a smile. "Upset with your best friend? Of course not. All right, I'll go change." She pretended to be cheerful, while biting her lip, knowing that she must never tell her husband the truth.

My Dearest Quanming:

I'm writing under a huge tree filled with the sweetest-smelling flowers, and Paul says to send you his warm aloha. I wish you could see him right this moment, wearing nothing but a pair of bright-colored shorts, standing on top of a ladder painting the weathered walls of our very small church. He looks like a different man from the one in San Francisco. He is much darker, a lot thinner, ten years younger, and twenty times happier.

Paul and I both feel we have found our paradise on earth. Our homes are two little huts built with dried palm leaves and mud. In order to go in and out, we have to climb a short ladder, for the huts are a few feet above the ground. We have very little furniture. We sit on straw mats, and when it's very warm we splash water on the mats to help cool it down.

There are no automobiles on this island; we travel

on the backs of mules. We ride between the palm trees and through the coconut groves. The primeval forests are so thick at times that we are happy when we finally come out of them and see the sky.

Most of the islanders are extremely friendly, though some are not yet sure whether they should trust us. Paul and I don't blame those who show distrust, because they have had some rather unpleasant experiences with the missionaries before us. We are certain that in time they'll learn to love us, as we already love them. Paul and I are supposed to be educating the islanders, but so far they have been the teachers and we the learners. There are only twelve letters in Hawaiian: a, e, h, i, k, l, m, n, and o, p, u, w. We are learning the language, and I'm doing very well. Paul, however, like all men, is kind of slow in catching on. We're also learning to weave mats, to dye fabrics, and to string flower leis.

I'm sending you a picture of me, wearing a muumuu, the Hawaiian dress. My lei was strung by Paul. The flowers he used are called plumeria; he gathered them from the tree underneath which I am now writing.

I love you, Quanming, and I always will.

Always yours,<br>Laurie

Through his blurred vision, Quanming looked at the picture. Laurie was barefoot, wearing a multicolored long robe. Her hair hung loose over her shoulders; her neck and shoulders were covered by large white flowers.

"Laurie! Laurie!" Quanming cried out, hating himself for not having the courage to choose her over his son.

Wu Da-chung was dying. People crowded around his bed, for Chinese custom demanded that no member of the family be absent. Death must be reached under public observation.

The man had traveled a long journey in life, and he was tired. He had a serene look on his face, accepting death as a welcome rest after his long illness. Sung Tinwei was looking at Da-chung's closed eyes and saying good-bye silently when an ear-piercing shriek broke the silence:

"My husband! Father of my children! You cannot leave us! What are we to do without you?"

The dying man struggled to open his heavy lids and focus his eyes. A troubled look replaced the tranquillity.

Sung Tinwei was furious. He bent toward Mrs. Wu and whispered in her ear, "You never understood your husband in his entire life, and now at the last moment you still can't see that he is ready to cut his earthly ties! Will you allow him the dignity of a peaceful departing, silly woman?"

Astonished by Tinwei's anger, Mrs. Wu hushed.

Sung Tinwei put a hand on his friend's arm. "Rest, Da-chung. Don't worry about anything. Quanming and I will take care of your family."

A smile appeared on the dying man's lips. The next moment he stopped breathing.

The funeral was the event of the year for the people of Chinatown. Besides the immediate families and friends, professional mourners were hired to make the procession look even grander. All who joined the walk were dressed in white, the color of death. An eight-man band played brass and string instruments next to the coffin; the noise was enough to wake the dead.

There were eighteen monks in charge of the funeral, each in either a yellow or orange robe. They burned incense to inform Buddha that Wu Da-chung was on his way. Paper money was burned to ease open the doors that led to the immortal world; paper clothes were burned for the wardrobe of the deceased. Half a dozen paper men and paper women were also turned into ashes; they would become Wu Da-chung's servants in a world hopefully still divided into classes. Mrs. Wu had especially ordered a paper automobile to be burned; she believed her husband deserved to travel first class through heaven.

A vegetable feast was provided by the family of the deceased. Children were running, playing, and laughing; no adult bothered to stop them.

While sitting next to each other for the meal, Sung

Tinwei said to Quanming, "I feel so empty now my best friend is gone."

Quanming understood how his uncle felt. His friends from the Pearl meant a lot to him, and he would be sad to lose any one of them. For an old man, when a person of his generation dies, he feels threatened and frightened by the realization that the next time it just might be his turn.

Loone and Fachai had come to offer Quanming their condolence, but Meiping wasn't there. She was again pregnant, and no pregnant woman was allowed to attend a Chinese funeral; it was believed that her presence would make the dead bleed through closed eyes.

The three Wu boys were now married with children. Each of them had established his own business away from San Francisco and all were sitting there impatiently, eager to go home.

The widow, her eyes still red from crying, had regained her appetite. Her worries were gone; Quanming had promised she could come to live with him and A-lin.

A-lin was wearing white, as all women were expected to at funerals; even their jewels must be white, such as pearls and silver, white gold and white jade. Underneath her jacket, A-lin had on the white jade pendant. Once in a while she would put her hand under the jacket to rub her fingers over the smooth surface of the phoenix. When she looked across the table at Quanming and saw the sadness on his face that was caused by much more than this death, she gave a chilly smile.

# 29

ONE DAY, SOON after his fourth birthday, Sung Hwa was sitting on the carpet and playing with his toy trains. He said to his father, who was reading a newspaper, "I like Saturdays, Baba. Because on this day you don't work. You stay home and play with me." Quanming laid down the paper and smiled at the boy thoughtfully.

"Is there a good story in your paper, Baba?"

Quanming frowned. "I'm afraid not." Seeing the boy waiting expectantly, he continued, "Well, there is a story about the American president. His name is Harding. He is talking about an Open Door Policy—"

"When the president wants to open a door, he has to talk about it first?" interrupted the child, his eyes open wide.

Quanming smiled. "The door we're talking about is not like the doors we have at home," he explained. "President Harding and the leaders from some other countries want China to keep an open door for all the foreigners to go in and out at all times, whether the Chinese like it or not."

"Is it a good thing to do? Does it make China happy?" Sung Hwa tilted his head, looking up at Quanming.

"No. The Chinese are very upset. I am very upset."

"I'm Chinese too, aren't I, Baba?"

"Of course, my little one. In Chinese your name, Hwa, has more than twenty meanings. One of them is also the ancient name for China."

"Oh." The boy frowned, thinking, then said after a while, "Don't be angry, Baba." He left his trains, walked over, and hugged his father. "When I grow up, I'll close all the doors for China."

The next second Quanming had his son in his arms.

"I love you, my little Hwa-hwa. I wish your grandparents were still alive to see what a wonderful grandson they have. You would have made them so proud. You had an uncle who would have loved to hear you talk about helping China . . . but he was killed many years ago."

"Killed by a bad man who wanted to open China's door?"

Quanming sighed. "No, by some other Chinese. Not all Chinese are good, Hwa-hwa, just like not all Americans are bad."

"But Mama says all American women are bad, and the worst are the ones with red-colored hair."

Quanming's voice turned hard. "Your Mama is wrong." Laurie had been gone for over a year, and Quanming had no idea A-lin was still brainwashing their son. "Your Mama doesn't need to hate redheaded women . . . not anymore," he murmured, thinking about the last letter he had received from Laurie.

In it Laurie had mentioned going to a Hawaiian luau and meeting a young man. His name was Palani, which meant Frank in English. He was a schoolteacher and was teaching Laurie to play the ukulele.

There was a picture enclosed. Laurie was standing close to the young man. Quanming's heart had ached as he looked at the handsome islander with curly black hair. The last time Quanming's heart had ached like that had been many years ago, when he had been a young boy in White Stone and thought he was in love with Kao Yoto. That puppy love, however, was nothing compared with his love for Laurie.

"Baba, why do you look so sad?"

The boy's innocent voice was filled with concern, and Quanming's heart melted. No, he could never leave his son. Not even for Laurie.

"Why should Baba be sad?" he asked, kissing the child on the forehead. "Baba has you, and you are a great boy. You are everything to me . . ." *When he grows up, I'll tell him about Laurie. He'll understand just how much I have sacrificed for him, and he'll know the extent of a father's love.* He took Hwa-hwa's hand in his and asked, "Would you like to go with Baba to see Uncle Loone? And later we can all go to China-town to visit Uncle Fachai."

Hwa-hwa jumped up with joy. As Quanming helped his son into the car, he was looking forward to see-ing his friends' reaction when they were told that at four, his son was already capable of discussing Presi-dent Harding's Open Door Policy.

Loone was going through all his sketches, looking for one to be used as the subject of a new painting. *The Pigeon Feeders* had been finished, but now he didn't feel it quite powerful enough to be the center-piece. *I need something more emotional, something with a strong feeling that the viewers can share.*

His eyes fell on the sketches he had done on Angel Island. He looked at the faces he had drawn, and won-dered what had happened to those people. Did this one get out of the island and become a part of Chinatown? Did that one kill himself like so many of them had before him? Could some of them still be living in that hellhole, waiting to be questioned?

He felt the pall of the barracks fall over him again. The old feelings had suddenly returned: frightened, not knowing what was going to happen, like a caged dog waiting to be butchered. *I need Moi. I need her to hold me and drive these terrible feelings away.*

He left his studio and walked to Moi's bedroom. Moi opened her eyes and saw her husband standing in the pale light of dawn like a scared little boy.

In a shy voice Loone murmured, "I was looking through my old sketches, and some of them reminded me of something unpleasant . . ." He pulled at her blanket. "I'm cold. Would you mind very much if I slept with you?"

Moi quickly made room for him and then held him in her arms. She felt like a mother comforting her baby who had awakened from a nightmare. She warmed Loone with the heat from her body, and he soon fell asleep.

Moi lay awake for a long time, then slipped out of bed. She opened the closet door quietly, took out a white blouse and a pair of gray slacks. When she opened her jewel box to get the pearls, she looked into the dresser mirror and saw that Loone had opened his eyes.

"Where are you going?" he asked sleepily.

Moi thought quickly. "I . . . today is Saturday . . . I'm going to Chinatown to buy you some dim-sum."

"All the way there?" Loone yawned. "I'd rather have you home with me."

"You need to sleep," Moi said, sounding like a mother soothing a naughty boy. "By the time you're up, I'll be back with the food. Then you can have me and your favorite meal all at the same time."

Loone smiled as he watched her put on the necklace. He murmured between yawns, "You are so beautiful . . . I like to see you wearing my mother's pearls."

Moi went back to the bed, kissed him on the cheek, and left.

Loone closed his eyes but couldn't go back to sleep. Without Moi's warm body the bed was cold. He got up and went to his studio, started to look through the sketches once more.

Between two unfinished drawings he found a yellowed sheet. It was a sketch he had done many years before, aboard the ship. There was the rolling sea in the background, with the wind blowing spray off the top of the waves. The sun was shining brightly, and the four friends were clinging together: Quanming, Fachai, Meiping, and himself with only one side of his face showing.

"We look so young," Loone mumbled to himself as he smiled at the drawing. Quanming had the air of a big shot, Meiping the expression of an angered tiger. Fachai was the perfect image of a dumb fisherman, and the reason Loone had had his face half-turned was that he thought of himself as too ugly to be seen by the world. *Well, I was wrong. I can't be that ugly, since the most beautiful woman on the earth has agreed to be my wife.*

"We were children . . ." he whispered. "Hungry and frightened and alone, sailing to a strange land. The children of the Pearl River."

Something began to take hold inside Loone. His body began to tremble. "Children of the Pearl!" he shouted, his voice reverberating from the walls of the empty studio.

Quanming and his son were just in time to catch Loone on his way out.

"I'm going to Chinatown to look for Moi," Loone said excitedly. "A new idea came to me a few minutes ago, and I want to tell her before putting the first stroke on the canvas." He said proudly, "Moi is my most dependable consultant. I always tell her what I am going to paint before I start. Moi is also such a considerate wife—she is buying me dim-sum right now. She'll probably stop at Yung Fa and go over some books with Fachai. She has been doing that boring job for me without any complaints."

The three of them got into Quanming's car, and as soon as Quanming started to drive, Loone began to talk. "My next painting is going to be a masterpiece." His face was aglow; he looked happier than Quanming could ever remember. "I'm going to call it *Children of the Pearl.*"

Loone swept a hand across the air, showing his friend what he was visualizing. "The sea, the sky, the ship, and the four of us. I'm painting a dream. A dream shared by all people from the Pearl, a dream that has remained unchanged through the years."

Quanming kept driving in silence. It was not often that his quiet friend made a speech, and he certainly didn't want to offer any interruption.

Loone continued, "As long as China is ruled by scoundrels, the Chinese will not stop trying to escape. We'll continue to search for a land where we won't be killed like ants." He then turned to face Quanming. "This painting is going to tell a truth, and truth cannot be destroyed. When you and I are gone, *Children of the Pearl* will live on. It'll stay in a museum, viewed by thousands of people. The viewers in years to come will have no problem understanding my message, because, I believe, there will still be a new generation of children from the Pearl.''

Loone turned quiet when they reached Chinatown. Washington Street, Portsmouth Square, Grant Avenue, Pacific Street—this was the area they had been thrown into in 1912. Though they had left this miserable district without the slightest regret, now, while revisiting it as outsiders, they still felt sorry for those who remained a part of it.

The streets were wet and filthy, crowded and smelly. Here a bum slept on a bench, there a group of old men stood around at the entrance to a dark alley. In front of a closed theater on Kearny Street, a few opium addicts squatted in a circle, shivering helplessly. On Taylor Street two men were fighting, and many people stood watching, taking a break from their boredom. A fish truck was coming from the Italian district, lumbering down the street and splashing water over everyone in range.

As they turned into Clay Street, Loone said, ''There is an old saying: 'Above every person's head the floating clouds change into a different shape.' Of the four of us who came on the same ship, three have been lucky, but one still lives with a dark cloud hanging over his head. We have to do something to help poor Fachai.''

''He could be happy in Chinatown if he were not all alone,'' Quanming said. ''I've tried to bring his wife and son over, but among all the forged papers on the market, none could be used by Fachai's family.'' Quanming continued with a sigh, ''The main problem lies in Fachai himself: he won't go to night school to study the English language. Even if the law changes, he still can't become a naturalized citizen by passing the tests. He has no property, and so he cannot sponsor his family.''

Yung Fa Restaurant could be seen half a block away,

and Loone suddenly raised his voice. "I know! I can transfer Yung Fa to Fachai's name! He'll then become a property owner and a qualified sponsor. I should have done this a long time ago. I have no interest in the business, and certainly don't need the money . . . " He thought for a while, then continued, "I guess the reason I have not done it sooner is that the Chus treated me like a son, and keeping Yung Fa in my name has been my way of showing respect to their memory. Well, I don't think Mama Chu and Papa Chu would mind my giving Fachai the place. They always liked him."

Hwa-hwa pointed out the window. "Look! Uncle Loone! Your car!"

Quanming parked his car next to Moi's, and the three started for the restaurant. The front door was not yet open for business, so Loone took from his pocket the key he had always had for the back door and inserted it into the keyhole.

"I love you, Fachai," Moi moaned, twisting her naked body under him. Her legs were wrapped around his back, pulling him deeper inside her.

Fachai looked over her shoulder at the clock on the bedside table. "I should go down soon. My new helper is an idiot. The customers will be coming for lunch in half an hour, and the door is not open—"

"I don't care!" Moi said, biting Fachai passionately on the neck. "Your customers can't be as hungry as I. There are other restaurants for them, but you are my only man."

"Moi, my love." Fachai nibbled on her breast, wanting her and forgetting everything else. "You've made my life meaningful again," he whispered hoarsely as he moved inside her more and more rapidly, and she came up to meet his every thrust.

Despite the fact that they had been in bed all morning, their lovemaking still held the same intensity. "I love you, Fachai. I need you, and I don't want you to ever leave me . . ."

The bedsprings were screaming in protest as their

bodies pounded one another. Their mouths were open, sucking in air. Both of them were bathed in sweat, and neither was aware of the footsteps on the stairway, followed by the opening of the bedroom door.

Loone stood staring at the two entwined bodies, his face drained of blood. Moi saw him first, then pushed Fachai off her. The lovers were not able to move farther, but remained frozen in time. The few moments seemed like eternity, and the silence was smothering.

Moi saw her husband eyeing her neck. She raised a hand to touch the pearls, and a cold chill went through her body. She was shaking uncontrollably and wished to die that very instant.

Without a word Loone turned and left. He could feel the bile moving up into his throat; he threw up on the landing before starting down the stairs.

Quanming had come upstairs with Loone, and in a glance had seen the two in bed. He shielded the scene from Hwa-hwa and quickly took the child downstairs.

"Aren't we going to talk to Aunt Moi and Uncle Fachai? What are they doing?" Hwa-hwa asked, and Quanming told him to shut up in a tone he had rarely used on his son.

Fachai and Moi jumped out of the bed. Neither could speak. As Moi rushed to get dressed, Fachai started hurriedly pulling on his pants. Looking at him, she was surprised to see that his body, so dearly a part of hers a moment ago, was now a repulsive sight. From his expression she knew he was feeling the same way.

Moi flew down the steps and ran into Quanming in the dining room. The look on Quanming's face told her that he too knew what she had done. She fled the restaurant and drove out of Chinatown at top speed, no longer caring if she lived or died.

When Moi reached home she ran into her bedroom, locked the door, stripped off her clothes, and bathed. She sat in the tub for what seemed like hours, trying to wash away the filth. Never had she felt so dirty in her life.

When she finally got out and dried, she refrained

from looking in the mirror, ashamed to look at herself. She put on a heavy robe, trying to drive away the freezing cold inside herself, then crawled into bed. She lay under the covers waiting and listening for her husband to come home. Not until the middle of the night did she hear his footsteps at the other end of the hall. Her body began to shake, for she knew that at any moment the door would be kicked down and Loone would burst in.

# 30

THE ENACTMENT OF Prohibition in 1919 became a noose around the neck of Chinatown. With time it became tighter and tighter, and eventually no one could escape. Wan Kon tried to bribe the wrong official, only to be arrested and heavily fined, then sentenced to six months in jail. After serving time he walked out of prison a broken man.

His affairs had not been going well for a long time. Kim Shinma had been imprisoned for life, and Wan's refusal to help the Korean had affected the loyalty of his other employees. One by one they had left the house.

David Cohen's attorney successfully untied the bonds that held Meiping to the House of Wan, which set an example for the other girls. Many went to the mission for protection, and eventually Wan Kon was forced to let them go without compensation. His whorehouse soon closed.

To be arrested caused too much loss of face, and now, without a liquor license, Wan lost his only remaining source of income. The once-powerful man was now aged and in poor health. His desire to fight was gone.

Limei, waiting for him outside the prison gate, welcomed him with open arms. She took him home and drew him a tub of hot water, and after he had bathed, she served him a hearty dinner. She smiled at him and kissed him frequently throughout the meal, never mentioning anything unpleasant.

"Limei," Wan said weakly, "let's get out of here. We have enough money to live the rest of our days comfortably. We can go to New York, where no one knows us. I don't want to see anybody . . . I only want to be with you."

Limei, now in her late forties, looked at her Lau Ban and started to cry with joy. She had never thought she would live long enough to hear these words coming from Wan Kon.

Meiping and her two children made a beautiful picture on the lawn. Rachel was two and the boy, Aaron, not yet one. The girl was being pushed on the swing; the boy was crawling on the lawn. Limei had come to say good-bye, and the two women had talked for hours about the past eleven years.

"You were so dirty and ugly," Limei laughed. "When we picked you up from the pier, the Lau Ban was certain he had made a bad deal. You smelled like a goat."

Meiping smiled at her friend. "You were so good to me. Without your help there is no telling where I'd be."

Limei shook her head. "I just showed you the way: you took it from there. It was your love for David that changed you from a wildcat into a gentle woman."

Meiping laughed. "I'm not so sure about being gentle. David claims that I have a terrible temper. Sometimes I don't know how he puts up with me. We do love each other so much, and that's what really matters."

Limei thought of the relationship between herself and Wan, and she sighed. "For better or worse, I guess I'm stuck. You know, through all these years I had always thought that I stayed because I wanted to be the number-one lady of the house, but now the House of Wan is gone and still I have no intention of leaving. What a fool I am, being in love with a man like him!"

As the two hugged each other, tears of farewell fell on their cheeks. As Limei walked away in a simple gray dress, Meiping stood watching her. Although on this day Limei was wearing no jewelry or makeup, Meiping had never seen her look so beautiful.

The sun shone warmly over the park along the bay. There was a strong breeze, and Quanming asked his son with concern if he was cold. The five-year-old stopped chasing birds and answered quickly, "Not at all. Feel me, Baba. I'm sweating!"

The father pulled the son close to him. Holding the boy's chin in one hand, he reached for his handkerchief. He dabbed the moisture from his son's pale forehead and pink cheeks, said slowly, "Baba loves you very much."

"And I love Baba," the child answered hurriedly, ready to go and play.

"Don't go," Quanming pleaded with his son. "Will you sit with me for just a little while longer?"

They sat on the bench. Quanming had trouble starting what he had planned to say. After a short time his son asked, "Are we going to just look at the water and do nothing?"

Quanming withdrew his gaze from the far horizon. "Hwa-hwa . . ." he hesitated.

"Yes, Baba?" the boy asked impatiently.

"Son . . ." Quanming stopped. It was a very difficult question to ask, a question he had wanted to ask for a long time. "Would you like to go away with me?"

The boy was immediately excited. "Oh, yes! Where are we going?"

Quanming pointed at the horizon. "Across the sea, where there's a group of islands. One is called Maui, and it's a warm and beautiful place. We'll have to sail for many days—"

Before the father had finished, the child was jumping up and down. "Let's go! Let's go today! Let's go home and tell Mama to pack!"

"Hwa-hwa . . . your Mama is not going with us."

"Oh? Will Mama come later, with Guai?"

"No, Guai will be Mama's girl, and you will be only Baba's boy. You and I will live on that island; Mama and your baby sister will live in San Francisco. We can visit them once in a while, but not live in the same house anymore."

In that instant the young face changed. The light disappeared from his innocent eyes, and the smile turned to a frown. "But, Baba, I'll miss Sister and Mama. Who is going to take care of me when you go to work, if we don't have Mama?"

"What if I could find someone else to take care of you? What if . . . I should find you a new mama?"

The child shook his head firmly, and he said furiously, "No! I'll never want a new mama! I want only my Mama, because she is my real Mama!"

"I see . . ." Quanming swallowed. "Well, that's all right," he said, looking at the boy sadly. "Forget what I said. Forget every word of it. I was only joking. It was a very bad joke, and Baba will never tell it again."

The boy was still pouting. But a few minutes later he looked up and smiled. "May I go and play now?"

"Sure," Quanming said. As the boy played, he sat and looked out over the water. He had realized that although A-lin had never been a wife as far as he was concerned, she would always be the only mother to his son.

"Laurie," he whispered toward the far horizon, "I guess I can never be with you."


The maid was a young Mexican girl. Through broken English she and Moi managed to communicate, and the girl had developed a great liking for her mistress. She was worried when Moi refused to get out of bed, and was angry with the master when he didn't seem to care. Staying beside Moi's bed to watch over her, she couldn't understand what Moi was screaming in Chinese.

"No! I didn't mean to hurt anybody! Honestly I didn't!" Moi was screaming again.

The maid picked up a wet towel and wiped Moi's face gently. The young girl was scared. Her mistress had been in bed for a long time, her food untouched; she never made much sense. How could the master just lock himself in his studio and keep on painting day after day?

She said to her mistress softly, "Please, Mrs. Chu, let me dress you. I've sent for a doctor, and he should be here soon."

Moi didn't fight with the maid. She let herself be dressed, but kept her eyes closed.

She felt like a pebble thrown into an ocean of shame. Each day she sank deeper, and there was no way for her to get out. Death was the only way to drive away the guilt and pain, but death refused to come.

She didn't even know how long it had been since it happened. Day after day she couldn't swallow her food; every morning she threw up. Night after night she lay awake staring at the ceiling. Her emotions were tied into a knot, her body frail from lack of nourishment.

She hallucinated frequently, and pictures of her past flashed in her mind. She saw herself as a child walking beside a young woman. "Moi, Mama has no choice but to sell you to the opera school"—the beautiful young woman was crying. "There are so many mouths to feed, and there's no food. You, being a pretty girl, are worth at least a few large bags of rice."

With her eyes closed, Moi still could feel the sun shining on her through the window. Her maid had opened the curtain. Then she saw floodlights shining on Yi Moi the actress. She was taking bows and smiling at the audiences, who were standing and applauding. She was now the young Lau Ban of a famous opera company, and she continued to bow.

A bald-headed man stepped out of the crowd, chasing her with a sharp knife pointed at her heart. She ran toward a large body of water, and reached the opposite shore. Waiting for her were two men: one was Fachai, the other Loone.

"I love you both!" Moi screamed. "Loone, you are like a brother! And, Fachai, you are my man! I didn't mean to hurt either of you, I really didn't!"

She kept on screaming, and then she heard the maid telling her the doctor was there. A stranger's voice spoke to her in English, and although she understood him a little, she didn't want to answer. She kept her eyes closed as she was being examined, and then she felt a needle jabbing into her arm. The pain shocked her, and through her parted eyelids she saw an aged white man smiling at her kindly.

After a perfunctory examination and several questions directed to the maid, the doctor reached a diagnosis. "Don't worry, Mrs. Chu," he said slowly. "You're just a little overwrought, which is not unusual during pregnancy. Now, have a long restful sleep, and you'll be fine when you awake."

News traveled fast in Chinatown, and everybody on Clay Street soon heard about Fachai's sudden strange behavior.

"It all started with his opening late for lunch one Saturday," the gossip went, "and then without a sign on the door to explain the reason, the place remained closed the rest of the day. When we went for lunch the day after, we didn't recognize the man. Polite, hard-working Li Fachai was gone, his body taken over by a drunken monster. He was rude to all of us. He had the nerve to tell us to quiet down because his head was killing him. The damn food was terrible. He dropped a pot of tea in one customer's lap, then broke a whole stack of dishes when he was busing a table. He threatened the dishwasher with a cleaver, and the poor man had to run for his life."

The gossip reached Chen Bai, the photographer.

For years, dressed in a tightly fitted shirt and a pair of pants that hugged his slender body like a second layer of skin, Chen Bai had greeted his male customers with a sweet smile and many gentle words. A young handsome customer would be touched gently by his fingers that were softened by perfumed lotion, and when encouraged, Chen would suggest a drink in the room behind the studio. What happened after that was one of the results of a bachelors' society.

The photographer had quarreled with his recent lover and didn't want to stay in his apartment to brood. He was looking for a place to eat, and upon hearing the gossip, headed for Yung Fa Restaurant.

He purchased a bottle of bootleg whiskey and walked into the place with the bottle concealed in a rolled-up newspaper. He looked around and was surprised to see only Fachai sitting alone.

"What happened to this place?" Chen Bai asked. "Not even one customer?"

Fachai looked up with bloodshot eyes. He tried to get to his feet to greet the customer, but he was so unsteady that he fell back to the chair. "No customer . . . no customer . . ." he repeated in a blurred singsong voice. "Nobody wants to come to eat . . . nobody likes me anymore!" He ended his mumbling with a loud burp.

A deep frown appeared on Chen Bai's face. He remembered Fachai as a young boy, when he had come to the studio to have his first picture taken in the Land of the Gold Mountains. Although Fachai had been infuriated by his hints and had turned down all of his advances, through the years Chen's eyes had continued to follow the handsome young man from a distance. He had always felt that Fachai was unhappy; he had noticed him on several occasions standing at the water's edge, alone, staring out across the bay. He had continued to reserve a soft spot for Fachai, but had never had a chance to let him know.

Chen pulled up a chair, and Fachai mumbled, "If . . . you've come to eat, I can offer you nothing b-but a bowl of noodles. I've been busy, and there's nothing p-prepared."

"Never mind the noodles." Chen patted Fachai on the arm. "I've come to visit you, like a friend."

"Friend?" Fachai shook his head. "I have no friend! I'm nobody's friend! I'm a . . . a misfit . . . a destroyer of friends."

Fachai's hands were shaking. Chen reached across the table to put his hand over Fachai's. "My friend, I can see that you are very down. That bottle of yours is almost empty, but I have a full one. How about you and me drinking it together and sharing our troubles? Who knows, maybe we can make each other feel better."

Day stretched into night, and Chen Bai still listened to Fachai spill out his sorrows. No one came to disturb them, and later Chen went to the kitchen to search for some clean pots and dishes. When he couldn't find any, he washed a few. He then managed to scrape up a few pieces of meat and some vegetables that were not ruined, and fixed two bowls of noodles for Fachai and himself.

The Chinatown gossip spread as the months passed. "No one knows what Li Fachai did to lose all his old friends. You know, the four of them came on the same ship from the Pearl. They used to visit him often, but now they never come anymore. Yung Fa is different from what it used to be, ever since that Chen Bai started working there. It's hard to say better or worse; it's the atmosphere. A new type of customer has taken the place of the old. Most of them are men, sweet-smelling men, if you know what I mean."

A full moon shone over the San Francisco Bay as a lone figure stood near the water, crying and laughing at the moon. "My name is Li Fachai. I'm a great fisherman! I've come from Willow Place and I'm going back with my suitcase filled with gold. Beneath the willows stands the most beautiful girl under heaven, and she is my Leahi. Leahi! Leahi! Can you hear me? I've been faithful to you all these years! I've never touched another woman, no, not even when women came to tempt me with bodies like snakes. Leahi, I remember our promise! I'm a good husband, I'm a good father, I'm a good man! My friends trust me. . . ." And then his voice turned into a wild scream. "Buddha knows that Chu Fong Loone is my best friend!"

Another figure appeared at the bay. "Fachai, you've worried me to death!" Chen Bai shouted, his hands resting on his hips. "Look at you, drunk and crying like a baby!" He lifted Fachai's arm and put it around his own shoulder, then continued more softly, "Put your weight on me. Just lean on me and let me take you home. That's right. I will take you back and give you something to eat, then it's off to bed with you."

Leaning on Chen Bai and still mumbling, Fachai stumbled back toward Clay Street.

Chen Bai's soft voice echoed in the night air. "You have been a very bad boy, frightening me by running off. I care a great deal about you and certainly don't want anything to happen to you, my friend."

Loone stepped back to look at the painting he had just finished. The large canvas was a stage crowded with Chinese actors and actresses. Their costumes were a mixture of Western suits, mandarin robes, and peasant clothes, all purposefully ill-fitted to give them a macabre look.

Their faces clearly showed the use of makeup to give their slanted eyes and flat noses the illusion of a frozen look of evil. As the viewer's eyes traveled the canvas, many different scenes of violence and crime could be observed. Here a man was stabbing another, there two men were picking each other's pockets. Some of the participants in the play were trying to climb a ladder, while others were shaking it from below to make the climbers fall.

People were lying on the ground in agony, with by-standers standing over them, grinning with satisfaction. Rape, robbery, children being beaten, old people stepped on.. . .

"Cruel, thoughtless, deceiving—that describes my fellow countrymen!" Loone spat out in anger as he paced back and forth. "I wish you were a bigger canvas and I were a stronger man." He threw his brush across the room. "I'm sure I've left some fornicating bastards out." He dropped into a chair and closed his eyes. "Damn, I'm tired. This will have to do, because I can do no more."

His bloodshot eyes narrowed as he gazed at the two figures center stage, larger than the rest. Their naked bodies were stretched on a bed, their legs entwined. The man had broad shoulders, the woman a slender figure. Each of them held a mask: her mask was the face of a beautiful woman, his a handsome man. But

their true faces were hideous and repulsive enough to
give any viewer a chill.

"My beloved wife, my trustworthy friend." Loone
began to laugh. "Did you know that you are now the
honored guests of my show?" He waved an arm to his
invisible audience. "Ladies and gentlemen, allow me
to present to you the lovely Yi Moi and the honorable
Li Fachai!" He screamed hysterically, then abruptly
his laughter ended, and he began to cry. His body
shook like a leaf in the wind. He spun around and
collapsed on the floor.

An article came out in *China News* telling the people of Chinatown about Chu Fong Loone's show:

> Mr. Chu has betrayed his own people by using oil
> instead of watercolor, and turned his back on tradition
> by creating his own composition instead of copying
> the masters. He used *The Betrayal* as a title for the
> centerpiece of his show, and although what he is trying
> to convey is not clear, it is obviously an ugly message.
> We strongly suggest that all who are patriotic to China
> stay away from Mr. Chu's show.

Meiping and David arrived at the gallery, but had to
wait outside the door because of the crowd.

"Half the population of California must be here,"
Meiping said. "But why no Chinese?"

"I believe that article in the *China News* that you
read to me has a great deal to do with it," David said,
escorting her through the people.

If that writer dares to show his face, I'll give the
bastard a piece of my mind!" Her anger rose as she
remembered what had been written, and her voice was
louder than she intended. "How dare he say such terrible things about Loone? Calling him a traitor to his
people! That stupid fool has no idea what little brother
Loone has gone through!"

People turned to look at the beautifully dressed lady,
and David whispered for her to hush. "I'm sure none
of these people are capable of reading Chinese, so the

article has obviously done little to hurt Loone's success. Look around: the cream of the city is gathered here. If you would only be quiet and listen, you could hear all the favorable comments."

Meiping bit her lip and tried to control her anger.

"Fantastic work!" she heard a man saying.

"Great talent! I have already purchased that one," a well-dressed man said proudly, nodding in the direction of one of the paintings.

"Each painting has brought tears to my eyes," a woman dressed in furs told her companion. "The artist is a heartbreaker!"

"I'm disappointed that the artist is not here. I was hoping to meet him in person."

Meiping's anger turned to pride. She couldn't keep quiet when she overheard people saying how much they wished to meet the artist, who was seldom seen in public.

"I'm a close friend of the artist!" she said, tapping a woman on the back for attention. David shook his head, even though he knew there was no stopping her now.

"We came on the same ship from China. He is like a little brother to me. He fell on the ship and twisted his ankle, and it was I who nursed him for many days . . ." She talked her way around, and only stopped when they reached the center of the gallery, where the spotlights were shining on a huge canvas.

When Meiping saw *The Betrayal,* her jaw dropped. "By the merciful Buddha!" she gasped. "What great pain has Loone suffered to paint like this! How deeply those two must have wounded him! I'm glad Quanming told me everything. We did go to Loone's house to tell him we were on his side, but he refused to see us. Still, he ought to know that we are his friends. My feelings are hurt now . . . looking at this painting, wouldn't you say that he hates the whole world, including me and Quanming?"

Still shushing her, David tried to reason with her that Loone didn't hate her.

"Poor Loone," Meiping said, her eyes riveted on

the painting. "He must think we would laugh at him, so he locked himself in his studio and refused to see us no matter how many trips we made. Oh, how I hate Fachai and Moi! Quanming and I have vowed never to talk to them again, and I wish them all the bad luck in the world!"

"I don't think we should be too harsh on Fachai and Moi. You know, none of us is perfect. To look at it objectively, we are all guilty to some degree. Quanming had an affair with Laurie, and look at our situation—"

Meiping turned, her face red in anger. David realized too late that he should have kept his mouth shut. "How dare you compare us with Fachai and Moi? We love each other and so do Quanming and Laurie! And . . . Rebecca is mean, and so is that A-lin! Loone is so devoted to Moi, and I'm sure there is nothing more than mere shallow physical attraction between Fachai and Moi! With those two it was just plain lust, and they are not fit to be on the same planet with my poor brother Loone." She took out her handkerchief and started to dab her eyes.

David didn't argue further: everyone seemed to be hanging on Meiping's every word. All he wanted was to leave, but Meiping was not finished.

She looked around with her head held high. "You are used to seeing the Chinese smiling and bowing at you. And you like to draw the conclusion that all these smiling and bowing people are kind and gentle. Well, you are wrong! Beneath all those smiles and bows, a lot of evil is carried out. What you see in this painting does show the true nature of many of my people, and my friend Loone is the only one who dares to tell the truth."

She turned and stormed out of the gallery, with David in pursuit. In the car he suggested that they grab a bite to eat.

"No, thanks, I'm not hungry," Meiping said so softly that David barely heard her.

"I can't believe my ears! You, who have the appetite of a horse, not hungry?" David teased. When she did not answer, he turned and saw her silently weeping.

His voice softened. "I am sorry, Meiping. I did not realize that the paintings had had such an effect on you."

Meiping nodded; the sound of her sobbing now filled the car. She pointed out the window at the moon. "The four of us . . . used to be so close. We had planned on celebrating this Moon Festival together. Now the moon is full, but we are drifting further and further apart. David, it's a shame . . . such a damn shame . . ."

David reached over and put his arm around her, gently pulling her close to him. She rested her head on his shoulder and closed her eyes. They drove silently through the moonlight.

At the gallery a salesman took one of his customers aside and whispered, "I heard that Mr. Chu is in poor health. According to someone in the know, that piece, *The Betrayal,* was painted by him night and day without eating or sleeping. This may be his last show, and someday this painting will be worth a fortune. I suggest that you buy several pieces. If he should die, think of what they will be worth."

# PART IV

## 31

DURING CHIANG KAI-SHEK'S PURGES of 1931, Wong Chung, a young communist from Kwangchow, escaped to Willow Place. Many villagers were eager to take him in, for his money would put food on their tables.

It was a sunny spring day, and in the house of Li, the mother and son were arguing. "Mother, let's get this young scholar to live with us,' Li Kwanjin said enthusiastically.

"No!" Leahi protested loudly. "We don't need the money, and I'm a woman living alone with a child. People's tongues will wag if a man moves in."

Kwanjin threw back his head and laughed. "A child? I'm eighteen, and this Wong Chung is not much older than I. Don't be foolish, Mama, you can't keep on living in the past."

Leahi would not relent until her son reminded her, "Since scholar Hsu died, I've never found another teacher. Maybe this Mr. Wong can become my new tutor."

Put this way, Leahi couldn't refuse, and on the same day Wong Chung moved in.

As soon as Wong walked into the simple farmhouse, he noticed many books, something he had never expected to see. He turned to stare at the middle-aged peasant woman and the broad-shouldered young man who looked like any other villager. "Have you read all these books?" he asked in astonishment.

Kwanjin smiled and told him about scholar Hsu. "He gave his collection to me when he died. The very last two books he bought were the ones by Lu Shum and Hu Shih."

Wong Chung picked up the two forbidden books and leafed through them. The books seemed well-thumbed, and he looked at Kwanjin with new respect. "I'm sure you're familiar with the passages by Dr. Hu relating to the harm of Confucianism. And what do you think of Mr. Lu's anger toward the invasion of foreigners?"

Kwanjin was thrilled. For the first time since the death of the old scholar, he had found someone to talk to. The two continued their discussion while Wong unpacked, and from his meager luggage Wong took out a few books and gave them to Kwanjin. "These are books about communism. The authors are Nikolai Lenin, Karl Marx, and their followers. You must read them, and then I'll help you to understand what they are trying to accomplish. You and I both know China's future lies in communism, and we must work together to educate the ignorant."

Through the entire spring, Wong Chung helped on the fishing boats and in the rice fields. When spring turned into summer, he had established himself among the villagers as one of them. One evening, when the fishermen and farmers had had their supper, Wong Chung gathered people along the banks of the Pearl and started to talk to them, using words they could understand. "We all want to live better, but the rich and the powerful won't let us. In order to survive, we must fight. We have no choice!"

There was a great deal of noise with the children running around and the older generation gabbing, but soon they became quiet. They stared at Wong Chung stone-faced. All their mouths were shut tightly. Everyone in Willow Place was used to submitting to fate. They believed that as country peasants their lot was to accept whatever was given to them. Wong Chung continued his monologues. He understood the reason for their lack of response, and he was prepared.

The cold winds of autumn soon arrived, and instead of sitting by the Pearl, Li Kwanjin offered his house as a gathering place. As his mother busied herself in making tea for the comrades, the villagers relaxed in the homey atmosphere, and became more willing to pour out their grievances. They complained about the landlords who never worked but lived in luxury, and the soldiers who had raided their village, killing, robbing, and raping. "It would be nice if this so-called communism really means that all Chinese are equal. . . ."

In the winter of 1931, after steady rainfall for over a week, the Pearl rose dangerously high, and the fishermen were forced to stay home. The farmers couldn't work either; their land had turned to mud. In the Lis' home, people filled every available space, sitting on the floor, standing, or leaning against the walls.

". . . Less than a month ago, our party leader, Mao Tse-tung, established a Chinese Soviet Republic in the province of Kiangsi," Wong Chung was saying. "The first assembly took place recently, and formally elected our leader the chairman." He paused dramatically and looked around. "Do you have any idea what this means?"

Everyone shook his head except for Kwanjin, who got up and stood beside Wong Chung. Then, with the assurance of a natural-born leader, he began: "This great news means that there is a new life for you, you, and you!" he said, pointing around the room. "This also means that China is now divided: one China for the rich and those who are willing to die as slaves; the other for all of us who are willing to work for a life of equality."

Sitting in her chair with her needlework, Leahi looked up now and then at her son. She tried to understand what he was talking about, but hadn't the faintest idea.

Kwanjin was a handsome young man, with his father's broad shoulders and handsome face. His eyes were like his mother's, large and round, but that's where the similarity ended. In his gaze was a passionate intensity possessed by neither of his parents.

Looking at her son proudly, Leahi thought of the past years. When Kwanjin was twelve, she had asked him whether he wanted to be a farmer like his maternal grandfather or a fisherman like his father. He had looked at her, shaking his head, "Mama, what can a fisherman or a farmer do for our country? I want to read more and understand more, so when I'm grown I'll be able to make China a better place!''

Kwanjin now had the villagers' attention: ''. . . Chairman Mao found a beautiful mountain called Ching-kang, right on the border of two provinces, Kiangsi and Hunan. Chiang Kai-shek asked the warlords of both provinces to arrest our chairman, but all the warlords said that the mountain was out of their territory. Safe from Chiang's reach, our leader and his followers worked the poor soil into usable farmland and grew their own food. There are now over three hundred thousand people living off this mountainous range.''

Kwanjin's eyes swept over his audience; then he continued, ''Believe me, my comrades, our Chinese Soviet Republic will be like a heaven on earth. Food, clothes, money, everything will be shared equally by all. Men, women, the old and the young, will work side by side. This republic will be like a big family, and Chairman Mao the father protector. Think about it, my neighbors, think hard, my friends. If you want to live a life free from injustice and torture, the only way is to go to Kiangsi.''

Leahi saw Wong Chung enthusiastically patting her son on the back. She heard the room fill with the mumblings of doubt. The villagers were debating if they would have the courage to leave Willow Place—the young eager and ready, the older insecure and afraid. She smiled as her son approached. ''Kwanjin, you're so clever with words. I would never know how to speak in front of so many people.''

Kwanjin got down on his knees and took his mother's hands. She tried to pull him up. ''You must never kneel to a woman, my son, it's not done.'' She looked around the room to see if anyone had noticed.

''Mama, please listen.'' Kwanjin held her hands so tightly they hurt. Looking into her eyes, he said softly, ''Mama, you and I are going to Kiangsi.''

The needlework fell from Leahi's lap. She stared at her son, confused. ''I, leave Willow Place? Part from the land handed down for generations?'' She shook her head.

"You're a young woman, Mama, only in your middle thirties. It's a shame that you've lived more than half of your life as a widow, and now it's time for you to come out of this widowhood. My father was wrong to leave you behind and go to America. I can't forgive him for selling himself to the filthy imperialistic dogs for a few pieces of silver!"

Leahi gasped. "A son must never criticize his father!"

Kwanjin ignored her. "It's a damn shame that our country forced our people to go to America to make a living. When the communists take over China, things like that will never happen again."

"Kwanjin," Leahi murmured, "your grandparents and I were very proud when the labor trader selected your father as one of the young men he wanted. How can you call it a shame?"

Again Kwanjin ignored her. "Mama, please say you will do as I ask. With you or without you, I have but one choice: I must go!"

For the first time Leahi understood what her son meant. She was dumbstruck. "You would leave me? If I don't go with you, I'll be left all alone? But how can I leave this place? What if your father should send for us? We're supposed to go to the Land of the Gold Mountains to join him—"

Kwanjin could not hold back his anger. "Mama," he snapped, "wake up from that stupid dream! Father is never going to send for us and you know it. All these years, I've never known him as a real person. The letters, pictures, and checks, that's all I've ever had for a father. Mama, I'm leaving with Comrade Wong in a few days, and if you don't come with me, you just may never see me again. Dammit, Mama, don't throw your life away for a memory!"

Fear appeared in Leahi's eyes, and her lips trembled. "No, don't leave me, my son! Please don't! I can't live through it once more. Nineteen years ago, I was young and strong, yet when your father left, I nearly went out of my mind. If it had not been for you, I would never have made it. You're all I have, and wherever you go, I will follow.''

Kwanjin took his mother in his arms and started to plan for a new and glorious future.

In the December wind and rain the banner of Yung's Teahouse flapped noisily. Since it was too wet to farm and too dangerous to fish, those who could spare a coin or two gathered in this cozy place for tea and company. The room was filled with steam and smoke; hot tea was being poured. Vegetables and meat were frying in the kitchen and the men were enjoying themselves as they ate, drank, talked, and smoked.

Yung Ko sat behind the counter on a stool, watching his wife run the business. The woman was as efficient in the front as she was in the kitchen. More important, she was a shrew when it came to collecting money. Credit had become a thing of the past, and their savings had grown steadily.

While smoking his pipe, Yung Ko listened to the noisy customers. He could easily distinguish from among them the voice of a young man wearing a blue cap, speaking in his city dialect: ''China is now divided, but will soon become one again. Chairman Mao will come from Kiangsi to liberate the rest of our country, and we'll all live as communists.'' He was among the handful of people his age who had moved into Jasmine Valley from Kwangchow since the beginning of 1931.

One of the aged customers asked, ''Son, I don't understand what you're saying. What is this communistic way? What is China being liberated from?''

Another young fellow, a friend of the one in the blue cap, straightened the red scarf around his neck and explained, ''The communistic way means we all have food to eat and houses to live in. China must be liberated, because for centuries it has been controlled not by people like us, but by a few rich and powerful men. China is weak, and foreigners have been taking advantage of us for too long. We must become strong and fight all of them: Japan, Great Britain, Germany, the Americans . . .''

Yung Ko took the pipe out of his mouth. "You wait, young man!" he shouted pointing the stem of the pipe at the one with the red scarf. "The Americans are good people. My daughter's husband is an American, and they have two lovely children. I'll never fight with my son-in-law, and no one can make me!"

"Your daughter is the woman of a white man?" the red-scarf speaker bellowed. "Are you sure they are married? Or is she only a plaything of his? It's disgraceful for a Chinese lady to—" He was interrupted by someone tugging persistently on his sleeve. He stopped, and turned in anger.

With a smile the blue-capped man whispered, "Comrade, be careful what you say. Don't forget that our mission is to win the villagers over. You must not argue with that old fool."

The speaker, realizing that he might be antagonizing his audience, changed his manner abruptly. "I'm sorry." He gave a slight bow to Yung Ko. "Did you say your daughter is married to an American? I thought you said an Englishman. Yes, you're absolutely right. The Americans are all right. And I'm sure you have beautiful grandchildren, as the result of a mixed marriage."

Seeing the anger had disappeared from Yung Ko's face, the speaker returned to what he was saying. "We Chinese must unite as one, first to fight the rich and the powerful, then the rest of the world. One day China will be a very strong nation, one that belongs to all the people, not just a select few."

The speech went on,, but Yung Ko stopped listening. He reached into a drawer and took out a stack of pictures. Laying them on the counter, he searched around for his glasses. When he located them, he slowly went through the stack.

He took his time studying the picture of Meiping and the white man, and wondered if they were married or, as the red-scarf man had said, she was just a plaything. He looked at the next picture; it was of a girl and an infant boy. *For your sake, my grandchildren, I pray that your father and mother are married.*

Mrs. Yung had been watching her husband out of the corner of her eye. Sensing his doubt, she came over to him and whispered, "Old fool, don't let those loudmouth punks bother you. Of course your daughter and this white man are married. They've been together all these years. If she was only his plaything, wouldn't he have left her a long time ago? No man stays with the same woman unless he is forced to do so by the bonds of marriage. Just think of yourself, you old fool!"

The rain was falling in torrents over the valley, and the wind began to howl. Old man Yung's heart leapt with joy at the thought that someday Meiping and her family would return to Jasmine Valley. *I'll show these people then that my Meiping has always been a good girl!*

The city of Kwangchow was soaked in water. Unlike the small villages, here the power of Chiang Kai-shek had reached into every crack, like the rain. People didn't dare to complain about the right-wing nationalists, or show any sympathy toward the communists. Chiang's spies were everywhere; people were arrested every day. Anyone who insisted on discussing politics whispered his opinions in a secure haven such as Fong's Pawnshop.

With the door locked and the windows closed, Fong Mao and his five grown sons were sitting around a table. "What bothers me the most," the old man said, "is that our national father, Dr. Sun, was pro-communism. Chiang Kai-shek is arresting all communists and killing them as traitors. This is contrary to Dr. Sun's beliefs!"

The oldest boy, Fong Ming, sighed. "Chiang has driven so many of the educated young men into exile, forcing them to go to Kiangsi. At the same time he has given the warlords their powers back and made them officials in his new government. It makes me furious!"

The youngest of the boys asked, "Baba, can we leave this miserable place and all go to Kiangsi to join Chairman Mao? I'm sick and tired of living in this police state!"

The father shook his head. "I can't. I promised your mother on her deathbed that I'd stay and mind the pawnshop for your cousin Loone."

"That doesn't make any sense!" another Fong boy interrupted. "Cousin Loone may not even be alive! All the years I was growing up, Mama talked about nothing but how much we owe our dear cousin. But he has never written us once in nineteen years. There is no reason for us to believe that he is thinking of returning . . . that is, if he is alive."

"I must keep my promise to your mother. You boys can go to Kiangsi if you wish, but I must stay in Kwangchow!" The father slammed his hand on the table.

The boys didn't argue with him anymore, but continued to discuss whether they should all go to Kiangsi.

An hour later, a conclusion was reached. The four younger boys would leave when they were ready, and Fong Ming would stay with his father in Kwangchow to mind the shoe store and the pawnshop that had been in the family for so many years.

Fong Mao sat shaking his head. "China is doomed. Our family is to be divided, and the dividing force is not the foreigners but our own people!"

On the same December morning, Yoto opened her eyes and looked at the bedside table: the little china clock showed eleven. She glanced from her clock to the window, where sheets of water were washing down the glass; everything outside was dark. She yelled for her maid, irritated that it was such a miserable day.

A young girl with long pigtails appeared at the door and asked if the Tai-tai was ready for breakfast.

"Of course I am ready! Can't you hear my stomach growling?"

The maid had a hard time imagining how her mistress could be hungry while still in bed, especially after her gigantic dinner the night before and the snack just before going to sleep. She hurriedly left for the kitchen, and in a short time came running back with a large tray filled with food.

Yoto sat with her back resting on several satin pillows and a silk cape thrown over her shoulders. She held a spoon in one hand, a pair of chopsticks in the other, and began to eat the large bowl of noodles cooked in thick oily chicken soup. When the bowl was empty, she lifted the cover from another plate, revealing three fried eggs and pork strips.

When she had finished, she rang for the girl to take away the empty bowl and plate and lift the lids off the stack of bamboo steamers. The top stack had meat buns, followed by different sweets in the next three containers: lotus cakes, sesame tarts, and almond cookies.

With a mixture of disgust and amazement, the maid watched Yoto eat. Being from an impoverished family, the young girl couldn't believe a human being, without doing any work, could eat so much food in one sitting. She looked at her lady's fat face and body, and found her repulsive. She remembered listening to the older servants talking about the Tai-tai being beautiful once, but over the years she had changed into a replica of a fat Buddha. The girl wanted to laugh but didn't dare; Mrs. Ma's appetite was great, but her temper was even greater.

Yoto felt better after the food. Picking up a soft towel to wipe her mouth, she asked, "Is the master home?"

"Yes," the maid answered, carefully removing the tray. "The master and the young lords are in the living room."

Yoto was happy to hear that. It was unusual for her husband to stay home these days. "Help me with the bath, and hurry!" she said, rolling out of bed.

The tub in the bathroom was filled with hot water brought in by two kitchen servants. Yoto stepped into it, but the water was so hot that she just stood there. She looked down but couldn't see her feet because of her stomach. She stared at the water and remembered vaguely how slim she used to be.

Slowly lowering herself into the tub with the help of the maid, she gave a sigh of relief. Getting out of the bed and standing so long had tired her. She rubbed the perfumed soap over herself slowly, thinking of the tiny waists on her two daughters. Once I was just like them, she thought. Soon they will be married and have children, and they too will become fat.

No matter what tradition said about the value of boys, Yoto found much more comfort in her two daughters than her three sons. Growing up in the shadow of their father, the boys had watched him chasing the maids and young village girls. As soon as they were old enough, they started following his example. The housemaids were either seduced by force or coaxed with favors. The girls outside the mansion learned to stay clear of the Ma terrors. Some unfortunate ones were raped, and money was paid to settle complaints from fathers with enough courage to approach such a powerful family.

Sitting in the water, Yoto remembered how she used to complain to her husband about the three boys' habits of drinking and gambling. He told her that these activities were normal for young men of their station, and she should be happy that they weren't smoking opium or involved in politics, especially communism.

Through the steam over the hot water, Yoto looked up to heaven and thanked Buddha for keeping her sons away from the communists. In the past few years the radicals had begun to move into White Stone and started preaching to the town's youth. Her sons, fortunately, showed no interest in these people, except occasionally ridiculing them for their chimerical ideas.

As she sank deeper into the bath, her thoughts returned once more to her daughters. She was happy that the girls were very much like herself twenty years before. They knew how to read and write, and had a talent for music and a love for poetry. They were content with their lives within the walled mansion, and went out only once in a while, always accompanied by their maids, who reported everything back to their mother.

Yoto thought about the girls going to the temple every year for the lantern festival, and could see the statues of the different Buddhas smiling behind the thick layers of smoke, as if laughing at all the mothers, telling them that no matter how well-protected the young girls were, there was still a chance they would get hurt.

She glanced at the rain, and wishing it would go away. Even in the security and warmth of the tub, she felt cold and frightened. Tears fell on her naked breasts; she was not aware of them. She realized she must not allow her daughters to go to the temple anymore, especially on the nights of the lantern festivals. A broken heart, unlike a bone, can never be completely healed. Years may pass, but whenever it rains, each raindrop will be followed by a teardrop.

She stood, and immediately the maid began to dry her. Her body was still, her thoughts in flight. *What if I was married to a poor man? Would I still have grown fat? I am only thirty-five. I shouldn't feel so old. If I had a husband who loved me, and only had eyes for me, maybe I would have a reason to cling to youth.*

As the maid helped her to get dressed. Yoto looked out the window, watching the storm. Some distance away, the rain was falling on that small red brick house at the foot of the hill. Under its roof she could have had a life with a tall, handsome husband. *It would be so cozy for the two of us to have a meal together, and later, while listening to the rain, I would feel so warm with his arms holding me close.*

She waved her hands in front of her eyes, trying to erase the image. "Go away! It's been too many years! Why won't you go away?" she screamed, frightening the maid. "I hate the rain. I hate it!"

After she was dressed, she rushed into the living room. "Good morning, Mama," her three sons greeted her the moment she entered.

"You've just missed Baba," the youngest one said.

"Have you any idea where he has gone?" Yoto asked casually, hiding her disappointment.

The three boys looked at one another, obviously trying to figure out the best answer. "He . . . We don't know for sure . . . To the town square maybe . . . or some teahouse. He was going to listen to the newest happenings about the communist movement," the eldest answered.

Yoto wondered why they always protected their father. Wasn't it she who had gone through the pain of their birth?

She decided to ignore their lies and changed the subject. "Tell me, then, what's the newest happening of the communist movement?" she asked calmly, easing herself into the nearest chair.

Her oldest son answered, "I'm not really sure. It has nothing to do with us, something about a group that calls themselves the Chinese Soviet Republic. Many ignorant peasants are forming a community that is growing larger every day." He shrugged.

Yoto was half-listening, for her thoughts had traveled to another time. A time that could not be brought back, yet would never be forgotten.

## 32

IN 1929, SEVEN months after Herbert Hoover's inauguration, the stock market crashed. Depression hit America like a giant sledgehammer. Most industries were either producing at a snail's pace or went bankrupt; even the car market plummeted like a spent Fourth of July rocket. And in every business the Chinese were the first to lose their jobs. The destitute Chinese carried their meager belongings in bags, and gathered under the trees in public parks or on the streets of Chinatown. They scrounged for food out of the garbage cans behind restaurants that were still lucky enough to be in business. Their wailing was carried on the winds of hopelessness:

"The sandy ground under our feet is sifting away! Our gold mountains are melting to nothing!"

"How can this happen to me? Does the Great Buddha have no eyes? I've given money and food to the poor beggars. What kind of reward is this?"

"I worked so hard, for so many years. I trusted all my money to an American bank. All gone! My dream of buying my own business, my hope of sending for my wife and children, my wish of going back to my village as a rich man envied by everyone . . . everything is gone!"

A national relief program was eventually established by the government. In every city there were long lines of people waiting for clothing and food. The poorest among the Chinese joined the line, and were able to survive for a while. Then, gradually, from state to state, authorities announced that they could no longer afford to take in the relief applications from the Mexicans, blacks, and Orientals.

A large number of starving Chinese were forced to beg, and in the cities they began being considered nothing more than a public nuisance. The police chased them with clubs.

The suicides of white Americans were publicized as tragedies; the news about the many Chinese who killed themselves remained untold, except by the *China News,* which was now reduced to four pages.

It was indeed a time of hardship, a time when the poor were starving and the rich had taken a sudden fall. In many cases, stepping down was just as impossible to bear for the rich as starving was for the poor; many millionaires killed themselves because they discovered they had but a few dollars left in their pockets; many beggars would have continued to live if they had had but a dollar or two.

In the spring of 1932, Quanming laid down the newspaper; what he had read filled him with dread. He sighed, looked out his study window, and sat deep in thought for a long while. A few white hairs had appeared at his temples, and deep lines showed between his eyebrows. In the past years his body had lost the slimness of a young tree, and now had taken on the look of a mature oak.

He pushed himself out of the chair and walked toward the kitchen. The place seemed empty without the large staff. The Depression had forced him to let most of them go. There were only two left: the old cook and a young maid. At the moment both were busy preparing a large pot of soup. At the sight of the Lau Ban they bowed, then continued to drop vegetables and pieces of meat into the broth.

Quanming watched, then suggested that the cook add some flour dumplings into the mixture. "That should make it more filling," he said, then turned to leave. He stopped by the door. "When it's ready, pour it into containers, and be sure to seal the lids tightly. Then put them in my car. Later we will bring them to Chinatown."

As soon as he turned his back, the maid made a face in his direction, then said to the cook with a wicked smile, "I guess we're going to stand on the damn street corner again, ladling out soup to those bums."

The old man gave the maid an angry look. "Where's your heart, girl? It's our own people we are feeding, and they are not bums. At one time they were hard workers just like you and me, until misfortune struck them. We could just as easily be on the receiving end except for the kindness of our Sung Lau Ban."

The maid shrugged. "Maybe you should tell that to our Tai-tai, and get her off my back when I have to leave her to go feed some dirty bums."

The cook continued to mix the water and flour with a large wooden spoon. "Tai-tai is a lucky woman. Not many men were able to keep their savings through this disaster. Maybe she should stop bitching and be thankful that she has that good man."

"You'd better keep your voice down, old man. If that witch hears you, I'll be ladling out soup for your starving ass as well. That's where the gardener and chauffeur probably ended up. They should have known better than to—" She was interrupted by the ringing of a bell high on the kitchen wall. The girl immediately dropped what she was doing and hurriedly left for her mistress's bedroom.

A-lin was sitting in front of the dresser looking at herself in the mirror. For the past few years she had been checking closely to see if any more of those hateful little lines had crept onto her face during the night. Never considered pretty when young, she nevertheless wanted to hold on to her youth for as long as she could. Rubbing between her brows with the tips of her fingers, she tried to erase the creases. She then leaned forward and studied her black hair for any signs of gray.

When the maid walked in, A-lin shouted, "What took you so long?" Without waiting for an answer, she threw a pair of tweezers to the girl. "Check the back of my head, and if you see any white hairs, pull them out. And I'll murder you if you touch any black ones by mistake again!"

The maid dreaded this chore; every white hair pulled

out had to be presented to the Tai-tai for examination, and through experience the girl had learned to dispose quickly of any accidentally pulled black ones. After a few pulls the girl exclaimed brightly, "There are no more. Your hair is so black that it shines like the hair of a young girl."

After checking in the mirror, A-lin tilted her head back and closed her eyes. The maid picked up the jar of cream and walked behind her. A-lin rested the back of her head on the girl, and the maid began to apply the cream to her face. A-lin believed that with massage, the lines on her face would be erased and her skin would regain the look of youth.

Youth . . . she had thrown away so much of her youth on a husband who did not appreciate her. *I'm almost forty. What a waste my life would have been if I had never found a man who makes me happy.*

The young maid's fingers were rough from hard work. *His* fingers were smooth and gentle with a particular scent. At the thought of him, A-lin relaxed; a warm glow surrounded her and she could feel herself becoming moist. *If only he could be here now, just he and I* . . . She became lost in a fantasy.

The maid was amazed when she saw in the mirror how her mistress had begun to smile. The grouchy woman appeared almost beautiful. "Mmm . . . mmm . . ." The maid never had heard her mistress purr like this before. The girl continued to work on her mistress's face as gently as she could, afraid to break this pleasant mood.

"Don't stop . . . please don't . . . never stop . . ." A-lin mumbled softly, picturing herself alone with her lover, the tailor Moa Lau.

For many years she had shopped frequently in his place, but had thought of nothing more than the goods in his store. Until ten years ago, when she found Laurie Eddington wearing the white jade pendant.

Trying to comfort her, Moa had told her that she was beautiful, right in front of her mother. He had said that her husband should treasure her instead of playing around with a white cow.

No man had ever paid her a compliment before, and

it had changed her life. The next day she had gone back, and after that she had started seeing him constantly.

For a while she considered him more than just a lover. One day after making love, she told him that she was going to divorce Quanming and marry him.

"Let's leave things as they are," Moa quickly replied. "You are the rich and respectable Mrs. Sung, and I'm a good friend of the family. This way we can have our fun without paying a price we can't possibly afford."

Of course, he was right. The price would have been too high. A-lin thought about it now and frowned. *It would have cost me my reputation, my children . . . and the pain of watching Quanming run into the arms of that waiting white whore.*

Moa had managed to please everyone in the Sung household. Everyone except, of course, Quanming. Hwa-hwa had accepted him immediately, and Mrs. Wu, although worried about Quanming finding out, was glad to see her daughter happy. The old woman had soon learned to accept the situation and began to enjoy Moa's company. For the past few years Moa had spent much of his spare time in the Sung home; the two women and the boy had frequently played mah-jongg with him, and that was what they were going to do today, after dinner.

In the past year, A-lin had been quite civil to Quanming. Their paths crossed seldom, because Quanming continued to lead a life which never included his wife.

A-lin opened her eyes and looked into the mirror, pleased by her reflection. Her face was smooth and her eyes bright. She looked at the expensive jar of cream and shook her head. No, it wasn't the cream. *A woman can only look young and feel young when she knows that she is wanted by a man. If it were not for Moa Lau, I would be as miserable as Quanming without out his whore.*

Many of the stores in Chinatown had closed. Street corners had become gathering places for the homeless.

Quanming left the cook and the maid in the town square to set up the free soup station, then drove on to Portsmouth Square. When he stopped in front of Sung Wu Company, he got out and looked at the building; his heart ached. He could not forget how this place had looked to him twenty years ago. The spreading white building had sparkled in the sunlight; the sight had taken his breath away.

He had been a naive young man then, and it had taken his uncle and Paul a long time to educate him before he earned the right to be called the young Lau Ban.

Quanming visualized the days of the early twenties, Chinatown's heyday. The gambling, prostitution, opium—a man could buy anything if he had the money. He also recalled the gang fights and the Tong killings, and had to admit that they were also responsible for making the old Chinatown an exciting place.

Even before the Depression, Chinatown's tentacles were being severed one by one. The police had put an end to the gang wars, and the smaller Tongs had been absorbed by two of the larger ones. Prostitution had ended, and then Prohibition tightened its grip. The bars and most of the restaurants had been gone for a long time.

The glorious days of the Sung Wu Company had come to an end as well. Quanming looked at the row of offices that faced the street, now empty with boards covering the windows. He remembered how the loan office had been taken over by the bank, and how the mission had lost its function once the prostitutes had disappeared. The classroom where Paul Eddington had once taught English was now vacant; there had been no one capable of taking his place.

He glanced over at the long building next to the offices, the now empty warehouse of the import-export business, another victim of the Depression.

To Quanming the building was a monument of a dead era. The trim was in need of paint; some bricks were missing and others were ready to fall. The pipes of the fountain were rusted. The largest window was

long gone, replaced by a piece of plywood. A loose
shutter hanging on a single hinge rapped against the
building in the wind.

Quanming looked across Chinatown and wondered
if the heart of this world of whores, thugs, and busi-
nessmen, good and evil, would ever again beat with
the exciting, vibrant, and colorful sounds of life as a
Chinese oasis in this land of the whites.

He took a key from his pocket, unlocked the door
to the main office, and went in. He walked down the
hall to the garden. As he took in the once-well-
manicured interior, he was appalled at the change. The
trees were so overgrown that the sun had trouble finding its way through. Last year's dead leaves made a
thick blanket on the ground; a pungent smell of decay
filled the air. The pond was nearly dry, and the once-
red bridge was now faded, with one railing lying on
its side. The pagoda, its base rotted away, was tilted
and about to fall. Although it was spring, there were
no flowers blooming.

The gazebo was in disrepair and matched the rest of
the wreckage. Quanming found Sung Tinwei in a black
robe sitting quietly, accompanied by his old servant,
now the only one left.

"Uncle," Quanming called, trying to sound cheerful.

Tinwei looked up, bewildered; he had been lost in
a reverie of the past and was now forced to come back.
"Ah, Quanming," he said, "how good it is to see
you." He immediately told the servant to get the young
Lau Ban tea and his favorite dim-sum.

Quanming was saddened by his uncle's gesture of
love. In the old man's eyes he was still a hungry young
boy. Quanming remembered how his uncle used to
order all sorts of dim-sum for him, and in those days
he had had such an enormous appetite that he was able
to devour everything in sight.

"No dim-sum," he said. "Thank you, Uncle."

The servant went for tea, and for a while neither
uncle nor nephew spoke. A soft breeze blew, rustling
the dead leaves, and the gentle melodic sound of wind

chimes floated across the garden, bringing back the lost, haunting beauty that had once abided here.

Sung Tinwei pulled his robe tightly around his frail body, trying to ward off the dampness.

"You seem cold, Uncle," Quanming said, taking off his jacket and draping it around the old man's shoulders.

Tinwei looked up at his nephew. "Quanming, I'm so cold that no jacket in the world can ever warm me." His voice was as thin as he.

Quanming reached for the old man's hands; they felt like ice in his grip. "Uncle, please let me take you to a doctor."

Sung Tinwei shook his head. "I'm not sick, it's just that this old body is worn out." A whippoorwill was calling, and a few seconds later, another answered. Quanming held his uncle's hands tightly, trying to will some of his strength into the old man.

Tinwei continued to talk, his voice calm. "I've lived a full life, but the warm days are over and the cold night is near. There is nothing wrong with my liver, my heart, or any other part of my old body. It is just time to give it up."

"Uncle!" Quanming pleaded. "Please—"

"You are acting like your mother-in-law when Dachung was ready to leave. I felt like strangling that stupid woman for her carrying-on," the old man said, showing his displeasure.

"I . . ." Quanming swallowed hard. "I'm selfish. I can't bear to see you leave. My life is so empty. If you were also gone, then I'd have no one."

Something in Quanming's voice made Tinwei ask with concern, "I thought you were close to your children."

"I've never been close to my daughter . . ." Quanming stopped, having difficulty explaining. "I love my son very much, but . . . through the years, he has changed. As a child he believed in me. When he grew older, though, he became indifferent." Quanming let go of his uncle's hand. He turned away,

ashamed of what he was feeling. "I just don't understand."

Sung Tinwei studied his nephew for a time, then
leaned back and said, "Quanming, tell me about your
son."

"Uncle," Quanming asked, "how is a child
formed? If he has my blood, at least half of his personality should be like mine. I've tried my best to
share with him my philosophy of life. But at fourteen
the boy is a male version of his mother."

Quanming stopped, glancing at his uncle. The old
man waved for him to go on. "He is clever, but de-
spises hard work. He is loved, but unwilling to love in
return. Take this Depression, for example. When I told
him about what's happening to so many people, his
only concern was whether I still had money stashed
away for the family—for him, mainly. He and I don't
agree on anything, and I've wanted nothing more than
for him and me to be close." Now that Quanming had
started, he poured out his sorrow, "I've been lonely
for many years. There were four of us who came from
the Pearl, and we were like siblings at one time. Then
someone came between Loone and Fachai, and their
friendship ended. Meiping and I had to take Loone's
side, because he was the one betrayed. He was hurt so
deeply that he blocked out the entire world, including
Meiping and me, and locked himself in his studio.
Even today he lives like a hermit. Meiping and I have
not visited Fachai, nor has he ever come to us. I don't
visit Meiping often, because, to be honest, each time
I do, I find myself envious of the love in their home.
She, David, and their two children are so close to one
another. . . . Now, tell me, my uncle, what did Meiping do right, and what did I do wrong, so that she
has a happy home and I don't?"

Quanming felt his uncle tapping him on the shoulder. Looking up, he was surprised by the change on
his uncle's face. Tinwei had thrown aside the warm
jacket and was sitting up straight. His eyes were bright,
the tiredness gone; he was once again his old self.

"My nephew, I have four things to tell you," Tinwei

began, sharpness returning to his voice. "First, you have to get out of Chinatown. The glory days are finished. From now on every Chinatown will be reduced to a few blocks of narrow streets where the Americans can go for a cheap dish of chop suey and a glimpse of a dragon dance during our New Year's parade. Those remaining in Chinatown will never be able to survive in the white man's world . . . they will be the uneducated, the poor, and those who have given up hope. Believe me, Quanming, in the future the Americans will see a different group of Chinese. They will not be the laborers from the Pearl. Our people will work side by side with the whites, and this new generation will look down on the children from the Pearl."

Quanming felt a chill at the old man's prediction, wondering if it was true that when a man was near death he could foretell the future.

Tinwei continued, "The second thing I want to say is that I was wrong to force you to marry A-lin. I have no answer to your problem with your son. But, believe me, all children are undependable. Through my whole life, I've never yet met one completely satisfied parent. But had you been happy with your wife, then you might not have been so easily hurt by your son. You are lonely and unhappy, not because you have lost your friends but because you have no love in your home. You see, my nephew, I never married, and I didn't know love was so important in a marriage."

Quanming was surprised at his uncle's perception. Had he been able to find comfort at home, even the Depression would have been bearable—

His uncle's voice interrupted his thoughts. "The third thing I want to tell you is a love story."

Sung Tinwei closed his eyes. The whippoorwills had resumed their love songs. The old man listened for a while, and then a smile appeared as he began to talk. "I was very young. Nineteen? Twenty? I'm not sure anymore. Da-chung and I had not been in this country long, and we were working hard to survive. Surviving, however, was not enough for us; we wanted to be ahead of all others. We went to a night school to learn

English. The teacher was a beautiful American girl working for the mission. I fell in love with her, and she was kind to me. I guess she was proud of having such an enthusiastic student. I followed her around like a dog for a long time, then asked her to marry me. She told me it was impossible, gave me many reasons. I was hurt. The wound was so deep that I never fully recovered. My love for her turned into hate, and I hated her for not giving up her people and her world. Did she turn me down because I was Chinese? Or did she say no because I was poor? I never figured it out—both were good-enough reasons, I suppose. If she had known that someday I would become the Lau Ban of the Sung Wu Company, would she have married me? Or would she have chosen to be the wife of a poor American? Well, I never saw her again, and my question has remained unanswered.''

The old man opened his eyes. "Quanming, when you told me you were in love with Laurie Eddington, I didn't want you to be hurt. I was afraid that she was no different from the girl I had known. But also, I believe, I was very envious. I couldn't accept the fact that I, who had built an empire here, had been turned down by this American girl, and you, who came under my roof with absolutely nothing, could have an American wife and be truly loved by her."

"You, Uncle, jealous of me?" Quanming asked, not believing what he was hearing.

The old man reached a hand toward his nephew. "Will you forgive this stupid old fool, Quanming?"

Even after living in America for twenty years, Quanming was still taken aback by hearing an elder apologizing to him. "Why, Uncle . . . of course . . ." He took the old hand in his.

"Thank you. You are generous with this old man." Tinwei gave the nephew's hand a squeeze. "Now, let me ask you, where is Laurie?"

"I don't know," Quanming sighed. "About ten years ago, when I decided not to join her in Hawaii because of my son, it seemed wrong to keep her waiting. I wrote her a letter and suggested that we should not communicate anymore. I haven't heard from either her or Paul since then. I imagine she is married . . ." Quanming couldn't continue, for at that moment he imagined the picture of the handsome Hawaiian, Palani. "Uncle, you said there were four things you wanted to tell me. So far you have told me only three."

"Ah," the old man sighed. "I must ask you a favor."

"I'll do whatever you say, my uncle."

"I want to be buried in White Stone."

"You're going to live many more years yet, my uncle. You're only tired—"

"Stop that nonsense. We all must die, and I most certainly shall die before you. Will you promise to take my body back to White Stone?"

When Quanming promised, Tinwei leaned back, relieved, and then started to talk about China, more to himself than to his nephew. "Even after all these years, I can still see the Pearl flowing though the small village and the white marble on top of the hill. I'll be happy to go back home. . . ."

## 33

WHEN CHINATOWN HAD been at the peak of its glory, its residents had dressed to emulate the Americans. Their choice of colors and combinations was at times ridiculous: bright yellows, flashing greens and purples. Most of the time the clothes seemed either too large or too small, but they wore them proudly, feeling more American. The Depression quickly changed all that. The Chinese were once again wearing the colors they had brought over with them: dark brown, gray, faded blue, and black. Their undernourished bodies shivered when the wind was too strong, and their colorless faces seemed more wrinkled as they looked up from bloodshot eyes. Dragging their feet and staring at the ground, they all seemed to belong in a funeral march.

When they walked by their favorite restaurants, none dared to stop. Some would reach into their pockets and finger the few coins they had left, then shake their heads and keep moving.

"Let's splurge and go to Yung Fa," one murmured with a weak grin. "As long as the tea is free, it doesn't matter whether the one who pours it is something less than a man."

All of Clay Street was in a shambles, and Yung Fa Restaurant was no different. For a time it had been the pride of the neighborhood, but in the past ten years it had begun to show signs of neglect. No new paint had been applied, and the interior had fared even worse.

Chen Bai, the photographer, had aged well. A gray shirt and a pair of white pants hugged his slim body; his graying hair was neatly combed, parted in a straight line. Eyeing the customers walking in, he smiled, and only then did a net of fine lines appear around his thin lips. "You must excuse us, my friends. Seat yourselves wherever you like, and I'll be with you in but a minute,'' he said, nudging Fachai with his elbow. "He has just received a letter from home, and if I don't finish reading it for him, he's going to kill me. Please, in the meantime, help yourselves to tea.''

People had grown used to Chen Bai, and now they were too depressed to make fun of the situation. They simply walked over and got their tea.

''Where were we?'' Chen Bai asked, looking at Fachai.

At thirty-seven, Li Fachai looked well over fifty. He had become bone thin, and his skin had a sickly pallor. There were dark circles around his sunken eyes, and his hands were trembling as he gave the sheets of paper to Chen Bai. ''Read the rest and forget the damn customers,'' he croaked, his voice unclear, as though his tongue were too thick. ''You left off about here, I think . . . I'm not sure. You know I can't read. Anyway, my son was saying it rained a lot last winter.''

''Ah, yes.'' Chen Bai cleared his throat. He took a pale blue handkerchief out of his pocket and dabbed the corners of his mouth delicately. Then he carefully folded the handkerchief and put it back.

''Dammit, can't you carry on?'' Fachai shouted.

As a few customers exchanged glances, Chen Bai pouted, looking hurt. ''Don't rush me. I have a cold, and my throat hurts, and you don't even care.''

Depression or not, the men smiled as they listened.

Chen Bai cleared his throat again and began to read. '' '. . . We left Willow Place last winter, during the long rainy season. My teacher, Wong Chung, led us northward from Kwangchow, and we were on the road for almost three months. We walked most of the journey, only occasionally caught a ride on a cart pulled by water buffalo, or on a train. There were twenty-two of us, and besides Mama, there were four other women—' ''

''Leahi!'' Fachai moaned. ''My Leahi left Willow Place!''

Chen Bai frowned. ''How can I read if you insist on interrupting me?''

Fachai ran his fingers through his unkempt hair, trying to keep his mouth shut. He knew the only reason his son was writing was that Leahi had forced him, and now the stupid boy was taking his mother to a strange place.

" ' . . . We arrived in Kiangsi two days ago, and were immediately assigned work. Mama belongs to the group of women who sew and mend clothes for the commune, and my job is to design and make inspiring posters. We eat in a common mess hall. The meals are nourishing, and Mama is thrilled by the fact that she doesn't have to cook; she feels like a rich lady to have others cook for her. She wishes you were here with us, and she told me that you'd be happy if you were assigned to be a fisherman.

" 'I didn't bother to tell her that this is a mountain area and there are no fish to be caught, because I know you won't come to us anyway. You've lived in that imperialistic country for twenty years, and my teacher, Wong Chung, said that by now you must be used to being a yellow pig owned by your white masters. My teacher and I have talked about you at times, and we laughed at your foolishness for talking about getting Mama and me to America. Your white masters would never allow us to enter their land, and we would never want to become slaves.

" 'Mama wants me to ask your forgiveness for breaking her promise. Was she supposed to wait for you forever in Willow Place, to rot and die with the willows? Anyway, I persuaded her to come with me, and I'm glad I did. Mama looks so young with her hair cut short; all the women here have short hair.

" 'Every night we gather in the open space to learn patriotic songs and dances, and Mama is beautiful when she sings and dances. Our leader, Chairman Mao, doesn't believe in wasting young women's lives, and Mama is a very young woman at thirty-five.

" 'My time belongs to the commune, and I've already wasted too much of it in writing to you. You are really a stranger to me, but since you are responsible for my being conceived twenty years ago, I guess you can expect to hear from me again sometime in the future.' "

Chen Bai folded the letter neatly back into the envelope, and when he looked up, Fachai had already left. Sadness fell like a curtain over Chen's face. "My poor friend, this is so unfair. You lost your twenty years of savings in the bank, and now this!" He dabbed his eyes with the back of his finger.

A crude man who had overheard shouted, "I'm sure you can cheer him up in no time at all."

Chen Bai glared at the man. Anger brought a flush to his face and his voice rose an octave. "Yes, I will try my best to comfort my friend. In the past ten years Li Fachai and I have been the best of friends—nothing more, nothing less. When I lost my studio, he was the only person kind enough to take me in. And when all his friends deserted him, I stood by his side . . . Oh, why am I telling you all this? You don't care and it's none of your business anyway!" Chen then excused himself and pranced to the kitchen to check on his friend.

Fachai was leaning on the kitchen counter, drinking out of a whiskey bottle.

"Oh, no, you don't!" Chen jumped forward, grabbing the bottle from Fachai. "You promised!"

Fachai's hand shot out and grabbed Chen Bai by his shirt, almost yanking him off his feet, and with an open palm he slapped him. "Give me back that bottle or I'll kill you!"

Rubbing his cheek, Chen started to whine, "You hurt me. I'm doing it for your own good, and you hurt me!" He reluctantly handed over the bottle.

After a long swig Fachai wiped his mouth with his sleeve. "I'm sorry about hitting you. I know you mean well, and I did promise to quit, but . . ." He collapsed over the counter, and his voice turned into a choking sob. ". . . what's the use of my going on? I am a man with nothing! Twenty years ago I came here with a dream . . . many dreams. My wife and child were to join me, and I was going to fish. We were going to have a happy life together . . . we were even going to become rich."

Forgetting his pain, Chen Bai walked over to Fachai to keep his friend from falling. Leaning on Chen, Fachai continued between sobs, "First, my grandfather died. Then my parents. I have a son who calls me a stranger and a yellow pig. I have a wife who has left our home. I used to have friends; they think I'm filthy. I used to have money in the bank, but now that's gone. Give me one good reason why I must quit drinking. Why must I continue living at all?"

"Now, now." Chen Bai put his arms around Fachai and talked softly into his ear. "Keep on talking. Let all your troubles out. Life is filled with injustice, and sometimes Buddha is most unfair. But we must be patient with life. After the worst of luck, good fortune is bound to come."

Chen Bai picked up a clean towel and started to wipe Fachai's wet face gently. "Go ahead, my friend, and have another drink, if that's the only way to make the pain go away. I, of all people, ought to understand what pain is."

Fachai looked at the bottle in his hand, then suddenly threw it against the wall. Looking at Chen Bai with gratitude, he said, "I'm going upstairs now. Let me be alone for a while."

"You are not going to do anything foolish, are you?" Chen asked, and when Fachai gave him a withering look, he added with a smile, "Of course you won't. I will take care of the customers. Don't worry about a thing. When you wake up, things will look better."

To himself he thought: *Hell, how in the name of Buddha can things get any worse?*

Fachai dragged his weary body up the stairs and fell on the bed. "Leahi, I'm sorry. I've let you down. I'm the one who has broken the promise, not you." He got up, walked over to the closet, and searched on his hands and knees. Finally he reached behind a box and pulled out a bottle. He sat leaning against the wall drinking until he became numb, the pain lost in an alcoholic haze.

* * *

In Royal Palm Heights there were no blue-blooded families with old money. Most of the residents had made their fortunes, and none of them felt any resentment for the Cohens. In fact, it was rumored throughout the development that the beautiful Meiping once had been the favored daughter of a powerful Chinese warlord, and David had been in China on a buying trip when he saw her. He immediately fell in love, and after a deal was made between him and her father, the two were married.

Meiping heard the bits and pieces of the story, and when she finally put them together, she laughed so hard her stomach hurt. She did nothing to discourage the rumor. On the contrary, whenever she invited neighborhood ladies for tea, she casually mentioned something fascinating that had happened at her father's mansion. The fantasies became so convincing that after a time she almost believed them herself.

The rumor reached the Jewish circle, and David's friends regarded him with envy. Those who saw him with Meiping anxiously passed on the information that the Chinese princess was very tall and beautiful and had an air of royalty. Like Meiping, David did nothing to disillusion the gossips, though he sometimes wondered: What would Limei say if she knew?

When Rebecca Cohen heard the rumor, she dismissed it with a wave of her hand. She knew she could make David miserable, but would it all be worth it? Her three sons were now grown and had lives of their own, and she was content not having to associate with her husband. As long as he continued to provide her with luxury, she could care less whom he bedded.

Meiping's paradise remained undisturbed until the Depression hit San Francisco. David didn't play the stock market, nor did he keep much cash. He believed in keeping his fortune in diamonds, because gems and gold were a universal exchange—solid, secure, not like paper. However, with the sudden drop in business, his cash flow stopped.

He had to ask Meiping to let her help go and tighten

the budget at home in order to provide for Rebecca's
needs. He kept his wife quiet this way until he learned
that a jeweler friend was selling out.

"If I bought him out," David explained to Meiping,
"then when this whole mess is over, I'd make a fantastic profit."

"I think you should," she said, encouraging him.

He went ahead, and as a result, in the spring of
1932, David Cohen had in his private vault a fortune
in gems. The transaction had all but wiped out his cash
on hand, however. He was now a very poor man sitting on a diamond mine. And Rebecca was no longer
happy.

Rachel Cohen was now eleven years old, Aaron ten.
As they grew older, it was more obvious that they both
had David's features and Meiping's color. The spring
sun was warm, and the children were told to play in
the yard until their parents had finished their discussion. When it was suppertime and no one called them
in, they ran into the house. They could hear their parents talking, so they tiptoed over to the closed door
and listened.

". . . So, the true reason behind her action is
money," they heard their mother saying.

"Yes," their father answered. "She heard about my
recent purchase, and thought I was rolling in money.
She was furious when I cut down her monthly support,
and went to her attorney . . ."

The boy nudged his sister. "Here they go again. She
must be a real mean old bitch."

"Aaron! If Mother heard you swearing, she would
wash your mouth out with soap."

"Well, I learned the word from her. I hear her use
it all the time, especially when she's mad."

"That makes no difference. When you are grown
up, you can do those things. That's why whenever they
want to talk about this *she,* they want you and me to
leave the room."

"She must be really bad. Every time they talk about
her, Mother flies into a rage. Before long we will probably hear her throwing something again."

Rachel told her brother to hush, because she wanted to hear what their father was saying.

". . . Actually, you and I should go out and celebrate. Finally she is asking me for a divorce."

Rachel turned to her brother with a frown. "I thought only married people could get divorced. Papa is married to Mama, so how can *she* ask him for a divorce?"

"Divorce must be like those other words that have more than one meaning," the boy said.

"It doesn't sound right." Rachel shook her head and continued to eavesdrop.

". . . She wants a fortune in cash, plus the house with everything in it, and the car, and an outlandish alimony, and my life insurance."

"She could have asked for all these a few years ago, and you would have been able to afford it. Why does she want it now?" From their mother's tone they knew that before long, things would begin to go flying—the prospect excited them both.

"She wants a divorce now because she thinks like everyone else: I'll go bankrupt soon, and she had better get everything she can before it's too late."

Meiping's voice was even higher now. "She is a despicable bitch! Do you remember how I threw that insurance man out? I could not live with myself if you bought life insurance to make me rich after you're gone. Why, it's bad luck! It's the same as wishing to get rich on your death. I hate her! I hate that fucking bitch!"

Aaron turned to his sister. "Wow, did you hear that? Mom must really be mad."

"Hush," Rachel said, putting a finger to her mouth.

The children could barely hear their father, and they edged closer. "Well, we have to do something, and soon. She is threatening me with an adultery suit. Her attorney said that she wants either a divorce, all on her terms, or me in jail."

The children looked at each other again, enraged at the prospect of their father going to jail—jails were for criminals, not their father. They ran into the room.

"Papa! We were listening and we heard!" shouted Aaron. "That bitch better not put you in jail! We'll fight and kill her!" He turned to Rachel, who was standing beside him.

With tears in her eyes and her fists clenched, Rachel nodded her approval. "Father, I have money. I have almost five dollars in my piggy bank. Will that help?"

David looked at his children. When the little ones were angry, they looked just like Meiping. He opened his arms to welcome them, and they jumped on the sofa to join him. David soothed them and dried the girl's tears, then kissed them both.

As Meiping watched, she felt in her heart a butterfly flapping its wings. In his sixties now, David was still handsome, with silver hair and a trim body.

*I must do something,* she thought. *For so many years my life has been built on quicksand because of that miserable woman. David belongs to me and the children, and I will do anything to protect that . . . we must go beyond Rebecca's reach.*

"My wonderful children," David was saying, "I'm sorry that you had to hear all that. Just forget all about it. Don't worry, no one is going to do anything to us. Don't ask me to explain now. But someday you'll understand." He then changed the subject. "Now, how about going to a restaurant for a big dinner with ice cream for dessert?"

Meiping was listening to the children's excitement when an idea dawned on her. "David!" she yelled so loudly that everyone jumped. "I have the answer! It's so simple! Why didn't you think of it?"

In the waiting room of the private clinic, sofas were placed along opposite walls. Loone looked across from where he was sitting and met the eyes of a buxom overdressed woman who was peering at him over her glasses. When their eyes met, she quickly turned away.

Her reaction nettled him. "You can't bear to look at me?" he mumbled under his breath. Talking to himself had become a habit. "Then why did you stare at me behind my back? Curious why a Chinese is in this overpriced hospital?''

Loone had convinced himself that he could read people's minds. ''I know what you are thinking, you white cow. 'My God, the Chinese are an ugly race! Look how thin and pale this man is . . . almost a ghost!' Well, for your information, madam, I don't represent all Chinese people. You should see Quanming—he is tall and handsome—and Fachai . . .'' Loone stopped, picked up a magazine, and began to flip through it hastily.

''Mr. Chu, the doctor will see you now.'' A young nurse had appeared at the door wearing a trained smile.

Just then Loone started to cough and couldn't stop. He tried to stand, but the sofa was soft and low; to rise from it seemed to require more energy than he possessed. He pushed on the arm with both hands and continued to struggle. He could feel all eyes watching him, and he was furious. The nurse rushed over to help, but he refused. ''Don't touch me! I can . . . manage . . . on my own.''

The nurse continued to smile, trying not to show her impatience. He managed to stand, then followed her into the inner office. The doctor was sitting behind a desk looking at the charts, and immediately Loone noticed his troubled expression.

''It's bad news, isn't it?'' Loone wheezed, collapsing into a chair, knowing he was about to hear the sentence. What little color he had was gone, and his heart was pounding in his chest.

The doctor nodded and began to explain what he had found.

When Loone came out of the office, his lips were one thin line, his eyes blank. Those in the waiting room couldn't tell by his expression what had transpired. They only saw a skinny Oriental gentleman in fine clothes walking quickly toward the door with his back straight and head high.

After he got into the car, he wilted like a week-old cut flower. His hands were shaking; he was wet with sweat. He could still hear the doctor: ''I'm sorry, it is cancer of the lungs. We can operate . . . however, I'm not at all sure of the outcome. I'm afraid the carcinoma is quite advanced. If you had come earlier, there might have been a better chance. If we do not operate, you probably have less than a year . . . ."

"I don't want to think about it!" Loone told himself, staring at the road. "No! This can't be true!"

He didn't see or hear anything on the way home. When he looked up, he realized he was in his driveway. He left the car in the drive; the servant could park it later. He stood looking across his land, and saw the gardener pruning the roses. The Depression hadn't forced him to reduce his staff, because he never trusted anyone, including banks. His money was in large bills tied into bundles, locked in a steel vault built into the wall of his studio. He looked past the old gardener and saw Moi and the boy at the far end of the property.

They had heard his car pulling up and turned in his direction. Even from a distance, he could see Moi's beauty. She still looked like a young girl rather than the mother of a nine-year-old. She waved, but when he didn't wave back, she let her arm drop. The boy was almost as tall as his mother, and he started to run toward Loone with a warm smile.

"No! Mon-fu! Come back!" the mother called, and the child stopped.

Loone headed for the house, wondering how it was that even though he had ignored Mon-fu all these years, the child still ran to him each time he appeared.

Ten years ago he had avoided the sight of Moi's swelling stomach, and when her time came, he had refused to go with her to the hospital. When she came home with the child, she had looked at him apologetically and murmured, "I named him Chu Mon-fu. I hope you don't mind." She had held the child for him to see, but he had turned his back on them, and from then on the three had lived under the same roof as strangers.

He held on to the banister as he climbed the stairs, then entered the studio, closed the door, and locked it.

Ever since the start of the Depression, no gallery had been able to put on shows. However, Loone had never stopped working, and now unframed paintings were everywhere.

In the middle of the room was a huge empty canvas. Loone pulled up a stool and sat staring at the easel without actually seeing it. He heard the wind blowing outside the window, even heard his own heart beating. Time passed slowly as he continued to sit, not moving, hardly breathing. Then, all at once, the dam of his emotions broke.

"I'm going to die! I'm going to die very soon!" He cried the words from the depth of his heart. "My life will be over in a short time, and I have never experienced the joy of being alive!"

Loone's entire body was shaking so violently that he almost toppled off the stool. He clasped the edge of the seat and called in a hoarse voice. "Mama, where are you? I'm so scared. What is death? Will it be painful? Will you and Baba meet me at the entrance of the world of the dead? I'm never very good in finding a place for myself among strangers—will the dead treat me badly? Baba and Mama, if only I could be sure that you both will be waiting for me . . ."

The dappled sunlight filtering through the trees near the window formed specks of dancing light and flickering shadow over the room. Loone watched the patterns on the canvas, and in each dark shadow he saw a face grinning at him. He could even hear them berating him.

"Hey, do you really think you should hate the world for your parents' death?"

"Loone, are you sure that your uncle and aunt have stolen everything from you?"

"You always feel the world owes you everything, but have you understood how much you owe the Chus?"

"Look back, Loone, can you remember how you treated Moi in the beginning of the marriage? You ignored her and never told her how much you loved her.

She wasn't your mother or sister; she was your wife.
What happened wasn't all her fault.''

"Don't you think Moi and Fachai have been pun-
ished long enough? For ten years now they have never
contacted each other. Moi hasn't even taken the child
to him; he doesn't even know Mon-fu is his. There is
a thing called forgiveness, you know.''

The sun was almost gone. The canvas was left
empty; the studio was completely silent.

Loone forced himself off the stool, walked toward
the window, and looked out. In the fading light he
could still make out the shapes of Moi and Mon-fu.
They were but two tiny shadows, both fragile and vulnerable.

"Is it too late to forgive?'' Loone murmured, leaning on the window frame, ignoring the tears that fell.
They were the first tears that he had shed in ten years.

# 34

QUANMING SAT IN his study staring through the window at an old oak tree. The autumn wind was gradually stripping off the red and yellow leaves. Quanming thought of his uncle. In the past six months, Tinwei had been very much like an autumn leaf, fading, ready to become a part of the earth. It pained Quanming to think of the dear old man. Pushing the thought of death aside, he picked up the newspaper and began to read about Franklin Delano Roosevelt, the governor of New York and the Democratic party's candidate for president.

In the living room, outside the study, a mah-jongg game was being played. "Your luck is extremely good today, Mrs. Wu. No one seems to be able to beat you." Moa Lau's voice penetrated Quanming's thoughts, and his stomach turned. He found the man's voice as repugnant as his skinny face and beady eyes.

"Well, you're not doing so badly yourself," A-lin's mother answered pleasantly. "Look at the chips piled in front of you, Lau!"

Quanming frowned. Apparently the old woman was fond enough of this weasel to address him so informally.

"Can the two of you stop congratulating each other and get on with the game? I know exactly which tile I need to win, but one of you has it and won't let go!" A-lin squealed excitedly.

Quanming raised his eyebrows. The only time his wife was cheerful was when she was with Moa Lau.

"It's my turn to meld! I didn't skip school for the fun of keeping you three company. I was counting on winning some money."

Quanming's heart sank. Hwa-hwa! He couldn't believe his ears. He glared at the door and had the urge

to go out there, grab his son, and shake some sense
into him. Fourteen years old, and skipping school for
a game of mah-jongg!

"Keep still, or when your principal calls I won't say
you're sick!" A-lin giggled. "The only reason you're
here is we couldn't find enough grown-ups to play with
us. Everyone is so upset with this Depression that they
won't even play mah-jongg anymore. I hope this stupid
thing gets over soon so I won't have to take a young
brat out of school just to play a game."

A young girl's voice joined in the conversation:
"Mama, you don't need Hwa-hwa. I've watched the
game long enough to know how to play. Will you let
me try?"

Quanming shook his head. So, she had also skipped
school! Ever since Guai was born, A-lin had claimed
the daughter as hers alone, and Quanming had little to
say in the matter. The girl's education, for the most
part, had been overlooked; she stayed home whenever
she wanted. According to her mother and grandmother, all she needed to learn was how to be a good
wife and mother. "I pity her husband and my grandchildren!" Quanming murmured.

"Okay, okay," Sung Hwa pleaded. "Hurry up and
play. I have to leave before the old man comes home.
He'll kill me if he finds out. You know how he turns
everything into a catastrophe!" Everyone laughed at
his remark.

*They don't know I'm here.* Quanming gritted his
teeth, using all his willpower to restrain himself from
going out and smashing the table, along with a few
heads.

He left the desk and walked to the back of the room.
In the middle of the wall was a small storage space
not much bigger than a closet, and no one but Quanming had the key. He walked in, pulled the string, and
a small bulb lit up. He closed the door behind him,
locking it to make sure he would not be disturbed.

He took a wooden box from the top shelf, and with
a key attached to his watch chain, he unlocked it, taking out one of Laurie's letters.

Dear Quanming,

It was so nice to hear from you again. In the past decade I have wanted to write to you at least ten thousand times, and several times I did, but I never mailed the letters, because I thought you were trying to make up with your wife.

I'm sorry to hear things haven't worked out at home. I'm extremely sorry to hear about your son. You had such high hopes for the boy.

I have so much to tell you. I'll start with Paul. He was married eight years ago, and now is the father of two boys. His wife's name is Lei, a beautiful Maui girl. Paul left the mission because they didn't approve of his marriage to a native girl. He and Lei started a private elementary school right after they were married, and now it is well-established, with students coming from all the Hawaiian Islands, and some from Samoa and Tahiti.

The mission fired me after Paul left, to make room for the next missionary and his assistant. Paul asked me to teach, but I turned him down. I have my own business now.

It all started with the shell necklaces and flower leis I made as a hobby. Some tourists asked to buy them, and gradually I had a stand in one of the hotel lobbies. There were travelers from all over the world, and they were all hungry for souvenirs. One stand expanded into several, and now I have a store. About a month ago I applied for a loan to build a larger place, with room for a small factory and also a workshop. I'll be teaching the Hawaiian crafts there.

I'm sorry to hear about your uncle. Thanks for sharing with me his story. Now I understand. I hope his health will improve, and I pray that when the Depression is over, the company will become prosperous again.

I wish you were here to help me with your expertise, since you know how to handle import-export affairs. I have someone working for me as assistant manager, but he is terribly busy. His name is Palani: I believe I told you about him once. He is married now; his wife is a good friend of mine. . . .

Quanming smiled as he looked over the picture of Laurie. She had aged, but looked good for a woman approaching forty. Her hair was held back with a large shell comb; she had on a light-colored suit. "We have both grown older," he whispered, "and I wish with all my heart we had done it together."

He was still looking at the picture when he heard someone opening the door to his study.

His body stiffened; he pulled the string and the light went off. He sat without making a sound, hoping whoever it was would soon leave.

"A-lin, my beautiful A-lin. If I had to sit near you one more minute without touching you, I would've died."

"I feel the same, my darling. Lau . . . oh, Lau, this is awful. Why must we pretend? Such torture, and I'm not sure how much longer I can take it. Hold me, hurry, before they start to look for us—" The rest of her words were muffled by kisses.

In between the sounds of kissing, Lau said, "Don't worry. They'll never find us here. This is your noble husband's holy sanctuary, and no one would dare to enter."

"I'm sure you're right. Oh, how I wish you were my husband instead of that arrogant bastard. I love you so much! Now, hold me tighter . . ."

"You smell so good, my A-lin, and you taste sweeter than anything I've ever tasted. It's difficult for both of us, but we've already put up with the situation for ten long years, and I'm sure we can put up with it a little longer. Soon his uncle will die, and who knows? Miserable people die young, and your husband certainly has been looking miserable."

"Forget him. Give me your hand, feel how much I need you. Oh, Lau, let me hold it! Take it out quickly! Look how it is ready. Give it to me now. I can't wait any longer!"

"I'll try . . . this damn couch is too short. Let me get on my back and you can straddle me . . . oh, God, that's it."

"I want to be your wife . . . don't stop . . . we

belong to each other. I love you . . . oh, oh, more, more . . .''

The sofa began to protest under their rocking. Moaning and breathing filled the room, and then all was quiet.

Much later Quanming heard his wife's voice again. ''Lau, I'm tired of having to hide like this. I love you with all my heart, and I know the children love you, my mother adores you. Let's make our move now. I can't wait!''

Moa Lau mumbled something, then the two left the room. Quanming didn't step out of his hiding place until he was sure that they were gone. When he entered his study, his face was drained of color. His hair was soaked with sweat, and his shirt clung to him. There was blood oozing from his lip where he'd bitten it; his eyes were two chips of ice.

Later that night, A-lin, her mother, and the children went out for dinner. Quanming heard them leave; he looked out the window until he was sure they were gone. He went to his bedroom and began to throw clothes into suitcases.

When he finished packing, he showered, put on fresh clothes, went to his safe, and emptied it. He looked around the room, then slowly walked to the front door. He took one last look around and left.

Moi was watching Mon-fu doing homework when a knock interrupted them.

The maid walked in. ''I am sorry to bother you, but Master Chu would like to see Mon-fu in his studio.''

''Me?'' Mon-fu asked in surprise.

Moi looked puzzled but smiled at the boy encouragingly.

Mon-fu hurried to the studio. He knocked only once, and the door opened. This was the first time in six months that he'd had the chance to look at his father so closely. He retreated a step at the sight that greeted him.

Loone's eyes were two dark holes; the skin on his face was taut and had a sickening pallor.

"Don't be afraid," he said, his voice hoarse and low. "Come in, I have something to show you."

Loone reached toward the boy, and Mon-fu let his father lead him into the room, although repulsed by the cold, wet hand.

Two spotlights were focused on a large canvas. Looking at the painting, Mon-fu gaped in astonishment. "Oh . . ." was all he could manage to get out. Then, after staring at it quietly for a time, he added, "This is the greatest painting I've ever seen!"

Stepping closer, the child pointed from one corner of the canvas to another. "I can feel the wind blowing over the sky. I can even see the clouds changing shape. It's like the sun is so bright I feel it warming my face, and I can even smell the salt water."

Loone nodded at Mon-fu approvingly, and the boy continued, "Who are these people? They all look so poor! This tall fellow here looks like he's posing as a kung-fu fighter. And this tall girl in dirty clothes with a dirty face looks like a tomboy! Ah! Here you are! Even in that funny little cap and with your face half-turned, I can still tell it's you. You are so young, almost a boy. Are you unhappy in the painting? You look so scared . . . so sad."

Loone didn't answer. He was afraid to speak. Something had blocked his throat, and if he opened his mouth, his emotion might get the better of him.

"Where is Mama?" Mon-fu looked over the painting. "How come she is not on this ship? And who is this man with the long pigtail and big shoulders? Is he a good friend of yours? You made his face look almost like mine!" The boy laughed. "Is this how you want me to look when I grow up?" He turned and met Loone's eyes; he never remembered seeing such tenderness in them before. He was about to say something when Loone began to speak.

"This painting must go to the gallery for my next show. Mon-fu, will you promise to tell the manager to put it in the center of the exhibition hall?"

Mon-fu looked confused as he answered. "I prom-

ise. But why me, Baba? Are you mad at the gallery
people, and won't talk to them yourself?''

Loone smiled, then started to cough, the pain cutting him like a knife. Each spasm came from deep
within, and by the time he stopped, there wasn't much
of his strength left. The boy became frightened when
he saw his father's face turning red, and was ready to
rush out of the room for help when he thought his
father was about to collapse.

With great effort Loone reached into his pocket and
took out five letters.

"Mon-fu," he said so softly the boy could hardly
hear him, "keep these for me until tomorrow, then
give them to your mother. One is hers, the others I
want her to forward . . .''

Mon-fu waited, because his father seemed to have
much more to say to him. But Loone started to cough
again and was having trouble breathing. Waving a hand
at Mon-fu, he gestured for the child to leave.

"Are you sure you don't want me to stay with you?''
Mon-fu asked, his young face frightened.

Loone continued to wave the boy away.

"How about bringing you a glass of water?''

Loone waved again.

The boy suddenly had a clever thought. "Shall I get
Mama? When I'm sick, Mama always makes me feel
better.''

Loone waved frantically. "Please leave," he whispered in a voice like sand.

The boy turned and reluctantly left.

After locking the door, Loone whispered softly,
"Yes, I want you, Moi. I want you more than life itself . . . .'' Wearily he turned his eyes to the painting.

"I can't bear much more. Life is too lonely, and the
awful pain . . . I've never been happy in the world of
the living . . . except when I was a child, and when I
thought I had Moi, but those days were so short. Even
when I was painting I was either angry or sad . . .''
He began coughing again. Quickly he turned, so the
blood would not splatter on *Children of the Pearl*.

Lying in bed, Fachai could hear the water dripping in the kitchen. He wanted to go downstairs to stop it, but hated to disturb Chen Bai and his latest boyfriend who was sharing his bedroom.

*Such a good man,* Fachai thought. *I was lucky that he came after everyone deserted me. Otherwise . . . well, I guess I would have killed myself. Hell! I'm too much of a coward to end my life, but is being a drunken failure better than being dead?*

His thoughts wandered. It had been twenty years since he went to Chen Bai to have a picture taken to send home to Leahi. *Twenty years. I was a dreamer then. My Leahi, the unborn baby, my boat, my future!*

There were loud voices coming from downstairs. Fachai frowned: not another argument between the lovers! Every time Chen Bai became emotionally involved, he inevitably ran into trouble. On the whole, though, most of his friends were nice people. Knowing by instinct that Fachai wasn't one of them, none of them had ever tried to persuade him. . . . He'd have to talk to Chen Bai tomorrow.

A loud banging broke into his thoughts, and Fachai jumped out of bed.

"Deu-na-ma! What's going on?" he yelled, half-stumbling on the stairway in his hurry to get down, hoping Chen Bai and his friend weren't trying to kill each other.

When he reached the bottom of the landing he realized someone was knocking on the restaurant's door. "Who is it?" he shouted, but there was no answer.

Robbery? No, a robber wouldn't knock first. He shrugged and advanced to open the door.

A streetlight silhouetted the visitor. Fachai squinted, trying to see, then blinked, recognizing the caller. This had to be a dream! But then he heard her calling his name.

"Fachai, have I aged so much that you don't know me anymore?"

"Moi!" he whispered. "Moi! Is it really you? Moi! Moi!" he kept repeating, lost for words.

"Yes"—tears began to run down her face—"and I've brought someone with me. Fachai, I want you to meet Mon-fu."

A boy appeared from behind Moi, and Fachai stared at his own image in miniature. "Mon-fu . . . ?" He looked up at Moi, and she nodded.

"Yes," she said, her voice trembling. "Mon-fu is our son, and on the way here I told him everything."

"Our son? What are you talking about?" Fachai was shaking so badly that he would have fallen had he not held on to the door.

While the boy stared at Fachai, Moi said, "The night air of autumn is chilly, Fachai. May we come in?"

"Certainly, I . . . Please come in."

Fachai had not heard Chen Bai coming up behind him. Chen had heard the knocking and also had come out to investigate. When he saw Moi, he knew who she was immediately. He bowed. "Allow me to introduce myself. We've never met, but I certainly know who you are. Oh, what an absolute delight meeting you. Fachai, be a sweetheart and find a clean table while I go make the tea."

Moi looked from Fachai to the man in the fancy silk pajamas. She could not hide her surprise and embarrassment. As Chen walked toward the kitchen, a young man entered from the back room. Chen whispered something to him; the young man looked at Moi and smiled. With their arms around each other, they walked into the kitchen. Moi let out a sigh of relief.

Fachai led Moi and Mon-fu to a table that looked fairly clean, and all three sat down without uttering a word.

In the kitchen, while boiling water for the tea, Chen smiled at the young man. "I'm so happy for Li Fachai. From the looks of it, he is not going to be lonely anymore. If things work out all right between him and that lovely lady, maybe I'll be free to go to the east coast with you, without having to worry."

# 35

CHILDREN OF THE FLUSH 37/

Leahi stared at the stranger, looked at him now. Sen
was a handsome, intelligent man... a widower in his
early forties... at ... [illegible] ... Kwanjin had ...

IT WAS A beautiful summer evening in 1933, and the
deep blue sky above the Ching-kang Mountain was
filled with brilliant stars. A fire was built in the open
field, and around it the comrades were singing patriotic songs. A crescent moon was gliding slowly across
the heavens; in its silver beam men and women began
to join hands and dance to the music played by a small
band.

"No, I can't," Leahi said to her son, stepping away
from the forming circle. "Your father has been the
only man who ever touched my hand."

Exasperated with her old ways, Kwanjin snapped at
her, "So, you're still a true believer of Confucius. 'A
woman must chop off her hand should that hand be
touched by a man who is not a member of her family.'
When are you going to change? You can't allow yourself
to be bound by the past anymore!" He took his mother's hand and dragged her back to the circle. "Mother,
Confucius is dead! So are all his sayings!"

Forced by her son, Leahi began to dance. The steps
were very simple, and she managed easily. After a while
she started to enjoy it. She had no idea how young and
pretty she looked in the moonlight, beneath all the stars
and in front of the glowing fire.

"Kwanjin, this is not as bad as I thought . . ." She
turned to talk to her son, only to discover that Kwanjin
was gone, and in his place a stranger was holding her
hand.

"You!" She stopped dancing, withdrew her hand,
and looked at the man angrily. "What did you do with
my son?"

"Comrade Kwanjin was called away. He asked me
to take care of you," the man said gently. "I am Comrade Sen."

Leahi stared at him. She remembered him now. Sen was a northerner, a party member and a widower in his early forties. She had seen him talking to Kwanjin frequently, and more than once the boy had tried to put in a good word for the man.

"I . . . I'm tired. I don't want to dance anymore!"

Heading back toward the communal bedroom she shared with several other women, she repeatedly wiped on her dress the hand that had been touched by a man, a stranger.

The next morning in the mess hall, Comrade Sen sat next to Leahi and Kwanjin for breakfast. Kwanjin tried to get her to talk to Sen, but she would only answer the man's questions by either shaking or nodding her head. Before the meal was over Kwanjin left, once again leaving her alone with the man.

In the middle of a monologue about the aims of the party, Sen suddenly blurted out, "You are a beautiful woman, Comrade Li. It's a shame that you're without a lover."

Leahi's face turned red. "I . . . I am a married woman. My husband is in the Land of the Gold Mountains," she stammered.

Comrade Sen laughed. "The word 'husband' is a feudal term, meaning, a ten-foot-tall man,' in contrast to the term 'wife,' which means 'the son-bearer.' In the new China, men and women are equal partners, and our chairman has decided that we must call our spouses 'lovers.' What I meant was, your lover left you many years ago."

Leahi sat mute as the man went on, "Well, my lover—or you can call her my wife—has been dead for a long time. It's our great leader's belief that when two lonely people are paired up, their working ability increases to benefit our country."

Dropping her chopsticks, Leahi brought her hands up to cover her ears. Comrade Sen laughed and shook his head.

From that day on, Kwanjin pleaded with her: "Mother, Chairman Mao can announce you are divorced, and you will be a free woman. Just say the word."

Leahi answered her son with a firm No. But the son persisted: "The chairman will marry you himself, and that'll be a very great honor."

"I don't care who says what," Leahi replied firmly. "In my heart I am married to Li Fachai, and I will always be his wife."

Li Kwanjin raised both his arms, then dropped them—he knew when he was temporarily beaten. He also knew the old Chinese saying: "With persistence, all minds can be altered."

Weeks passed. At first, in spite of the constant pressure from her son and the continued persuasion of Comrade Sen, Leahi refused to change her mind. But by the time autumn began, she started to soften. Kwanjin and Comrade Sen would not give up, and she couldn't fight them forever, all alone.

The wedding took place on top of Ching-kang Mountain, under a clear sky. People of the commune stood in a circle, and in the center was Chairman Mao. The bride and groom were wearing work clothes; their only ornament a red flower on each of their shirts.

"Comrade Sen," the chairman began, "you are a loyal party member and a hard worker." He turned to Leahi. "Comrade Li, you have been most useful to our cause, and a good laborer. From this day on the two of you shall work side by side, contributing to our righteous aims for the future of China."

Music and feasting were considered decadent pleasures at weddings, since marriages were meant to help the comrades in their determination to reach the party's goals. After the service a poem was read to wish the newlyweds success in fighting jointly against the imperialistic dogs. Li Kwanjin usually read the poems, and he was very proud to read for his own mother's wedding.

"Please," Leahi had pleaded with her son. "For once, don't tell me to follow Chairman Mao's footsteps or be a good comrade. Read something beautiful, something you learned from the old scholar Hsu as a child, long before you became interested in communism. Perhaps something about Willow Place? Or a willow . . . ?"

Kwanjin thought about it for a long while. He didn't want to show his softness in front of all the comrades by reading a sentimental poem. But then he remembered that his mother had always given him whatever he wanted without ever asking for anything in return. *Well, for her wedding I can bring back something of the old feudal days, and no harm will be done.* A love poem by Quan-tsi came to his mind. He smiled at his mother, and cleared his throat.

> The wind blew a leaf from the willow,
> And it fell lightly upon the water,
> Where the waves carried it out of my sight.
>
> Time gradually erased the leaf from my memory,
> As I watched a new leaf floating away.
> Since I have forgotten you, whom I love,
> I dreamed away the day in sorrow,
> Living at a new water's edge.
>
> But the leaf kept floating back to me,
> And I knew that inside my heart,
> The memory of you shall forever remain.

Kwanjin regretted reading it. His mother never stopped sobbing through the entire poem, much to his embarrassment.

In the graveyard of White Stone, Sung Tinwei's cremated body, which had been transferred from a little wooden box to a porcelain jar, was placed under the ground. Dirt was piled to form a mound; a shrine would be built later. Next to this burial plot stood three other shrines, belonging to Quanming's parents and brother.

The grave-digger was a very young man, and the only assistant he had was a thin, shabbily clothed old woman. "She is my mother," the digger explained, shaking his head in shame.

Quanming examined the woman without quite knowing why. Her long hair was completely white, dirty and unkempt. She moved about on bare feet with her back stooped. Her patched blouse and pants were covered with dirt.

She met Quanming's eyes, grinned, and started to sing in a broken voice:

> All graves have names,
> all except one.
> They planted a tree over his head,
> for what he had done.
> There was the red blood,
> and there was the pale moon—

"Stop it, Mama!" her son yelled.

The squeaky voice faded, but the old woman continued to stare at Quanming with an empty smile.

Quanming studied her face carefully. The features were distorted, but the faint traces of an innocent girl remained. He felt a chill racing down his spine. "Please," he asked the young man, his voice strained, "what is your mother's maiden name?"

"Bao A-teem," the man answered. "My father was a miller, but my grandfather on my mother's side was a grave-digger. People have stopped taking rice or wheat to our mill since flour became available in stores. But people keep on dying and graves have to be dug. I must make a living, so I took on my grandfather's trade."

In a flash, Quanming saw that autumn night of twenty-one years before. He charged into the grave-digger Bao's house, found the couple crying on the ground and their daughter lying there naked with her legs covered with blood. The male servant from the Ma house pulled a knife. *It was on this spot where I am standing now that I killed a man!*

Quanming looked at the old woman again. This time he could see clearly a young girl resting in her mother's arms, being rocked like a baby and smiling into space with vacuous eyes.

*My Great Buddha? I thought she would recover from the shock with time, but it's obvious that she never has.*

A man . . .
A tree . . .
A moon . . .

While singing, her lips parted to reveal a toothless mouth; her eyes were the eyes of a dead fish.

Reaching into his pocket, Quanming took out several bills. "Take this," he said to the young man. "Go buy some fabric and have new clothes made for your mother."

He then walked away quickly, leaving the young man to his digging and his mother to her singing of the same refrain over and over, like a needle stuck in a scratched record. The bright summer-morning sun beat mercilessly on him, and he was soon soaked in sweat. He didn't remember White Stone being so unbearably warm, and wondered if a person's tolerance to heat was reduced by age. Soon he stopped in the shade of a tree to rest, and saw some of the village children passing by. He waved at them, but they didn't wave back. They only looked at him, giggled, and then ran away. He watched the farmers in rice fields working knee-deep in water, and the fishermen coming home from their boats, struggling with the tubs filled with their catch. He did not recognize any of them. They looked at him the way they would a stranger, an outsider. *I guess I don't look like one of the people of the Pearl anymore,* Quanming thought, and began to wonder if a life span was so short here that all the villagers he had once known were now dead.

He wandered over to the temple, and recalled Master Lin and Kao Yoto. They were two of the many yellowed pages in a book of bygone days. He knew they had existed once, but he couldn't see more than two vague images. The old master had been long dead, and Kao Yoto had faded away in his memory.

On the temple steps beneath the arch, young men in school uniforms had gathered and were engaged in a heated discussion about saving China through communism. He listened for a few minutes, standing in the shadow of a post, then shook his head. China had not changed. Maybe it would never change. The young were still unhappy with the government and willing to risk their lives to change things. They were forever trying to save their beloved country from the cruel hands of bad rulers, but their chance of winning was always slim. He looked at all the young faces and wondered how many of them would be killed, how many hearts would be broken by their deaths.

"I'm too old to fight for China," he mumbled sadly. "I am leaving my country in the hands of the next generation, though I will always love my homeland."

He walked inside the temple, only to discover that what had appeared to him in his youth as a majestic structure was now dirty and neglected, without any of the peaceful beauty he had expected to find. "I wonder if they still hold their lantern festivals here," he whispered to himself. "Maybe even the lanterns were never really as bright as I remember."

He left the temple and walked to the front of the hill. Standing there, he looked up at the white marble boulders; they at least had remained the same. As he approached his home he heard the sound of hammering coming from the workers fixing up the old place. The red brick house had deteriorated so much that when he first had spied it he had not recognized it. He had gone to town and hired a group of men to work on it immediately.

"Mr. Sung," the chief carpenter shouted through the window, "a servant from the Ma family was here. You are invited to dinner tonight."

"The Ma family?" Quanming asked with a frown. "I don't even know them." Well, he did know one of them, but he hadn't planned on visiting her because he hadn't forgotten the days when he was considered far from good enough to associate with them.

A bricklayer yelled from his scaffold, "I wouldn't give up a fabulous spread if I were you! The Mas are the number-one family in White Stone now. The Kaos stepped down long ago. Old man Kao died, and the young Kao lost the family fortune . . . smoked it away in an opium pipe. A daughter of the Kaos is married into the Ma family, and now she is the lady of the house of Ma . . . she's big enough to make two ladies and more!" He broke up laughing, joined by several other workers.

"Yoto is fat?" Quanming mumbled, disbelieving his ears. Flashing in front of his eyes was a beautiful girl standing in the soft light of a lotus-shaped lantern. The sleeves on her pale-colored dress were flapping in the spring breeze like butterfly's wings; her tiny waist wrapped in a green sash was like the delicate stem of a flower barely strong enough to support her fragile body.

The workers had stopped laughing, and they reminded Quanming that in a village the size of White Stone, news traveled fast. "Everyone knows about your returning from the Land of the Gold Mountains, and rumor goes that you've brought home large bags of gold. Being the head of the number-one family, Ma Tsai-tu feels he is obligated to welcome you."

As soon as Quanming entered the living room of the Ma mansion, a man in a maroon-colored silk robe stood up, walked through the roomful of people, and greeted him with an outstretched hand. "My name is Ma Tsai-tu. My humble dwelling is honored by your presence, Mr. Sung Quanming."

So, this is the man Kao Yoto married, Quanming thought. He studied the well-groomed, portly host. Like all the affluent of China, he was extremely pale, and carried himself with a self-assured air.

Ma Tsai-tu gave a slight bow. "Please, let me present my unworthy family."

Quanming was introduced to the three Ma boys. The father proudly told him that his two younger ones were in their late teens; the eldest was twenty. "Please excuse my lack of humility, but they are the most clever and extraordinary young men."

According to custom, the boys addressed Quanming as Uncle Sung. But though they bowed politely to their honored guest, Quanming noticed on their faces that they found him beneath their station and rather amusing. They did not even have the decency to hide their contempt. Quanming smiled to himself at the foolishness of a father's pride.

"My two daughters." Ma motioned for the young

ladies to come forward. "The younger one is fourteen, her sister is sixteen."

When Quanming smiled at the younger one with two pigtails, she looked shyly at Quanming, then looked away. When his eye fell on the face of the older one, his heart skipped a beat. *Yoto!* he called silently. *The girl's shining long hair hung straight to her waist, held back with a jeweled comb. Why, she shouldn't be standing in a heavily furnished living room. She should be in a temple under the glow of a thousand lanterns, and walking through the swirling smoke of incense burning in iron urns. Will she recite a poem soon? Why, I kissed her in the presence of the statues of Buddha, and she told me that she would always be mine . . . . Now I remember: I loved her once for a short time.*

"And this is my wife," said Ma Tsai-tu, snapping Quanming back to reality.

What the workers had implied did not prepare Quanming for what stood before him. Yoto's face was without blemish and her hair was shiny black, but her eyes were lifeless, her expression blank. Her most astonishing feature, though, was her size. She managed what was supposed to be a smile, but it did not hide the embarrassment she felt in his presence.

Quanming bowed, trying to smile as he looked into Yoto's eyes, but his lips quivered. *How cruel is life! It's a one-way journey, and there is no way to go back. Yoto is no longer sixteen, and I can never be nineteen again.*

Ma Tsai-tu was now saying, "And this is my brother-in-law, Mr. Kao."

Quanming turned away from Yoto to look at a man who appeared to have one foot in the grave. The skin covering his stooped frame was as sallow as old wax. His thin lips smiled, displaying a row of yellowed teeth. His bow was only a slight lowering of his head, which was considered rude.

Quanming returned the insult by ignoring the formality of a greeting, remembering what the workers had said about this man's addiction to opium.

"Please sit down, Mr. Sung, and share with us a

fine bottle of wine," Ma Tsai-tu said, leading Quanming to one of the cushioned chairs.

The wine was poured into thin crystal glasses, and a
servant brought in a variety of dim-sum on silver trays.
Turning the glass in his hand and looking at the wealth
with which the Mas surrounded themselves, Quanming
thought of the majority of people he had seen since his
return. In Hong Kong, Kwangchow, and White Stone,
the poor were still struggling and starving exactly like
they had been twenty-one years ago. *Is China the only
place where wealth will always be so unevenly distrib-
uted? Is it so far behind the rest of the world?*

"Mr. Sung." His thoughts were once more interrupted
by his host. "Please allow me to welcome you back
home."

Quanming raised his glass. The host looked at his
guest, thinking of the stories he had heard about Sung
Quanming: a poor man whose brother had been beheaded. Smiling broadly, Ma Tsai-tu said, "Please
pardon my forwardness, Mr. Sung. We have never met
before, and you may be wondering why my invitation.
You see, my behavior is the result of a parent's love
for his children."

Quanming waited. He focused his attention on his
host, avoiding the eyes of his hostess. He could feel
Yoto's gaze, and his heart was filled with pity: yesterday's emotions were gone, but not the memories.

"You see," Ma Tsai-tu went on, "the communists
are threatening China, and if they should succeed, we,
the rich, will be in trouble. I wish to send my boys to
the United States with a large sum of money. They can
live safely and in comfort, and the rest of us can join
them in case of an emergency. Will you help us, Mr.
Sung? Of course, I'll pay you for your trouble."

Quanming took a deep breath. A dozen thoughts
flashed through his mind. Most of all, he wanted to
tell this arrogant bastard to go to hell.

From the corner of his eye he caught Yoto lifting a
handkerchief to cover her mouth, a gesture he remembered well. Every time she had been afraid he would
lose his temper, she had performed this little ritual. *I*

*will not hurt her feelings by being rude to her husband. I must get out of this place in a hurry.*

"I'm very sorry, Mr. Ma," Quanming said, smiling politely. "I will not be able to help you. And since I won't be of any use to you, I feel I have taken enough of your time, and have given up enough of my own. So if you will excuse me," he said, getting up from the chair, "I shall be on my way."

As he walked out of the room, his eyes and Yoto's met briefly. The sorrow in hers was so deep that his heart ached. Could she have been happy with her husband? he wondered.

Not until he had passed through the outer doors and was on his way back to the house, did he realize he and Yoto had not exchanged a single word.

The shrine was completed, and Quanming stood for a long time saying good-bye to his family.

"Mama, you were right to send me away. But you were wrong to hope that someday China would become a livable place. I'll be leaving the Pearl once more, and I'm not sure if I'll ever return again. Baba, you have your brother lying next to you now. You two must have a lot to talk about. And, Quanli, if you had left China a long time ago, your head would not have been chopped off."

He finally dried his tears and turned to the young grave-digger, who had been waiting patiently. "Here," Quanming said, handing a key to the confused young man. "This will open the door to the red brick house, a gift from me to you and your mother. Please take care of the Sung family graves in the years to come, because I'll be leaving tomorrow for Hawaii, a beautiful island very far away."

That night, Quanming stood by the open window inside the little house at the foot of the hill, looking out at the night sky. The moon was full; the stars looked lifeless and pale against its bright glow. The fading stars were all his yesterdays; in them he found the sadness in Yoto's eyes. The brightness of the moon seemed to represent his future, for he could see Laurie's smile in the moonbeams.

He went to bed to catch some sleep. He would be on a long journey from the Pearl again early in the morning. Lying there with his head propped on his hands, he saw in the darkness once more the image of himself and Yoto, both young, walking through the courtyard of the temple, from one Buddha to another. The flickering candles . . . the dancing smoke of the incense . . . the poem written by Li Po, a poem that he and Yoto had shared once . . . a beautiful poem . . .

He was trying so hard to recall the words in that poem that he did not hear a wagon stop down by the road.

A woman got out to look at the red brick house bathed in the moonlight, and her body trembled. She took a few steps toward the house, then halted. The moon cast her shadow clearly on the ground: a very large shadow. She looked down at the huge black spot and covered her face with her hands. After a long while she started to slowly back away. Even with the help of her maid, it took all her strength to lift herself back into the wagon. She sat sobbing, her frame shaking so hard it rocked the carriage. She eventually told the driver to take her home.

Finally Quanming remembered the words and recited them slowly:

> Gold shining brightly as the finch's wings,
> Shall brighten the house where I must go.
> But the thought of you,
> Standing and weeping by the ancient gate,
> Shall steal my sleep as I lie alone.
> Watching the dying moon of dawn,
> Tears shall be with me wherever I roam.

## 36

IN THE DINING room of the Peninsula Hotel, the Cohens were having breakfast. In the room there were women from India dressed in saris, men with turbans, Japanese in kimonos, English gentlemen in tailored suits and ladies in large straw hats covered with flowers.

"Did you say Hong Kong is China, Papa?" Aaron asked, looking around, puzzled. "How come, except for the waiters, I don't see any Chinese?"

"We arrived in the middle of the night. We haven't been on the streets of Kowloon yet. You just wait, you'll see plenty of Chinese everywhere. This hotel is very expensive, and most of the Chinese can't afford it," David said, ruffling the boy's hair.

Rachel, also looking at the people, whispered, "Are they all running away from someone, like we did from *her*?"

David and Meiping exchanged a glance. "Children . . ." David cleared his throat. "From now on, you must forget *her*. Your Mama and I are starting a new life here for all of us, and in the future you shall never hear about *her* again." He went on to describe the city of their future home. "We are very close to your Mama's original home, the Kwangdung province of China."

He went on to tell them other facts about Hong Kong, and when he had finished, he kissed the children; he knew better than to kiss Meiping in public. He then left for the Star Ferry to go to Hong Kong. While in San Francisco, he had corresponded with a jeweler who had promised to introduce him to the right people to help him get started in business.

Meiping decided to take the children shopping. Leaving San Francisco in such a hurry, they had taken nothing but a few suitcases. Once in the streets, she was as excited as Aaron and Rachel. The day quickly passed and they were exhausted by the time they returned to the hotel laden with packages.

That evening in the hotel's dining room, the children began to tell David about their exciting day before they even ordered.

"It's so warm here, Papa," Rachel began. "But Mama said this is only spring, and it'll get much hotter when summer comes. Aaron and I felt we would suffocate in the sun, but it didn't seem to bother Mama. She bargained with every peddler on the street in Chinese. Sometimes it sounded like they were really mad at each other, but Mama said they were not; it was just their normal way of doing business. Mama told us we'll have to learn Cantonese, but I don't know if we'll ever be able to learn it. It sounds like the firing of machine guns—"

Aaron couldn't wait any longer. "Are you going to talk all night? We ate in a whole bunch of different places, and—"

"I counted six places," his sister interrupted. "It was so warm! Aaron and I became very thirsty. So, after every few blocks, Mama took us to eat. The eating places were all dirty, but at least there were large fans—"

"Shut up! It's my turn," the boy said, upset, ignoring his sister when she stuck her tongue out at him. "Mama said the last time she tasted such delicious food was twenty-one years ago. She told us that all the Chinese restaurants in San Francisco are no good. Guess what we had, Papa? Eels, frogs, steamed buns, and something that looked awful but tasted great . . . and Mama wouldn't tell us what it was."

Meiping finally got a chance to talk to her husband. "All of a sudden I'm not a foreigner anymore. No one thinks that I speak with an accent, nor did anyone look at the children strangely. It seems like many foreigners in Hong Kong have Chinese wives. I spotted several children with mixed blood just this afternoon. Oh, David, I'm so happy here, I truly am."

David waited patiently until his family had finished, then calmly described his fruitful day. "I'll be in business within a month, and I've found us a home. A man whom I met this morning took me to his home on Victoria Peak. He showed me a house for sale in the same area, and I could not resist it. I found the agent and put down a deposit."

"What does the house look like? Is it big? When can we see it?" Meiping and the children asked excitedly, all at the same time.

David smiled at his impatient family. "The house looks like a castle, and it is very big, with three stories and many rooms. It was built by an Englishman. And you won't believe the beauty of the view. From several rooms you can see the South China Sea. I stood on the balcony for a long time looking at the small fishing boats and the misty mountains in the distance. I felt so peaceful there, and was certain that we made the right move." He looked at Meiping with a smile. "Our troubles are behind us. We'll have a good life here."

David told the children that there was a British school on the Peak, where all subjects were taught in English. But he agreed with their mother, that like all people of Hong Kong, Rachel and Aaron would have to learn Cantonese.

A month later, the Cohens were comfortably settled in their new home. Leaving the house in the care of two servants, they traveled from Hong Kong to Kwangchow. On a warm day in the summer of 1933, they arrived in Jasmine Valley.

Although a smattering of automobiles had already appeared in the larger cities of China, in the small villages along the Pearl River, a car was useless. No gas could be purchased anywhere and there were no suitable roads. Meiping, David, and the children arrived in a wagon.

Long before they had reached Yung's Teahouse, swarms of village children had begun to run alongside them, shouting, pointing, and begging.

"A white devil! But the lady is one of us! The little

ones are half him and half her!'' they shouted in the
Pearl dialect.

"Mama, you didn't look like that when you were a
little girl, did you?'' Rachel asked, pointing at a bony
dirty young girl running barefoot on the hard ground.

Meiping eyed all the running children and answered
casually, "They are much better-looking. I was often
told that I was the ugliest child in the whole Jasmine
Valley.''

"I don't believe you!'' Aaron said, dropping his jaw.
"You are so pretty. You couldn't possibly have ever
looked like one of them.''

Meiping smiled and nodded. "But I did, honestly.
Life is hard along the Pearl. It always has been this
way. That's why my people would do almost anything
just for a chance to get out of here.''

David didn't say much, for he was intent on taking
in everything. Noticing a shirtless farmer in a rice
paddy and a small boy riding on the back of a water
buffalo, he said to Meiping, "Your people and the
Jewish people are very much alike. They suffer, they
work hard. Next to them, those born in the USA are
hothouse flowers. These people can endure so much,
and when given a chance, they can achieve an enormous amount in the world.''

Meiping didn't answer. Already she could see the
faded banner of the teahouse dancing in the wind, and
her eyes began to moisten. "Home,'' she whispered.
"After twenty-one years I am home . . . the daughter
of the Pearl has returned.''

The wagon stopped. People ran out of the teahouse
with eyes staring and fingers pointing and mouths jab-
bering.

"Look at the tall lady in her gray silk suit! She's so
beautiful! It thought you said that Yung Meiping was
ugly!''

"Well, I was told by someone, who was told by
someone who used to know her a long time ago. Look
at all the diamonds she has! Her father hasn't been
lying after all!''

"Look at the big white man! How odd that he and

the boy are carrying the suitcases while the woman
and the girl are empty-handed. Look! The man and
the boy are walking behind the woman and the girl!
Have you ever seen anything so strange?"

"How in Buddha's name can a man grow to be so
big? What do white devils eat, I wonder."

Two women giggled as one whispered something
into the other's ear. Meiping overheard and blushed.

"What did they say?" David asked.

"Never mind!" was all that Meiping would translate.

Most of the comments were aimed at Rachel and
Aaron, since the villagers had never seen such children before. Frightened by the stares and jeers and
pointing fingers, the boy and girl stayed close to their
parents as they walked toward the teahouse door.
"They're not nice!" Rachel said, about to cry. "Why
do they point at us and laugh at us? Don't they know
that they're not supposed to stare?"

Meiping told her daughter that the children in China
had a different set of manners, and she must not be
bothered.

"What are they saying about us?" Aaron asked.
"And how come they talk about us right to our faces
as if we were all deaf? Aren't they very wrong to treat
us this way?"

Meiping told her son that in China it wasn't considered wrong for people to talk about others to their
faces. "You see, when they treat you as if you were
deaf, then you must act deaf to suit the situation."
And then she lied: "Don't be upset. They are saying
that you and Rachel are the two most beautiful children they have ever seen."

The noise stopped abruptly as the crowd stepped
aside.

The old man who appeared was short and fat. His
white beard was blowing in the wind. He stared at
Meiping, and his eyes filled with tears. He raised his
trembling arms toward his daughter, and Meiping ran
to him.

"Baba, you've shrunk!" Meiping cried loudly. She

put her arms around her father and looked down at him. "Why did I always remember you as a big man who could easily beat me up? Have you always been so short?"

Yung Ko held Meiping tightly, his words running together: "My good daughter! My precious Meiping! I missed you so much all these years. I wasn't sure if I would live long enough to see you again." He reached up to hold Meiping's face between his hands. "How have you been? Were you really given the honest job of a maid in a rich house when you landed in the Gold Mountains? You didn't have to do anything shameful through the years, did you? I have been so worried! I could never face your Mama when I see her in heaven if you were forced to do indecent things! How I hated myself for letting you go! I've had many terrible dreams! Tell me, is that big white man over there truly your husband? Is he good to you? He doesn't beat you often, I hope. My Buddha, he is big! You must tell me all about my grandchildren."

Before Meiping could begin to answer all the questions, a plump woman appeared at the door of the teahouse wearing a dirty apron. "You old fool," she shouted at Yung Ko, "keeping your daughter and her family standing in this blistering sun all day. Don't you know how to ask people to come in?"

Yung Ko quickly obeyed his wife, and Meiping liked her stepmother immediately. The villagers automatically followed without invitation, standing around and watching without missing anything. Mrs. Yung brought out her best dishes and started to serve dim-sum and tea in the correct order: first David, the visiting man, then Aaron, the honorable number-one son. Then came the host, Yung Ko, followed by Meiping, the female guest. Mrs. Yung herself was next, and poor Rachel had whatever was left, being the youngest woman in the group and the most worthless.

"Baba," Meiping said, holding the old man's hand across the table, "the greatest thing you did for me was sending me to the Land of the Gold Mountains. Yes, I did honest work in a rich house, and yes, my

David and I have been married for a long time. He is good to me, and he never beats me. Your grandson is very smart, and even your granddaughter is not doing too poorly in school. . . . Baba, you really shouldn't worry. Mama will thank you for what you've done when you see her in heaven."

Then Meiping took from her purse the gifts they had brought for her father and stepmother. As the gifts were being unwrapped, the villagers stretched their necks to see what was being given.

"Ahya!"

"Oooo!"

None of them had ever seen a solid jade bracelet or a gold Rolex watch before. The sounds of awe and envy filled the tearoom.

Mrs. Yung looked at the apple-green bracelet on her wrist and felt a lump in her throat. She looked at her husband's glowing face, and for the first time in the past twenty-one years she was certain that the old man was laughing from the bottom of his heart, truly free of guilt and worry.

"Thank you, Meiping," Mrs. Yung said sincerely, "for a beautiful bracelet, and for the priceless gift of making your father happy. I shall never know whether you have told him the truth or a lie, but it doesn't matter. I don't think my poor old man will ever moan in his sleep again."

Meiping and her family stayed in Jasmine Valley for a few days, and on the early evening before their departure, she took them through the woods in search of her hill.

They climbed a narrow path to reach the top, and on the plateau by an old tree Meiping found a large sheet of flat rock. Sitting on the rock, they looked out over the valley below.

The trees were of different shades of green, and it was the season for the jasmine to bloom throughout the valley. Small houses could be seen through the foliage, and out of the chimneys thin columns of smoke danced slowly in the soft breeze. Squares of farmland stretched toward the horizon, and the banner of Yung's Teahouse waved in the wind. The Pearl was flowing beyond the valley like a dark gray dragon resting in the setting sun.

"Take a deep breath," Meiping told her family. "And remember the smell of the most beautiful place on earth. My home, my valley, my jasmine . . . " She stopped in mid-sentence.

A large bird was flapping its white wings, soaring from the bottom of the valley toward the graying sky.

Everyone's eyes followed the bird as it flew higher toward a horizon that was becoming one with the Pearl in the deepening dusk. They watched the majestic creature turning slowly, changing into a silhouette as it flew across the surface of the full moon that had silently appeared.

Meiping swallowed, her voice quavering with emotion: "Many years ago, a woman held the hand of a little girl, and the two climbed the mountain to come here to look for ginseng roots. As time passed, the woman died, and the little girl grew up. But the woman had sung a song to the girl, and if you listen carefully, you can still hear the melody echoing in the valley." She began softly to sing:

> Flowers of the valley bloom,
> Then they must fade and die.
> While wild geese fly on the wind,
> And the moon plays idly in the sky.
> How far is the moon?
> And how clear is the night!
> I'll fly on the wings of birds,
> In search of my heart's delight.

## 37

LOONE WAS RIDING in a rickshaw, going from Kwang-chow harbor into town. He didn't remember summer ever being this warm. He had trouble breathing; he looked at the crowds in fear, and wondered why everybody was shouting so loudly. His head began to pound.

"Sisan," the rickshaw-puller called over his shoulder, using a term of respect for such a fine gentleman, "did you say Fong's Pawnshop?"

"Yes. It's still there, I hope?" Loone asked apprehensively.

"Oh, yes," the coolie answered. "I was just there myself a few days ago. Best pawnshop in Kwangchow. Always gives a fair price, and lets you buy your stuff back even when the ticket is overdue. If all rich people were like the Fongs, there would be no need for communism."

Loone started to cough. He covered his mouth with a handkerchief, and soon the white cloth was dotted with fresh blood. Cold sweat made him shiver in the heat, and as he tried to catch his breath, he saw another rickshaw beside his, carrying a mother and a young child.

He turned to follow it with his eyes, and it seemed that the child had transformed into himself, the woman into his mother.

"Look, Mama, look over there! Will you buy that beautiful picture for me? Mama, will you?" the child was pleading with a smile, knowing that his mother never could deny him anything—anything except to stay with him forever.

"Sisan, are you all right? Do you want me to stop and get you a cup of tea?" the coolie asked when Loone couldn't stop coughing.

"Go on," Loone said, struggling to speak. "I haven't got much time."

Time . . . yes. As the rickshaw started up again, Loone kept thinking how a few months ago, when he had been in San Francisco, he had worried he wouldn't have enough time to finish *Children of the Pearl*. When that was done, he had then worried about whether he would die before the ship reached China and be buried at sea. Now that he was finally on the soil of his native land, he knew he must hurry to get home.

He saw the pawnshop from a distance. The old sign was gone, and a much larger and brighter one gleamed in the summer sun.

Again the image of a child appeared in front of his eyes, this time coming home from school. His young parents were waiting at the door, greeting him with love and specially prepared food.

"Baba! Mama! I'm home!" the child called.

*Baba! Mama! I'm home again!* Loone said silently. A sharp pain hit him with such intensity, the world started to turn black.

Loone fainted in front of his childhood home.

When he opened his eyes, Loone found himself in the room he had occupied twenty-one years ago.

"Cousin Loone . . . my cousin," a kind-faced man and a shy-looking woman, both middle-aged, were calling from the foot of his bed.

"You are . . . ?" he whispered weakly.

"I'm your oldest cousin, Fong Ming," the man said, then pointed at the woman. "This is my wife, Jade."

Fong Ming explained that the rickshaw puller had come running into the pawnshop, asking for help. He had told Fong Ming that a customer, who was coming to the shop to look for someone, was now dead in the rickshaw. "We rushed out, discovered the rickshaw man wrong. We knew you were alive, but did not know who you were. I took the liberty of looking at the passport that was sticking out of your pocket, and couldn't believe that you had finally come home." Smiling at Loone, Fong Ming continued, "You gave us a scare, Cousin Loone. We've sent for the doctor, and he should be here any minute now.''

"I don't need a doctor," Loone said. He looked at the couple and then his eye was caught by a yellowed picture hanging on the wall behind them. That picture had always hung on this very same wall. Loone's father was standing, his mother sitting and holding a baby.

Following his eyes, Fong Ming explained, "We've tried not to change anything in this room. It should look the same as you left it twenty-one years ago.''

"You mean . . .'' Loone started to cough. When he finally stopped, he wiped his mouth and continued, ''. . . your father and you knew all the time that I would come back? You mean, you wanted me to come back?''

Fong Ming nodded without hesitation. "Of course. When I was small, I used to hear my parents talk about how sorry they were for letting you go. As a matter of fact, my mother spent her last few years talking about nothing but you. My father refused to leave Kwangchow because he had promised my mother to wait for you.''

Loone's eyes moistened and he changed the subject. "Where are your brothers? There were five of you, if I remember correctly.''

Fong Ming answered, "My four younger brothers left Kwangchow for the Ching-kang Mountain to join the communists some time ago. I haven't heard from them for a while now.''

They were interrupted by the arrival of the medicine man. He was not the kind of medical doctor Loone had become accustomed to in San Francisco. His beard still showed traces of what he had just eaten, and his clothes were in need of washing; dried blood still clung to the fabric. His hands and long fingernails were filthy, and as he came close, Loone could smell his bad breath.

He checked the patient by tapping Loone on the chest, and when Loone told him the trouble was cancer, his expression didn't change. He quickly prescribed several medicines: the gallbladder of a snake and the roots of some unheard-of trees. "Cancer is easy to cure," he said, "as long as the patient is able to pay the doctor's fees and the cost of the medicine."

Jade paid the man, and he said he would be back to check on the patient the following day. "Will there be any problem with further payments for the visits?" he asked with concern.

"Oh, no. We'll be able to pay," Fong Ming said quickly.

Jade added, "We'll give everything we own to you if you can make our cousin Loone well again."

In a hoarse voice Loone told his cousins that they must not make any useless sacrifices. "There is nothing to be done, believe me. I've come home to rest, not to get well."

But before he could finish, his cousins had already left. They had to start searching for the needed live snakes and tree roots.

Loone awoke from a long but restless sleep to the sound of peddlers barking their wares.

"Buy my steaming meat buns!"

"Buy my fresh vegetables!"

"My watermelons are large and sweet!"

"My soybean milk is hot and nourishing!"

So this was the sound of home. In the past twenty-one years Loone had heard the same hawking of wares repeatedly in his dreams. He closed his eyes once more, and felt like a child again. As a child he had stayed in bed, listened to the city coming to life until his door was opened by his mother carrying a tray in her delicate hands.

For a brief moment Loone was confused. The door actually opened, and a woman appeared with a tray. "I hope you've rested well, Cousin Loone." The petite woman smiled as she laid the tray down. "This is not a quiet neighborhood, being in the center of a business district."

Loone sighed. No, neither his mother nor his childhood would ever return again. "Thank you, Cousin

Jade, I slept many hours, more than I ever slept else-where.''

Jade smiled, arranging the dishes on the tray. "It is not much, just a bowl of rice gruel and several small dishes of meat and fish. I'm a very poor cook, but please try to eat."

Loone forced himself to take a few bites, and re-gretted not coming back earlier, when he was still in good health and had a good appetite. Jade watched him picking at the food. When he stopped, she left the room and came back in a few minutes with two bowls.

"Please, Cousin Loone, first, the gallbladders of snakes.'' She gave him a small bowl half-filled with wine. Floating in the wine were two green things, each about an inch long. "I killed the snakes myself," she said, making a face. "And I removed the bladders while the snakes were still wiggling. The doctor said you need four bladders a day, and I have arranged with the snake restaurant to deliver us live snakes every day.''

Loone stared at the woman and resigned himself to the ordeal of putting the repulsive concoction into his mouth. He immediately understood the meaning of "as bitter as gall.''

"I'm swallowing this awful thing not because I be-lieve in it, but because I owe you an apology for being wrong all these years,'' he mumbled. The woman smiled at him without understanding.

The larger bowl was filled with soup made from the tree roots, and this, at least, was palatable. Loone was drying his mouth when the door opened and Fong Ming walked in.

There were several large ledgers in his hands. He laid them aside; then from his pocket he took out a folded sheet of paper. "Please, my cousin,'' he said, "check and see if all this is correct.''

Unfolding the paper, Loone saw it was the deed to the pawnshop; the owner's name was Fong Loone. He was then handed the ledgers, which contained detailed records of the shop's profits for the past twenty-one years: half had gone to the Fongs; the other half had been deposited in the bank in Loone's name.

After a long coughing spell, Loone dabbed the blood from the corners of his mouth and asked his cousin to send for a public notary. "I want to give everything here to you and your family. No," he cried as they began to protest, "don't argue with a dying man."

That night, lying in bed, Loone thought of the five letters he had left in San Francisco with Moi. There was one for Moi and Fachai; two were for Quanming and Meiping; one was for his attorney; and the last was for the manager of the gallery. He had given the house to Fachai, Moi, and Mon-fu; he wished them happiness in that home. He hoped Meiping and Quanming had received his letters of good-bye; it had been so many years since he had contacted them that he hadn't even been sure if their addresses were still the same.

*I wonder if they will ever come back to China . . . as all children of the Pearl must come home one day.*

Summer turned to autumn, and Loone dragged on, his waking hours ever fewer. At the Mid-Autumn Festival, the Fongs gathered many relatives for the feast. Loone, too sick to come down, stayed in bed.

He tilted his head toward the window and looked out at the moon. He listened to the hubbub of people downstairs, talking and laughing, and tears began to fall on his pillow.

*This is the story of my life: I am always on the outside, looking in.*

Reality began to become unclear, and gradually he slipped into a world mixed with memory and fantasy.

He saw another Mid-Autumn Festival of long ago: a table was covered with food, and Loone was very much within the picture. His handsome father was sitting at his left, and to his right sat his mother, young and beautiful, with a string of pink pearls luminous around her neck.

"Loone, my son, look at the moon," said his father. "It's a symbol of unity. You, your mother, and I will never be parted once we've shared the view of the mid-autumn moon.''

"Loone, my baby." His mother placed a loving arm around him and held him close. With a kiss on his cheek she asked, "Why do you look so somber, my love? Come now, my serious little precious, smile for your Mama. There is nothing for you to worry about. Mama and Baba are here. We love you and will protect you from all the hardships of life. Nothing will ever change that.''

Loone cried out, "Baba! Mama! I'm coming to you! Wait for me!" His voice became a desperate bellow as he continued to yell, "I want to be with you! Take me along! Don't leave me alone! Please . . . you promised!''

The faces of his parents towered over him. He saw their smiles lighting up everything around him and chasing away the darkness. He felt their warmth covering him like the hot rays of the sun and driving out the freezing chill in his body.

A peaceful look came onto Loone's face; the pain of a lifetime had finally ended.

Downstairs, the feasting people started to sing a song that was centuries old, one that was sung always during the Moon Festival.

When the Autumn moon is large and glowing,
Once again my lonely heart aches for home.
I can see the waters of the river flowing,
And a small room I call my own.
It has been written that few men go wandering,
Without the hand of fate and that alone.

# Epilogue

PRESIDENT ROOSEVELT WORKED diligently to fight the Depression, and by the end of 1935, many art galleries had sprung back to life. A year later, the owner of a prominent art gallery in San Francisco decided to highlight Christmas with a very special show—a presentation of the works of the deceased artist Chu Fong Loone.

On December 22, 1936, the show opened with over one hundred paintings.

*The Valley of Jasmine, The Mountain of White Stone, The Pigeon Feeders, Memories of a Better Day, The Betrayal, Behind the Bars on Angel Island, The Dreams of a Willow* . . . and in the middle of the room, a gilded easel on which stood a huge canvas covered by a veil.

The viewers, most of them the cream of San Francisco society, talked and sipped champagne as they browsed in the company of trained salespeople. All of a sudden a hush fell upon the room. Everyone stood still, and all heads turned toward the three new arrivals, who looked out-of-place—they were Chinese.

The man and woman could both be in their early forties, but it was obvious that life had been much kinder to her than to him. The man's face was deeply lined, while the woman's was smooth. He was already turning gray and moving with an older gait; her hair was still black and she carried herself with a youthful lightness. Between them walked a young boy in his early teens, dressed neatly in a blue suit.

The gallery manager made his way through the staring crowd, approached the boy, and guided him to the podium that had been placed alongside the veiled centerpiece.

The room remained silent as the boy stood on the

podium before the people and glanced from face to face. He waited until the tension was at its peak, then began to talk. "My name is Chu Mon-fu. I am the son of Chu Fong Loone." His English was perfect, without a trace of a Chinese accent. He turned to face the easel, then slowly lifted the veil.

The only sound that could be heard was the intake of breath. Then, like a distant rumble of thunder, a soft murmur began to fill the room. It grew gradually in volume, and finally burst into an explosion of applause.

The viewers felt themselves leaving the walled gallery, entering an endless ocean. They were warmed by the sun, buffeted by the wind. They were sailing with four young Chinese; they were extremely close to all four of them.

They felt the pride of the tall, handsome young man. They shared the aggressiveness of that wild-looking young girl. In the eyes of the pigtailed boy they saw homesickness, and when they looked at the thin, pale, shy boy with a funny-looking cap, their hearts ached.

It was only a half-turned face hidden in the shadow of a cap, as if the boy was unwilling to look the world straight in the eye. But the combination of his fear, anguish, and loneliness formed a strong force, moving them with irresistible power. The ladies started to wipe their eyes; the men let out reluctant sniffs.

Chu Mon-fu didn't look at his audience; his tear-filled eyes were focused on the boy in the cap. "We Chinese are the descendants of Huang-ti, who separated heaven from earth. We are in the United States of America for different reasons, and we came from various provinces of China. My father and his friends were among the earliest immigrants in this country; they came from the Pearl River. Fong Loone was only fourteen at the time, and his friends were not much older."

Mon-fu paused briefly, then proceeded. "If you look closely at their eyes, you'll see the dreams of the children of the Pearl. Some of the dreams were turned into reality, while others died away." Mon-fu lifted a hand to tap gently on the canvas, touching the boy in the funny cap. "But Chu Fong Loone hasn't really died. He will be with us forever . . ." The boy couldn't continue.

He left the podium abruptly. With tears rolling down his face, he ran through the applauding crowd to the other end of the room and joined the waiting man and woman. "Mama, I'm sorry," he said in fluent Chinese. "I couldn't finish what we rehearsed together. I thought of Baba, and a terrible thought came to me . . ." He let out a sob. "Baba never knew that we loved him, did he?"

The woman was also crying unashamedly. She touched the string of pink pearls around her neck, trying to find words to answer the boy. "I don't know . . . I hope he did. He never gave me a chance to tell him . . ." She turned to the man. "Fachai, do you think he knew?"

The man gave a deep sigh, put one arm around the woman and his other arm around the boy, and started them toward the door. "Moi, I'd give anything to have a chance to tell him. But"—he turned to look at the large painting once more—"whether he knew we loved him or not, he did forgive us. Of that I'm sure."

## ABOUT THE AUTHOR

Ching Yun Bezine was born in northern China in 1937, just before the Japanese invasion which forced her family to flee to Shanghai. There her father's shipping business flourished and she grew up surrounded by luxury and waited on by servants. But when the Communists came to power in 1949, Ching's family fled once again, this time to Taiwan. Ching obliged her parents by becoming a lawyer (her brother is a doctor) and by entering into an arranged marriage to a Chinese physician she did not know. Twenty-five years old and pregnant, Ching left her husband and emigrated to the United States where she has lived ever since. While struggling to survive as a single mother in a foreign land, Ching earned her bachelors and masters degrees in fine art and wrote fourteen best-selling books in Chinese, published by Crown Taiwan. In 1973, while working toward her Ph.D., Ching met Frank Bezine, an American psychologist and educator. They were married one year later in Hawaii. Children of the Pearl, Ching's English-language writing debut, is a remarkable achievement in itself and a beautiful expression of the author's respect for the East and love of the West.